RACKETEERS

Nick Deffenbaugh

*To my awesome
friend Ryan.
Thanks, man.
—N Deffbgh*

authorHOUSE®

AuthorHouse™
1663 Liberty Drive
Bloomington, IN 47403
www.authorhouse.com
Phone: 1-800-839-8640

First published by AuthorHouse 6/17/2009

ISBN: 978-1-4389-7669-3 (e)
ISBN: 978-1-4389-7667-9 (sc)
ISBN: 978-1-4389-7668-6 (hc)

Printed in the United States of America
Bloomington, Indiana

This book is printed on acid-free paper.

For my family and friends.

And of course, for Baby.

PREFACE

There were nights when she thought she could see the whole city from the rooftop. This was not one of those nights. Tonight the cramped buildings of the neighborhood appeared to be nearly on top of one another. The gray and brown stone buildings with their wood facades stood sentinel to the quiet street, looming so close that Dottie had to reevaluate the size of her little world.

This morning eighteen-year-old Dottie had buried her mother next to the place her father had been laid to rest three years earlier in 1914. It had been a quiet, solemn ceremony with only a handful in attendance, including Dottie herself and the priest. And of course, there was Tommy.

There was always Tommy.

But Dottie had, however—to the astonishment of the neighborhood—opened up the saloon at the usual time and remained as chipper and gay as she ever had been during the last five years she had been running the place. At two o'clock in the morning she closed the saloon, wiped up the bar, washed the glasses and swept the floor. Then, with all the chores done, she turned down the lights, sat in the stillness by the bar and wept bitterly.

Afterwards, she went to the roof, where it seemed she always did her best thinking.

A horse and buggy strolled by on the street below. The horse carried its head low, as if chagrinned by the racket of its loud clip-clopping hooves in the stillness of the night. Dottie frowned as the horse cocked its tail and emitted a stream of feces onto the pavement in front of the saloon. Having finished its business, the horse ambled down the street with its rickety buggy close behind until it disappeared into the darkness, leaving only the echoes of its footfalls.

Dottie flapped her old skirt in the wind and gave thanks that the shorter hemlines were here to stay. America had joined The Great War three months ago and with the new wartime demand for material, there was less to use in dresses and skirts, which was just as well. It was simply too hot.

It was too hot for the long heavy dresses, it was too hot for thinking. And it was too hot to feel sorry for one's self. Not that Dottie ever did much of that. No, this was not a place for brooding. It was an escape—a few moments of peace and quiet after running a busy saloon all day long.

She sat on the edge of the roof with her feet dangling over. After a moment's consideration, she removed her shoes, hitched her dress high above her knees and began rolling off her stockings. She paused and scanned the city. It did not seem so wide and open anymore. It had once seemed endless.

A year ago her mother had insisted that Dottie change the name of her father's saloon; her father would have been proud to see the way Dottie had taken charge and kept the old place going. But now that Mamma was gone, Dottie was all alone in the world.

All alone except for the boy who wasn't even fourteen yet who was standing in the shadows watching her. She didn't know how long he had been there, but she suddenly felt his presence. With a sly smile, she hitched her dress even higher, finished removing the other stocking and placed it in her shoe—moving very slowly as she did so. "Hi, Tommy," she said without turning around.

His feet shuffled over the tarred roof as he joined her. He stuck his legs over the edge and returned her smile. "Hi, Dottie. I... I didn't know if you'd want to be alone." He handed her a shiny red apple.

Dottie smiled at it, "Apples. Always apples. What would I do without you, Tommy?"

Tommy shrugged, "You wouldn't have as many apples."

During the lean times when Dottie's father was gravely ill and she was working full time at two jobs to pay the doctor bills, Tommy had known she was regularly skipping meals so her father could eat. And so eight-year old Tommy had started bringing her apples, in spite of the fact he was little more than a bag of bones himself; malnourished, thin and sickly. She never quite let on to how much those little acts by a homeless boy had touched her.

"Dottie?" His voice was no longer that of the dirt-smudged little boy she had met so long ago. "You're not gonna pack it in are you?"

"People keep asking me if I'm going to sell the place," she said thoughtfully. She turned her eyes to Tommy and asked, "And do what?" Her life for the last five years had been the saloon. Cheering up the neighborhood working men with beer and funny stories and sound advice was all that Dottie knew. She was going to add 'Work in one of Rocco Petrelli's bawdy houses?' but she did not like to use that name around Tommy.

Tommy shrugged and looked out over the city. "Get married. Move away. You could have any man you wanted..."

Dottie smiled wistfully and patted his hand. "No, Tommy. I'm going to stay right here. Come hell or high water."

The streetlamps tried in vain to bring light to the old neighborhood, and the darkness hid the relief in his eyes. "Good. I'd... I wouldn't..."

Dottie patted his hand again to let him know she understood what he was trying to say. "You shouldn't have sent those flowers this morning, Tommy. They probably cost a fortune." A bouquet of roses had appeared on her doorstep the morning after her father's funeral three years earlier. She pretended not to know where they came from, but she knew that little Tommy had stolen them, just for her. But the flowers he brought to her mother's funeral this morning had been purchased with Tommy's hard-earned money.

"If you ever need help, Dottie, me and the guys'll—"

"No, Tommy. You guys have enough to do. I'll be alright." Dottie sighed and lay back on the rooftop, her feet hanging out over the edge. She wriggled her bare toes in the delicious breeze. The moon peered out from behind a cloud, illuminating her face. Tommy studied it for a long moment before lying back beside her.

Dottie was his best friend on earth and the most beautiful girl he would ever lay eyes on. She could have wooed any man she wanted, but she seemed content for now to be married to her father's bar. It was as though she knew there was something else coming down the long road ahead and she was merely waiting for time and circumstance to fall together.

"Do you remember when we met?" Tommy asked softly.

"Of course."

"Did I… did I ever thank you? Or your parents?"

Dottie smiled in the moonlight and patted his hand again. "In many ways, Tommy." They fell into silence for a long time watching the clouds veil the moon and then move on. It made Dottie think of a magician she had seen at a carnival playing now-you-see-it, now-you-don't with a magic cape. "Tommy? What do you think the future will be?"

Tommy's answer was as natural and as sure as all his answers. "Whatever we make it."

"It is here at last—dry America's first birthday. At one minute past twelve tomorrow morning a new nation will be born. Tonight John Barleycorn makes his last will and testament. Now for an era of clear thinking and clean living."

—Anti-Saloon League proclamation, January 16, 1920

"Let's misbehave!"
—Cole Porter

1

FAT'S WAS A MUSTY, SMOKY POOL HALL THAT was a second home to most of the young thugs of the neighborhood. Though most of them appeared at Fat's at one time during the day or another, the ones in attendance at this hour were the less-ambitious and the less foolhardy. The foolhardy—those with money—were at Ruby's on 49th street sipping cut wood alcohol flavored with juniper juice or swilling a green beer concoction which was supposed to resemble lager. The ambitious were out on the streets looking for a way into the ever-expanding rackets.

This breeding ground for thugs of the future was operated by an aging hood known as Fat Eddie DiStella, who had done a half a dozen years on a pissant stick-up job when he was a teenager. But now Fat Eddie was older and fatter if not wiser, and made his living fencing the trinkets these neighborhood kids picked up, running a couple of speakeasies—including Ruby's—and operating crooked poker games.

Fat Eddie kept watch over the bootlegging operations in the neighborhood in the name of Rocco Petrelli. It was Eddie's job to make sure that things went smoothly, which was much easier said than done. Every time something went wrong with his operations, Eddie would hear from Rocco Petrelli's right hand man Patsy. And a call from Patsy Guarino was a *bad* thing.

Eddie's neighborhood bordered Sean Conway's territory on the north side and Eddie always claimed it had the highest percentage of young turks running around and getting in people's hair. Though most of these kids would be dead or in prison by the time they hit their mid-twenties, there would always be more to come along to fill the void, giving Eddie *agita* by starting street fights with the Irish kids to the north, knocking over neighborhood fruit stands and mom & pop stores or by merely lusting after Eddie's daughter. These juvenile delinquents were a plague—more than enough to keep Eddie busy without his crew's constant skirmishes with Sean Conway's gangsters.

It was no wonder Eddie started losing his hair at an early age.

His stomach churned as he thought about these things while waiting for Tommy Trent. "Where the hell is this goddam kid?" Eddie said to no one.

Tommaso Trentino was one of the more ambitious neighborhood products. He was somewhere around twenty-one years old and already had his hand in several pots. He ran his small band of men as efficiently as any of the real gangsters. He was known to the people of the neighborhood as Tommy Trent. He had dark wavy hair, olive oil-colored skin and dark blue eyes that always seemed to see three steps ahead of everyone else. There was an air of sophistication around the young man, an air of confidence and placidity, as if there was some great secret fortune heading his way and he was simply waiting for it, taking everything else in stride. Fat Eddie was the only person in the neighborhood who never fully recognized that there was something out of the ordinary about Tommy Trent. At most he might admit the kid had *some* potential.

Eddie's right hand man Mo Cimmino, among others, spoke highly of the young man. "You'd have a helluva lot more trouble with the other kids around here if it weren't for Tommy. The troubles with the kids we've got ain't nothing. There's a crime wave of kids in the other neighborhoods, but here, they're all afraid to step on Tommy's toes. You should thank the kid, Eddie." But Eddie didn't care to listen to Mo; he always took the advice of his underlings with a grain of salt.

A lot of people around the neighborhood never knew what to make of Tommy Trent and rarely crossed his path. There was a deep ominous intelligence lurking behind the dark eyes that none of the other neighborhood hoodlums seemed to possess. His close band of friends added to the mystery by never talking much of their leader.

And the dames loved him.

But to Fat Eddie, who hadn't noticed the Great War until it was over, Tommy Trent was just another two-bit punk who just had a little more balls than most.

Impatiently, he paced back and forth in the back of the pool hall. He had nearly given up when Trent walked in, his snap-brimmed hat cocked at an angle casting a shadow over his intelligent eyes. He was no more than five feet ten inches tall but he had a certain presence that made him seem larger.

Eddie raised a hand for Tommy to stop in his tracks. Tommy did so, removed his hat and pretended to study the crowd. He had already seen everyone in the room before he stepped through the doorway. "Tommy, let's step outside."

Tommy led Eddie into the darkened streets. "I been hearing things, Tommy. That you're capable of more than just busting heads, no?"

Tommy did not answer. Eddie closely studied his shadowed face beneath the streetlight for a moment. When he couldn't read anything, he laughed. "All right kid. Let's go to my office."

Eddie DiStella's office was upstairs from a good-sized furniture store across the street from his pool hall. This was legitimate occupation—he'd been selling furniture for nearly three decades now. He and his daughter lived in the comfortable apartment upstairs and his office was off of the living quarters.

Being taken into Eddie's office was a step closer to graduating to the real world of gangsters.

* * *

Marco Messinio turned onto Seventh Avenue in his new Chrysler and smiled contentedly at the motor's sound. "Don't she purr pretty? Ain't no sound better in the world." Mo did not reply.

"Somethin' the matter, Mo?"

Instead of answering, Mo Cimmino chewed a thumbnail and shook his head almost imperceptibly.

"We got this buncha kids in my neighborhood," Marco went on with a sigh. "These punks have been knockin' over the wrong stores, stealing the wrong cars..." He shook his head. "Real fuckin' headache. Is Eddie having any problems with the kids?"

"Nah, not too much," Mo said, coming to life for the first time in a mile. "There's only one real organized gang of kids. They tow the line and none of the others fuck with them. You know, it's just Eddie... Well, he's got enough things to worry about with the fuckin' Micks."

"Go on," Marco urged, but Mo seemed not to hear. "C'mon, Mo," Marco groaned, "You're givin' off waves of gloom over here. You wanna say Fat Eddie doesn't know his ass from an applecart, go ahead. I ain't gonna rat on you. Ain't like the whole world don't know."

Mo suddenly became animated. "Look, all my life I've been a street-level guy. It's all I ever wanted. I didn't want none of the headaches of leadership or organization. I'm happy where I am, in what I've chosen. So I got no right to complain about the hierarchy."

"'Hierarchy?'" Marco chuckled, "What books you been reading?" After another half mile, Marco pulled the car against the curb and turned the motor off. He pointed to one of the office buildings twenty yards from the intersection. Mo acknowledged with a nod. After a few minutes of waiting Marco said, "Look, Rocco knows. There ain't a thing goin' on in the whole city that Rocco Petrelli don't know about. He knows Eddie'll never be another Sally Nose. He just... wants everyone to give Eddie a little more time. Eddie's old man was a real stand-up guy in the days of Big Joe. And for that Eddie at least deserves a chance."

"Sure, I know," Mo shrugged, not taking his eyes off of the building. "I ain't making a beef."

"Yeah, I understand. Yer a lot smarter than anybody gives you credit for, Mo." Marco laughed, "Even when you bend my ear, you don't actually *say* anything."

"There he is," Mo said softly.

Marco leaned over the steering wheel. A man had stepped out of the building and into the rainy night. The wet pavement glistened at his feet. He hefted a briefcase in his hand, as he scanned the street for his car, as though the briefcase weighed a ton. His walk was obviously impaired by more than a few sips of bootleg gin. "Yeah. That's our pal. Go to, Mo."

Mo Cimmino nodded and stepped out of the car. He moved quickly and quietly for a man of his size. He watched the man as he switched the heavy briefcase from one hand to the other and stepped out into the street. Mo timed his walk so that he met the man as he opened the driver's side door.

"Mr. Kuehl?" Mo said with a smile in his voice.

The man turned around with a grin as though expecting a friend, only to find himself starring into the barrel of a .38.

Marco Messinio watched from the corner as Mo shot the man between the eyes. The muzzle flash split the night like lightening, but the sound was a surprisingly modest 'pop.' It sent the man's head snapping backwards, knocking his hat off and tumbling over the opened car door. The body bounced against the door and crumpled to the pavement. Cimmino leaned over the dead man and shot him through the head two more times. Then, calmly, he turned around and dropped the gun into his coat pocket as he returned to the car.

Marco nodded approvingly as Cimmino filled up the passenger side of the car. The car leaned a little to the right as the tires settled. "Anywheres I can drop you?"

Mo thought for a moment. "Take me to Dottie's place."

* * *

No one ever called him Joe The Peg-Leg to his face. He had returned from the Great War as an amputee only to discover that his wife had run off with a policeman while Joe had been serving his country. Since then, Joe spent most of his time in speakeasies. It was a common sight in the neighborhood to see Joe hobbling from one speak to the next with a crutch under his arm and a flask on his hip. But only a few dared look him in the eye as he passed by.

Joe didn't care for many people; his outlook on the world had been soured long before. But he did like the people who ran the speaks in the neighborhood and he liked the kid Tommy Trent. The kid liked to listen to anyone who wanted to talk—he always seemed to be learning about people, places, and most importantly, human nature. Joe was a citizen of the street, and Tommy had been raised in those same avenues and alleyways. It was their common bond.

Joe was commenting on the young girl at another table across the speakeasy who was giving Tommy the eye when Mo Cimmino found them. "Tommy. Can I join you?"

Tommy sat upright in his seat, slowly so the gesture would not be mistaken for eagerness. "Sure, Mr. Cimmino. Have a seat. You know Joe?"

The two nodded towards each other without looking the other in the eye. "So what's going on?" Mo asked.

Tommy shrugged, but Joe spoke first, "He and that red-head across the bar there have been battin' their eyelashes at each other."

Mo followed his gaze to the girl. She was a pretty young thing, not more than twenty. Her dress was so short that her garters were exposed as she crossed her legs. Mo grinned. "Shit, can you get me some of dat?"

Tommy smiled and took a sip of his beer. "If you don't mind seconds."

Cimmino and Joe laughed. "But whattaya wanna do that fer?" Joe said. "You could have The Deuce any time you wanted." He turned to Mo and addressed him without looking at his face, "The whole world knows he and The Deuce have an understanding."

Shuffling in his seat, Tommy said, "Even if that were true, Joe, for the time being The Deuce and I are permitted to play the field." He looked back to the red-head who met his gaze with a shy smile. "And it looks like a good night for a ballgame."

Mo leaned across the table, "I hate to spoil any plans, Tommy…"

"What can I do for you, Mr. C?"

"Personally? That red-head would suffice. But Eddie was hoping you'd drop by tonight. He's anxious to see how that…." His eyes flashed to the crippled war vet, "*thing* went."

"It's okay to talk in front of Joe. He won't cross me."

Mo eyed Peg-Leg Joe suspiciously. His voice dropped to a hoarse whisper, "Well, Tommy, word's gettin' around. People are talking. I been telling Eddie for a while he should take you more seriously. You're a good kid. You got brains and Eddie needs more of that in his crew."

Tommy nodded his appreciation, then shrugged. "I don't know who's been saying what." He wondered if he was really going to be offered a spot in Fat Eddie's crew or if he was going to be taken for a one-way ride. "But sure. Lemme take care of one thing and I'll stop by to see Eddie in a little while."

Mo stood up from his seat, his mission completed satisfactorily enough for him. "Good. I gotta run. See ya' round."

As he reached the entrance of the speakeasy, he turned and watched as Tommy crossed the room. He stopped by the red-head, leaned over and whispered in her ear. The girl giggled and looked up to him with wide eyes full of youthful vigor.

Mo shook his head and left chuckling.

* * *

Candace laughed and tossed a lock of red hair back from her brow. "You know, Tommy, when I first saw you tonight, I had no idea you were so popular."

"I'm not," Tommy shrugged. "But a man's gotta make a living."

A curious smile spread across her face. "Doing what?"

"I'm a beer taster. I go around to all the speaks and breweries checking the beer for quality."

The girl laughed again. It was a musical laughter. "Alright, Tommy, don't tell me. But will I see you later?"

Tommy winked and then smiled. "I wouldn't be surprised."

"I'm not the kind of girl to be kept waiting forever, you know."

He ran his hands over her shoulders. "No… No, I bet you're not. But I'm not the kind of guy who breaks a date without making up for it ten times over."

Candace gave him a quick peck on the mouth, then winked. "I'll hold you to that."

"Sure. Go on inside and then if I'm not back in an hour, you have my permission to blow me off."

The girl gave him a final wink before disappearing back into the speakeasy. Tommy chuckled, shoved his hands deep into his pockets and strolled down the street to The DiStella Furniture store.

Tommy knocked on the door of the residence and waited for Fat Eddie. "Tommy. Come in." He held the door open for the young man and closed it behind him. He ushered him into his office and studied him for a long moment. "So?" Eddie finally said. "How'd it go?"

"No problems," Tommy said with a shrug. He produced a thick

envelope from an inside pocket and handed it over. All counted, he had just brought in eleven hundred dollars, probably more money than he had ever seen in his entire life. However, he gazed upon it with the same nonchalance as if it had been a ten spot.

"Swell, kid." Eddie fingered the bills lovingly. "Sure there weren't any problems?"

"Nah. In and out. Piece of cake."

"Good. C'mon. Let's have a drink." They adjourned to the living room where Fat Eddie poured them each a brandy. Trent sat down on the couch and took the drink graciously. "So, how much of that is mine?"

"How about one bill?"

"And six for the big guy and four for you?" Tommy Trent smiled, "How about I use that chair and break your head open and take it all?"

For a moment Fat Eddie was not sure whether to laugh or reach for a gun. He chuckled and shook his head, "You're a character, kid. You got balls." Tommy's grin broadened.

Eddie's laughter died when his tall shapely young daughter entered the room, unaware her father was entertaining a guest. She was dressed indecently in nothing but a nightgown and robe, and Fat Eddie was filled with rage as he saw Tommy Trent's eyes following her contours. She was bent over a table, looking for a magazine, oblivious to the eyes on her. "Sarah!" Fat Eddie barked.

The young woman looked up and saw Tommy's dark eyes fixed on hers. "Oh!" she exclaimed, clutching her robe shut to hide her goods, which Tommy could see were very good indeed.

"Get outta here!"

"Sorry, Poppa," she said over her shoulder as she hurried out of the room.

Fat Eddie smiled an apology for the interruption. "Where were we?"

"How about your daughter?"

"Wha?"

"Your daughter. I'll take one hundred dollars and your daughter."

"You're crazy!"

"Maybe."

"How dare you?" Fat Eddie threw two hundred dollars at the young man and hollered, "Get out of here. Get out of my sight, you pig!"

* * *

Sarah DiStella was eighteen years old, and one of the prettiest young girls in the neighborhood. She had big, dark, mystical brown eyes that peered out at the world beneath a shade of thick lashes. Her nose upturned ever-so-slightly, and a lot of the guys who hung around the pool hall—all of whom she had shot down—said it showed she was a snob. When she smiled, a dimple appeared on either side of her full lips. It was often said that she could have been big in the moving picture business—that was if Valentino wasn't the only Italian name allowed in the movies. To look at her, one would never guess that the corpulent and uncouth Fat Eddie was her father.

Her beauty had often caused a lot of annoyances for Fat Eddie. Every one of the young neighborhood thugs wanted a piece of her tail, but Eddie had sworn to her mother that he would see to it that she was raised properly, and that meant keeping her from running around with the 'gutter thugs.'

But things were a little easier for Fat Eddie in that sense ever since he had one of the thugs sent to the hospital for propositioning his daughter. (And say, wasn't it Tommy Trent he paid to do the job on that kid? Eh, doesn't matter.) Since then everyone who hung around the pool hall knew that Sarah was off limits if you didn't want to spend the rest of your days limping.

A set of steps led from the second floor above the furniture store outside to the side street. It was on the side of the building, hidden from view of the pool hall, allowing Sarah (and the occasional 'important guy') to come and go without being spotted by the thugs. She had just come down the stairs when a figure emerged from the darkness. The guy obviously thought he was suave—the way he dressed, the hat, the grin. Just another masher. He took off his hat and nodded to her, the streetlight showing his black hair was wavy. "Good evenin', Miss."

Sarah didn't give him a second glance; continuing on her way as if he wasn't there. "Take a hike," she said.

"Hey-oh! What's this?" He was walking along side her now, putting his hat back on at a cocky angle. She kept walking faster and faster but he kept right along side of her. "Since when is that a polite way 'a speakin'?"

No response.

"Is it a crime to say good evenin'?" He grabbed her arm and turned her around to face him.

"You better get out of here, friend, and don't come back, cause my father'll—" she stopped herself, looking at his face for the first time. "Haven't I seen you bef—"

"Yeah, sure. Up in the parlor. I was talking business with your father."

"Oh. I guess that means you're not really a gutter-thug."

"I'll take that as a compliment."

"Now you've graduated to the curb." She started walking faster now.

"You know, that's no way for a nice young lady to talk. Especially to people she don't know."

"You're right. My mother said to never talk to strangers."

"Hey, now, will you at least stop long enough so I can tell youse my name?"

"'Youse'? My, my, very poetic. Lord Byron, I presume?" By now, they had reached the drugstore and stood in the light that spilled out from the windows onto the sidewalk.

"You know, you'll get a reputation as being snooty with that attitude."

He admired the way her dress hugged her hips as she went up the steps, opened the door, and turned saying, "For your information, mister, I already have." The door slammed behind her.

When Sarah emerged from the store a few minutes later with her bag full of goods, the masher was leaning against a street-lamp, cleaning under his fingernails absently with a small pocketknife. She went on as if she hadn't noticed him. He quickly caught up to her. "Good evening, Miss."

"You again?"

"What?"

"You again, huh?"

"No, no. You must have me confused with somebody else."

"Oh, a guy who *looks* like you."

"Yeah, must be. Lucky devil."

"He wears the same clothes, has the same face, the same thing on his mind."

He grabbed her arm again and stopped her. "Hey, let's not be rude."

She looked down at the sidewalk and said softly, "You're right, I apologize."

"That's better... So, you want I should walk you home?"

"No."

"—to my place?"

He had no sooner gotten the words out when she slapped him hard. He barely flinched. A wide grin spread across his face and the light of the drugstore glinted against his eyes as they followed her hips down the street.

* * *

Sarah set the bag down on the kitchen table and stood silently for a moment listening to her father bellowing over the telephone. "Whaddaya mean it never got there?" There was a long pause. "Dammit, who was security?... G's gonna be pretty pissed. They got it all, huh?.. Fuckin' Micks." She heard him slam down the receiver and curse fervently under his breath and waited a moment before joining him in the other room.

"I got your medicine."

Fat Eddie's face grew soft, "Thanks, darlin." He paused and studied her. "Is there something wrong?"

"Eh," she shrugged, "Another masher, that's all." She debated whether or not to tell him that the masher was the young man she had seen in the parlor. She decided it could wait until morning. "No big deal. I'm gonna go to bed now. G'night, Poppa."

For all of the alleged secrecy surrounding the workings of the bootlegging and liquor smuggling business, word of a stolen shipment or a daring raid by a rival gang spread quickly through the streets. Tommy Trent and his band of men stood in a small circle near Dottie's speakeasy, their hands buried deep in their pockets and their coat collars turned upwards with hats pulled down low against the autumn chill.

"It's frustratin'," Joe Mitchner complained. "We got us a sweet little set up, milkin' those Irish kids out of their money. But it's like we're stuck in the middle between Fat Eddie and Conway's boys."

"It's just not safe anymore," Tony Palermi took the toothpick he had been gnawing at and flicked it into the gutter. "We're gonna have to move the game somewhere else. Away from the border. I mean, one of the stray bullets nearly took my ear off."

Tommy and his gang had been running a small card game in an old flophouse on 87th, the dividing line between Sean Conway's territory and Rocco Petrelli's. Most of the customers were from the north side of the border and were careless players. During one of the games, Sean Conway's men hijacked one of Fat Eddie's trucks just outside of the flophouse and several stray rounds from the ensuing gun battle had smashed through the windows.

Marty Rossini snorted, "When Sally Nose was running the neighborhood, those Irish pricks'd never have the balls to heist a load. But Fat Eddie? He's a pushover and the whole neighborhood's gone to shit."

"Even *our* action's been down since he took over. He don't spread the wealth like Sally did."

"Yeah," Gaetano said with a shrug. "But he's got old ties to Rocco."

"Tommy," Palermi said, "you know that he charges Dottie twice what Sally Nose did?"

"Yeah," Tommy sighed and let his irritation show. He looked down the street to Dottie's speakeasy. "I know. But Rocco put him in charge. We'll all just have to suffer until he changes his mind... Or, until someone shows Eddie how to do things right." Tommy grinned and Gaetano imagined he could see a light bulb appearing over his head. "Hey, Marty, your uncle the cop, he's about my size, right?"

"Yeah, I guess."

"You know what the next night he's off duty?"

"Uh, Friday, I think. Yeah, Ma said he's comin' over fer dinner."

"Good. Do you suppose that it would be possible for somebody to borrow a cop's uniform when he's off duty? Without anybody noticing?"

"I wouldn't be surprised."

Gaetano interrupted, "Whoa, pally, just what's runnin' through that mixed up mind of yours?"

"Nothing..." He scratched his lower thumb with a thumb-nail and then pointed a finger at them, "You guys all have presentable suits, right?" The guys all nodded cautiously. "Fine. That's fine. I want all you guys to meet me here tomorrow night at eight. I've got a nice little idea."

Jimmy Brisone had been a bit reluctant to take this job from Fat Eddie. The assignment came to him as something of a shock. From what he had heard, Fat Eddie had just started to use the guy for bigger jobs, and now this? It didn't make much sense to him. The only way he could reason it out was that the guy must have done something to Eddie's daughter. Anyway, it didn't matter. Jimmy was getting twice the usual ten-spot.

He used half of that extra ten to bribe a buddy into helping him.

Jimmy knew that Tommy Trent's little band of thugs hung around Dottie's speakeasy. And afterwards, the gang would probably all split up and go their own ways, with Tommy Trent always the last to leave.

And so, after waiting for an hour and a half, Jimmy's nerves were getting frayed. The alley where he and Sam stood was wet and formed a wind-tunnel. He pressed himself closer to the side of the empty two-story office building. He just wanted to finish this, get his other ten from Fat Eddie and go home. As if to make him more miserable, the wind kicked up again and tore through him. His mind began wandering. He could not be exactly sure how much more time had passed when somebody tapped his shoulder, making him jump.

It was Sam. He pointed towards Dottie's. Just as he had expected, the group had broken up an hour earlier and Tommy Trent was the last to leave at two o'clock in the morning. He was now heading right towards them. The two ducked into doorways and waited breathlessly. The stick Jimmy had once used to play stickball seemed heavy in his hands. He waited.

When Trent wandered between them, Sam pounced, trying to wedge his arms beneath Trent's to lift them up. Jimmy had already stepped into the alley when he saw that his buddy had blown it. Trent wriggled out of his grip effortlessly and delivered a sharp elbow to Sam's groin. Jimmy had almost forgotten that he was holding a weapon, but by the time the initial shock was over, he found Trent's fist smashing into his throat. As Jimmy lie on the pavement gasping, he saw Tommy Trent pounding Sam with the stick. Tommy moved easily, as though he had all the time in the world right now, delivering each blow with great deliberation and care, as if he were hammering out a piece of art. When he finished with Sam, he turned to Jimmy, who was still on his back, gasping for breath. Tommy Trent spoke softly. "You two had better stay away from Fat Eddie for a couple of days." The last thing Jimmy would later recall was the sound of the stick breaking over his head.

2

Micah Collins stepped outside of the warehouse for a smoke and a breath of fresh air. It was a chilly night and Micah was sure that meant it was going to be a tough winter. As he applied the lighter to the end of the cigarette, his eyes scanned passed the flame and into the darkness, knowing that he was being watched. He smoked slowly, fighting back waves of nausea and making sure that the cigarette end burned bright enough to be seen through the light mist that hung in the cold autumn air.

Out of the darkness he heard the sound of a large engine rumbling towards him. He took a deep breath and held it.

* * *

The phone rang in the darkness next to Fat Eddie's bed, jarring him out of a sound sleep. It startled him so that his legs kicked out, causing a shock wave to ripple over the waves of fat. He struggled to roll over onto his side and lift the receiver. "Hello?"

"Eddie?"

"Yeah, it's me," Eddie grunted, wondering who the hell else would be answering his telephone at this time of night. "Who's this?"

"Mo. I got some news."

Eddie didn't like the quaver in the voice. "What is it?"

"Well, I don't know exactly how or who..."

"Come on, come on, spit it out, you dope."

"One of the trucks is gone."

"What? Hijacked again?"

"No-no. Not really. It was empty. But just the same, somebody stole the damned thing."

"Don't go nowhere. I'll be there in a few minutes." Fat Eddie slammed the receiver in its cradle and threw back the covers. The night was chilly and all he wanted was to stay in his nice warm bed without having any crises to worry about. This was all he needed. And so soon after one of his shipments had been hijacked. Just great.

The phone rang again. Fat Eddie stopped, one leg in his trousers. He gave the phone a blazing look. The disarming stare had no effect on the ringing. He hoped to himself that it was Mo again and that he had simply forgotten that he had parked the truck up his ass and everything was alright and that Fat Eddie could go back to bed.

"Yeah?"

"Eddie, you hear about any trouble?" It was Mickey Gurgone, who ran one of the distilleries in the neighborhood.

"Yeah, one of my fuckin' trucks is missin'."

"Well, there's more."

"Now what?"

"Somebody broke in over here and well, they walked off with five or six shot guns."

"Oh, holy hell," Eddie groaned. "Are you sure?"

"Eddie, I'm staring at the fuckin' cabinet right now."

"Alright. Alright. You hear anything, call me here, or I'll be with Mo." He hung up again and pulled his trousers up. *Oh, great. G's gonna love this.*

* * *

The tremendous crash broke the steady hum of men at work inside the warehouse. They whirled around simultaneously to see a huge truck parked in the middle of the floor and coppers jumping out of it. The large wooden doors of the entryway hung crazily along the sides of the truck. Only one of the men was in uniform; the rest must have been Prohibition Agents following his lead. He held a shot gun on Micah Collins as he marched ahead with his hands up.

"What's this shit, now?" Felim Strong bellowed at them. He had been pumping wood alcohol into a barrel of near-beer and tossed the needle-like apparatus to the side with disgust.

The cop spoke. "Everybody against that back wall, and nobody will get hurt. You are all under arrest."

The Irish men obeyed, muttering among themselves. They were lined up against a wall of whiskey crates stacked seven high. Each of the crates bore a red maple leaf emblem. "That's a lot of alcohol boys. Don't you know it isn't legal?"

"What's the matter, Officer?" Felim called out, "Didn't you get your payment?"

The blue-eyed cop pushed him up against the wooden crates, and began patting him down. "Not enough, boy-o."

When all of the men were searched and disarmed, they were herded into the back of one of their own trucks like cattle. Felim's men hadn't even finished unloading it yet and had to seat themselves among a handful of Canadian whiskey crates. The back gate was closed and secured before the engine was started. As the truck pulled away, they saw some of the remaining agents turning the warehouse upside down. "Hey, Felim," the man next to him whispered, "What's going on?"

"Looks like we've been sold out."

"Huh?"

"Somebody out bid us in City Hall."

They fell silent and watched the floor with grim consideration. The Irishmen who had never taken a pinch before were nervous. The rest knew it was more or less routine, something that went along with the business they had chosen. But, boy, oh boy, wouldn't the wops get a kick out of this? Felim could almost see Patsy Guarino laughing now, not to mention the fat smiling face of that loathsome Eddie DiStella.. "And that fat pile of shite, Rocco," he said softly to no one in particular.

The ride to the station was a long and slow one. The night breeze was a little cold, but at least the rain had stopped. *Thank God for small favors,* Felim thought. *Now how about some big ones?* The streets and buildings shrank behind them as the truck rattled onward, bouncing its uneasy and unnerved cargo. The street lamps stared down at their reflections in the rain puddles along the potholes as though they were bowing their heads in shame and disbelief for poor Felim Strong and his boys.

Finally the truck stopped behind the precinct house which appeared huge and ominous in the darkness. They all steeled themselves to the unpleasant process of getting booked. *Why are they taking so long?* Felim wondered. He looked into the darkness and saw nothing. For a moment he considered making a run for it until he heard the approaching footsteps. A flashlight was held on them; Felim held up an arm to shield his blinded eyes. "What's going on here?"

Another policeman shined a light on a small crate of booze. "What's that?"

The first policeman, who Felim recognized as a sergeant, whispered to another, sending him on an errand. In moments he came back leading a veritable army of armed policemen. "Alright, out with you. You have some questions to answer." As the men started filing out of the truck, the sergeant grabbed Felim and pulled him aside. "Jaysus, Felim. Sean's going to be mighty sore about this. Don't you know better than to park outside a police station in a truck full of your merchandise? Now we'll *have* to book you."

It was then that Felim realized that they had been had.

* * *

Fat Eddie was pacing up and down the spot where the missing truck should have been. This would most likely be the end of him. Rocco and his right hand man Guarino would not be pleased at all. In fact, to put it simply, they'd be pissed. First a bunch of Micks from the Conway gang walk off with another truck load of booze and now this. *He's gonna find somebody else, that's for sure. Yes,* a nasty voice in the back of his mind said, *but what'll they do to vacate your position?*

The phone rang at that moment and Fat Eddie nearly jumped out of his skin. He looked at it with wild eyes, *My God, has he found out already?* He envisioned Rocco Petrelli drawing a line across his throat with his index finger and Patsy Guarino smiling at the order.

One of the guys who had been staring at the truck's vacant spot with Eddie answered the telephone, "It's for you, Eddie."

"What do they want?"

"They won't say."

Eddie took the phone from him and muttered, "Hello?"

"Hiya Eddie, ole' boy. I understand you're likely to get in a bit of trouble with the guys upstairs."

"What? Who the hell is this?"

"That ain't important. What is, is the fact that a certain somebody is willing to get your fat out of the fire, *if* you will remember his kindness. Understand?"

"What are you talking about? Look, who the hell is this?"

"That ain't important," the voice repeated. "Now, do you want help or don't you?"

"I don't need nobody's fucking help."

"If that's the way you feel about it, Eddie, alright. But I have to warn you that this certain somebody is going to go straight to G if you won't take his help. Good-bye."

"Wait! Wait! Let's not be hasty," Eddie giggled nervously. "Let's talk this out."

"No talk. Do you want this guy to help you out, or not?"

"Yeah, sure. But what's he gonna do?"

"Are you going to remember he did you a favor?"

"Of course, if he can do anything."

"Alright. Listen carefully. Stay right where you are. In five minutes there will be a honk at the south entrance. They're bringing your truck back. Open the door and let 'em in. Alright?"

"Okay, got it."

"Good. It's the smart thing to do, Eddie," the voice said and hung up.

Fat Eddie replaced the receiver and stared at it for a few moments. Finally Mo spoke, "What is it, Eddie?"

"I don't know, he said softly, thinking. "Somebody wants to talk. Sounds a bit fishy. Could be a hit." He turned to Mo and spoke with authority. "I want you to get all the trigger fingers you can in five minutes. Get them here on either side of the south entrance. Me and a few others will be by the back exit, watching the other side. You'll hear somebody honk in a few minutes. Let them in, but don't nobody fire until you're sure there's trouble. Got that?"

"Yeh, sure. You watch the back exit," Mo said. When Eddie walked away, Mo muttered under his breath, "Yeh, so you can beat it at the first sign of trouble, you fucking chickenshit."

The warehouse was silent when the horn sounded outside. Mo thought he could feel the engine rumbling through the concrete floor. He nodded for the guys to open up the door. The door swung open and the headlights of a large truck spilled into the warehouse. The truck pulled in, followed by another. Fat Eddie had been watching this, peeking around the corner, prepared to hop into the car that one of the guys already had running in the alley. He could feel the beads of sweat popping out on his forehead. He remembered to breathe when he recognized the figure that emerged from the first truck.

"Tommy," he said in half-whisper of disbelief. The young man was wearing a partial policeman's uniform, polishing the cap with his elbow. Fat Eddie appeared from his shelter and stalked towards the young thug. "What kinda fuckin' game are you playing?"

"No game, Eddie. Take a look in the truck."

Fat Eddie slowly rounded one of the trucks, as if expecting an ambush to blow him away. Instead, he found barrels and barrels of beer stacked behind crates of Canadian Real McCoy. It was a fortune in alcohol. He almost lost control of his bowels. "Holy shit," he whispered. "What the—" he turned to Tommy Trent and lost his train of thought.

The young man showed a hint of cockiness behind the steel eyes. "There's more. You have a contact man at the precinct house over on 87th, right?"

"Sure."

"Give him a call and ask if anything interesting has happened on the north side lately."

Fat Eddie hesitated for a moment, looking for a trap somewhere. Then he went into the office and chatted on the phone for a few minutes. Meanwhile, Tommy's men had piled out of the trucks and had begun helping Mo's crewmen unload the alcohol. "They didn't soup 'em all. Put the ones without corks over there."

"Hey, Marty," Tommy called. Marty Rossini put down a crate of whiskey and joined him. Tommy handed him back his uncle's cap. "Thanks for the uniform. You think you can get it back before it's missed?"

"Sure," Marty grinned, "no problem."

"You know, that came in handy," Tommy said with a grin. "Might have to get us some of those."

Eddie returned with a stunned expression plastered on his chubby face. "What's going on?" Mo asked. Fat Eddie didn't reply, his eyes going over Tommy Trent waiting for some sign of what was to come.

Finally he couldn't wait, "What's all this about, Tommy?"

"Simple. You agreed to let me help you, and here I am. I mean, Rocco and G gotta be unhappy and unimpressed with your operations, Eddie. But now I've changed that. Tell you what, you go over to that telephone and tell him that your guys just got back the hijacked liquor three-fold and landed the Micks in a heapa trouble. You tell him that, Eddie. And that one of your right hand men carried it out."

Eddie was slow to respond. "What else?"

"Well…" Tommy extracted a loose cigarette from his breast pocket with an effortless sleight of hand. "For starters, you could apologize to Jimmy Brisone for making me have to put him in the hospital."

"Oh, well, that," Fat Eddie giggled nervously, "Tommy—that was just all a misunderstanding. No hard feelings, right, Tommy?"

Tommy Trent's only answer was a vague sardonic grin.

3

Dottie's had become a popular speakeasy and with its charming hostess, its fair variety of liquor and the beautiful dancing girls, it was no wonder. It was the brightest spot in the neighborhood. So it was not unusual to find Tommy Trent and his band of men, Gaetano "Tano" Amato, Marty Rossini, Tony Palermi and Joe Mitchner, sitting at one of the side tables. Nor was it unusual to see Tano sitting at the piano when the band took a break, singing in that smooth laid-back baritone of his that seemed to melt broads like warm butter or to find Connie Banks sitting on Tano's lap at the table, not minding his hand resting high upon her thigh beneath the flapper's dress. There was a celebratory atmosphere tonight, although Tommy had not yet told them what they were celebrating. All evening they had been pressing their leader into letting them in on what was spinning in those wheels in his head, but he held out until Connie went back to join the dancers.

When she was out of sight and Tano's attention was no longer on the swaying of her hips, Tommy cleared his throat loudly to gain his attentiveness.

"So," Tano started, packing the end of a cigarette on the table, "What's all this about?"

"Gentlemen," Tommy raised his glass in a toast. "To moving up in the world."

They all drank to the sentiment and let Tano, the closest to Tommy Trent, speak for them. "I don't exactly get it, Pally. So we did a nice thing for Fatso. So now he might treat us with a little more respect. Then what?"

"Yeah," Joe said, "It's not like he's gonna introduce us to the Big Guy as heroes or something."

Tommy took a slow sip from his glass and placed it on the table carefully, letting dramatic tension build. He was a master of this. "You guys really think that much of me, huh? This is just stage one. But before we get to stage two, we have another matter to attend to."

"What's that?"

"Well, those guys on the North Side aren't going to be too thrilled about having monkeys made out of them. They're probably looking for the responsible parties right now, and they are probably getting close to home."

"So what are we gonna do?"

Tommy answered with a shrug, as if it were the most natural thing in the world, "Confess."

* * *

Sean Conway had grown up in a slum in the Irish section of the city that was like a thousand other slums across the nation: packed with hoards of people who had fled the old world to find nothing but poverty and crowded, unsanitary conditions in the new one. The neighborhood had been so isolated that many first and some second generation Americans still carried a bit of the Irish brogue with them. His father's family had been wiped out by one of the many famines that ravaged the Emerald Isle and sent those who could escape scattering to the four corners of the earth. At a very early age he decided that neither he nor anyone else in his family would ever go hungry again.

He had devoted his life to stock piling all the wealth he could to prevent any future disasters. Decades of hard work, political finagling, pay offs, and murders had put him on top of the Irish neighborhoods. If anyone had a problem, they could come to Sean Conway. If anyone wanted somebody roughed up, they could come to Conway. If anybody wanted some booze, they could come to Conway.

Together with Hyman Amberg, Conway and Rocco Petrelli owned equal percentages in the Sondern brewery, one of the largest in the country. Conway had significant political pull in the 42nd and 43rd wards and was being courted openly by both political parties looking to gain and keep his favor. One of the parties had recently held a banquet in his honor and a county clerk awarded him a platinum watch set with rubies and diamonds.

His position was a precarious one, however. Conway had always disdained prostitution and banned it from his district, leaving his chief rival's predecessor, Big Joe LaCava, open to create a massive empire of bawdy houses and opium dens, a monopoly which raked in mountains of money of which Conway could only dream. LaCava had amassed greater amounts of political clout and greater fortunes and his heir, Rocco, had used them to purchase large interests in most of the other brewery and distillery operations. This left Conway and most of the other mob bosses feeling they were living under Rocco Petrelli's thumb. If they could not produce enough beer and bathtub gin to satisfy their neighborhoods, they would have to buy it from Rocco's mob. And the prices Rocco charged Conway were dangerously close to being usurious.

Conway had respected Eddie DiStella's predecessor, but not Fat Eddie. He would never be half the gangster that Sally Nose had been. Everyone knew it, even Rocco Petrelli. He had been put in months after the amendment went into effect and had yet to catch up with the times. He was weak, and therefore fair game.

But the raid on the warehouse by these new boys from Eddie's neighborhood had enraged Conway. Lifting an occasional truck or two was considered fair play, but cleaning out an entire warehouse and getting a whole crew sent to the can was a different story. That was just asking for trouble.

But Sean Conway wasn't ready to take on the entire Rocco Petrelli organization.

So he had sent his right-hand man, Pat Michelson to get Felim Strong's men out of jail and to find out what really happened.

Pat Michelson was a bit of a mystery and his background was vague. Few people knew anything more than the fact he arrived from Ireland suspiciously soon after the Easter Rising in 1916.

Michelson's sudden appearance at Felim's warehouse unnerved Micah Collins. Collins felt it was only a matter of time before Michelson found the traitor. He certainly hoped that Tommy Trent had a few more tricks up his sleeve.

Micah Collins admired Tommy Trent and believed in him. Many hours they had spent drinking together and discussing how the gangs should be working together against the common enemy: the law and the Prohibition Agents. It was just a shame that Trent was a low-level guy, otherwise everyone in the city would be spending all their time making money hand-over-fist instead of trying to kill each other.

"It's a helluva mess," Michelson said, surveying the remnants of Felim's warehouse. Tommy and his boys had done a thorough job of cleaning it out. Felim and Micah could only nod in agreement. Pat Michelson lit a cigar and squinted his eyes against the smoke. "But I might have something that'll help you guys. C'mon. Let's go for a ride."

The hair on the back of Micah Collins' neck stood on end. For an instant, he considered reaching for his gun, but thought better of it. Shoot first, ask questions later might have worked in the moving pictures, but not in the real world. Michelson led them to an anonymous black sedan with an anonymous blue-chinned driver behind the wheel. "I've got a guy cross town who wants to sell me an old beat up still," Michelson explained. "I need you guys to let me know if you can think it can be fixed before I bother."

Micah and Pat got in the backseat. Felim sat beside the driver. They drove for a long while, chit-chatting idly. Micah Collins was beginning to wonder just where the hell this still was supposed to be. *They're gonna kill me,* he thought. *The sonuvabitch knows.*

Occasionally Michelson would throw in a question about the raid. Felim answered easily and seemed to be in a pretty jolly mood, which was more than Micah could have said about himself. His innards were tied in knots and he was willing himself not to break into a sweat. He was sure they had discovered he had set up the warehouse for Tommy Trent. But what the hell? There had been good money in it and Tommy had been an old friend. It had been worth a gamble, anyway.

The car pulled over near the rail yards while the driver got out to relieve himself. The driver stood with his back to the car and whistled a happy little tune. Pat Michelson pulled a small revolver from under his coat. Micah Collins reached for his own gun, certain that this was it, but Michelson made a quieting gesture.

Micah's jaw drooped and his eyebrows furrowed.

Felim, in the front passenger seat, was in the middle of a funny story when Michelson placed the muzzle of the gun to the back of his head and pulled the trigger. The windscreen was showered with blood and fragments of brain and bone as Felim Strong's body pitched forward in the seat. Pat shot him once more at the base of the skull just to be sure, and let out a heavy sigh.

When the echoes of the gun blast died away, Michelson frowned at the corpse in the front seat. "It's a bloody shame. He was a good man." He turned to face Collins, "It's your warehouse now. But just remember what happens to people when they get greedy."

Pat Michelson stepped out of the car and Micah followed. "How-how did you know it was him?"

Michelson led Micah to another car around the corner as if he were out for a Sunday afternoon stroll. As he opened the door, Pat grinned over the roof of the car, "We have a guy working for us in Fat Eddie's neighborhood."

4

SARAH DISTELLA SAT AT THE VANITY TABLE IN her room, brushing her hair and wondering about her own sanity. It had been swimming around in the back of her mind for days now, but it had not really surfaced until last night. And when it did, it was like a wave crashing into the ocean.

She had been sitting here in this very spot, going through the same repetitious motions with her brush when she heard her father letting somebody in. She recognized the voice but could not place it. After mulling it over for a few, she stood from her chair and ran her hands over her thighs, smoothing out the blue dress.

She found her father sitting in the front room sharing his cigars with the masher—the gutter-thug who had graduated to the curb, Tommy Trent. *He thinks he's so suave,* she thought contemptuously, watching him sitting in the large chair across from her father, holding a cigar in one hand and toying with his hat with the other.

Her father was just finishing the question, "Do you really think they'll stop screwing around with us?" when she started to cross the room to the front door, circumventing the two to avoid interruption. She nearly jumped when her father stood up, and exclaimed "Ah!" directing Trent's attention to her. He too was now standing, holding his hat in both hands, leaving his cigar smoldering in the ashtray next to his chair. "Sarah, have you met Tommy Trent?"

Being polite for only the sake of her father, she extended a courteous hand. "We've haven't been formally introduced," she said trying to mask the hauteur behind her words.

Trent took her hand delicately, and, knowing that kissing it would have pushed her father too far, opted for a polite bow. "Pleasure to know you, Ms. DiStella."

He thinks he's so debonair, it's sickening, she thought, all the while her father's voice was booming, "Call her Sarah."

Trent smiled a little and redressed himself, "Sarah."

It was then that she looked into his baby-blue eyes and the waves crashed against the shore. *Of course he thinks he's suave. He is. Most people who think they are, aren't. But not this guy. He is and he knows it. And boy, handsome to boot.* The thought startled her and she looked away from him shamefacedly. "Pleasure," she muttered before excusing herself from the room.

And ever since then, she had been wrestling with a quandary: Was she becoming infatuated with this guy? The thought frightened her, and what made it worse was that deep down, she knew the answer was yes.

She put the brush down and pinned her hair back with a pair of barrettes. Then she put on a hat, adjusting the angle properly and examining the effect in the mirror. When all was satisfactory, she grabbed her purse and left the room.

Her father was in the kitchen and she called to him from the front door, "Poppa, I'm going down to get your medicine." When he called back thanking her, she opened the door and headed down the wooden steps to the street.

She walked out of sight, oblivious to Tommy Trent in the phone booth near the pool hall. He made a quick call and then studied his pocket watch for seventy five seconds before heading across the street and going up the same stairs she had just descended. One of the guys in the pool hall watched through the window and wondered why Tommy

Trent never came in anymore.

He had graduated to bigger things.

* * *

Her mind was still on the subject of Tommy Trent when she reached the drug store. She went in past the soda fountain to the drug counter. "Hello, Mr. L." she said brightly as if it would call her full attention to the here and now.

"Hello, Ms. DiStella. I'll get it now." The small man disappeared for a moment, gone to fetch another bottle of Eddie's medicine. It was for his stomach, and considering how high-strung he was, and the way he reacted to pressure, it was no wonder he went through the stuff like it was water.

She paid for the bottle and walked through the drug store, ignoring the soda jerk who was always ogling her shapely body, most particularly her posterior. She might have told him to buzz off and keep his eyes in his skull, but he was just a dumb kid. He was only sixteen.

Outside, she noticed for the first time just how clean and crisp the air seemed. She took a deep lungful of the air and smiled with satisfaction at the small ghost-like billow her breath produced. She pulled up the collar of her coat and pulled down her felt cloche hat. She thought to herself that winter would soon be pulled in by those long fingerlike clouds that stretched inward from the north. But that was fine by her. There was something purifying about winter. The whole world went to sleep beneath a blanket of ice and snow so that it could awake anew and refreshed come spring.

'Besides,' she thought, 'you can't have Christmas without winter.' She looked up the sky and smiled. The sun would be setting before long and it would enter into her favorite time of day. A true romantic at heart, she always loved walking during the sunset, regardless of the time of year.

Her mind wandered this way and that as she made a conscious effort to *not* think about Tommy Trent. It was no use. That was the burning question, wasn't it? Tommy Trent: Gutter Thug or 7th Avenue Valentino?

She was not very far away from home when it happened. Suddenly, out of the blue, yanking her back to reality from her daydreams, a strong man had leapt upon her from behind, clamping a hand over her mouth, the other arm wrapped around her middle, pinning her arms down to her sides. Her eyes bulged outwards as she tried to scream. *My God!* she thought, *He's going to rape me!* "Shut up, lady," the voice demanded.

A dark pillowcase was pulled over her head as the man dragged her into a car. She managed to bite her assailant's hand as he adjusted the pillowcase and she scrambled blindly for the door latch. But the man grabbed her and pulled her back, almost like a football tackle. Another man, sitting next to her attacker, forced her head down against his knee, exerting a tremendous pressure on her skull with one hand while the other tied a gag over the pillowcase. The gag cinched tight, pulling so much of the pillowcase into her mouth that she thought her jaw would break. The first man had his arms wrapped around her legs, busily tying her ankles together. Now the second man was tying her hands behind her back in a painful angle. She could feel that her dress had ridden up in the struggle and they could probably see everything. She started to cry.

* * *

Fat Eddie had already taken to complaining to Tommy about his many woes and had been at it for a long while. "And all these kids—I got little kids, twelve years old, runnin' round, upsettin' apple carts, pickin' pockets, rollin' drunks. They're a nuisance."

"They want a piece of action," Tommy said. Not so many years ago he had been one of those untamed kids Eddie was complaining about. "Everybody wants in. Even those kids. So give 'em something to do. Let 'em wash the trucks or empty bottles. Let 'em act as look-outs in front of the speaks. Make 'em feel they're part of it."

"You mean, pay them?" Eddie laughed. "These fuckin' delinquents?"

"Well, you either give 'em a few quarters for sweeping up warehouses or you let 'em run wild and spend all your time trying to knock sense into them. Besides, if they gotta put more coppers on the beat to deal with these kids, then it becomes harder for the coppers to pretend that they don't see anything." Tommy set his glass down on the table and crossed the room to the window. "C'mere." Eddie followed Tommy as he pulled back the curtain and threw the window open. "Look out there. Take a deep breath. …You know what that is? Money. It's hangin' on the air, Eddie. All you gotta do is grab it."

Eddie grinned. He liked the sound of that.

"But if you get distracted by all these little things, you miss it."

"All right," Eddie said pulling his head in from the window. "You think that'd help? Okay. Tomorrow you round up all these little punks and give 'em something to do—trial basis, of course."

"Me? Why me?"

Eddie chuckled. "It's your idea, chum. Then, if I think it's worth it, I'll keep it and it will be my idea, see?"

Tommy nodded.

Eddie looked out the window again and his grin faltered. The sun was beginning to set and he realized he was hungry. "Hey, Tommy, how long you been here?"

"'Bout an hour and a half. Why?"

A dull panic started sinking in through the fat. "Sarah. She shoulda been back an hour ago." He went on, interpreting Trent's grunt as a sound of concern. "She was just going to the drug store."

"Maybe she ran into some friends."

"No. No. She'da called."

Tommy Trent looked at the clock against the opposite wall. "You want me to go look for her?"

Fat Eddie, somewhat incoherent, glanced up at him with wildly frightened eyes. "Wouldja?"

"Sure." Trent went to the hall tree and grabbed his coat. He had just one sleeve on when the phone rang. They both froze.

It rang a few more times before Eddie got up the nerve to lift the receiver. "Hello?... Yeah... What?... Holy— Okay. Okay... How much!?!... I don't have that fuckin' kinda money— Okay, okay. Please, whatever you ask... Where?" Here he shakily grabbed a magazine and scribbled on the cover. "...When? Okay. Okay." He replaced the receiver and held his head in his hands for a long moment before looking up at Trent.

"What's the matter?"

"Somebody's kidnapped my daughter."

Tommy Trent did not speak, and Fat Eddie knew instantly the crazy wheels in his head were spinning. Finally, "How much are they asking?"

"Ten grand."

Tommy whistled.

"You wouldn't happen to have that kinda money on you, huh?"

"No."

Fat Eddie sounded absolutely defeated. "I guess I'll have to go crawling on my knees to Patsy." Patsy Guarino seemed perpetually dissatisfied with the lack of miracles Eddie could work and the less contact they had, the better. The thought of going to him for any kind of help made Eddie's stomach turn.

Tommy finished putting on his coat before reaching to the small of his back. He pulled out a revolver and checked the loads. "Where and when?"

Eddie handed him the magazine with the address. "Three hours."

"Alright. Let me have a crack at this first. If you don't hear from me in an hour, go ahead and call G. Okay?"

"What are you going to do?"

"Round up some of my desperadoes. Usually when there's a ransom-drop off, there's a bum watching for cops setting up a sting. I'll find him and try to shake it out of him."

"Be careful, Tommy. Jesus, be careful. This is my daughter we're talking about."

"Alright. Just remember, an hour and call the big guy." With that Tommy left. Fat Eddie stared at the door for a long while and then burst into tears.

5

She was locked in some kind of small broom closet. She did not know why or where or by whom. But nonetheless, here she was. She had been sitting on her feet for what seemed like days and they were painfully asleep. Her hands were still tied behind her and she could not change to a more comfortable position in the cramped quarters. She had been crying for so long her throat hurt and her lungs were burning. She felt suffocated with the gag still tied in her mouth and the pillowcase over her head. She was cold and in pain and had never been so frightened in her entire life. But at least they had not molested her. Yet.

Sarah heard occasional voices, but nothing distinct enough to understand. Nor could she even guess how many men there were. From what she could tell they were all in another room. She was not foolish enough to hope that this was some kind of horrible nightmare from which she'd awaken. It was too real, too inconceivable.

She wanted to go home and, yes, juvenile as it might sound, she wanted her mother who had been dead for eight years now. Why she should miss her departed mother so much at a time like this, she did not know. She wanted to be anywhere but here.

And thinking about her mother, and the seemingly very real possibility of her own demise, Sarah found herself being tortured by the vivid memories of her mother's funeral and all the horror and hell and grief she and her father went through.

She had never believed that she would ever go through more horror or hell. She had never had any reason to think otherwise.

Until now.

How long had she been here? How long was it going to be before they dragged her out and stripped her and raped her? How long before they were going to murder her? How long before she would see her mother again?

Another wave of racking sobs tore through her, making her feel as if her lungs were going to stop working. Well, at least that way would be easier.

She now saw what a sheltered life she had. The newspapers were always full of stories about violent crimes, kidnappings and murders, but her father had done such a thorough job of protecting her, all the stories seemed like fiction. She had never witnessed any of the violence or ever been in need of anything. Whatever she needed, her father bought for her. Whatever she wanted her father bought for her.

But all she wanted now was to be away from this place and home. But this seemed like something that *no one* could buy for her.

* * *

Sarah didn't know whether she had fallen asleep or just blacked out but it now seemed as if a great deal of time had passed. She could hear somebody fiddling with the closet door handle. Whoever it was was having trouble. A groan escaped her throat but was strangled by the gag. The door opened and she braced herself for the worst.

A pair of lips pressed almost to her ear, "Sarah," the voice said in a barely audible whisper. She somehow recognized it immediately and felt like fainting. "It's me, Tommy." He removed the pillowcase and brushed her hair back with a tender hand before using a small knife to cut the ropes that bound her ankles. He leaned in again, reaching behind her for her wrists. "Now keep quiet. We're too out-numbered for a shoot-out. Do you understand?"

She nodded deliberately. He carefully helped her out of the closet, but her legs did not seem to want to work. The tall man with him was watching another door carefully, cradling a deadly looking Thompson machinegun in his arms. After such a long time in utter darkness the thin beam of light spilling out from under that door was almost blinding. Tommy lifted her off her feet and carried her to an open window. The other man set the machinegun on a table by Trent and climbed out first. Tommy passed her through the window to him. "My name's Tano," the tall man said softly.

"C'mon, save the chit-chat," Tommy said as Tano passed her back to him. Tano leaned back in through the window to retrieve his machinegun. They slunk down the fire escape to a dirty alley that came out on a small side street. Tommy carried her to the car. Tano got in behind the wheel while Tommy deposited Sarah in the back before climbing in beside her. "Alright, let's get her home."

"Thank you," she managed in a cracked egg-shell voice as the car started moving.

Tommy Trent seemed to have not heard. "Are you okay?"

"Yes, I think so."

"They didn't hurt you?"

"No."

"They didn't molest you?"

"No," she repeated and rested her head on his chest. She let him put his arm around her and immediately felt safe. "Thank you."

6

Jesus. Fat Eddie sighed. running a hand through his sparse hair. "I don't know how to ever thank you, Tommy."

It had been an hour since Sarah had finally fallen asleep. Tommy had carried her in through the door, escorted by Tano, and helped the girl's father get her into bed. She had not wanted to sleep in the dark, demanding that the light stay on in her room. And she didn't want to be alone when she fell asleep, so Tommy Trent had sat in silence holding her hand until she drifted off. And even then, he had sat holding her hand, watching her face calmed by the world of slumber, the rise and fall of the blanket as her breathing steadied itself through the gentle pout of her lips.

And now, an hour later, the two men sat in the front room as Eddie realized he would have to completely re-evaluate his opinion of Tommy Trentino. "Jesus, I just… Thank you," Eddie said for at least the third time in the hour.

Trent held up his empty glass and Eddie wordlessly got up, took it and filled it at the drinks cupboard across the room. He paused, topped off his own glass as well, and turned to face Tommy. "Next week all the boys are meeting with the Big Guy." He waited for some reaction from Tommy. "The boss. You know, Mr. Petrelli." He watched Trent and his lack of emotion incredulously. Rocco Petrelli was to crime what Babe Ruth was to baseball. He was *the* big hitter. He was the guy every young gangster in America looked to for inspiration. "What? You never heard of him?"

"Sure, I heard of him. Who hasn't?"

"You know he's the guy we work for, right?"

Tommy knew that and a lot more, but remained placid. He needed to know how Fat Eddie really felt about his tiny little toe-hold in the vast empire that was crime. Eddie went on, "I answer to G. And *he,* even though he's like a king in his own right, answers to Mr. Petrelli." Trentino nodded, waiting for what he already knew was coming.

"Well, to be honest with you, Tommy, just because you saved my daughter's life, I would like for you to be there with me, when I go. You can be my chauffeur and bodyguard."

Tommy stood up and looked Fat Eddie over from head to foot. He caught Eddie's eyes in his and raised his glass.

Tommy Trentino nodded and smiled.

7

Tommy Trent parked the car along side the Welman Hotel and opened the rear door for Fat Eddie. "You look sharp, kid." Eddie said as he stepped out. He cast his eyes upwards to the starless night and sighed, turning up the collar of his coat. "Sure hope it don't rain." Eddie pulled him close as they approached the front steps. "Maybe, I'll introduce you to Patsy when we go in. All you have to do is stand around and look tough and like you're ready in case of trouble. Can you do that?"

"Sure."

Eddie led him inside the hotel and down a long marbled corridor. They came to a lounge filled with other well-dressed tough looking men. "Patsy," Eddie called. "Patsy." The crowd seemed to part before the tall gaunt figure. "This is Tommy Trent. One of my new guys."

"Nice to see a fresh face from that neighborhood," Patsy said to Tommy. "You got him here on time."

Tommy shrugged. "All in a day's work."

"Tommy's the one who took care of that little problem." Eddie said.

"Which one?" Patsy Guarino asked, "The hijackers or the kidnappers?"

Fat Eddie's smile faltered. "I, I didn't know you knew—"

"Come on, Eddie," Tommy said quickly. "There's probably nothing in the city that he or Mr. Petrelli don't know about."

"You got that right, kid." Patsy said.

"I took care of both problems," Tommy said with as much modesty as was possible coming from a gangster.

Patsy grinned. "Swell. C'mon, Eddie, Tommy. Rocco will be here in a few."

* * *

Rocco Petrelli had been about Tommy Trent's age when he went to work for his uncle, Guiseppe "Big Joe" LaCava. LaCava owned a string of whorehouses throughout the county ranging from flea-ridden $1 bordellos to the luxurious $50 ones frequented by the rich and powerful. Rocco's first job was to rid his uncle of the Black Hand nuisance who had been trying to extort money from him. Rocco's solution was simple. He waited for them to arrive at the designated drop-off point and shotgunned them to death.

He then became Big Joe's number one enforcer and collector. He only had to burn down one store and one apartment house before the people of the neighborhood began to shape up and pay LaCava the appropriate tributes.

Then he became a bouncer in The Victoria, the grandest whorehouse of them all. Those were good years—he lived the high life in the bordello and the guests were rarely any trouble. It seemed as though Big Joe was paying Rocco to drink champagne by the gallons and to have all the sex he could handle.

It was there that Rocco fell in love with one of the girls, but beat her to death when he learned she had had his child scraped from her womb. Rocco Petrelli's belief in love was short-lived.

But it made his move into the white slavery end of the business all the easier. He used his handsome charm to lure girls who were between the ages of thirteen and seventeen and were either orphaned, desperate or just gullible to his "place of business" offering them a job. There he would lock them up and rape them or "break them in" as it was known in the profession, before he handed them over to the "keepers." The keepers would further torment the young girls before moving them to one of the whorehouses. They'd work there for a few weeks before being sold to other white slavers in other cities for anywhere between $200 and $400.

To this day Rocco would still have thirteen year old girls brought to him when he felt particularly lively.

As he moved into the white slavery business, he also became a Black Hand extortionist. Usually his targets were the guests of the $50 whorehouses.

And when Big Joe died, Rocco took the helm. He developed an army of gunmen and skull breakers to muscle in on other racketeers and whoremasters. It was a simple step from that to offering protection across the board to businesses of all varieties. His army of henchmen soon attracted the attentions of local unions who needed a way to stop the strikes and discourage the scabs.

Ah, there were a million rackets, but God had truly blessed Rocco Petrelli with this Prohibition. He was a king among kings and a public hero. He gave the people what the government would deny them: gambling, girls and booze. All nice, clean, victimless crimes.

It was no wonder Rocco Petrelli was the most popular man in the city.

* * *

Tommy Trent and another man were assigned to stand inside the large double doors of the meeting room "just for show" as Eddie said. Two other men stood on the opposite side of the room from them, near Rocco's place setting. It was no secret that the chauffeurs and bodyguards of the upper echelon were among some of the most trusted men. They heard everything and were expected to keep their mouths shut.

In spite of Eddie saying the guards were there merely for show, Tommy figured that in this day and age to be as powerful as Rocco was to be in a precarious situation. He knew it would only be a matter of time until some of the other gangs decided to challenge Rocco's position.

Tommy wondered to himself what Dottie would make of the sight of Tommy Trent standing across the room from Rocco Petrelli.

"Gentlemen," Rocco Petrelli said standing at the head of the long table. "I want to thank you all for being here. Not that any of you mugs had a choice." A good-natured laugh echoed through the room.

"There comes a time when… any business enterprise needs to reorganize itself and merge with others. Any large corporation in the world. The old days are over and with them go the old ways. This is the twentieth century and we've been hanging on to nineteenth century ideas too long. We're finally moving forward."

"Just so's you know," he said, smiling, sticking his thumbs behind the lapels of his evening jacket, "I'm still the boss." The men laughed again. "And Patsy here, he's still number two." The men pounded and tapped on the tabletop in applause as Patsy stood briefly and took a quick bow. "Marco Messinio, will still be a captain along with the rest of you mugs," he said indicating the men sitting on the left side of the table. "But he is also our consigliere. Marco's sharp and whenever Patsy and I need a third head, he'll be the man."

"Now, you guys," he addressed the men on the left side of the table directly, "You're our eyes and ears on the streets. You have a lot of responsibilities, but I know that we won't be disappointed. You're the ones that everyone goes to with their beefs, when they need advice… when they need to know where's the best place to pick up a broad, whatever." The men laughed again.

"And you all know Joey Bones?" Guiseppe Osso, a short stocky man, stood up and repeated Patsy's quick bow. The men applauded. "Bones has decided to come over and join us. From now on, he'll be an equal to the rest of the captains, and he'll run his turf with the same free reign. He is to be treated as an equal with the rest of the outfit. If he needs help, you guys help him. If you need help, you can go to Joey, see?"

The men applauded once more, more enthusiastically.

"Now, I know that you're all thinking that the other groups might get nervous about this… *merger*. But Hyman Amberg has assured me he has no complaints and that he will talk sense to that hot-headed Irishman. The others…" he shrugged, "They're small potatoes."

"So I thank you all for being here. I hope you enjoy your dinner." He picked up his glass of champagne, "And here's to decades of prosperity for us all!"

Echoes of "Hear! Hear!" and the clanking of glasses filled the room.

Rocco Petrelli surveyed the group with a satisfied grin. His mob was now an army. Complete with officers.

8

Hey, kids! Tommy called and then whistled. The five young boys abandoned their game of stick ball long enough to eye Tommy suspiciously. He wasn't one of the shop owners coming to harass them and he didn't dress like a cop. He dressed like a gangster.

The tallest of the boys, who Tommy guessed was about twelve, nodded to the others who ranged in age down to about eight years old. They gathered in a semi-circle around Tommy, folded their arms and studied him for a long time, squinting from beneath their dirty caps.

Tommy let them look sinister.

Finally the oldest boy shifted a wad of candy from one side of his mouth to the other and said, "What do ya want?"

"How'd you kids like to make some money and maybe get Gores off yer back for a while?" Officer Gores was the neighborhood flatfoot who seemed to spend most of his shifts chasing these kids from one rolled drunk to the next.

The youngest of the kids, a cherub-faced boy of about eight stepped forward and did his best to sneer, "Doin' what?"

"I need someone to be my eyes and ears out here on the street."

"How much?" the oldest boy asked.

"The five of you?" Tommy said and began thumbing through a wad of singles, "A buck and a quarter a day."

"That's only a quarter a piece," another boy scoffed. "We can get that in an hour snitchin' apples and coal."

"Okay," Tommy said and put his wad of money back in his pocket. "But I don't want to hear you kids whinin' when Gores takes his nightstick to you."

The oldest boy grabbed Tommy's elbow. "Wait a minute, mister." Tommy turned back to them. "You mean to tell me you wanna fork out eight bucks and change every week just have us stand around doin' nothing'?"

Eight bucks was nothing. That would come out of the shop owners' protection money. "Sure," Tommy said, "But it wouldn't be for nothing."

The little one spoke up, still trying to master a sneer, "Wha'd we have to do?"

"Well, just hang around out front here like you are now. See, some of the boys have something going on in one of the buildings over here. Now you guys would let us know if there was trouble on the way. If a copper comes by, you'd give a signal."

"How?"

"You can all whistle?" The boys nodded. "Then it's that simple. If you see a cop other than Gores you let out three short whistles and a long one, like this." Tommy demonstrated. "Can you do that?"

All of the boys except the youngest repeated the whistling. He couldn't quite get the hang of it. Tommy smiled. There was something about this little boy that reminded Tommy of himself at that age. It was tough on a cute little kid like this when acting like a tough guy was a matter of survival. Tommy patted the kid's shoulder. "Don't worry, fella. You'll get it. So what do you say?"

The boys exchanged glances, shrugging. This was their first opportunity for regular work. "Sure," the oldest one said. "We'll see how it goes."

Tommy smiled, making the kids think they had just made his day. "Swell." He addressed the little one. "What's your name?"

Another boy answered, "They call him Jackrabbit."

"Why's that?"

"Because he can jump over anything when a copper's after him!" The boys all laughed.

"Alright," Tommy pulled the money out of his pocket again. He thumbed up five pairs of singles and began passing them around. "Here's eight days in advance, alright?"

The boys eyes lit up as they took the money. Tommy wondered if any of them had ever seen that much money at once. "Thanks!"

"I'll have a little chat with old Gores for you."

As Tommy began walking away, the oldest boy called after him. "Hey, wait up!" He caught up with Tommy and gave him the narrowed eyes again. "My name's Vinny. What's yers?"

"They call me Tommy Trent."

"All right, Mister Tommy Trent," the boy said, sticking out his hand like a businessman. "It's nice doin' business with you."

* * *

Mo Cimmino had spent most of the day looking for Tommy. He had tried talking Jimmy Brisone into helping him, but after meeting Tommy in that darkened alley and getting his face smashed in, Brisone politely refused.

He had almost decided to give up when he spotted Tommy and his friend Tano heading towards Dottie's speakeasy. "Tommy! Hey, Tommy?" The two men whirled around with their coats unbuttoned. "C'mere," Mo motioned them towards his car. "Where the hell you been? Eddie asked me to find you hours ago."

"Here and there. You know Tano?"

The men nodded to each other and muttered "How's it goin'?"

Tommy leaned an arm on the car door and lit a cigarette. "What's up?"

Mo shrugged. "I dunno. But Eddie wants to talk to you. Private, he said."

"Sure." He turned to Tano, "You wanna come?"

Gaetano looked at his watch. "Nah. At six I'm gonna go see if I can find Connie."

"Okay. I'll catch up with you later." He climbed into the car and closed the door behind him.

"One of the guys in yer gang?" Mo asked as he made an illegal turn-around.

"Yeah. You remember. You met him the night we cleaned out that warehouse on the north side."

"Oh, yeah," Mo grinned. "That was pretty funny. You know, when Eddie got that mysterious phone call that night, he thought he was gonna get whacked."

"Why? He got enemies?"

"Naw. Eddie ain't done nothin' to nobody."

Trent smiled, "Then why was he nervous?"

Mo shrugged. "Eddie's always been a skittish fuck. And those Irishmen on the north side's enough to make anybody a little antsy." He grinned again, "That was a helluva way to get Eddie to notice your gang, though."

Tommy shrugged it off. "Well, I was just tired of Conway's boys always startin' trouble around here. It was disrupting a game I was running."

"What do you guys call yerselves?"

"Who?"

"Yer gang."

"Nothin'."

"Aw, come on," Mo Cimmino laughed. "Every gang's gotta have a name. I mean, when me and Eddie was kids we ran with the 22nd Street Prowlers."

"We're not a gang… Just me and a few friends with a few sidelines, is all."

"A few?" Mo laughed. "That ain't what I heard. I heard you ran a gang of Irish kids outta business."

Tommy shook his head. "Just a rumor. We've always kept our heads down."

"Well, whatever," Mo chopped the air with his hand in a dismissive gesture. "Anyway, it was a good thing you guys got in with Eddie before one of the other gangs demanded protection money."

Tommy didn't say anything. He had been paying protection money directly to the police. "Ah, small shit's all we do. We've never gotten into anybody's hair."

"I'm just sayin'. Any of the gangs see someone standing on his own two feet, they're gonna want a piece, y'know what I mean? Here we are." Mo made another illegal U-turn and pulled the car against the curb by the back entrance of Fat Eddie's home. "You go on up. He's expecting you."

"What about you?"

"Me?" he administered another dismissive chop to the air. "I'm goin' home. I don't wanna hear him bitch about how long it took."

Tommy went up the wooden steps to the top floor and knocked. The door opened, "Tommy!" Eddie said. "Where you been?"

"I was in the theater most of the day."

"Come in, come in. You wanna drink?"

"Sure."

Eddie poured them each a small whiskey. "I got a favor to ask, Tommy. An important one."

"What is it?"

Fat Eddie handed him his drink and motioned for him to sit down. Eddie thrust his hand into his trouser pocket and stood over Tommy for a long moment, studying him. "I gotta go out of town for the weekend. I need someone to look after Sarah."

"She's a big girl. She doesn't need a sitter."

"I know, I know. But I'd feel better, Tommy. I mean, someone tried to kidnap her once, what's to say nobody else'd give it a try? And with all those hoodlums in the pool hall…" He shrugged. "I'd ask Mo, but Sarah'd be miserable. With you lookin' after her, she could go out with her friends and take you along without making her… uncomfortable. Embarrassed. But…" Eddie sat down and looked into his glass for a moment. He chuckled nervously. "Look… I know my daughter is beautiful and any young man who's got a drop of blood in him'd be… *interested*. And I know you're a good lookin' kid yerself and you probably play hell with the dames, but… You saved my daughter's life. She trusts you. *I'm* gonna trust you. You know what I mean?"

"Eddie," Tommy smiled, "I gotta reputation that these days is almost unheard of. Sure, the dames like me, but it's because I'm a gentleman. Not some wandering playboy."

Eddie's eyebrows arched high on his puffy forehead. "A gentleman gangster?" he laughed, regarded Tommy for a moment and then laughed again. "Well, it's good to know, Tommy. I'll be gone a couple of days, but I'll call her every night to check in. There's a spare room across the way. I want you to stick around with a gun handy. I don't want some piece of shit breakin' in and assaulting her."

"Eddie, I'll be the ideal bodyguard and keep my hands to myself."

Eddie grinned. "That's what I wanted to hear. Now, Sarah likes you, Tommy. You'll get along fine. You can go out with her friends or take her to the theater—have some fun. Just don't let nobody fuck with her."

"On my honor."

"Good." Eddie finished his drink and slapped Tommy's leg. He stood up and stretched. "I'll be leavin' round ten tomorrow. Sarah'll be opening the store and if you can keep an eye on the shop, I'd appreciate it."

"Sure." Tommy finished his drink and placed the glass on the table. "You don't have anyone who's sore at you for anything and might be lookin' to take it out on your daughter once you leave town, do you?"

"No. No. But better safe than sorry, Tommy. She's my only daughter, y'know."

"I understand."

"Alright. 'Night, Tommy. See you tomorrow."

* * *

Tommy Trent arrived at the DiStella furniture store just in time to see Fat Eddie holding his daughter at arm's length by the shoulders and smiling. As he stepped into the shop, he could hear Eddie say, "But I don't have to tell you anything. You're a good girl." He gave her a hug and a kiss on the cheek. "Be good."

"I will, Poppa. Be careful."

"Don't worry," he said as he crossed the room to welcome Tommy. "There he is. You remember everything I told you?" he said softly.

"Sure."

46

Eddie wondered for a moment if he should tell Tommy to keep his paws off of her and decided against it. There would be no need. "Okay. Grab my bag, wouldja?"

Tommy picked up the small suitcase and followed Eddie around the corner to his car. "Can I ask if this is business or pleasure?"

Eddie smiled. "A little of both, I think. I *hope,* anyway. It's good for the soul, y'know what I mean?" Tommy nodded. Eddie stepped closer and his face grew serious. "You know a year ago I'd've never thought of letting any of the guys from the neighborhood near my daughter, let alone look after her. Thanks, Tommy. It's a load off my mind. I know when I come home, I won't be disappointed." He nodded to himself and climbed into the car. "She can close up shop early tonight, if she wants to. Nobody buys furniture on a Friday night." He closed the door and waved as he started the motor. "Least ways, not unless they're completely drunk."

Tommy raised a hand politely as Eddie drove away. Leaning his back against the side of the building, he let out a sigh. He fished a cigarette from his pack and lit it. He had been doing odd jobs for most of the captains in Rocco's turf for a while now—the jobs that weren't important enough to give to any of the actual members of the outfit. But this was to be the oddest job yet. Babysitting an eighteen year old blonde beauty with big brown eyes and big…

But still, Tommy would rather be at Dottie's.

It wasn't anything against Sarah. Since the kidnapping, he had learned that she wasn't nearly as aloof as the neighborhood thought. She had just been sheltered very well by her father and she knew surprisingly little of how the neighborhood she had grown up in really operated. There was an innocence about her that you couldn't find in any of the other young girls in the neighborhood.

He had finished half of his cigarette when Sarah appeared by his side. She joined him looking across the street at the crowd of people milling around the sandwich shop. "Hi, Tommy."

He turned and smiled. "Hey, Sarah. How's the world treating the DiStella Angel?"

Sarah felt herself blush and cursed herself for it. "Fine," she smiled and then joined him in leaning with her back against the wall. She folded her arms and smiled. "This how you spend your days? Holding up walls like this?"

"Hey, you gotta union card?" Tommy said sternly, stepping away from the wall and pointing a finger at her.

"A what?"

"Wallholders Local 518. If you don't have a card, I'll have to ask you to step away from the wall, miss."

Sarah grinned. "And if I don't?"

Tommy toyed with the idea of threatening to move her physically, but thought better of it. "Then all the other wall holders in the city will go on strike and buildings will be falling down right and left."

"Oh," Sarah said moving a half step from the wall. "I wouldn't want to be the cause of civil unrest."

A car drove by and the horn honked. A man and woman inside both waved, "Hi, Tommy!"

Tommy raised a hand and smiled until the car rounded the corner. "Friends of yours?"

Grinning, Tommy chucked her under the chin. "A very astute observation, kid."

Sarah laughed at herself. "I imagine you're a pretty popular guy."

Shrugging, Tommy said, "Eh. I know a lotta people."

The oldest of the five boys Tommy had taken to calling The Jackrabbits spotted him and crossed the street. "Hi, Tommy!"

"Vinny, how's it goin'?"

"Fine," the boy said and then tilted his head back so his twelve year-old eyes could study Sarah from beneath the brim of his cap. Vinny then gave Tommy what was supposed to be a knowing look.

Tommy cracked a grin and fished some money out of his pocket. He handed a few bills to him. "Say, at noon would you grab a couple of sandwiches and bring them back to the store here for me?"

"Sure," Vinny said, looking over his shoulder at the sandwich shop in case it had grown legs and walked away. "What do you want?"

Tommy shrugged and looked at Sarah, "Any preference?"

"Naw."

"We'll have what ever you and the other boys have."

Vinny looked at the wad of bills in his hand. "Gee."

"And keep the change."

"Sure! Thanks Tommy!" Vinny was now running down the street, looking for the others. He turned and continued running backwards long enough to say, "I'll be back at twelve sharp!"

"Who was that?" Sarah asked.

"One of the kids I pay to play stickball. They remind me of m'self when I was a kid." he said absently. When he saw Sarah had raised one eyebrow, he explained, "To keep them out of trouble."

Sarah DiStella smiled and thought that was the sweetest thing she had ever heard. She suspected that Tommy had a great number of similarly noble ventures.

Sarah seemed unable to stop smiling around him. "We got in a big radio this morning. Would you help me get it out of the crate?"

"Sure," Tommy said and followed her into the shop. She led him through the crowded showroom and into the storage area where a large crate awaited him. "You sure it's a radio in there and not an elephant?" he asked.

She blew out a puff of air and put her hands on her hips. "I don't know where on earth we'll put it out there."

She watched as Tommy went to work, pulling off his coat and tossing it aside before finding the crowbar. He had the top and the four sides of the crate removed in no time. "You're quick."

"Practice," he said and stepped back to look at the radio. It was a huge thing with more dials and knobs than seemed necessary. "You know, I think I saw something like that in a science fiction magazine once."

She laughed. "It *is* a bit much. But it's supposed to be able to receive broadcasts from overseas."

"No kiddin?" Tommy stepped forward and twisted a knob. "Can you get Sicily on this thing?"

"That, I don't know," she said, still smiling. "But look," she stepped forward and lifted a section of the top. "It plays phonographs too."

"I'll be... Does it open cans too? Hang out the washing?"

Sarah laughed. "No. It does everything else, though. You could even use it as a paperweight. ...A really *big* paperweight." Tommy smiled at her and she laughed. "We've got some radios in the showroom all ready to go. Wanna see if we can find anything to listen to?"

"Sure."

Tommy settled down on an overstuffed sofa in the showroom as Sarah worked the knobs on an Atwater-Kent floor model radio. After the vacuum tubes warmed up, the radio plucked voices out of the air as if by magic. "My father said this was just going to be another fad," Sarah said. She left the volume low to keep it from interfering with the conversation and joined Tommy on the sofa.

When they weren't non-existent, most daytime programming was primitive at best. They alternated listening to the radio with listening to the shop's demonstrator phonographs and Sarah's personal collection of records.

The only person who came into the DiStella Furniture shop the rest of the day was Vinny when he delivered lunch for them at twelve o'clock on the dot. As Vinny left the shop, he cast another of those knowing looks over his shoulder for good measure. Tommy supposed that he'd have to play twenty-questions with the Jackrabbits next time he saw them.

They spent most of the afternoon sitting close together on a sofa only half-listening to the broadcasts and phonographs. Sarah DiStella was getting ideas, but Tommy succeeded in avoiding her advances and deflected any questions he deemed too personal. Sarah noted it seemed he didn't want to talk about his family at all.

In the evening they went to the theater and at one point, when the house lights were low, Sarah worked up every inch of nerve in her body and put a hand on Tommy's knee. He quickly moved it away. "Cut it out. There's a million people here."

She nodded apologetically. Sarah had fancied Tommy even before the kidnapping and she knew that she would have to be very careful. Tommy worked for her father and she had the distinct idea that guys had been put on crutches for looking at Fat Eddie DiStella's daughter the wrong way. After the theater they went dancing at a small dance hall she and her friends frequented. Tommy was a good dancer and a perfect gentleman. He made sure to have her back home in time for Eddie's phone call.

* * *

Sarah DiStella made sure to get up extra early the following morning so that she would be dressed and have her hair and make-up fixed before Tommy saw her. She let him sleep until after nine o'clock and then decided to wake him up when the coffee came to a boil.

She quietly stuck her head past the doorway of the spare bedroom.

A Thompson sub-machinegun rested on a chair next to his bed and a revolver sat on the pillow beside his head. Apparently he truly meant to protect her.

He had only removed his shoes, suspenders and his tie before falling asleep. "Tommy?" she said softly and rapped on the doorframe. His eyes came open immediately and his hand reached for the revolver. He sat up and grinned at her. "The coffee's done," she said.

"Thanks, kid." He swung his legs out of the bed, stretched and then ran his hands over his face.

"Do you always sleep in your clothes?"

"No," Tommy said as he passed her and followed the smell of the fresh coffee. "I usually sleep in just my shorts, but I didn't think that would be appropriate."

Sarah smiled devilishly, "It'd be fine by me."

Tommy poured himself a mug of coffee and said without looking at her, "But not with your father." He took a sip from the mug, "You make good coffee. That's a prime qualification for being a good wife."

She understood that he was not making any suggestions about himself. Last night he had given her the third degree about her dating habits and had successfully dodged any questions about his own love life. She imagined it was quiet active.

"What would you like to do today?" She put her hands on the kitchen table and leaned forward. "I don't *have* to open the shop. We could have the whole day."

Tommy lit a cigarette and squinted through the smoke as he leaned back against the kitchen counter. "First thing is you're coming with me to my place long enough for me to take a shower and change. Then we can worry about what's what."

In the car she cleared her throat and said demurely, "I had fun last night, Tommy. I hope we can do it again sometime… I mean, after my father returns."

Tommy's only reaction was to toss the cigarette end out of the window.

Tommy lived in a tiny apartment near the poor section of the old neighborhood. Sarah could smell the tenement on the breeze. "It's not much, but it's where I come home to rest my head... Once in a while." He let her inside and she was surprised her by how neat and well kept his home was. She hadn't expected a bachelor pad to be so orderly.

"It's… cozy," she said.

Tommy grinned incredulously. "Well, I think it's a dump, but thanks for being polite about it. But I'm not gonna live here forever."

"Oh?"

His grin became a crooked one. "You don't think I'm ever going to amount to anything?"

"No, Tommy!" she sounded alarmed and put a hand to her throat. "That's not what I meant. I just…"

He laughed. "Relax, kid. Make yerself t'home while I freshen up a bit." He paused and took the revolver from his waistband and motioned with it. "I'm gonna leave the door open a crack so I can hear what's going on. If there's a problem, holler."

"You don't think there will be, do you?"

He smiled again. "Look, Angel, your father asked me to protect you and that's exactly what I intend on doing." He winked and disappeared from the room.

There wasn't much furniture to choose from so she lowered herself on to the sofa and chewed her thumbnail while listening to him rummage around in the next room. She visualized him walking down the hallway as she heard the footsteps. She couldn't resist herself.

She got up carefully, counted to ten and then crept slowly from the room. Her heart was racing as she crept forward, her hands on the wall. The bathroom door was a jar. She considered it for a moment, licked her lips nervously and leaned forward. Through the crack in the door between the hinges she could see Tommy's backside as he climbed into the shower stall. He was naked and surprisingly muscular. Sarah's heart was pounding in her eardrums and she forced herself to turn away as Tommy turned around to pull the curtain closed. 'What's wrong with me?' she thought, her hand to her chest. 'Acting like a naughty school-girl.'

Her heart had only slowed a little and her face still felt red several minutes later when a knock came at the door. She peered through the peephole to find a dark-haired girl waiting. At first glance Sarah thought it was the one and only Clara Bow. She opened the door a crack and the Clara Bow clone seemed as surprised to see Sarah as Sarah was to see her.

"Oh!" the girl said. "Is Tommy here?"

Sarah nodded and slowly opened the door. "My name's Connie," the girl said as she stepped past Sarah. She narrowed her eyes and turned to her, "Aren't you—"

"Gloria Vanderputty," Sarah said quickly and put a hand out. Connie took her hand with an eyebrow raised in suspicion.

"I'm looking for my boyfriend, Tano. I thought maybe Tommy might have seen him around."

Sarah smiled, "I know Tano! But," she shrugged. "I haven't seen him. I've been with Tommy since yesterday morning," she said, liking the sound of it.

"That's the way rumors get started, you know." Tommy was standing in the doorway behind them tucking his shirttail into his trousers. "Hi, Connie. This is Sarah DiStella. F—" he paused, "…Eddie's hired me as her bodyguard."

"Oh," Connie said and then repeated herself. Sarah didn't like the way she sounded so relieved. "I guess Tano's out on another of his sprees, huh?"

Tommy grinned and held Connie by the shoulders, "Don't worry, doll. He loves you. Just give him time. You'll get him settled down."

"Oh… I know you're right. But if you see him, tell him I was looking for him, huh?"

"Sure," he walked the girl to the door. Connie gave Sarah one last suspicious glance before stepping into the hallway. "Say—" Tommy said, tapping Connie on the shoulder. She stopped and turned to him. "Don't say anything to The Deuce, huh?"

The girl gave a knowing smile and winked her heavy dark eyelashes. "Mum's the word, Tommy."

"Thanks." He closed the door and was smiling to himself when he turned around. As he sat on the sofa next to Sarah, she grabbed his hand and put his arm around her shoulder as though she were cold. Tommy rested his head on the back of the sofa and sighed.

"Who's The Deuce?"

Tommy shrugged. "No one… Just a dame I've been in love with since I was twelve years old."

Sarah's "Oh," sounded very small. "Does she love you?"

"I think so. In her own way." Tommy smiled again and leaned forward to light a cigarette before changing subjects. "Tano's my best friend on the face of the planet. Connie's determined to tame him. But he's not half as wild as people think. The last time he went to a whorehouse, he spent the whole night playing the piano in the parlor. Never so much as looked at one of the dames." He pointed his cigarette at her, "But don't tell him I told you that. He's got an image to live up to."

"Is… is anyone taming you?"

The crooked grin returned to his face. "Why you scatter-brained little angel," he chuckled. "I *am* tame."

"The Deuce… that girl… You really love her?"

"Uh-huh."

Sarah put a hand on the side of Tommy's face. "Could you love me too?" She pressed her lips against his and then pulled away with a shy smile. "I hope you don't think I throw myself at every man…"

"I don't. Otherwise you wouldn't have the reputation you have."

"What's that?"

"That you're a snob and that anyone less than a Harvard professor wouldn't be good enough for you."

"That's what all the guys think of me, huh?"

Tommy scratched his lower lip with his thumbnail. "Well, that's putting sugar on it…"

She scooted closer to him and kissed him again. "Let me show you I'm different."

He grabbed her hand from his face and squeezed her fingers gently. "This isn't good."

"It *is* good," Sara said and kissed him. He hesitated for a moment and kissed her back. It reminded Sarah of the warm glow that had accompanied her first sip of whiskey. "I love you, Tommy," she whispered and lay back on the sofa, pulling him with her.

Tommy thought of the beautiful and glamorous Dottie Deuce. He loved her. There was no evidence of another man in her life; there had never been anyone serious. Tommy and Dottie spent many hours together—they were still the best of friends after all these years and Tommy believed she wanted to be more than that as badly as he. But neither he nor Dottie seemed able to make the first step. It's insane, he thought. I would kill or die for Dottie…

But Dottie Deuce had been locked into the role of tavern matron at an early age. When she was thirteen years old her father became ill and could no longer run his tavern. So Dottie quit school and went to work in a garment factory by day and ran her father's saloon by night to earn enough to feed her family and pay the doctor's bills. Every night since she was thirteen had been spent in her father's saloon. She was a fixture in the neighborhood; the city would not have seemed quite the same without her. For all but a few old timers, there had always been a Dottie Deuce working behind that bar.

She had passed beyond being human into being a legend.

Tommy Trent and Dottie Deuce could only be lovers when Tommy himself became a legend.

Tommy's eyes snapped open when he came to the realization. His lips were on Sarah's neck, his hand on the smooth skin of her thigh above the stocking. He had been trying for a very long time to figure it out, and it had come to him while in the arms of another woman. "I love you, Tommy."

The hand pulled away from her leg, the lips from her neck. Sarah opened her eyes to find Tommy sitting up, smiling and wiping away the rouge from his lips. "Let's go get some lunch."

"But, Tommy—"

He was already up and holding out her jacket for her.

She smiled. She was content—she had found some answers. She had pressed her thigh against him to find that she had aroused him. He did want her.

It was a step in the right direction.

She smoothed down her skirt and slipped into the jacket. "Okay. Let's go."

* * *

He had made breakfast the following morning. When she asked him about his cooking skills, he shrugged and said, "I've been makin' my own meals as long as I can remember."

"Oh," she said softly. "It was good." She began to clear the table, and Tommy insisted on helping. It was rather odd, she had never dreamed she'd fall in love with one of her father's employees before. But it seemed that every little moment with Tommy was golden. This weekend had been the most thrilling of her life. She couldn't help pretending that they were married and this was her husband helping her with the dishes and not a bodyguard hired by her father.

Fat Eddie returned to find Tommy helping Sarah wash up the breakfast dishes. Sarah dried her hands on a towel and hugged her father. "Poppa!"

"Hey, how's my beautiful angel?"

"Fine, Poppa." She smiled back at Tommy.

"You two stay outta trouble?"

Tommy grinned, "She was a handful, but I managed to keep her outta prison."

Eddie laughed. "Well, good." He shook Tommy's hand and led him into the next room. "Everything okay? Really?"

"Yeah. It's been quiet. You've been acting like you were expecting a hit squad or something."

"Well," Eddie chuckled. "You know, the over-protective father-thing, I guess."

"Your daughter's a good kid, Eddie. She should find herself some handsome millionaire and settle in."

"I know what you mean. She's been seeing this banker's kid. He's a quiet, legit guy. Got money."

Tommy smiled to himself. Sarah hadn't even mentioned him. "Well, I'll go get my gear and clear outta here so you can catch up on your sleep."

Sarah met him in the hallway as Tommy emerged from the guest room. She walked with him to the front door. "I'll see you soon, I hope," she said.

"Sure. I'm always around, ain't I?"

She smiled and bit her lower lip. "Well, I mean more than that."

He smiled at her, "You're a good kid. I gotta go."

She put her arms around him and gave him a hug. He leaned into it awkwardly as he had the machinegun hidden beneath his coat. "I love you, Tommy," she whispered in his ear.

He pulled away from her. He was still smiling, but his eyes were dull. "Stop with that," he whispered. "I'm poison, kid." He kissed her forehead and opened the door. "See you around."

When Eddie finished putting his suitcase away, he stepped into the parlor. "He gone?"

"Yes," she said leaning her back against the closed door. She couldn't suppress the long sigh. Poison? And who was this Deuce?

Her father stood by her and took her hands. "He didn't try anything... funny, did he?"

"No," she said and thought: *I only wish he had.* "He was a perfect gentleman... It's a shame all men aren't like Tommy."

9

"Y EAH R OTH SAID SHOVELING A SCOOP OF BUTTERSCOTCH candies into a white bag. "I remember when you were yay tall and'd find a penny. You'd come in here and get a bag of these." He chuckled, "You'd think it was Christmas the way your eyes'd light up."

Tommy was leaning on the counter, grinning and gnawing at a toothpick. Jim Roth was now beyond seventy and had owned the grocery store for as long as anyone could remember. He had always liked Tommy and he had felt sorry for him when he was a boy. He had had some tough breaks, but he made it through okay.

He was becoming a fine young man. Respectable.

"I remember I always felt bad for you and those other kids who had nothing to do other than wander 'round the streets." He shrugged and put the bag on the counter. "It's a hard ole' world, I guess."

"Ah, phooey," Tommy said with a smile. "It's a grand life if you don't let it beat you down."

The old man's face loosened as though someone had just flicked a switch to turn him off. Tommy followed his gaze to the tall slim man who had just entered the store. "It's Chucky Spano," the old man whispered softly, as though to warn Tommy to get out of the store and head for the hills. But Tommy already knew who it was. Spano was idly poking through a basket of apples. He selected one and strolled up to the counter as he ate.

"Hi, Roth!" he said sputtering apple juice onto the counter. "You think any more about what we talked about?"

"Mr. Spano, I—"

But Spano had turned his attention to the handsome young man who still leaned against the counter, chewing a toothpick, watching him impassively. Spano glowered. "What's your story, chum?" He asked. "Why don't you beat it?"

Tommy slowly removed the toothpick from the corner of his mouth. The cold blue eyes were locked on Spano's. "Uh-uh," Tommy said and flicked the toothpick so it whizzed past Spano's left ear.

Spano chuckled. "What's this old Jew to you? Why don't you beat it?"

"I happen to like the old Jew."

"Oh, yeah? You hang around niggers too?"

"No... I've stomped the shit out of a few..."

Spano cracked a smile. "Some kind of tough guy, huh?"

"Not particularly."

"Look, kid. Don't you know who I am?"

"Sure. I just happen to not give a damn."

Chucky Spano turned to grin at the old man behind the counter. The old man seemed to be growing shorter and shorter until only his eyes remained peering over the counter. In a minute or two he'd end up disappearing behind the counter altogether. "This friend of yours has balls, old man." He turned back to Tommy. "You know me and I don't know you, chum. Why is that?"

"I keep a low profile." Tommy leaned away from the counter. "Just so's you know, this old Jew is paying Rocco Petrelli for protection."

"Oh, yeah?" Spano grinned. "Since when?"

"I just picked up the third payment."

"No kiddin'? Rocco's recruiting from the juvenile delinquent hall, now?"

"You look like you just got sprung yourself."

Spano smiled again and looked Tommy up and down. He licked his lips and nodded before turning and walking away. He stopped in the doorway and turned to point a finger at Tommy. "I'll see you around, kid."

Tommy inclined his head in a polite bow. When Spano had gone, he put a quarter on the counter. "Keep the change."

The old man had reassumed his full height behind the counter, but the color had not returned to his face. "No, Tommy. It's on me."

But Tommy pretended not to hear. He had the bag in his hands and was halfway down the center aisle. "Take care, Mr. Roth."

* * *

Sarah DiStella smoothed down the sides of her dress and checked her hair, scolding her heart for pounding like a school girl's. She put her hand on the door handle, counted to three and then opened it wearing her best smile. "Hi, Tommy."

"Oh, excuse me. I must have the wrong place."

"Wha?"

"I—Oh! It's you!" he said with a grin, stepping inside. "When you opened the door, I thought you were an angel and I was about to get myself checked into the Big Hotel in the sky or something."

Sarah laughed and scolded herself again, this time for melting at his very touch as he put his arm around her shoulder. "How you doin' kid?"

"I'm great, Tommy."

"Swell." He held the white paper bag out to her. "Butterscotch?"

She smiled and took a piece from the bag. She watched him carefully as she popped it into her mouth.

Tommy looked at the bag, frowned and then shrugged. "I started out with a lot more, but I ran into the Jackrabbits."

"Those kids who you pay to keep out of trouble?" She was now holding the piece of candy between her index finger and thumb rolling it between her lips.

Tommy nodded.

"Are you interested in children, Tommy?" Her big brown eyes glowed with mischief.

The crooked grin spread across Tommy's face. "In theory, doll. Not in practice." His smile faded, "There's already too many kids out there facing too many bad breaks."

Sarah fell silent for a moment and decided to consume the butterscotch. Finally she asked, "You're here to see Poppa?" Tommy nodded. She turned her eyes away from him and asked softly, "When are you going to come to see me?"

Before he answered, Fat Eddie stepped into the room. "Tommy! How's it goin? No, no, no, leave your coat on. We's gonna take a tour of the neighborhood." He ushered Tommy outside, turned and kissed his daughter on top of her head. "I'll be back in a little while, Sarah."

"Here," Tommy said, tossing the bag of candy to her. "Knock yourself out."

She smiled, "Thanks, Tommy. Bye, Poppa." She watched them walk down the steps. When they had disappeared around the corner, she closed the door and put her back to it. She let out a long heavy sigh and ate another piece of candy.

* * *

Fat Eddie winced as they went down the stairs and Trent reflexively reached out a hand to steady him. "No, no," Eddie said. "It's alright." He grimaced until they reached the street. "Just the bullet I took… I ever tell you that story?"

"No."

"Well," Eddie chuckled gleefully, cherishing the idea of reliving his brief spell as a hero. "You're in for a treat: Remember the Election Day Riots? That's what the papers called 'em, but what did they know? It was just… *panic*. Of course," he chuckled, "if I'da been on the receiving end of those baseball bats, I'da panicked too.

"See, Rocco and the boys were worried about the outcome in one of the districts. And you know Rocco. There's no way he'd let the political machine get derailed.

"So the day of the election, everyone—and I mean *everyone* was dispatched to make sure things went our way. Some of the guys were assigned to nab poll workers, but the rest of us… Me and Sally Nose were at this polling place. Now, Sally used to run this neighborhood and I was just one of his boys, like you. Sally with a gun and me with a bat. When the voters got their ballots, we'd ask them how they were gonna vote. If they gave the wrong answer, we'd say 'uh-uh' and take their ballots and mark them for them. If they gave us any shit, we'd just beat their brains out.

"Things were moving along nice and smooth like that all day until—somehow, coppers from another district got called in. And they didn't stop to ask questions, they just started shooting. They were shootin' at everybody. I forgot how many voters got hurt. So we start shootin' back, all over the district it was like the fuckin' Wild West all over again.

"So anyway, all I had was a bat when these coppers come bustin' in. Sally got two of them before they got him. They got me in the leg while I was scrambling for the gat Sally dropped. I got it and shot the other two.

"I tried to get Sal to a doctor, but he died later that night." Eddie had been so engrossed in his tale, he had to look up to the street sign to see where he was. "C'mon. Ruby's down here."

Ruby's was a blind-pig. On 49th avenue, the storefront appeared empty; indeed there was nothing on the first floor of the building. All the business was downstairs. Fat Eddie led Tommy around the block and down the dim alleyway. A set of stone steps led beneath street level. At the end of the steps was a solid door with a tiny peep-hole. Eddie rapped on the door and motioned to Tommy they'd have to wait a second. "This is another one of my places. If they offer you any booze—don't take it. It's all rot-gut in here."

A shadow obscured the tiny hole in the door and a moment later a large bar was removed from the inside. The door was opened by a sandy haired clean-cut college boy a few years younger than Trent. "Hi, Mr. D. Come on in."

Eddie led Tommy past the kid and through another door. A warm gush of stale yeast-smelling air hit them as the door opened. The small room within was packed with kids from the local high school and the college across town. A young girl who couldn't have been sixteen had passed out in the arms of her male companion. He didn't look so hot either. Fat Eddie chuckled. "Heh, before the Amendment nobody ever heard of high school kids boozing' it up. But now it's the *in* thing. Defy authority, all that. Makes 'em feel like tough-guys, big-shots."

A few derelict old men sat in the corners and Tommy wondered if they hadn't been drinking wood alcohol all their lives. Tommy gestured to the mummified men hovering over their glasses of hopped-up near beer. "Those guys an advertisement for what this junk'll do to you?"

"Nah," Eddie said smiling. "Not everybody can afford Ms. Dottie's high-falutin' liquor."

Tommy didn't care for the tone of voice Fat Eddie used when speaking about Dottie Deuce, but he let it go. Fat Eddie was from an entirely different era and a good part of him was still there.

A pleasant old man greeted them from behind the bar. He looked like the old guy who had run one of the neighborhood fruit stands when Trent was a toddler, but he knew it couldn't be the same man. "Eddie, how's it going?"

"Abe, c'mere." The old man leaned across the bar. "I want you to meet Tommy."

"Hi, kid. Welcome to Ruby's."

"You're gonna deal with Tommy from now on."

"Oh?"

"Yeah. I ain't got time for you bums no more."

The old man grinned. "Movin' up in the world, eh, Eddie? Good for you. 'Bout time. How about a toast?"

Eddie waved him away, "Get outta here with that junk." A blast from a trumpet on the other side of the packed room distracted him.

A plump black man in a derby sat on a bar stool by the piano blasting the kids with licks of hot jazz. One of the college boys was keeping time on a ukulele. Eddie turned to the old man. "What's that nigger doing in here?"

"Hey, Eddie—"

"Get him out."

"But Eddie, the kids *like* that kind of noise. They go for it in a big way."

"I don't care, get the fuckin' coon out."

"Aw, Eddie—"

Fat Eddie grabbed the glass ashtray on the bar and hammered it across the side of the old man's head. The old man fell behind the counter, his limbs flailing. The kid who had been watching the front door noticed Tommy's fists clench as though he was going to jump Fat Eddie. But he did nothing.

Eddie DiStella pushed his way through the crowd to confront the trumpeter. "Get the fuck out of here, nigger." The man stopped playing, his eyes wide and confused. "This ain't no fuckin' black and tan joint. Get the fuck out." The man hesitated for a second longer and Eddie took his trumpet from him and smashed it into his head, knocking the bowler and a piece of scalp onto the piano keys. The man toppled to the floor. He held his head, trying to ward off the blows as Eddie held him by his neck tie and pounded him with the trumpet until the instrument was so misshapen it looked as if a giant had used it as a toothpick.

Finally he threw the trumpet aside and delivered a swift kick to the trumpeter's ribs. But he wasn't moving. "Go back to darkie town or visit Messinio's black and tan joint. Cocksuckin' nigger."

The boy who had been cradling the unconscious girl in his arms, dropped her and she fell like a limp rag doll. He trotted over to a corner booth and vomited on his nicely shined shoes.

Eddie motioned for a couple of the kids to pick up the trumpeter. "Dump him in the alley. Tell the cops he got hit by a car or something."

10

These Spano brothers, I don't know what to do with them," Patsy Guarino sighed.

Rocco Petrelli sat at the head of the huge early nineteenth century French dining table with his breakfast laid out before him. He was shoveling a fork into a mountain of eggs and then piling the yellow curds onto a triangle of toast. "I suspected Chrissy and Girlie Boy would give us trouble eventually. They don't have the... *finesse* for this business. Coffee?" He lifted the small silver pot.

"Sure." Patsy handed his hat wordlessly to the maid and stepped through the wide portièred doors into the dining room. He pulled a chair out from the table and sat down. The silent maid placed a cup and saucer in front of Patsy and disappeared again. Rocco tilted a platter of sausage links towards Guarino who politely shook his head. It was a quarter past ten and Patsy had eaten hours earlier.

"Now, Sally knows how to run an operation without making trouble for everybody else." A piece of the toast stuck in his craw and he made a face and swallowed hard to get it down. "And Hymie knows that it isn't how much turf you have, it's how hard you work." He waved his egg-greased fork at Patsy. "People should take a lesson from him. He knows there is more money in working than complaining. Conway, well..." he shrugged. "He's gonna be problem. Sooner or later. Before too long, I bet. I mean, look at the feud he's been having with Eddie." He crammed another piece of egg-smothered toast into his mouth and said, "Say, how are things in the fat boy's neighborhood?"

"Eh," Patsy shrugged. "They called a truce with Conway's boys."

"Good. Good."

"Eddie put that kid on to taking care of the flow for him. You know, the kid that rescued his daughter."

"Hah!" Rocco laughed and waved his fork in the air again, "I lay you eight to five the kid pulled the job himself. How's that working out?"

"Okay. No complaints. The precinct captain says the kid's easier to get along with than Eddie."

Rocco snorted, "Who isn't?"

"The kid's been recruiting some cowboys from all over. Petty thieves, yeggmen, hold-up men, wanna-be torpedoes. It's like another army."

"Oh?"

"Don't worry. He's not keeping them for Eddie or himself. He's sent some over to Marco and some to Art, Bones. ....spreading them around to everybody."

"Well, good. A few extra shooters never hurt anybody."

"Especially when it keeps them off the street and outta everybody's hair with their petty bullshit bank jobs. Everybody's dying to get away from that small time stuff and get into the booze."

"It is the biggest employment opportunity in history," Rocco grinned. He wiped the toast crumbs from his mouth with a fine linen napkin. "Tell you what to do about the Spanos. Go talk to The Jew. Under bid them by... ten bucks. Maybe that'll get the point across."

"Okay."

"Now... Eddie..." Rocco trailed off with a shrug.

"What about him?"

"Well… You tell me, Patsy."

Patsy Guarino shrugged. "He's always been eager to please. But he's just…"

"Incompetent? Twenty years behind the times?" Rocco held up a hand defensively, "Now, don't get me wrong. Being eager to please is fine and dandy… if you can deliver on it."

"Yeah," Patsy said and then chuckled, "But they can't all be Roccos."

"You got that right, buddy boy. There's only one Rocco."

* * *

During the months following the dramatic rescue, Sarah DiStella saw more and more of Tommy Trent, but only because her father was relying more and more on his help. From what she understood, not only was Tommy Trent a knight in shining armor, but he had a good head for business too. Her father's opinion of Tommy Trent had changed dramatically. Fat Eddie had gone from grudgingly giving the kid some things to do in the neighborhood to grooming him as his heir. Often he sent Tommy on errands to lighten Eddie's load, which was a relief to Sarah. For years she had watched as the stress ate her father alive. And now Tommy was handling more and more things for him everyday. Fat Eddie had once remarked, "Twenty, thirty years from now when Rocco retires, that kid'll be tough competition for the top spot. Mark my words."

Sarah had never fallen in love with one of her father's employees before. It seemed so improper, but she couldn't help it and she certainly couldn't imagine admitting it to her father.

Her father had always kept her away from the young men of the neighborhood. They were "a bunch of bums who'll never amount to nothin'," he said. But surely if he believed that one day Tommy Trent would be a contender for the position of boss, that meant *he* was going somewhere, that *he* was going to amount to something. Surely, her father would make an exception.

She tried dating other guys and she'd probably continue to do so until Tommy showed his interest more openly. But all the time she was out with someone else, she'd be thinking of Tommy Trent. She supposed that wasn't fair to her dates, but she couldn't help it.

Sarah DiStella was in love.

She pictured Tommy, naked, climbing into the shower stall and immediately shook the thoughts away. "Hey, what's wrong?" Bobby Dorini asked.

Sarah smiled apologetically and saw her friend Anne and her husband on the dance floor. "I'm sorry, Bobby. I was just— Shall we dance?"

Sarah enjoyed dancing. It was something she had discovered about two years ago when her father began permitting her to go out with boys—as long as they were accompanied by another couple. That pattern still persisted simply because she enjoyed the company of her dwindling number of friends. Most of them had married and moved away or had gotten jobs elsewhere. Anne was among the last of the old gang.

There was a pretty hot jazz band tonight, whose enthusiasm seemed to be catching. They were just as tireless as the kids who were dancing. One number seemed to roll into another and as they danced right along with it, Sarah wondered what her mother would have thought of the scene: all the young girls in scandalous knee-length skirts, many with their stockings rolled down, showing their knees, all the make-up and all the youthful vigor…

She suddenly realized that Bobby was talking. He was waiting for an answer. "I'm sorry?"

Bobby shook his head, "Sarah, I don't know what to do with you."

"What do you mean?"

"Never mind," he sighed.

Anne and her husband Paul had returned to their table where they rested for a few drinking soft drinks. "Come on," Sarah said and led him back to the table.

"You guys want to get a beer?" Paul asked.

Sarah laughed, "Sure. You want my father to tear my hide?" Sarah had never been allowed to cross the street and walk past her father's pool hall, let alone look at one of the speakeasies.

"Oh," Paul said softly and looked away. It was hard to remember that this sweet and pretty little Sarah's father was one of the thugs who ran the speakeasies in the neighborhood.

The conversation moved onwards but left Sarah behind. She was thinking about Tommy Trent and she imagined he spent a good deal of time in a dark mysterious speakeasy somewhere. She couldn't picture him getting spifflicated (as she believed the hep college kids called it) but she could certainly see Tommy sipping a glass of anisette and sitting around a dimly lit table with a bunch of other big swarthy young men, telling them funny stories and being suave and handsome and debonair. Then she had the unhappy vision of young flappers crowding around him, begging him to take them for a spin on the dance floor, or just sitting very close to him with their heads on his shoulders and their hands feeling his heartbeat.

She sighed.

"—think, Sarah?"

Oh, no! Bobby was talking to her again and she was a hundred miles away, secretly wishing she were one of those wild flappers on Tommy's arm. Poor, Bobby! The poor guy must have been completely in love with Sarah to put up with this. "Think?" she said, trying desperately to save the situation. "Well, I— Tommy?"

Tommy Trent and Gaetano Amato had just walked past her table, heading towards the front door. She hadn't seen them until now. Tommy was absently rubbing the knuckles on his right hand and almost jumped when she called his name. He stopped and led Tano to their table. Sarah stood up to greet them, but made no motion to shake hands or even dare to attempt a hug. "What are you doing in a place like this?"

Tommy looked around the crowd of young kids dancing and drinking soda and grinned sheepishly. He felt a little like a preacher caught in a whorehouse. "We just had to... talk to a guy."

"These are my friends, Annie and her husband Paul, and Bobby. This is Tommy and his friend Tano."

Tano smiled, "You remembered." The last time he had seen Sarah, he had been carrying a tommygun, helping Trent rescue her from the kidnappers.

"Of course."

As Bobby was occupied shaking Trent and Tano's hands, Annie gave Sarah a certain look that said a whole lot. *My God,* Sarah thought, *is it that obvious?* She managed a nervous smile and looked back to Tano and Tommy. "Why don't you guys join us?"

Bobby seemed a little steamed at the suggestion, but Sarah took no notice. Tommy was tempted to accept just to see what the mild-mannered banker's son would do. But he smiled again and shook his head, "We'd love to, but we have errands to run."

Sarah couldn't resist and held her hands out, "How about a quick spin 'round the floor, then?"

Tommy licked his lips nervously and tried not to laugh, "Sorry, doll. I don't have time right now. Some other time."

"Promise?" Sarah asked hopefully.

Tommy acted as though he hadn't heard. "It was nice to meet you all."

Anne, Paul and Bob echoed the sentiment.

Sarah watched them a little more intently than she should have as they left the dance hall. For the rest of the night Annie kept shooting secretive smiles at her. She now understood why Sarah was acting like a Dumb Dora, her mind constantly a million miles away.

Sometime, when the men weren't around, she'd have to pry the juicy details of her obviously consuming infatuation with the mysteriously handsome and debonair Tommy.

* * *

They look like a pair of mad weasels, Paul Linwood thought as he saw the Spano brothers get out of their car. Linwood had been carrying a sack of groceries home when the white Olds pulled up along side him. He looked away from them quickly and stepped up his pace. "Paulie," Chucky Spano put his arm across Linwood's shoulders. "My brother and I need to talk to you."

"I can't, I'm very busy. Maybe some other time," Linwood walked faster now, almost breaking into a jog.

Chucky grabbed him by shoulder and whirled him around. "You can make time." Linwood saw Chris Spano had kept a slow leisurely pace behind them. He had his hands in the pockets of his long black coat and looked as though he might be out for a pleasant afternoon stroll. Chris Spano was in no particular rush to catch up with them and there was something unnerving about it. Chucky put his arm around Linwood's shoulders again as though they were old chums. His lips peeled away from sharp pointed teeth in a bizarre imitation of a grin.

Chris Spano stopped walking when he was about three feet away from them. He studied Linwood with emotionless eyes. "Who are you buying your booze from?"

"Come on, Mr. Spano—"

"Rocco?"

"Look, I'm getting it for forty bucks a barrel. I gotta family to feed."

"Okay. So it's the *price* of my merchandise you object to. Not the quality." Spano reached out and plucked an orange from the top of the man's grocery sack and peeled it with his thumbnail. "I just thought I'd ask you to reconsider. Think about it."

Chris inclined his head towards the car and turned around. Chucky pinched Linwood's backside before joining Chris in the car. The pair smiled politely and waved as they drove away.

Paul Linwood heaved a heavy sigh of relief. "Stupid," he cursed himself softly. He had been buying his beer from the Spanos at fifty dollars a barrel until someone from another crew offered to sell to him for ten bucks less. An extra ten dollar-per barrel profit seemed too good to resist at the time.

But at the time he hadn't thought of the Spanos' reputation. It was rumored that they liked to torture people for fun for the slightest infraction. His mind began to wander over the possibilities and kept returning to the vision of his speakeasy being burned to the ground. But how could he go to his new suppliers and say he changed his mind? They would be just as likely to torch the place.

Someone had him by the lapels, recalling him to his immediate surroundings. He barely had time to look up at the man's face before a second man slammed a heavy stick into Linwood's back. The groceries went scattering over the street as the two men dragged him into an alley. All he could do was curl up into a ball and hold his arms over his head to ward off the blows. But it didn't do any good. They beat his sides in until he couldn't take anymore and had to uncurl himself. They went to work pounding him in the face, chest and groin with the stick, fists and feet. Paul Linwood was sure he was going to die.

The world was getting fuzzy and dark as the two men lifted him up and dragged him around the corner. The last thing Linwood remembered was crashing through a store-front window.

* * *

Anne ran a hand over the mattress and pressed down on it hard to test it before she plopped down. "This is nice," she said and then sat up long enough to look at the price tag. She flopped back down in defeat. "Oh." Her husband worked in the rail yards and it would be a while before they could save up the cash for this bed.

She rolled on her side and propped her head up on her hand. "So, tell me about that handsome young man at the dancehall the other night."

Sarah blushed and shook her head.

"Oh, come on. Please?" Anne begged. "I won't buy any furniture at all if you don't tell me."

Sarah looked around her father's store as though someone might have snuck in and would be listening. She sat gingerly on the bed, remembering how she had been scolded for jumping on them when she was little. "He's a guy…"

Anne was now lying on her stomach, propped up on her elbows and her feet kicking the air behind her. Her face was strained with expectation. She waited, but it seemed as though Sarah's shoes had suddenly become immensely interesting. "Well, hell, kid. I could see *that!*"

Sarah chuckled, "No, it's— He's a guy who works for my father."

"Oh." The look of expectation turned to a frown. Everyone knew that Fat Eddie wasn't just a furniture salesman. But Anne had never judged Sarah for it. Sarah was a good kid.

"But he's different, somehow," Sarah trailed off.

"Well, he looks like the adventuresome sort, I'll give you that." Anne sat up and scooted over to sit next to Sarah. It was plain that Sarah was trying to spit something out but it wouldn't come.

After a long internal struggle, Sarah said with a shy little smile, "He's just a nice looking guy."

"Oh, you kid!" Anne laughed and nudged her friend in the ribs. "Don't give me that! You've got it big time for this guy, don't you?"

Sarah's eyebrows arched upwards, "Is it that obvious?"

Anne nodded.

"You think Bobby noticed?"

Diplomacy was the best tactic here, Anne decided. "I couldn't say."

Sarah's face clouded and she began nervously toying with a pencil. "It's ridiculous, I know. But, I can't help it. He's just so… I'm in love with him, Anne."

Anne's heart went out to her when she looked up with those big brown eyes that were now very moist. She put an arm around Sarah's shoulders, "Look, Sarah. I know I don't have to tell you anything. I know it's really not even my place to say anything." She put her other hand on Sarah's elbow. "But if he works for your father, you know what that means."

Sarah sniffled and said "Yeah" without looking up. "My father hired him as a bodyguard for me when he was out of town for a few days. If he even suspected that Tommy and I kissed… he'd have him killed." She blinked her eyes, heaved a heavy sigh and shook her head. When she lifted her face up, it was brighter. She laughed and turned red and grabbed Anne's hand. "Can I tell you something?"

"What?"

Sarah giggled and put a hand to her face, "I don't believe I'm going to say this… I peeked at him while he was in the shower. I felt like such a naughty little school girl."

Anne roared with laughter. "You dirty little thing, you!" The eagerness returned to her face. "So what did you see?"

"Nothing…" Sarah was absently drawing a figure-eight on the mattress with her finger. She giggled again and admitted softly, "He's got a cute little behind."

Anne laughed again. "Oh, Sarah, what am I gonna do with you?" She chuckled and then became serious. "But doll, even if he's got the cutest ass on the planet, it's still dangerous."

"Yeah, I know." Sarah sighed sadly. "I guess that I'll either have to get over him or hope that things might change…"

* * *

As the months rolled on and summer waned into fall, Tommy Trent was thus far satisfied. Before he knew, it had been nearly a year since Sarah's kidnapping and he had gone from running floating crap games, cracking safes and knocking heads in to collecting protection money, arranging security for booze shipments, making bargains and alliances with other crews and mobs.

There was no doubt about it: Tommy's feet were firmly in the door.

Fat Eddie was as good as retired now, even if he didn't realize it. Tommy Trent ran the entire neighborhood for him. Often Fat Eddie's right hand man, Mo Cimmino would ask Eddie for instructions and he'd shrug and wave him away saying, "Talk to Tommy."

On one hand it was almost sad to think that Fat Eddie had virtually given away his position without realizing it. On the other hand, Fat Eddie running things was the last thing the neighborhood needed. Things were too sloppy and the money wasn't rolling in as it should. Fat Eddie's neighborhood was dead last among earners and respect.

But that was slowly changing as Tommy Trent took the reigns.

11

Fat Eddie's hands sweated as he ascended the staircase to Patsy Guarino's office in the LaCava-Petrelli Imports building on 27th Avenue. He had been summoned here before on several occasions, which always coincided with Patsy's monthly appearance at the building to check the books for Rocco.

And it had always been unpleasant.

Patsy Guarino looked more like a murderous undertaker than an accountant; being alone in the same room with him was enough to make Eddie nervous. But to be called in to be berated by him… It was nearly unendurable. Most of the time when Eddie made his appearances here, Guarino ranted and raved about his neighborhood's lack of profits, or confronted him about the skirmishes along the northern border with Sean Conway's mob. Each time it seemed to take years off Eddie's life. He had developed a deep-seated revulsion to the L-P Imports building the way some dreaded the dentist's office.

For the first time, Patsy smiled when Eddie stepped in with his hat in his hands. Eddie was flabbergasted and quickly convinced himself that it was a new trick. "Siddown, Eddie. Drink?"

"N-no. Thank you."

Guarino grinned. "Don't look so worried, Eddie. For once you're not here for me to bust your balls. Tell me, how are things going?"

"Good. Real good. Things are lookin' up. We got new speaks openin' all over..."

"This kid Tommy's working out for you?"

"Yeah. Oh, yeah. He's like my right hand now. All these young turks I got prowling around, they relate to Tommy. I've had him take some of these hot-headed kids off the street and give them something more constructive to do."

For a moment Patsy Guarino wondered if Fat Eddie believed what he was saying. Although Tommy Trent went through the motions of doing things for Eddie and doing them Eddie's way, it was becoming apparent to the outside world that a new force was slowly taking command of Eddie's neighborhood.

But neither Patsy Guarino nor Rocco Petrelli were going to argue with the profits.

"And by makin' him my go-between," Eddie continued, "everybody on the street's thinking that I've been bumped up and they listen more... He's a good kid. And I don't just say that because my daughter's sweet on him."

"Is she?"

"Yeah," Eddie shrugged. "She doesn't think I can see it, but I know. She's sweet on him, but there's no funny business."

Guarino nodded to show his satisfaction. Eddie continued, "Tommy's energetic, reliable... keeps his gang towing the line. I tell him to do something, I know it's gonna be done."

"You've given him Dottie's place, huh?"

Fat Eddie hesitated. He hadn't so much given it to Tommy as he had turned a blind eye to the take-over. After all, the kid had saved his daughter's life and was making Eddie's work easier. "He bought out the building next door to it and he's expanding it into a nightclub." Fat Eddie smiled sheepishly and shrugged. "Sorta a reward."

"Well, Eddie," Guarino sat back and shuffled through a sheaf of paper. "You know I'm always the first to tell you when Rocco's pissed about you or your neighborhood. So it's only fair that I be the first to tell you when he's pleased."

"Really?"

"Yeah," Guarino said, consulting the papers. "We've seen a steady increase in profits from your turf." Guarino was not about to tell him that the neighborhood had brought in 1.5 million more during the last year than it had any year before. He doubted Eddie fully realized how well Trent had organized things into an efficient machine and he doubted too that Eddie was getting much of the new-found profits. Tommy even handled Eddie's paperwork now. But as long as Guarino and Rocco got their sizable sum, they wouldn't make a beef.

"Rocco and I are really pleased. So whatever changes have been made, Eddie, keep 'em."

* * *

Francis Sirico looked a great deal older than any twenty one year old should. His eyes, which once were the happy sparkling eyes of a boy growing up on the street, were now glassed over with a dull sheen, the result of five years in a correctional facility. He had missed a lot in those five years, he knew, but he did not fully realize just how much until he got in the car with his old pal Gaetano Amato.

"Frankie!" Amato cried, "You look great!"

"Tano," Sirico said shaking his head with a grin, "nobody looks good after five years in the can." Frankie Sirico was handsome in a rough way. His smile could be warm and charming, but when agitated his lips would pull tightly together in a small disdainful sneer and the nostrils in the slightly bulbous nose would flare. The effect was dramatic and rather frightening. His forceful voice and tone was simply a reflection of his personality.

"Ah, bull. Come on. Let's go for a ride."

Sirico looked at the car's lush interior approvingly. "Where we going?"

"We're going to Dottie's, a little joint Tommy owns."

"*Owns* it?"

"Eh, half. With Dottie Deuce. You remember her, right? Nice lookin' broad, big—" he made a gesture with his hands to finish the sentence.

"Sure, Tommy's friend. The one with the knockers and the mile-long legs."

"Yeah, that's right."

"Tommy's moving up in the world, huh?"

Tano shrugged. "Tommy's got brains. Fat Eddie and his pals don't. They realized they need us."

"What about that Black-Hand bastard Petrelli?"

Tano paused and shifted uncomfortably in his seat. "We're working for him."

"Oh, hell, Tano. Tell me you're kidding. I mean, I heard rumors. But, no. Tell me you're yanking my chain. Please."

"Nope."

"But what the fuck? Tommy always hated that *stronz*."

"Frankie, calm down. First of all, it's a way into the rackets. And the old neighborhood," he shook his head as if he couldn't quite believe it himself, "Things are getting so much better there now. Things are improving all around. Secondly, things aren't going to stay the same forever." Tano smiled and put a hand on Frankie's shoulder. "Times are changing, amico mio."

* * *

It was without a doubt that Dottie Deuce was the most admired and respected woman in the neighborhood. She was charming, intelligent, warm and a keen observer. She had learned the fine art of serving alcoholic beverages from watching her father. She had now taken the art to new levels.

Her father, rest his soul, would not have recognized the old place now. In the two decades following the Civil War, the neighborhood had been predominately Irish. Then, during the final two decades of the 19th century, a flood of Italians and Sicilians had moved in and the Irishmen moved to the north side of the city.

The old building, erected somewhere in the 1870's, had been an Irish pub, complete with a flagstone kitchen and a small wood burning stove that provided heat, and at the hands of an ancient Irish wizard, whose name has been lost to the ages, managed to produce a veritable cornucopia of hot dishes to help soak up the rich thick ales.

When Dottie's father took over the pub sometime in the mid '90s, he had erected a partial wall, sealing the old kitchen off from the rest of the saloon and made it his business to provide the working Italian men with cold beer and warm spirits—a means of revitalizing the energies that had been worn down to a nub while doing the hardest and dirtiest jobs in the city for mere pennies—the jobs once relegated to the Irish, and before them, the Negro.

By the time Dottie's father had taken ill in 1912, the position of the immigrant Italians had somewhat improved, but the old saloon remained an important gathering place for the men of the neighborhood to discuss the news of the day and how to better their positions further still.

The regulars witnessed an amazing thing unheard of in those days before The Great War: As Dottie's mother spent more and more time taking care of the ill master of the house, young Dottie Deuce, age 13, slowly began to run the entire business. By the time her mother had passed away in the summer of 1917, Dottie was a successful business woman.

It was, perhaps, due to the magical phenomenon that was Dottie Deuce. She was a charming, and now, very beautiful young woman. Upon entering the saloon, a new comer would feel that Dottie was an old friend within minutes. She had a remarkable memory for faces, names, stories and facts. One man, his first time by the tavern, off-handedly mentioned dropping a brick on his toe while erecting one of the city's new skyscrapers. His second time in, some two and a half weeks later, Dottie's first words were: "Hi, Jim. How's your toe?"

And this coming from a young woman who saw dozens of different faces and heard twice as many different stories each and every day.

If someone had a problem, the chances were that Dottie could come up with a solution or that she knew somebody who could. At any given time there might be a doctor, a lawyer, a bricklayer, a street sweeper, a locksmith, a plumber or a policeman bellied up to the bar and all would be willing to do a favor or take on a new client on Dottie's recommendation. "Any friend of Dottie's is a friend of mine" was a saying often heard around the old saloon.

Dottie soaked up knowledge like a sponge. She had quit school at the age of thirteen, but by the time The Great War ended, Dottie was as educated as some of the high school and college graduates who returned to the bar again and again.

She was a friend to everyone in the neighborhood. The women and men both admired and respected her. She had done what was unheard of in those first decades of the twentieth century, and she had done it with honesty, intelligence, an instinctive business sense and boundless charm and grace.

Since she turned sixteen, Dottie had received countless marriage proposals. Much of the time it was the alcohol talking, particularly when the proposals came from neighborhood men who were already married. But there had also been a number of serious proposals of courtship. Dottie gave as much credence to these as she had the others.

Upon her mother's death, Dottie hired two out-of-work construction workers to open up the old flagstone kitchen. The two men were willing to work for the excuse to hang around a saloon all day and drink beer with the attractive young lady.

She then convinced the Widow Strantini to stop her mourning of her long-dead husband, stop hiding in her small tenement slum and start cooking. The Widow Strantini, who was seventy if she was a day, refused Dottie's invitation to come and live with her. The rooms upstairs where Dottie had grown up now seemed eerily empty with only Dottie living there. Dottie thought she might have enjoyed the company. Besides, an old lady should not have to live alone with nothing but her memories to keep her company. But working over the ancient wood burning stove, whipping up various stews and pasta dishes to sell to the beer drinkers at lunch and dinner time seemed to give the old widow a second lease on life. Indeed, she was happy for the first time in years and would often say she hadn't enjoyed herself so much since she had been a girl in the days before the War Between The States. The widow's last three years were happy and busy, thanks to the kind and generous Dottie Deuce.

In the early days, Dottie would hum or sing to herself when in a good mood while swabbing down the old bar with a rag. On many occasions, a customer, with a few too many in him, would call out for a song and Dottie would simply laugh. But after two years of this, resistance wore thin and Dottie decided she would either have to demonstrate to one and all that she could not sing or give up her happy little habit of humming. On the memorable night, a customer seated himself at the tinny piano in the corner as the rest of the evening crowd waited expectantly. After the first few quavering notes, her voice rang true and clear and to her astonishment alone, it was beautiful. This only added to her popularity, her growing legend. Not only was she beautiful, witty, brilliant and just plain fun to be around, but she was a damn fine singer to boot.

It then seemed that every time one of the neighborhood men was a bit blue, he would stop in to Dottie's for a drink and request a song. This inspired Dottie to institute Friday Night Sing-Along. The whole crowd would gather and drink beer and sing into the wee hours of the morning. Dottie always monitored the contents of the songs depending on who was present in the saloon. The bawdy songs were saved for the nights when only the most boisterous and roguish were in attendance. As an added attraction, anyone who purchased one of the sandwiches Dottie and her friends Connie and Julia made on these Friday nights, got their first bottle of beer free.

Dottie's saloon was a hugely successful and popular place long before Prohibition came into being.

Sally Nose ran the neighborhood in those days. He was medium height, medium build and all gangster. But Dottie never judged anyone too quickly or harshly, even if Sally did work for Rocco Petrelli. Sally Nose was pleased that Dottie was not among the neighborhood saloon keepers who had decided to throw in the towel when the 18th Amendment was finally ratified. The neighborhood would not have been the same without Dottie's or Dottie herself.

Of course, what were Dottie's other choices? Living in the streets with little Tommy Trent? Becoming a prostitute and living in one of Rocco Petrelli bawdy houses? And besides, Dottie loved running the saloon. She loved the people. She loved the neighborhood.

The numerous regulars packed themselves into Dottie's saloon on January 16, 1920. At midnight, The Volstead Act became the law of the land. A moment of silence was observed when the old grandfather clock in the corner began ringing. It was Dottie who broke the silence. She motioned to her young friend Tommy Trent—who was either sixteen or seventeen at most—to join her behind the bar. She threw an arm around his shoulder. "Everyone?" the charming young woman announced. "This is my dear friend Tommy. He's not old enough to drink. But, since the next drink I pour will turn me into a criminal anyway, I might as well go all the way."

She then poured half a tumbler of whiskey for the young man, who drank it to the accompaniment of hearty cheers. Then the saloon's guests surged forward, everyone wanting to go down with Dottie and become this new kind of criminal: a drinker.

Things had gone very well for the first few years of Prohibition. She had been able to hire Connie and Julia and a few other girls to wait tables and join in with the sing-alongs, which had become nightly affairs that evolved into a regular floorshow. Pretty girls brought in new customers and Dottie's charm kept the old timers coming back for more.

But then Sally Nose died and Fat Eddie DiStella took over the neighborhood. Eddie had no business sense, and there were times when Dottie would wonder if he had any sense at all. Eddie began pushing the rot-gut harder—it was cheap to make in vast quantities and the more he sold spared him the hassle of having to import the real McCoy. Eddie's very existence seem to irritate the Irishmen on the north side and as they began hijacking Eddie's shipments more and more, Dottie found herself paying three times what she had paid Sally Nose.

She was being taken advantage of because she was the only female speakeasy operator who was working without the immediate backing of a tough-guy. Sally Nose had admired Dottie and respected her, but Fat Eddie didn't seem to respect much at all and without a gangster partner, she found herself being squeezed under Eddie's fat greasy thumb.

But there was a remarkable coincidence in the works.

Perhaps it was not a coincidence. Perhaps time and circumstance were beginning to mesh, bringing their destinies closer to hand.

The hearts of some women might have ached to see a young friend like Tommy work his way into the rackets. But not Dottie Deuce. She knew there wasn't much of a choice for Tommy. He had never trusted anyone to take him in because he thought they would turn him over to the authorities, who in turn would send him back to the disease-ridden house of death from which he had escaped at the age of five or six. By the time he met Dottie, he was already wise to the ways of the street, and in any event, he was too proud to allow Dottie's family to take him in. What else was there for a little boy in the 1910's, when the cops were all either Irish or Polish and didn't particularly care what happened in the Italian neighborhood, as long as it stayed among the Italians? In the streets it was survival of the fittest. You were either a tough-guy or you paid a tough guy for protection. Otherwise you might as well not have bothered being born at all.

But Tommy *had* been born, somewhere between 1903 and 1905—no one would ever be sure. And the good Lord had dealt Tommy a bad hand to start with. But Tommy played it as no one else could. A lesser man might have been dead years ago, but Tommy had something very special to live for: Dottie Deuce, the Queen of the Neighborhood.

They already loved each other. The whole world, with the exception of the DiStellas knew that. It was only a matter of time before time and circumstance fell into place and brought them together.

Since Fat Eddie DiStella had asked for Tommy's "input," everyone in the neighborhood—everyone but Eddie—began to realize that Tommy had taken over. Suddenly the DiStella neighborhood was ranking among the top earners. Thanks to a tenuous treaty with Conway's Irishmen, inspired by Tommy's bold liberation of the liquor in Felim Strong's warehouse, and thanks to Tommy's intuition and innovations, the booze was flowing virtually hassle free. And the gambling take was up, too. DiStella was praised for finally putting fresh blood into his crew, but he was also the one who took the hit when something didn't go as well as it should. Fat Eddie was about the only one around who didn't realize that Tommy Trent got 'all the fame and none of the blame.'

Behind all great men—in the legitimate world and otherwise—there is usually a woman. Dottie Deuce was that woman for Tommy. She was his motivation and his inspiration. She was also the one who called his attention to how much influence he now wielded.

Although Tommy Trent had always spent a great deal of time at Dottie's, his merry band of men had become regulars too as soon as The Volstead Act went into effect. Dottie's was, they might have said, the gang's headquarters.

It was not unusual for Tommy to stay long after the speakeasy closed. He would often join Dottie upstairs in her living quarters for a nightcap. Many nights he would fall asleep on the sofa and not wake up until morning. But, unknown to Dottie, Tommy had been sleeping in the building for years. During the harsh winters when Tommy was just a boy, Dottie's father would rig the back door of the saloon to make it easier for Tommy to "break in" and sleep on the floor and out of the cold. The little boy, too proud to ask Dottie's family to let him stay, would always sneak out before dawn, believing the family was none the wiser.

After five or six months had passed since Eddie DiStella decided to let Tommy "take care of" the flow of booze and manage the speakeasies, the neighborhood had vastly improved. Dottie knew it was time for Tommy to stop pleading ignorance to his rising importance and influence. It was time for Tommy to stand up and take destiny by the balls. She decided to prod him forward in a way Tommy could not refuse: she would ask him a favor.

"Sit down, Tommy," she smiled, handing him his whiskey. She stood beside him and placed and arm around his shoulder, bumping his arm with her hip. "Tommaso, you know you're my boy, right?"

"Sure, I do, Dottie."

"And I love you." She pressed her hip a little harder against his shoulder. "And I'm proud of you."

"For what?"

"Come on, Tommy," she laughed. "Everybody knows you're in charge now. You move your fingers and make Fats dance. Everybody knows that." Dottie waited for some response. When none came, she pulled a chair in front of him and sat down so her knees were nearly touching his. "I need your help, Tommy. I can't afford to keep this place going. Not like this. It's not worth it. I don't want to pay Fat Eddie. I don't believe in paying ghosts. I want you to help me. Be my partner, Tommy? Please?"

Tommy leaned over and brushed the hair back from her face before sitting back again. He looked at his glass of whiskey. He considered it for a long moment and took another swallow. "You're a wonderful woman, Dottie. You're beautiful *and* you're a genius. You don't find too many broads like that in this life. And, I will admit, it has occurred to me that Fat Eddie has been strangling this place… Not letting you bring it up to its potential. This is a great place and you're a great girl. Yer *my* Dottie." He looked at the floor for another long moment. "You don't have to pay anymore. From now on."

"Oh, thank you, Tommy," she smiled, grabbed his hand and squeezed it

Tommy kissed her hand and then smiled, "In a few weeks this will be the classiest joint in the city."

And Tommy Trent had been better than his word. Within two months some of the regulars at Dottie's were the same men who would sit and chat with Rocco Petrelli as his friends. People from the legitimate world, people whose names showed up in the newspaper gossip columns and the showbiz fan magazines, as well as policemen and politicians from all over the area began frequenting the speakeasy. Even a famous mystery writer made sure to stop in at Dottie's whenever he was in town. The booze was high class and there were twice as many dancers for the floorshow—so many that Dottie had to promote Connie Banks and put her in charge of them. And pretty girls never failed to pack a speak. There was even an honest-to-goodness band now instead of the four tired old men who used to provide the music. Tommy booked singers, vaudevillians and Broadway dancers for guest appearances. Dottie's was now bigger, brighter and better than Hyman Amberg's extravagant Pharaoh Club. And she didn't have to pay Fat Eddie a penny—she was actually making money now, able to afford the kinds of things she had always wanted. Instead of handing over almost seventy percent of her take to DiStella every week, she and Tommy would whack up the take every night with much joking, laughter and drinking.

And for Dottie Deuce, the beautiful Queen of The Neighborhood, the owner of the brightest spot in town, every moment she spent with Tommy Trent was priceless.

* * *

Prohibition would be remembered as The Jazz Age with good reason. He supposed that Bob Harris and His Orchestra was only one of hundreds of bands spawned since the Volstead Act went into effect, but Harris liked to think they were among the best. This was not without reason either.

Bob Harris's first love had always been music. He could read musical notation better than he could read English by the age of twelve. His first band, like many, started as a quartet that landed jobs playing in the local vaudeville theaters. Harris had always been something of a musical innovator and he kept his music fresh—as he said, "honest." He wasn't much more than a boy when he landed the dream job of working in a print shop that produced sheet music of the newest tunes. He would swipe copies of nearly everything that passed through his hands, take them home and spend hours studying the composition, dissecting each number as a biologist might dissect a frog. Bob Harris had been thirteen when he wrote his first musical arrangement of a popular tune.

He chose his music like he chose his band members: using only the best elements from piano-roll ragtime, barrel-house and the countless other forerunners of jazz. Over the years his band had created their own unique sound unlike the many other musical aggregations that had been accused of merely playing "sanitized nigger music." His formula was simple: if it excited him or made the hair on the back of his neck stand up, he'd incorporate it into his own unique arrangements.

His band had grown by several members when they tasted their first success and were booked to tour a ring of vaudeville houses in Australia.

It seemed that the Australians didn't know what to make of Bob Harris and his frenzied clarinet and cornet-guided band. A young comic from New England on the bill with Harris was one of the few people who consistently encouraged him during the trip.

Bob Harris returned to the United States with his band and a new wife.

And then along came prohibition and its thousands of speakeasies wanting entertainment to keep their customers awake and buying. Gone were the days when jazz bands were novelty acts in vaudeville and steady work was only found in the more progressive bawdy houses. Work for a good jazz band was everywhere and Bob Harris And His Orchestra began touring the country, building something of a reputation for themselves.

But with success comes trouble and Bob Harris found it in a man by the name of George Torino. The band had played an engagement at nearly all of Torino's clubs and speakeasies and had planned to move on to another city when they were told otherwise. "I like you and your boys," Torino grinned. "You work for me, now."

They got into a heated exchange over it; Harris hadn't signed any contracts and did not intend on staying in the city. Later that evening his piano player came staggering into Harris's hotel room, bleeding. Torino's boys had taken a hammer to his fingers. The pianist wept, "They said to tell you it's the same for you and the other boys if we don't stick around."

Late that night Bob Harris gathered his pregnant wife and as many of his band members who weren't too stoned or hung-over to travel, stole a bus and drove nearly twelve hours without stopping to return home.

A lesser musician might have given up or been frightened off, but music was all that Bob Harris knew or cared to know. Instead of being discouraged by the fact that his former pianist's fingers were so crippled he had taken a job driving a truck down south, Harris began working even harder.

He called in old favors, sold family treasures and begged, borrowed and stole every great musician he could get his hands on.

The newest incarnation of Bob Harris And His Orchestra was the greatest yet.

But then a new and more personal hurdle needed to be jumped: his wife, afraid of reprisals by the Torino gang, refused to travel in her advanced stage of pregnancy. It was a tough decision. Harris had been around long enough to know what happened to most marriages when the musician husband left his wife behind to resume the itinerant lifestyle of the wandering minstrel. They always promised to be true and to come home faithfully as ever, but most of the time they didn't, and when they did, they often found there was nothing to come home to.

It was then that Tommy Trent came to the rescue. Tommy was an old boyhood chum of Bob's and had just taken over a saloon from Fat Eddie DiStella. He had expanded and remodeled the speakeasy and turned it into a lavish nightclub. All he needed was a good hot band.

There was no need for a written contract with Tommy Trent. His handshake was better than anything put on paper. Bob Harris And His Orchestra became the house band of Dottie's and landed (with Trent's influence, Harris suspected) a recording contract with the Conroy Label. The only condition to the agreement was that Harris and his boys were free to appear on the radio or cut records whenever and wherever they wanted, as long as they were awake and sober enough to play in the speakeasy. Harris had heard stories of other gangsters who would have demanded a cut of any radio or phonograph income for sponsoring a band. But Tommy Trent was more than just another gangster. He was an entrepreneur.

Working with Tommy and Dottie was a joy. They respected Harris's knowledge and instinct for the business and gave him a much freer hand than a lot of the people he had worked for in the past. Harris also worked closely with Dottie and her right-hand-gal, Connie Banks in creating (and constantly updating and revising) the ten o'clock and midnight floorshows.

The girls were all young, beautiful, talented and easy to work with. Harris had instructed his boys not to get too involved with any of the Dottie's girls, though. A certain amount of flirting was just fine—in fact, in some ways essential to adding to the festive atmosphere of the club— but that was as far as Harris wanted the boys to go. As the club became more and more popular, Harris didn't want his orchestra boys to make themselves competition to the rising number of big gangsters, coppers and politicians for the affection of the girls.

He had learned first hand that grudges born in speakeasies and nightclubs were always dangerous.

Bob Harris's wife was ecstatic about the set-up too. Their children would actually have their father around to be with them, instead of traveling the country, hopping from one saloon to the next.

Harris had just finished playing his solo and looked around the club with a satisfied smile as he kept time with his foot. Dottie's was packed tonight. It was a good crowd, and it was turning out to be a really good life.

There was something of a special occasion tonight: one of Tommy's friends had just gotten out of the reformatory (Harris couldn't help but wonder if Tommy had arranged the release) and they had made a list of Frankie Sirico's old favorite tunes. Harris had made new hot arrangements of them all, bringing them in line with the jazz era.

Earlier in the evening Gaetano Amato had given in to Harris's requests that he join them on the piano for a couple of tunes. Tano was a good pianist and a good singer, and Harris always believed he could have been big in the music world.

But just as music was Bob Harris's first love, so was being a gangster to Tommy Trent and his boys.

* * *

Alice Byrd was nearly a fixture in Dottie's. She was the daughter of a wealthy alderman and seemed to spend her life flitting from one social gathering to another, never seeming to have a care in the world. There were those who whispered she didn't have enough intelligence to care about or even notice much of anything.

When she wasn't attending a governor's ball or another of her father's political social gatherings, she was most often in Dottie's. She loved large gatherings and deep in her heart, she preferred a night in Dottie's to a night anywhere else in the world. Often in the gatherings of the political elite, she felt a little lost and anonymous, but here in Dottie's she could maintain the benefits of anonymity and still be a fixture; a familiar face and a friend to everybody without being her daddy's air-headed little girl.

She was five two, slim and pretty, and wore her head of raven black marcelled hair like a crown. When Max Fleischer would go on to create the character of Betty Boop, there were those who would wonder if he had ever met Alice. She even had a high, soft almost child-like voice.

Often Alice would stop by Trent's table where he was holding court with his gang and their girls before flitting off to make her rounds of the tables. Tonight Trent's gang was in an especially celebratory mood, each taking turns and toasting Frankie Sirico and his return to the world of the free.

It was unusual to see Alice take a shine to any one young man in particular; in fact, no one was sure whether she had seriously dated anyone in her entire life. But Alice found Frankie's intensity electrifying and hung on to his every word. She leaned very close to him with her head nearly on his shoulder, gazing up at him with starry eyes.

"Are you new around here?" she asked.

"No," Frankie said. "I just come back."

"Where have you been?"

"Eh," Frankie shrugged. "I was up the river for five years."

"What did you do?"

"Nothin'. I was framed."

"Boy, that's terrible," Alice said. "What did you do with all that time? Five years?"

"I wrote a book."

"Really?! What about?"

Frankie shrugged again, "I never learned to read, so I dunno."

"Oh," she said, quite seriously.

"Jesus," Frankie chuckled, pointing a finger at the girl. "Is this broad a Dumb Dora or what?"

Everyone laughed, including the girl, her high pitched giddy laugh making it apparent she was unaware of any insult. Frankie leaned close to Tommy and said in Italian, "I think somebody pulled the plug and let her brains leak out."

Tommy nodded gravely. "I think you may have something there."

Frankie grinned and put his arm around her shoulders and squeezed her tight. She giggled. "I think I'll take you home with me tonight and see what you *do* know."

"Okay," Alice said and giggled again.

Tano lifted his glass, "Not out twelve hours and he's got himself a dame. Good for you, Frankie!"

The gang echoed, "Salut!"

12

Tommy? He turned to see to whom the sad egg-shell voice belonged. "Hi, Tommy."

Tommy Trent's face sagged. "Candace?" The girl nodded.

She was unrecognizable from the girl that Tommy had once run around with. In those days she was a gorgeous red-head with a bright and happy smile for everyone. But now she looked like a cruel mockery of her former self.

Her eyes were dark and sunken, her skin which had once been smooth and flawless, reminded him of a dead white fish. Her cheek bones were so pronounced and her cheeks so hollow that she resembled a corpse. The full lips had gone thin, as had her figure. She wore a thin blouse through which he could tell the skin he had once loved to touch was stretched tightly over the ribs. He could practically count them. The breasts which had once been high and firm now sagged helplessly. "Tommy, can I talk to you in private?" A tear rolled down her cheek. "Please?"

He led her to his car and helped her climb in before rounding to the driver's side. "Candace, what's the matter?"

The girl looked at the shaking fingers in her lap. The fingernails were jagged and gnawed. "I need a fix," she said softly.

"What?"

"You know…" Another tear fell from her face and into her lap. "I know you know everyone in the city, Tommy. I went to Fat Eddie for help, but he told me to get lost. Freddy Kesner won't give me anymore." Her sunken eyes were wide and wet when she looked up to him. "I know you don't deal in junk, but you gotta know someone who does, right? I'll do anything."

Tommy Trent was stunned. "When did you get mixed up with Fred Kesner?"

The girl shrugged. "Well, you know… I was always too fond of the bottle," she gave a brave effort to smile. "I lost my job after we split up and I met Freddy… At first…" She put her head in her hands and wept.

He put his arm around her bony shoulders. "What happened?"

The girl sobbed and Tommy repeated his question softly.

"I'm a whore, okay?" she wailed. "I'm just a junkie whore, Tommy. Freddy got me hooked on it and then said I had to work for it. A dollar for each man I lay. Oh, Tommy—" The skeletal body collapsed against his side. He was surprised that someone so frail could weep so bitterly. "But Fred got mad at me and tossed me out. I had nowhere to go, no money, no clothes—nothing. If I don't get a fix soon, Tommy, I'm gonna die."

Tommy took her hand and squeezed it gently. She had needle tracks in the bend of her elbow and a fresh knife scar on her wrist. Growing up on the streets, Tommy had seen many unpleasant things. But the desecration of Candace Maccadro's beauty was the greatest tragedy.

He buried his nose in the stringy hair that had once been so full and beautiful. A mental snapshot of her hair bouncing in the sunlight in the old days flashed across his mind's view screen. "Why didn't you come to me sooner, Candace. If you needed a job, you know I—"

"It just happened, Tommy," she said weakly. "I thought that… I was too proud, I guess. I loved you Tommy. And it just didn't seem—" She trailed off.

Tommy let go of her and nudged her to sit upright in the seat. He put his fingers to her sunken cheeks. "Okay, Candace."

"You'll get me a fix?"

Tommy shook his head. "No. I know a doctor. He can help you with this. Get you better. Then you can come work for me."

"I… I didn't know you ran a whorehouse."

"I don't. Your days of whoring are over, Candace. There are a lotta other things a bright beautiful girl like you can do. You'll get better, I'll set you up with an apartment and a good job. You'll get to start over again."

There was a long silence as the weight of his words sank in. Finally, "Thank you," the girl cried. "Thank you."

* * *

The Bridgeview Sanatorium was one of the most famous convalescent homes in the nation; one of Flo Ziegfeld's stars had just spent time there recovering from surgery. Dr. Raymond Talbert was well respected by the legitimate world and the underworld. A boyhood friend of Meyer Lansky, Talbert was a gangster's best friend when he needed a bullet removed without hospital staff alerting police.

Dr. Talbert briefed Tommy on the girl's condition in the hallway outside her room. "I'll be honest with you, Tommy. She's pretty far gone now. Her heart's weak, she doesn't remember when she last ate, she's dehydrated, and I haven't even checked to see what kind of venereal diseases we may be dealing with here."

"Come on, Doc," Tommy grinned. "You're a wizard among the medical profession." He stepped close to him and placed a hand gently on the back of the doctor's neck. He produced a roll of bills and handed it to him. "Whatever she needs, she gets. There's a thousand dollars for right now. Make her better, doc. You may not be able to tell it, but she was a beautiful girl once. Make her beautiful again, okay?"

* * *

The five men sat at the round table in apartment 217 enveloped in a haze of cigar smoke. The curtains were all drawn and the only light was a bare bulb that hung above the stacks of chips and bills in the center of the table. Everyone was looking back and forth between Carl and his partner Fred Kesner, each on opposite sides of the circle. "I believe the expression is 'so you hear a pin drop,'" one of the others said.

"Yeah," Freddy glared at him. "Shut your fuckin' mouth and let's keep it that way."

Finally Carl took the cigar out of his mouth. "I call."

"Fuck you," Freddy smirked. "You don't have shit."

Carl spread his cards in front of him, smiling, *"Cacciatelo in culo."*

Freddy Kesner sneered and tossed his cards on the table. "Shaddup with that guinea talk."

Carl laughed and hugged the stack of chips to him, "Come to poppa!"

The door burst in and in an instant Freddy Kesner found himself sitting alone at the table in a haze of gun powder. Three men in suits had kicked the door in and began blasting. Four shots sent Kesner's four companions toppling from their chairs with holes in their foreheads.

The cigar drooped from Kesner's mouth as he held his hands up. He looked from one of the gunmen to the next. They wore handkerchiefs over their faces. "Take whatever you want. Take whatever you want."

"Hey, scumbag!" one of the gunmen cried cheerily. "This is from Candace." A bullet tore through Kesner's throat. His fingers groped at the wound frantically as he tried to stand up. After a moment he collapsed forward, sending the poker chips and cigar butts scattering across the floor.

* * *

The Shamrock Club was only identifiable from the street by its green painted façade and the small shamrock painted on the front window. But everyone knew it; The Shamrock club was the swankiest nightclub on the north side.

Although Sean Conway disdained prostitution, he had no qualms against selecting his mistresses from the club's employees. This week it was Bessie.

She had just finished putting her costume back on when Pat Michelson knocked. "Alright," Conway said, leading Bessie to the office door. "Go back to work." He gave her a gentle shove past Michelson. "Come in, Pat."

The boss of the Irish mob poured a tumbler of whiskey for Michelson and motioned for him to sit down. "Any idea who killed Kesner?"

Pat Michelson took a sip of his drink and shook his head. "Nah. The guy was a scumbag. Coulda been anyone."

Conway sat on the corner of his desk and lit a cigar. "Oh, well. Doesn't matter. So tell me, Pat, what have you learned about this guy, the dago's new Golden Boy? This punk who knocked over Felim's warehouse and now thinks he's some kind of big shot."

"Well," Pat began, referring to his notes as needed, "this kid used to run a burglary ring. Crackin' safes, knockin' over warehouses, what-not… Few dice and card games… He and his buddy Gaetano Amato have recently been bringing in a lot with hijacking trucks. Not booze, other things. Fur coats, whatever."

"Gaetano Amato," Conway snorted, "Gaetano Amato. Sounds like a fuckin' nursery rhyme."

"His friends just call him 'Tano.'"

"Go on."

"Well, it seems that the Fat Boy's daughter has a little thing for this kid. At least that's the rumor that's been going around the speakeasy Fat Boy has in back of that ice cream parlor."

"She's gotta thing for this guinea? That Sarah girl *and* Dottie Deuce? Jaysus, there's no fucking justice."

"What makes it worse is Fatty seems to think she could do worse that this Trent. And that's how he got his foot in the door. Now the kid's practically bigger than Fatty. G has decided to put Trent onto the security for the trucks."

Conway chuckled. "I bet Fat Boy's not too happy."

"Eh, it was the smart thing for G to do. This kid has more experience with that sorta thing than that fat ass sitting around, watching his fucking pool hall every night. Fat Boy goes around as though it were his idea."

"This cease-fire's not going to last forever," Conway sighed. "I hope the dagos don't wise up too much."

"It gets worse," Pat said. "Trent has been talking with the Jews. He's been getting friendly with some of them. That's… that's not a good thing. When the shit flies, if the Jews side with the Dagos, it will be like three on one. We'll be fucked."

"It won't come to that. Hyman's too smart for that."

"What do you mean?"

"Well, if any of us ever makes a move on one of the others… It'll be to last man standing. And that old Jew knows it. He knows that he'd need us to help him wipe out Rocco's mob. He'd side with us until Rocco was finished and then *he'd* come after us."

"So what do you think? What do we do?"

Conway looked out of the window for a long moment, taking in the dark silence that seemed to be draped over the city. He knew it was just the calm before the storm. Finally he turned to Michelson.

"We're going to have our cake and fuckin' eat it too."

* * *

In the popular parlance, it was known as a 'petting session' and Bobby Dorini was getting hot and heavy with Sarah DiStella in the back seat of his new Lincoln. He had been waiting for this moment for a very long time. "Sarah," he panted between kisses. "Can I… can I touch your breast?"

She pulled his lips back to her neck and cooed, "Yes, Tommy."

Dorini paused and then jerked away from her, his eyes wild. "What?"

"What?" she said, puzzled. Then Sarah realized with horror what she had said. "Oh—"

"You just called me 'Tommy!'"

"No, I didn't—"

Dorini was tucking his shirt tail back in. "Look, you think I don't know? Think I don't know who Tommy is?" He sat beside her, angled away from her with his head in one hand. "Jesus, Sarah…"

"Bobby, I'm sorry. It's just a sli—"

"You know what? Get out."

She looked around the darkened street. "What?"

"I said 'Get out.' You want to fool around with your father's gangster friends, then go ahead." He leaned across her and threw the door open. He pushed at her shoulder, but she was a big girl and didn't move. Bobby Dorini felt completely impotent. "Get out!" When he shouted, his voice took on a high glass-like quality. "Go on! Be their whore."

"But, Bobby—" Sarah sniffled. "I—"

"No. Get out. Get the fuck out." He turned and began kicking at her with his legs, forcing her out of the car and onto the pavement. He stepped out of the car after her and hissed, "You wanna be some gangster's whore, go ahead. Christ, Sarah, I thought you were different."

She was crouched in a heap on the pavement weeping. "But Bobby—" She reached a hand up to him but he slapped it away.

He leaned over and hissed, "I don't ever wanna fucking see you again!" Then he spat in her eye and got behind the wheel of the car. He drove off into the night leaving her alone.

She looked around the empty street and bowed her head, sobbing.

She was still crying when Tommy found the telephone booth she had called from. "I hurt my knee," she whimpered, showing him her torn stocking. He helped her into the back seat and sat next to her. He patted Tano on the shoulder and the car began to move.

Holding her hand, he brushed a lock of hair from her face, "Calm down and tell me what happened."

"He— I—"

"Did he rape you?"

"No." She collapsed in his arms and let him hold her close. "He was kissing me and I... I called him Tommy. He got mad and kicked me out in the middle of nowhere. Called me a gangster's whore." She began crying again. "He spit in my face, Tommy."

"Shhh," Tommy said, rubbing her shoulder. "It's okay, doll. A piece of shit like that? Don't matter what he says or thinks."

She looked up at him, "I love you, Tommy. I want to be with you."

"Come on, now," he said stroking the back of her neck. "Stop with that. Just be still."

* * *

"My father's a rich man. He'll pay lots if you let me go."

The canvas sack was torn off of his head and he found himself blinded by a dim light bulb hanging down from the ceiling above the table. He held a hand up to try to block some of the light. His eyes squinted, "Please, if this is about money—"

"We don't want your money," a man said. Bobby Dorini tried to focus on the face, but it was hard to see. The place smelled as though someone had dropped a can of motor oil in a mildewy basement.

"What do you want?"

"We just want to slap you around and knock the shit out of you a bit," the man said in a polite conversational tone. "Then you can go back to work." A hand lashed out like a snake, grabbed Dorini's tie and slammed his face down into the table.

Dorini bounced off the table and rolled on the ground. He held his face while blood and snot bubbled between his fingers. A foot kicked him in the gut. "Wha'd I do?"

The man leaned over and lifted him by the neck tie. He put his face very close to Dorini's, "You don't recognize me, asshole?" He kneed Dorini in the groin and let him crash to the floor. It all became clear.

"Oh, God! Tommy! I'm sorry, Tommy. I didn't mean to hurt Sarah. I loved her…"

Another foot kicked him in the ribs and Dorini wailed in pain. "Jesus," Tommy chuckled. "Is this guy a pansy or what? He's already about all in."

He lifted Dorini by the tie again and kneed him in the groin before slamming his back on the table. "Today is Thursday. If I haven't heard by Saturday morning that you called Sarah and apologized profusely and begged her for forgiveness… I'll have to have another little chat with you. Do you understand me?"

"Yes."

"Then if you really love this girl, be a man. Get me?"

"Yes," Dorini sobbed.

"Good." Tommy rolled him over and grabbed the back of his coat collar and dragged him across the concrete floor and out into the alley. A moment later, Dorini felt himself sailing through the air and into a row of battered garbage cans. He lie still, staring up at the sky until he heard the car drive away.

He lay there for a very long time looking at the gray sky over head and the side of the brown brick building beside him. Dull waves of agony flowed up from between his legs and he wondered if he would ever be able to father a child now. For the second time since the night before he wished he had never seen Sarah DiStella. After a long while, he sat up, wincing and holding his side. He was sure he had broken a rib.

It took his last ounce of strength to stagger into the police station and collapse into a chair before a policeman's desk. The policeman stopped writing in his ledger and looked up at him with narrowed his eyes. "And what happened to you?"

"A guy named Tommy… works for Eddie DiStella… beat me up."

"What for?"

"A girl," Dorini said, panting.

"You don't need a cop. You need a doctor to set that nose of yours."

"You gotta help me," Dorini panted.

"Eh, get outta here," the policeman waved his hand as though he were swatting a fly.

"Please! You gotta find him and arrest him!"

The policeman leaned back in his seat and scratched his chin. "Looks to me like you fell down a flight of stairs. How do I know that's not what happened and you're just trying to get this guy locked up so *you* can get the girl?"

Dorini was horrified and repulsed. "How can you— I demand justice! Do you know who I am? I'm Robert Dorini the Third."

"Well, now, I'm Lieutenant Jim Oliver the First. Now get the hell out of this station before I run you in for vagrancy."

"What?!?"

The policeman had returned to his writing. Without looking up, he said, "Quit wasting my time. If you need to find another girl, there's a whorehouse three blocks down."

"But—"

"—Or would you like to be booked for disorderly conduct and assaulting an officer?"

13

When Tommy Trent met Fran Barrey, he understood why Max had fallen in love. Maximilian Aaronson kept one of Miss Barrey's Parisian postcards in his automobile and had shown it to Tommy. In the photograph, a girl sat in a swirl of fog, her blonde curls peeking from beneath a silk headwrap. Her body was enswathed in a sheer length of black gauze, leaving very little to the imagination. She was a well-endowed girl. The eternally youthful face, her dark mesmerizing eyes, the pouting lips and the devilish smile only hinted at the woman's dynamic personality.

There was something darkly captivating about her.

She had been a wildly successful model in Paris and she also had a reputation as a fabulous chanteuse, though the Parisian police had her listed among the city's six thousand five hundred prostitutes. It was unclear how she met the young American infantry captain during the war, but she left all her success and her glamorous Parisian life behind, marrying him and coming to the United States.

Fran had struck up an immediate friendship with Tommy and Dottie when Max began work on his business proposal. Fran and Dottie knew they had something in common beyond being beautiful and held with an almost mystical regard. In some ways they were kindred spirits.

Fran's reputation was much harsher than Dottie's—the arrest in Paris for prostitution had been made by a police official Fran Barrey had refused to sleep with and she had never been able to shake the scandalous brand. The common knowledge that Paris was 'the sin capitol of Europe' during the first decades of the century, coupled with Miss Barrey's *joie de vivre,* her love of art and her career as a model—both with and without clothing—certainly hadn't helped either. "I'm not half as dirty as I'm supposed to be," she would confide in friends.

She was now holding onto Max's elbow as they toured Dottie's speakeasy. They looked like an incongruous couple. Max was tall and gangly. He could be handsome when he smiled, but there was something fish-like about his large eyes and the way the corners of his mouth drooped when he wore his natural relaxed expression. Fran Barrey was much shorter and ravishingly beautiful. Whereas Max spent a good deal of time grooming to make himself presentable, Tommy imagined that Fran, with her youthful face, was beautiful even after just tumbling out of bed in the morning.

"That half of the club used to be a grocery store," Tommy said pointing to the left side of the building.

Dottie stood close to him and elucidated, "When Tommy took the place over from Eddie, he bought out the guy next door and knocked out the wall. He brought it into the twentieth century."

Tommy grinned, "Ah, don't listen to her. She's the one who's always made this place swing."

Fran Barrey stepped up onto the low stage and ran a hand over the piano top. "It's beautiful," she said. Her accent was peculiar, not entirely Parisian. She studied the piano top for a very long time, thinking of her days as queen of the Parisian nightlife.

The old saloon was now nearly three times its original size. Tommy Trent had put everything he owned into remodeling the place. The newly expanded Dottie's had seating for eighty people at the round tables between the low stage and the bar. Another thirty five customers could belly up to the bar comfortably. "The whole place is lovely," Fran said. She pointed to the microphone and raised her eyebrows.

Tommy understood and grinned. "There's a speaker in the building across the alleyway." Customers in the mood for gambling could slip through a back exit and across the alley into a small casino that matched Dottie's décor. The speaker piped the music and happy sounds of drinking across the way to remind the gamblers to come back and spend their last few dollars on a couple of glasses of beer before calling it a night.

Dottie squeezed Tommy. "Tommy set it up that way to keep me out of trouble."

"On paper," Tommy explained, "the property the casino's on is owned by a figment of our imaginations. Nobody'll bother Dottie about the booze, and they can't touch her for the gambling."

Fran smiled. She couldn't help but admire them. A man who would go to such precautions to protect his woman…

Dottie joined her on the low stage, surveying the speakeasy. "It always looks best when it's packed with people and the band is playing their hearts out." Dottie said. She took out her cigarette case and offered one to Fran. She took it graciously and placed it in a long cigarette holder before lighting it.

"Of course," Fran agreed. "You can never completely tell about a place until it's filled with music and life. I remember one of the biggest spots in Paris looked like a dilapidated saloon during the daylight hours."

"During their off season, Tommy's been bringing in some top-notch vaudeville comics for the floorshow. And of course, our girls really work hard, too. They bring in a lot of thirsty guys."

"I have heard much about the floorshow. It's nearly as famous as you."

Dottie laughed, "I hope you haven't heard anything too terrible."

"Not at all. In fact, I think if you were to go to Paris, you could be the most popular woman in all of France." Fran leaned back against the piano and appraised Dottie. "I think that you and I will always be good friends."

"Well, I hope so," Max said. He motioned Tommy to join the girls on the stage. He extended his arms and looked around the speak, "See, this is what I want, Tommy."

"How's that?"

"I'm going to open a place on the far west side. I want it to be second only to Dottie's. I want you to help me run it."

Tommy moved his glass in a small circle to hear the ice jingle. He watched the ice cubes swirl for a moment before speaking. "Why me?"

Fran answered for him, "Just look at this marvelous place. It's become the biggest thing in the city. We want your help to make ours just as big."

Aaronson slipped an arm around Fran's waist, but she showed no signs of noticing. "I'm gonna name it in Fran's honor. Le Paris or something."

Fran Barrey seemed unimpressed with the honor. "But I am a citizen of the world." She addressed Tommy and Dottie, "True, I was born in Paris, but I spent six of my first ten years in England." She added shyly, "That explains my accent."

"And why you speak better English than I do," Tommy said.

Fran did not seem to be the kind of woman who would blush unless it could get her something. She blushed now. "Thank you, Tommy. But sometimes I forget my grammar."

Dottie turned to Max, "Your uncle has The Pharaoh Club. That's the swankiest joint in the city."

"Nah. It may be a bit over-the-top, but it's not nearly as popular as your place now." Max smiled, "Besides, I want a place that I can feel is my own, you know what I mean?"

Tommy's eyes narrowed, "Your uncle won't help you?"

Max smiled. "Naw. Uncle Hymie's planning on retiring as soon as the Repeal comes. He's grooming me to take over and doesn't want me spending all my time in a club. Dave'll be running the place most of the time." David Gold had been one of Tommy Trent's boyhood chums and had introduced him to Max Aaronson, Hyman Amberg's nephew. "What do you say, Tommy? We can be equal partners."

Tommy considered and shook his head. "Uh-uh. If we open this place together, I'll take twenty percent and Dottie will take twenty five. She's the reason this place is what it is."

Dottie started to protest, but Tommy gave her a squeeze to quiet her. Fran watched admiringly. "But I gotta tell you, Maxie, a high-class place is a lot of work. There's overhead to figure; you got the supply, you got the girls and entertainment… There's a million things to watch over and you've got to have people you can trust on all levels. Dottie and I won't be able to be that much help, I'm afraid."

"I know. I know. You've got your hands full running the neighborhood for Eddie. But I would appreciate anything you two could do to help me out."

"I would even come and sing for your customers once or twice a week, if you like," Fran offered. She looked to Dottie, "If you could help us put together a floorshow…"

"Why don't you stop in tonight and catch the show first, before you decide whether or not you like it."

Fran laughed. "Max's word is good enough for me. He says you've got the hottest band in town and the hottest girls. He raves about it all the time."

"You have a spot picked out?" Tommy asked.

"Sure."

"Let's go see it."

* * *

It took more than two months to put together the nightclub on the far west side. Le Paris would indeed be a grandiose club. Both Max and Fran had been enchanted with the atmosphere at Dottie's and had used it as the model for Le Paris; it would be a French-themed replica of Dottie's. An intricate dark cherry-wood wainscoting wrapped itself around the lower half of the walls all around the club. The top half of the walls were papered in a rosy pink shade, decorated by ornate gold framed mirrors and imported rose woodcarvings. Max Aaronson had chandeliers imported from France and wired to a dimmer switch so they would not interfere with the special lighting for the floorshow. Hung throughout the club were colorful French posters—mostly advertisements for alcohol and famous Parisian nightspots.

"I need your help, Dottie," Fran said as she led Tommy and his entourage into the empty club. Tommy, Dottie, Connie Banks, Tano and Frankie Sirico sat with her at one of the large round tables. Two old French magazines sat opened on the tabletop. She pointed to two colorful full page ads bearing her likeness. "Which do you prefer?" One was a cartoon of Fran Barrey seated upon a fingernail moon, obviously enjoying a glass of wine, laughing and kicking up her heels. The second was a simpler ad with a line drawing of Fran Barrey smoking a cigarette. They all voted for the first one.

"We're going to have it reproduced and blown up to hang on the wall," she explained.

"Well, why not one of them nudie postcards?" Tano asked with a grin. Connie jabbed him in the ribs with her elbow.

Max Aaronson entered with twelve men close behind, all carrying instrument cases and music stands. "Good afternoon, everyone!"

"Hiya, Maxie," Tommy said. "These the boys you settled on?"

"Sure. Your bandleader recommended them."

"Well," Tommy said. "If there's anyone who knows anything about music, it's Harris."

The musicians were setting up on the low stage. Max motioned for the bandleader to step over to the table. "Jimmy Revel and His Reveleers, meet Tommy Trent and His Racketeers."

Tommy laughed. "That's pretty good, Maxie."

"Tommy here and the delightful Miss Dottie Deuce are part owners," Max explained.

Jimmy Revel was a short lean man and Tommy wondered how he had the lungs to produce some of those sounds from the clarinet. Revel smiled politely and shook their hands. "I used to play in the Bob Harris band." He pushed a lock of black hair away from his eyes and polished the lens of his round glasses. "He let me start my own band because he knew nobody'd ever beat his."

"I've seen you boys in Marco Messinio's place, haven't I?"

"Sure, Mr. Trent. We've played most of the clubs on the East and North Sides. This is our first engagement on the West."

"And it may be a permanent engagement," Max grinned. With the club opening in less than two weeks, Max reminded Fran of a kid during the final week before Christmas.

"Well, I hope so," Tommy said and turned his eyes back to Jimmy Revel. "And just call me Tommy, huh?"

"Why, sure boss." He inclined his head towards Dottie, "And the lady?"

"Call her anything but Dorothy," Tommy said with a sly grin. He pinched her thigh lightly. "You only call her that when yer sore at her."

"And when you do, she's liable to gouge your eyes out," Fran said.

They all laughed. Max's ebullience was catching.

Jimmy Revel whirled around on one heel; his clarinet seemed to appear in his hands as if by magic. "Okay, fellas," he said to his orchestra, "Let's show 'em what we got!"

The band tore into a hot jazz number that seemed to shake the walls with its heavy thump-lump-tah beat. Tommy held onto his glass to keep it from dancing off the end of the table. When Jimmy Revel took his solo he showed that his lean physique betrayed a massive set of powerful lungs. His cheeks puffed out and turned red as he seemed to try to blast the roof off. Dottie thought he nearly succeeded.

When the song ended with a double tap on the hi-hat, everyone at the table applauded and cheered. Tommy was satisfied. He leaned close to Fran and Max and said in a low voice, "If it'll sweeten the deal, I can talk to the boys over at the Conroy Label about a contract for them."

Fran beamed. "An arrangement like Bob Harris has with you? Oh, that would be great, Tommy! You are a doll!"

Max shook his head in disbelief. "You and Dottie are the greatest. None of this would have been possible without you guys… If ever there's anything Fran and I can do for you, say the word, huh?"

"Sure, Maxie." Tommy pointed to the empty bottle on the table, "I think we could start with a fresh bottle, huh?"

"Sure." As he stood from the table, Max tapped Tano on the shoulder. "We've got a whole bevy of beauties coming to audition for the floorshow. They should be here any moment."

Tano laughed and clapped his hands together. "Well, bring 'em on!"

Connie kicked him in the shin.

Tommy leaned back in his chair and sighed. He raised his glass in a toast. "Ah, to all you Women's Temperance dames and Anti-Saloon dolls with yer big mouths and little axes, wherever you are, thank you."

* * *

Whatever the stereotypes might have been, Tommy always thought that the girls who sang and danced in the countless floorshows in the countless nightclubs across the nation were some of the hardest working people on earth. Most of them were hanging onto dreams of Broadway and Hollywood stardom and even though the odds were against them all, they still stuck with it and nearly worked themselves to the point of collapse.

That was evident by the fact the girls were still working with Connie Banks and Jimmy Revel's band hours later when Tommy returned to Le Paris. Connie was going through some of the finer points of keeping their dance steps in unison when Tommy joined Fran Barrey at the table. "Dottie go home?"

Fran had been sitting alone and lost in thought. "Oh, hi, Tommy. Didn't see you come in." She sat upright in her chair and slid a spare glass over to him. "Yes, Dottie went home to open up the club. We're borrowing Connie for the evening. The kid's got talent."

Tommy nodded in agreement. "This is going to be a great place," he said and lit a cigarette.

"But not without your help and Dottie's help," Fran said.

"It's gonna give us a run for our money."

"Don't worry. Dottie's will still be the crème de le crème."

"You got all the girls you need for the floorshow?"

Fran nodded. "I think we have enough. We've kept the runners-up on as waitresses like you suggested."

Tommy topped off his glass, "Believe me, it'll be worth the extra dough to keep 'em around. If one of your showgirls get sick or gets herself in a family way, you already have the talent waiting tables."

"You're a wise young man, Tommy. Are you just wise in business, or with women, or what?"

He grinned, "I'm just wise when it comes to anything relating to booze."

Fran was smiling into her glass. She swirled the ice cubes and laughed. "America in Prohibition! I've seen many things and gone many places, but I've never found anything quite like it."

"I take it from your tone you approve?"

Fran thought about it for a moment. "Yes. I think it's a ball. But I think that it's men like you who make this such an interesting time and place to live."

"How do you mean?"

Fran shrugged, still staring at her glass and smiling. "I like you, Tommy. You couldn't find another man like you in all the world." She paused a moment and then sat up in her chair suddenly. "I forgot! I have something for you!"

She disappeared for several minutes and returned with a small frame. Smiling shyly she handed it to Tommy. The frame contained one of her pre-war postcards in which Fran Barrey was lying quite naked on a bed of flowers. She had signed it for him, "To Tommy, Love always."

"Well," Tommy said. "That's—that's really nice. But I don't know if Dottie would approve."

"See?" Fran said, her lower lip pouting ever-so-slightly. The pout turned into a smile. "This is why America will never produce a famous artist who will live through the centuries. This country was founded by puritans and it remains puritan. If Michelangelo had been American, his statue of David would have gotten him arrested. This is not pornography, Tommy. It is *art*. This photograph was taken by the greatest of all photographers in the world. I'm sure Dottie'll understand."

Tommy put the frame on the table and considered his drink during the long pause that followed. "Can I ask a personal question, Ms. Barrey?"

Her dark eyes shot up to lock on his. "Anything."

"You came to America with a husband. What happened?"

She looked back to her drink and spoke softly. "He became a policeman. Six months after we were married, a nigger stabbed him to death."

"I'm sorry," he said. Fran shrugged. "Have you ever thought of going back to Paris?"

She took her time answering. "I don't think so. Paris is not the same now as it was before the war. I had many adventures and knew many interesting people in Paris…" She laughed softly at a memory, "One of them, a famous painter whose name I won't mention, told me I had the most beautiful breasts in the world… But those days and those adventures are all past." She put a hand on Tommy's. "And perhaps I stayed in America to see if I could find a man like you."

"What about Max?"

She smiled out of the side of her mouth, "It's a shame that you and Max are friends and that Dottie and I are friends."

"Why?"

"Because I should like to fuck you very much." The frankness of the statement was disarming.

Tommy put his other hand on hers, "Now, look, Frenchie. Don't start getting any ideas in your head."

* * *

Each Christmas Tommy Trent had appeared at the DiStella's apartment with presents. Last year he had given Eddie a box of cigars and a beautiful little handheld mirror to Sarah. Sarah had been mortified; she hadn't expected him to give her anything. She remembered how horrified she felt, in her robe on Christmas morning, her hair still uncombed, no make-up, standing in front of the man she had been infatuated with for so long, holding the beautiful gold mirror with nothing to give in return. She felt like a dope.

But this year she vowed not to make the same mistake.

Fat Eddie was sitting in his office marking off a list of kitchen chairs that had just been delivered to the store downstairs. "Poppa?"

He looked up and pushed the papers aside with a smile. Since her mother's death, Eddie had always tried to make enough time for her. "What can I do for you, kiddo?"

She sat down on the desk. "Last year Tommy surprised me with that Christmas present..."

"Yeah, that was nice of him."

"Well, I felt terrible about it. I almost died! I didn't have anything to give him."

"You really like him, don't you?"

Sarah nodded and felt herself turning red. "Yes. Yes I do. I liked him before..." She stopped herself. She didn't want to mention the kidnapping. "I want to get him something this year."

Fat Eddie looked away from her and thought for a long moment.

"He's not seeing anyone is he?"

That was the question. For all Eddie knew he was seeing every broad in the city. And then there was Dottie Deuce. The Deuce and Tommy Trent would always be a mystery. The whole world seemed to know they loved each other very much, but no one was sure how far their relationship had gone.

"I don't know, Sarah. But you're seeing that nice Bobby boy, aren't you?"

Sarah looked down at the floor and shook her head. "I had to break it off with him."

"Why?"

"Because every time he'd take me out to dinner, I'd be sitting there… thinking about Tommy." She looked up to her father, "I just couldn't keep doing that to him."

"You really like Tommy." It was more of a statement than a question.

She nodded again and then her eyes grew wide with horror. "You're not gonna stop letting him come over are you—" She thought of how Tommy always came in with a big smile on his face, would toss his hat and have it land on the hall tree before giving Sarah a hug or a kiss on the top of her head, saying "How's the DiStella angel?" No matter how urgent the business might be, he always took time to say hello and make sure she was doing okay and make her laugh. And the way he looked at her made her melt.

Fat Eddie let out a long sigh. Then he stood up and patted Sarah's shoulder. "I'll see if I can get a copy of his Christmas wish list from one of his friends."

* * *

"Hey! Hey!" Gaetano Amato cried cheerily as he stepped into Tommy Trent's apartment. "Christmas is coming early this year!"

"Come on in, have a drink."

Tano wiped the snow from his shoulders and hung his jacket up by the door. "Carlson's not paying anybody for protection."

Tommy nodded as he poured the drinks and handed one to Tano. They sat down on opposite sides of the small coffee table piled high with stacks of ten and twenty-dollar bills Tommy had been counting.

"Tuesday morning they're getting a shipment of fur coats in," Tano continued. He took a sip of his drink and then looked at the glass as though he had just discovered alcohol, "Ooh, that takes the chill away!" He took another sip. "Anyway, I talked to a guy on the inside, and we've got dibs."

"Good," Tommy said, shuffling some bills together and stuffing them into an envelope. "Sounds good. It'll be nice to get out for once." He tossed the thick envelope on the table and sat back with a sigh. "That's for the police captain."

Tano laughed, "Yeah, you've been doing too much of Eddie's work and not having enough fun. Not that going to Dottie's every night and having to sit through those routines the girls do is a burden or anything." His smile widened, "And then having to go all the way cross town to watch Fran's girls... Oh! Murder!"

Tommy laughed and refilled his glass. "I couldn't be happier with the way things have been going with Dottie's. I'll never understand why Eddie treated it like it was just another speak."

"Because Eddie doesn't have any imagination."

* * *

The snow was coming down hard and making it increasingly difficult to see the road. Eli Jacobs was leaning over the truck's steering wheel, straining his eyes to see past the windscreen. This was his last haul before he got a couple of days off for the holidays. In the old days, he would have worked straight through the holidays, but now that the trucking firm had a new boss this would be the first time in years that he'd get to spend the holidays in their entirety with his family.

His reflexes were faster than the rest of him. They forced his leg down on the brake while he was still wondering if it had just been a phantom on the road. The truck tried to fish tail as it came to a halt in front of the figure standing in the road.

It wasn't a phantom. Phantoms don't carry tommyguns and smoke cigarettes.

The cab door opened and a man with a pistol was pulling his arm, "Alright, pal. Your holiday break starts right here."

"Don't hurt me," Eli pleaded as he stepped down out of the cab.

"Don't worry." The man directed Eli to the roadside. "Sit there."

Eli looked at the pile of snow the plows had scooped up, and then back to the gunman as if to protest. He thought better of it and sat on the dirty pile of snow.

The man with the tommygun stepped forward and tossed a blanket to Eli. "Stay warm, pal." The blanket was followed by two fifty-dollar bills fluttering down like big beautifully green snowflakes.

The two men climbed into Eli's truck and waved politely as it moved past. A car motor started to his right, startling him. It pulled into the road and the truck followed it into the dark snowy night.

14

THE ONLY TIME THAT THE DISTELLA APARTMENT LOOKED as bright and alive as it had when Sarah's mother was alive was during the holidays. The rest of the year the house seemed to have something missing; even outsiders who had never known her mother could feel it. The apartment always felt happy, but people would step inside and feel that there was something out of place, that an essential part of the picture was missing. Except at Christmas. Sarah always liked to think that mama came home to be with them during Christmas.

It was Christmas Eve, that most magical of all nights in the year when such miracles could occur and Sarah and her father were decorating. "Poppa," she said, standing on the ladder. "Hand me some more tinsel."

"You should let me get up there. It's dangerous."

"Oh, posh," she sighed, placing a bit of glimmering tinsel next to one of the shiny purple ornaments.

When she turned around again, her father was looking up at her with the most peculiar expression. "What is it, Poppa?"

"Nothin'," he smiled. He had been thinking that his daughter had somehow become a full grown woman, even prettier than her mother and that someday a nice young man was going to marry her and take her away from him. And then Fat Eddie would rattle around like a ghost in the old apartment where his daughter had been raised. It was such a blend of bitter and sweet that a lump crawled up his throat. "Ready for the angel?"

"Sure!"

He fished the small hand painted angel from the box of Christmas memories. "Remember when you were little? I'd always pick you up and lift you high so you could put the angel up there."

"Yeah," she smiled wistfully.

"Heh, I don't think I could do that now."

He passed the angel to her and cringed inwardly as she leaned far over on the ladder. He held it with an iron grip until she had gotten the angel just right and stood straight again. He helped her down the ladder, folded it and put it to the side. Then he put an arm around her shoulder and they both looked at the beautiful tree.

A knock came at the door and the girl jumped. "Oh!" She put a hand to her hair, "I'll get it!" She darted towards the door, stopped and turned around again to retrieve her shoes from where she had kicked them off before climbing the ladder. She made one more pause on her way to the door to check her make-up in the small mirror on the wall.

Fat Eddie couldn't help but grin, but part of his heart ached. He knew who the girl was hoping would be at the door. His daughter was passing from infatuation into love. But it could be worse. Maybe having a capable guy like Tommy Trent for a son-in-law would be a handy thing.

She opened the door and smiled. "Tommy! Come in."

Tommy wiped his feet and stepped inside the room. He had a package under his arm. "Hey, that's a pretty Christmas tree."

"Thank you. We just finished decorating."

"Hi, Eddie."

"How you doin', Tommy?"

"Filled with the Christmas spirit! Here—this is for you," he handed

Eddie a large box wrapped in bright paper.

"I hope it's another box of those cigars!" Eddie grinned as he tore open the package. "Aha!" he cried as though he had discovered gold, "I knew it! Thanks, Tommy." He threw an arm around the young man's shoulders. "Merry Christmas kid."

Tommy took a thick envelope out of his pocket and handed it to Eddie. "And Happy New Year, Eddie."

Eddie chuckled as he put the envelope in his pocket. "Thanks, Tommy. You know, that's a good idea! Let's drink a toast! I'll get the wine!" Eddie scurried from the room and Sarah took it as her cue.

But before she could speak, Tommy produced a small package from an inside pocket and handed it to her. "You didn't think I forgot you, did you?"

"No," she smiled. Her brow furrowed and she licked her lips in concentration while struggling with the package's ribbon. She finally removed it and peeled away the paper. Opening the box she discovered a stylish platinum bracelet with diamonds. "Oh, Tommy! It's beautiful." She threw her arms around him and gave him a squeeze.

"Merry Christmas, kiddo."

"Not so fast," she said scurrying to the stack of presents by the tree. She pulled out a small package and returned to him. "This is for you."

"Oh, you didn't—"

"Go on, open it."

He unwrapped the package and discovered a pocket watch inside of a black velvet box. "Wow, this is great, Sarah. It's beautiful. Thanks."

She smiled slyly and pointed to the ceiling above. Tommy looked up. "Oh, mistletoe. So that's how it is. I see—"

Before he could speak further she threw her arms around him and kissed him. He thought she'd never let go. "Merry Christmas, Tommy."

"Oh, it is," he grinned giving her a squeeze.

She laughed and pushed herself away from him. Her father returned with three glasses and a bottle of wine. "This is from the old country, Tommy, so I hope you like it."

"What should we drink to?"

"The future. What else?"

The delivery boy stood on the corner stamping his feet and blowing into his hands. His cheeks were blue from the cold and pumping his legs to get his bicycle through the snow. He watched as Tommy Trent left the DiStella residence and climbed into his new car.

The boy noted the time on a small pocket watch and waited the five minutes he had been instructed, wondering if freezing like this was worth an extra five dollar tip. By the time the five minutes were up, he decided that five bucks was indeed worth it.

He knocked on the door with frozen knuckles and waited. He shifted the package under his arm and called out, "Delivery!" and rapped on the door once more.

When Fat Eddie took the package without giving him a tip, the boy made an obscene gesture at the closed door and cursed. "Merry Christmas to you too, fatty!"

Eddie read his name on the address label and scratched his head as he took the package to his office. He took his time opening it as though it might be a bomb. Inside the box he found a fur coat and an unsigned note. "Give this to your daughter."

"That devil," Eddie chuckled.

"What was it Poppa?" Sarah came into the room as Eddie turned around, showing off the coat with a flourish.

Her eyes grew as large as saucers. "From Tommy," Eddie announced proudly.

"Oh! Oh, my!" she rushed forward and hugged the coat and her father at the same time. "Oh, Poppa!"

* * *

"How many of those coats did we give away?" Tano pushed a black curl of hair away from his forehead and kicked his feet up on the coffee table. Connie was in the next room fussing with the Christmas tree.

Tommy too, put his feet up on the coffee table and began counting on his fingers, "One to Dottie, one to Frenchie, one to Alice, one to Connie—"

"Those don't count," Tano said gruffly. "The ones for our broads don't count."

"Oh," Tommy chuckled. "Alright. One for Fat Eddie to give his daughter, one for Rocco to give his broad, one for Patsy, uh, Marco Messinio and we sent one over to Hymie."

Tano laughed. "What's that Jew gonna do with *another* fur coat?"

* * *

Sarah DiStella had been strictly forbidden from ever going into one of the neighborhood speakeasies. But the man she was falling helplessly in love with had given her the most beautiful fur coat in the world and it still took her breath away when she thought of it. And the journey to Dottie's would be a tremendous opening for her to push the relationship along. It was also dangerous—if her father found out, he'd hit the roof, but after weighing the consequences, she had to find Tommy and thank him.

And she also wanted to see with her own eyes the famous Dottie Deuce.

As she walked, she ran over a myriad of lines to use on Tommy, but none of them seemed satisfactory. But she was convinced that if she just let the words come straight from the heart, it would do the trick.

The bright cheery atmosphere, the laughing voices and the hot jazz nearly overwhelmed her as she stepped into the speak. It was nothing at all like the dark dingy mysterious places she had imagined. She scanned the room for Tommy while adjusting her coat to make sure it had the proper effect. She saw a strikingly beautiful woman showing a similar fur coat to a couple of girls who oohed and aahed and pawed at it.

It was The Deuce. Sarah knew it instantly.

She was very beautiful.

The beautiful woman turned around and draped her arms over Tommy's shoulders and kissed his cheek. Sarah could read her lips as she said, "Thanks, doll."

Sarah DiStella's heart skipped a beat and she suddenly grew dizzy. Her mind began racing in a hundred directions.

"Can I help you, miss?" asked the large man by the entryway.

"Um, no," she said quickly. "I just… I remembered I forgot something." She made a hasty retreat.

She had just come dangerously close to making herself look like the biggest fat-head in the world. It was only for a second that she saw the beautiful buxom blonde with her arms around Tommy's neck, but if felt like a lifetime.

So that was the beautiful and glamorous Deuce. And wearing a coat like Sarah's. Sarah DiStella's head began to ache.

15

After the discovery of King Tutankhamen's tomb in 1922, anything remotely Egyptian was hot. Hyman Amberg had been quick to jump on the bandwagon, opening The Pharaoh Club early in 1923. It was the swankiest joint in the city. Hieroglyphics were carved and painted on the walls which were made to look like the sandy stone the pyramids were built from. Elaborate mummies, coffins and statues adorned the club. The waitresses all wore beaded Egyptian headdresses, chokers and breastplates which were just big enough to conceal their nipples. Their make-up was *à la* Cleopatra, modeled on Theda Bara's theatrical make-up.

The Pharaoh Club was so grand that even Hyman Amberg enjoyed spending time there, though he only drank when discussing business with his rivals and partners.

It had been the number one club in the city until Tommy Trent created an equal to rival The Pharaoh Club by remodeling and expanding

Dottie's. But that was fine. A little competition was healthy.

But when his nephew Max opened Le Paris—in a vain attempt to get that French hooker to spread her legs for him—Amberg began to fume. And he became irate when he learned Max was giving half the profits to Tommy Trent and Dottie Deuce.

The Pharaoh Club was now only the third greatest in the city. He might not have objected to Le Paris stealing away customers if all of the money had stayed on the west side. But giving half to Tommy and Dottie wasn't much worse than Max coming in and robbing The Pharaoh Club at gunpoint.

But this was not the time to brood about such things. It was New Year's Eve and another year of prosperity was in the offing. There would be plenty of time to fret over his nephew later. He sat, drinking a cup of tea, frowning at the degenerate nigger music, but smiling at the scantily clad waitresses. June was seated next to him, sipping a whiskey sour.

"I been wonderin'," a voice startled them. Hyman Amberg turned in his chair to find James Poulhaus standing behind him. "Isn't it strange for a Jew to be running a place that honors the Egyptians? Didn't they keep your peoples as slaves in the desert for forty years or some such shit?"

Amberg smiled. "Hi, detective." He nodded towards the group of men standing behind Poulhaus. "You boys out celebrating?"

"Sure! In't ev'rybody? We're making the rounds." Poulhaus was swaying almost imperceptibly. His nose and cheeks were very red. "I didn't see you when we came in, or I'da come over to say hello. We're gonna hit your nephew's place next."

"Going to see the French tart?" June asked. A baleful glare from Hyman made her look back to her drink and keep her head down.

"Well," Poulhaus said uncomfortably, "I'll see you, Mr. Amberg."

"Sure, Jimmy." As the men moved towards the exit, Amberg called after them, "Steer clear of Prohibition Agents!"

When they were gone, Amberg took June by the hand and then slapped her with an open fist. The girl barely flinched. "What the hell's the matter with you?"

June turned her green eyes to him, "I'm sorry."

Amberg looked away from her and sighed through his nose. "You tryin' to start trouble? Don't say shit about the French whore."

* * *

As Sarah looked around the dancehall and counted, she came to the conclusion that seven out of ten people there were spiking their drinks from their flasks. But why not? This was New Year's Eve, and if ever a night had been made for drinking, this was it.

There were two flasks being passed surreptitiously around at the table where Sarah sat with Anne, her husband Paul, and Victoria "Vilma" Wolfe. Sarah had made sure to wear her new platinum bracelet and her new fur coat. Anne had been skeptical when Sarah proclaimed the fur coat to be a sign that better things were on their way. "If a guy gave me and another girl a fur coat, I'd be awfully mad."

"Don't you see?" Sarah said. "He gave me the same gift he gave that other girl! I'm gaining ground."

"It couldn't be that they were stolen? I read in the paper…"

"I don't believe that," Sarah said flatly. "Besides, what about this beautiful bracelet?" She pulled back the sleeve of her fur coat to show it off.

"To guys like that, money is nothing."

Sarah pretended not to hear and did not take from the flask as she passed it to Paul. "In any case, let's not ruin the evening by getting into a debate." She got up and started towards the dance floor, smiling over her shoulder. "I have a feeling this is going to be a very good year!"

* * *

The crowd in Dottie's roared as the clock struck twelve. Noise makers blew as confetti rained down on everyone. The place was packed tonight. Frankie Sirico hugged Alice Byrd close. Alice had skipped her father's political celebration to be at Dottie's tonight. "It's the only place to go on New Years!" she said.

Connie Banks broke away from the chorus line long enough for Tano to pick her up and whirl her around before giving her a big happy New Year's kiss. Tano turned to find Tommy giving Dottie a long passionate kiss. "Hey! *Amico Mio!* Happy New Year!"

Tommy paused long enough to wave his hand over the crowd to him before sweeping The Deuce back into his arms and gave her another long kiss. "This," he smiled, "looks like it's going to be a big year, doll."

16

RUMORS AND STORIES ABOUT GANGSTERS TRAVELED QUICKLY AND there was usually some shred of truth behind them. Rumors about their girls, on the other hand, traveled even faster and leaned towards the bizarre.

Although Dottie Deuce was famous and beloved in the neighborhood, she felt there were only three people who were really knew her: Tommy Trent, Fran Barrey and Connie Banks. Connie was her friend, confidant and because of her remarkable resemblance to Clara Bow, her headline girl in the floor show. She had always thought of Connie as a kid sister.

Dottie's was closed for the night now and Connie sat on one side of the bar while Dottie absently dried the glasses with a towel on the other side. Her thoughts were a million miles away.

It was strange, Connie thought, how easily a woman could get a peculiar reputation in a town like this. Fran Barrey was believed to be a sex-crazed maniac in spite of the fact she refused the countless propositions made to her. She was supposed to be wild and crazy, but underneath it all, she was a lot like most of the girls Connie knew.

Dottie was a legend, known as the toughest broad in the neighborhood. She could drink anyone under the table and still be able to dance on top of the piano without missing a beat. Or so the stories said. No one had ever actually witnessed such a spectacle. Some people seemed to believe she was a pistol-packing saloon doll from the old days of the Wild West. Sure she was a tough gal, alright, but beneath it all she too was just like any other woman.

It was the price the women paid for popularity and their small degree of fame. Connie Banks was very pleased she was rather anonymous, referred to only as "the girl who looks like Clara Bow."

"Remember when little Frankie got sprung?" Dottie said suddenly. Connie was so startled she nearly sloshed her drink.

"Sure."

"I overheard something." Dottie finished polishing the final glass and came around the bar and took up the stool next to Connie's. She lit a cigarette and took a sip of her drink. "Frankie pulled Tommy and Tano aside…"

"And?" Connie urged.

"He thanked them and swore an oath of undying loyalty. Apparently all the time he was up the river, Tommy and Tano were giving money to his sister to help support the family."

"Really?"

"Yeah. All that time they took care of little Frankie's family. I had no idea."

"Neither did I."

Dottie thought of the little half starved boy who used to bring her stolen apples because she wasn't eating enough. Dottie put her elbow on the bar and supported her head with her hand. She let out a long wistful sigh. "It's the sweetest, most noble thing I ever heard."

The morning air spilled in as the front door opened. Connie swiveled around on the stool. "There they are!" she cheered as Tommy and Gaetano entered the speak. "Our sweet and most noble men!"

"What the hell are you talking about?" Tano said taking her into his arms. He laughed and then sighed, "All right, how much do you want this time?"

"Nothing, doll face," Connie patted his cheek. "Long night?"

"Uh-huh. But I think it was worth it."

Tommy put his arms around Dottie and gave her big squeeze. Tommy and Tano sat on either side of the girls and each held a fist in front of the women's eyes. Simultaneously they uncurled their fingers, letting the diamond necklaces dangle before the girls' eyes.

Dottie smiled and threw her arms around Tommy. "Oh, you *are* the sweetest and most noble guys!"

* * *

Sarah DiStella was hurt that the beautiful and charming Dottie Deuce didn't even regard her as competition. It was as though she was unaware of Sarah's intentions, and she didn't treat Sarah any differently than she did the other girls in the place.

The Deuce had even intimated that if she could sing and dance, Sarah would be welcome to join the chorus line.

A chorus girl! The nerve! Sarah DiStella, a chorus girl!?!

Sarah had prepared herself for this evening with the same focus as a prize fighter in training for the big bout. But instead of being cold, jealous or suspicious, Dottie Deuce welcomed her warmly and offered her friendship freely. She was a nice woman, a good woman, and Sarah cursed the part of her that admitted she actually liked Dottie.

Damn her!

Sarah had come here expecting a psychological game of chess, not a friendly 'Welcome To The Neighborhood' party. Dottie introduced her to some of the girls. There was Connie—whom she had already met—a girl named Julia, a Marie, a Harriet, a June, a Louise… and then there were Tommy's friends: Tano, Frankie, Marty, Tony… and none of them seemed to have the slightest idea that Sarah was Dottie's rival.

Sarah was surprised by the amount of flirtatious banter the girls exchanged with Tommy and how Dottie seemed to think nothing of it. Was it all an act? Had Dottie coached them all on being so receptive and friendly, to act as though Sarah was just one of the gang and nothing more?

She wasn't one of the gang! She never wanted to be! She had nothing in common with these barelegged, sequin-dressed hussies. She was the one who was going to steal Tommy away from Dottie; she was the one who was going to be the love of his life!

What made it worse was that by the end of the evening, Sarah found herself liking some of these barelegged, sequin-dressed hussies. She laughed openly and freely with them, even though they often shocked her with their free way of speaking.

But wasn't that what speakeasies and nightclubs were all about? Being naughty? Drinking illegal liquor, listening to degenerate jazz music and flirting with members of the opposite sex?

Tommy was his usual self, except he had the nerve to hold Dottie's hand right there, a few feet away from Sarah, when all along he knew how she felt about him. 'Oh, God!' she thought queasily, 'Doesn't he even think of me as Dottie's competition?'

No. That couldn't be it. That night outside the drug store when he had followed her like a lust-mad wolf, the first time they had kissed and she had felt how much he wanted her—

But Sarah could not have known that she had met Tommy at the very end of his days as a roaming ladies' man. Sarah didn't realize that Dottie had spent years waiting until their age difference would no longer be a factor and that Tommy had been waiting until he was as much a legend as the great Dottie Deuce. All along Tommy and Dottie knew that when time and circumstance came together, they would be together. And time and circumstance would leave no room for Sarah DiStella.

17

It was their first girls-night out since Anne and Paul were married. The girls had known each other since their school days and tonight they seemed to be having one last wing-ding before adulthood had claimed them irrevocably. Any day now Anne would be pregnant and their little clique would forever be changed.

They intended on going all out as well; Flo and Victoria, who for the last few years had insisted upon being called the more vampish name of Vilma, had even coaxed Sarah into wearing a "headache band"—a ribbon headband—the purpose of which was dubious other than as a badge of honor which stated that the young lady wearing it was hep and ready to raise a little hell.

Florence Palermi, age 20, was driving fast in her father's Lincoln. Vilma was passing a silver hipflask around. The girls had just concluded a round of teasing Anne about the benefits of married life when Sarah surprised them all by taking a long pull from the flask. "Hey, take it easy. That's the real stuff," Flo said, glancing behind her. "My brother got it for me."

"Since when do you drink the hard stuff?" Vilma asked.

Sarah lowered the flask from her mouth and wiped her lips with the back of her wrist. "Tommy introduced me to the joys."

"Who's Tommy?" Vilma asked with a devilish look in her eye.

Anne answered, "He's the good-looking tough guy she's been drooling over for a year now. Longer, actually."

"Ooh!" squealed Vilma.

"Holy!" Flo exclaimed, and turned her head to look to the back seat until the car began swerving wildly across the road. "You don't mean Tommy Trent, do you?"

"Mm-hmm."

"Oh, you kid!" Flo roared with laughter. "You're kidding me!"

"No." Sarah sounded a little insulted.

"My brother Tony's in his gang!"

"What a small world," Anne observed without enthusiasm and took a drink from the flask.

Flo sighed dreamily, "He *is* a doll. You two kids serious?"

"Well, *I* am." Sarah said and the girls laughed.

"Hey! I know where they hang out! It's this speakeasy called Dottie's. Let's go see if they're there!"

"No!" Sarah protested. "My father'll hit the roof! Uh-uh!"

"Aw, come on," Vilma wheedled. "Let's go see your lover-boy."

"It's not a good idea. Besides, the girl that runs the place is Tommy's other woman."

"Why don't you and her duke it out over him?" Vilma asked.

Sarah tossed her head back and said haughtily, "It t'wouldn't be lady-like."

"Oh, poo!" Vilma exclaimed and began sulking. The girls giggled again.

"Well, I'll tell ya' this, kid," Flo said. "If you can land Tommy, half the girls in the city will be wearing black armbands on accouta you."

"Oh, no!" Vilma cried, her period of sulking having lasted a satisfactory amount of time. "We have to find your brother, Flo!" She turned the opened flask upside down. "It's empty and I can still feel my legs!"

The girls roared with laughter again. Sarah brightened up. "Hey, I *do* know a place where my father won't hear about me going."

Flo nearly drove off the road again. "Where? Where?"

"Its way over on the west side. A place called Le Paris. Tommy took me there. My father doesn't have anything to do with that one."

The car turned wildly in a U. "Flo," Anne said, surprised at how calm her voice sounded. "maybe you should let me drive."

"Oh. Am I that bad off?"

"Well, you just narrowly missed hitting a tree. Pull over."

Flo did as Anne asked and they changed places. Anne was doing her best to be carefree and giddy, but things just weren't the same now. She knew that they would go into the speakeasy and Vilma, Flo and Sarah could all ooh and aah over the guys. "It's the price you pay when you get married," she muttered softly.

"Wha?"

"Skip it."

When they arrived at Le Paris, the doorman was reluctant to let them enter. "Why don't you dolls go home and dry up, huh?"

"Listen, Mister," Vilma growled, but Sarah yanked her out of the way before she could get herself into trouble.

"I've been here before," Sarah said.

"Sure you have. But this isn't the delicatessen anymore. Beat it."

A new voice joined the conversation, "What's going on Cockeye?"

"We got four dames here, who..." Cockeye stepped aside as a young man in a tux appeared at his side.

"What do you kids want?"

"T'get drunk!" Vilma demanded.

He started to say something but paused when he saw Sarah. "I seen you before."

Sarah nodded. "With Tommy."

"Yeah. That's right. Does he know you're here?"

"Sure," Sarah lied.

He withered her with a skeptical gaze. "Now, look," he said pointing a finger at them. "My name is Dave Gold. I've known Tommy since we were kids. If I find out you're pulling my leg, I'll be in trouble. You wouldn't want to get an old friend of Tommy's in trouble, would you?"

"No."

He looked them over for a minute trying to decide if they were dressed well enough. "This is a high-class place. If I let you girls in, you have to promise to be on your best behavior."

"We swear," Sarah said and looked to the other three. "Don't we?"

The girls all nodded.

"Alright," Gold said and then whispered softly to Cockeye, "If they start getting loud, toss 'em out on their ass."

"Yessir."

Cockeye opened the door all the way and motioned them in. The club was darkened and Jimmy Revel and his band were playing softly behind a beautiful woman who was crooning a song in French into the microphone. They settled around a table at the midpoint of the club. A handful of couples were dancing with their heads on each other's shoulders.

"Wow," Vilma said. "This place looks like a palace."

"Were you expecting a dim and dingy little saloon?" Sarah asked.

"No. No."

Anne laughed, "Instead of standing there and looking like a tourist, kid, why don't you go fetch us some drinks?"

Vilma nodded and disappeared into the crowd. She returned a few moments later shuffling her feet while juggling the glasses. The other three were watching the singer. "That's a pretty song," Flo said. "I wonder what it means."

Sarah shrugged.

"Am I drunk, or does she keep looking at us?"

They joined in the applause when the woman finished the song and took a bow. She thanked the audience graciously, stepped aside and with a sweep of the arm sent the band into a hot jazz number that nearly knocked Vilma out of her chair.

"Hey, she's coming this way," Flo said.

Anne got a bad feeling and grabbed her purse. "Maybe we should leave."

But it was too late. Fran Barrey was standing at the side of the table, her dark mesmerizing eyes fixed on Sarah. "Haven't—haven't I seen you here before?" Sarah nodded. "With Tommy, right?"

Sarah nodded again. She couldn't bring herself to look into the woman's eyes. The other girls felt a wave of ice flowing from her. Fran could not fathom why Tommy ran around with this young girl. She remembered the sappy look of love in the girl's eyes when Tommy brought her in. Fran was by no means a violent person, but there was something about Sarah that just made Fran want to smack her.

"I'm sorry," Fran said, closing her eyes and shaking her thoughts away. She said warmly, "How is Tommy? I haven't seen him in a couple of days."

A couple of days? Sarah thought, and wondered if Tommy brought other girls here. "I haven't seen him in a couple of days, either." But it had been much longer than that.

"Well, Tommy's a busy guy." Her thoughts wandered off to a daydream. The dreamy look made Sarah's heart sink. She had thought that The Deuce was her only competition, but now she was beginning to wonder.

"How—how well do you know him?" Sarah seemed to be addressing her drink.

Fran tossed her head back with a throaty laugh and put a hand to her bosom. "We are dear, *dear* friends." She snapped her fingers and called out, "Jen?"

A young waitress appeared at the table immediately. "Yes, Miss Barrey?"

"This is a friend of Tommy's. Give them a round on the house."

"Yes, ma'am."

"Well, it was nice to meet you—" Fran said extending a well manicured hand.

"Sarah." She took the hand lamely.

"Sarah. I have to run along. If you see Tommy before I do, tell him Frenchie was looking for him, huh?" Frenchie was a nickname that she would tolerate only from Tommy or Dottie.

"Okay."

The girls were silent as they watched the woman move on to mingle with other guests. "Jesus," Flo sighed softly.

"Didja catch that look? Talk about a cold stare," Vilma said. Then she was the first at the table to smile again. She elbowed Sarah, "Think she's jealous of you, kid."

Sarah frowned. "Me too." But she knew that wasn't it. Old Frenchie was obviously very protective of Tommy and Dottie and her own relationship with them.

A long pause followed. Finally Flo spoke up, "Well, girls, I don't know about you, but I'm gonna find me a man to dance with."

"Me, too!" Vilma said and got up so quickly she nearly knocked her chair over backwards. She remembered the warning about being too loud and put a hand to her lips and giggled. She repeated, in a whisper this time, "Me, too" and joined Flo as she headed into the crowd.

"There they go man-hunting," Anne said. She nudged Sarah's glass. "Why don't you go find somebody?"

Sarah wondered how on earth she could be in a room full of people and feel so suddenly isolated.

"Oh, hell, Sarah," Anne groaned when Sarah did not answer, "I keep telling you this Tommy guy is bad news."

* * *

Fat Eddie DiStella couldn't get over how much the place had changed in such a short time. It was a bright, beautiful place now, a world away from the place it used to be. Sure, it had been a popular spot in the neighborhood, but now it was the jewel of the city. Every table had matching gold-trimmed settings. The white tablecloths and china were impeccably clean. And one waft from the kitchen told him that Tommy had raided the staff of the Café DiNapoli. It wasn't just a speakeasy anymore. It was a full-blown nightclub.

And there, in the center of the low stage, leaning against the piano, dazzling in a red sequin dress, singing into the microphone as if she were making love to it, was Dottie Deuce. Having to say something, he turned to a man at a near-by table, "If I was a few years younger, *Madonn'!*"

Dottie was coming close to the end of the song now, and Eddie knew that she was living a dream, thanks to Tommy Trent. It seemed he had that effect on a lot of women. Including his own daughter. Fat Eddie was torn in two over his daughter's love for Tommy.

Dottie finished the song and regarded Eddie from across the room with a smile. The band members were returning from their break and taking up their places around the pianist as she left the stage. The chorus girls—twice as many as there were before—came dancing out from the wings doing high kicks and singing in unison.

"Eddie!" Dottie cried, and threw her arms around his neck. The sweet smell of her perfume was enough to make Eddie's knees weak.

"Dottie. You've got the voice of an angel."

"Ah, get outta here," she laughed. "What can I do for you?"

He blinked once and cleared his throat. "Uh, has Tommy been in tonight?"

"No, not yet." The drinks were placed before them even before Fat Eddie and Dottie sat down at the table. "So how's things going, Eddie?"

That was a tough question. Two years ago he was coming in here to make his big collections but now it Tommy's place. But what could he do? He owed Tommy Trent his life. The man had saved his daughter and his daughter was now in love with him. Besides, Eddie had asked Tommy to help him clean up the neighborhood. So what could he do? "Couldn't be better," he said. "You?"

"Things are definitely on the up, Eddie. Thanks to you and yer boy Tommy."

"He's a good kid."

"Sure… So are you here to see Tommy socially or on business?"

"Maybe both. Why?"

"Well, I don't know…"

"What?" Eddie snapped, "I need a fuckin' invite to talk to him now?"

"Jesus, Eddie. You always take things the wrong way." She lit a match, applied it to the end of her cigarette and shook it out violently before tossing it into the ashtray.

Fat Eddie stood up and pointed to the bar. "Look, when he comes in, tell him I want to talk to him, okay?"

"Sure, Eddie," she smiled sweetly. She watched him walk away, tapped the ash from the end of her cigarette and muttered, "You fat fuck."

18

THE WASHINGTON NEIGHBORHOOD WAS A LUCRATIVE TERRITORY. THERE was a speakeasy on virtually every corner, strategically placed between the factories, mills and warehouses that lined the south side of the neighborhood. And the speakeasies all did a booming business.

The territory had been awarded to the Spano brothers for their help with Hyman Amberg's number rackets. West 83rd Avenue was the main drag in the Washington neighborhood and there the heart of the Spano operations lay in some 250,000 square feet of warehouse.

The territory was separated from the smaller ones by Hyman Amberg's to the west and Rocco Petrelli's to the southeast. The north and northeast borders met Sean Conway's turf.

The southern sections of the county were in turmoil. Two of the three mobs, Sal Careli and Jimmy Doyle's were in constant battle with the encouragement of the Rosen-DeMeo combine in the north. Nate Cohen and his mob were always trying to negotiate a peace. Doyle and Careli were the source of daily headlines and acute embarrassment to city hall and the county seat.

Had Amberg and Petrelli not separated Chris Spano from these territories, he'd have been all too happy to bring them under one banner by force. Spano, like Sean Conway, and unlike his other neighbors, had no qualms about flexing his muscle.

In fact, the Spano brothers were feared in their own neighborhoods. More than one saloonkeeper had lost a finger or an eye for trying to get their alcohol elsewhere. A couple had ended up dead. Five times now Hyman Amberg had had to use his political connections to have charges of assault, attempted murder and murder against one or both of the brothers dropped.

The fifth time had been the last straw. "No more," Hyman Amberg told Chris Spano. "If you and your bother can't keep out of trouble, then you're on your own."

"Hyman—"

"No! My friends in city hall aren't going to be friendly very long if they think I'm backing a gang of cold blooded killers."

"It was just business."

"Business?" Amberg nearly shouted. "When a guy tries to buy from someone else without your permission, you rough him up a little bit. You don't shoot him six times in the middle of 83rd Avenue!"

"But—"

"No! No buts about it. If you and your boys can't keep your shit together and think before you act, then the law can have you!" Amberg left without another word.

More often than not, they could be seen strutting through their neighborhood alternately giving money to poor newspaper boys and frightening old women with equal pleasure. But without assurance of political backing, the Spanos were unusually quiet following Amberg's warning.

Three days had passed when Hyman Amberg was on his way home from a luncheon meeting with Rocco Petrelli. A long black car roared out of an alleyway and pulled along the right side of Hyman's car. The red curtains in the car parted and two men with pistols in each hand leaned out. Amberg's driver shouted, "Duck!" and cut the wheel sharply, but

Amberg was already crouched in the backseat, fumbling for the revolver beneath the seat.

The two men opened fire on Amberg's car and the driver swerved up onto the sidewalk. Two pedestrians dove for cover as the second car chased Amberg's. As the car rode abreast of Amberg's, Hyman pointed his gun out of the side window and fired blindly. The men in the other car opened fire again. Three rounds found Amberg's thigh and he dropped his gun. A fountain of blood obscured the windscreen. Amberg's driver let go of the wheel and clutched the side of his neck. The car careened into the side of a police station. Amberg flew forward, his shoulder hitting the back of the front seat, cracking his collarbone. The long black car roared off into the distance.

Amberg pressed his hand against the holes in his leg and looked at the dead man behind the wheel. His eyes moved to the police station the car had crashed into. "Shit," Amberg muttered and then passed out.

When interrogated by the police later, he insisted, "Nobody shot at me."

He and Rocco Petrelli would take care of things in their own way.

* * *

Rocco Petrelli was something of a hero with the press. He was honest and candid about his bootlegging, referring to it as a "service to the great American people." He was free with his money and quick with his jokes. The suave gangster's charm and charisma attracted reporters like honey attracts flies. There were always two or three newspapermen in the lobby of the luxurious Carlisle Hotel. They eagerly awaited Rocco's appearances on the red carpeted mezzanine above. He never failed to be surrounded by his entourage: bodyguards, lawyers, go-fers, yes-men, and usually one or two blondes or brunettes, depending on his mood. When Rocco appeared the reporters would rush up the red carpeted staircase to meet him with cries of "Mr. Petrelli!" and "What do you think of—?"

But the reporters never seemed to notice Pasty Guarino as he led Tommy Trent up the long lavish staircase. They passed four bodyguards on the fourth floor until they reached the large double door of a penthouse suite. Two burly men were seated outside of the doors. Guarino merely nodded to them that the kid was okay and they let them pass.

Guarino led him into the lush suite. It was obvious from the first glance that Rocco's favorite color was dark red and that he had an affinity for gold. Various shades of red, each one darker than the last, seemed to cover everything. Dark red, dark wood and bright gold were everywhere. On the couch in the front room a girl with short-bobbed black hair sat indiscreetly in nothing but a flimsy robe, reading a magazine and smoking a cigarette. Tommy could see that black was not her natural hair color. She seemed oblivious to their presence as they walked past. Gloria, the maid, smiled. "Hi, Paul," she said to Guarino. "This a friend?" She looked Trentino over hungrily.

"Yeah. This is T. Is The Man awake?"

"Sure, let me see." She knocked on the door of the bedroom. "Mr. Petrelli? Mr. Paul is here to see you."

"Shoo 'em in, Gloria doll."

She turned and smiled at Patsy and Trentino. "You may go right in," she said pushing open the wide double doors, revealing the interior of the huge bedroom. The room was carpeted in red as well and the silk sheet that covered the man's legs were blood red. His pajamas were purple silk. He put aside the newspaper and grinned, his trademark cigar sticking out of one corner of his mouth. "Heya, Patsy. This the Golden Boy?"

"Tommy Trent, meet Rocco."

Tommy inclined his head slightly. "Mr. Petrelli."

"Please, kid, call me Rocco." He plucked the cigar from his lips and offered Trent his other hand. Trent took it and found it was soft and flabby. The hands of a man who hadn't done a lick of work in years. "So how is Fatty taking your success?"

Tommy resisted the urge to smile. Rocco wasn't that much slimmer than Fat Eddie. "I don't think he's noticed. He thinks all the innovations and improvements are his idea, and that's fine with me."

"How so?"

Patsy interrupted, "T and Fat Eddie's daughter are—" he made a gesture with his hands to show they were more than causal acquaintances.

Rocco grinned. "I see. Yeah, I bet you play hell with the dames. I hear Dottie Deuce has her eyes on you, too. And that little French dish." Trent shrugged. "Well, kid I can see how you might not want to embarrass your future father-in-law, but never let a dame or her family come between you and business." Tommy briefly considered denying any rumors he was romantically involved with Fat Eddie's daughter, but knew better than to disrupt Rocco's train of thought. Rocco replaced the cigar between his lips and went on, "I heard a lot about you kid. Since you made that peace with the Micks, things have been goin' pretty smooth. Things are lookin' up across the board. Pat, you tell him about that other thing?"

"Not yet. We were gonna talk it over over a few drinks."

"You two go do that. I just wanted to see you, kid. Thanks for stoppin' by." He reached out a hand and Trent shook it again.

"Thanks, Mr. — uh, Thanks, Rocco."

"Sure, kid. Keep up the good work."

"Come on," Patsy said, leading Trent out of the bedroom. "Let's go have a drink. There's something we need to discuss."

19

Michael Bock owned a chain of the most fashionable clothing stores in the city. His wide range of materials and styles made his small chain of stores *the* place to go if someone wanted to look sharp and wealthy. But it hadn't been easy. He started out with his father's little store twenty years ago and devoted nearly every waking moment since then to the creation of a fashion empire. Bock made mountains of money selling clothes to gangsters, athletes and entertainers but he was always too involved in working to spend any of it.

And like any successful businessman, he had to make certain arrangements to protect his business. He had been paying Rocco Petrelli's mob for years to make sure there were no union problems to prevent his merchandise from being delivered to the stores. It was a worth while investment. Rocco wasn't trying to bleed him dry like some might. There were times when Rocco would order a new suit which he would take instead of the monthly payment.

Michael Bock felt he had something in common with Rocco: they had both started with nothing and built empires for themselves.

But when Chucky Spano arrived at Bock's office two months ago to demand a tribute for his mob, it was a bit much. "You pay Rocco to keep the trucks moving," Spano explained. "But you don't pay no one to make sure your stores don't burn down."

Ever since then, Bock had been toying with the idea of making a beef to Rocco about it. The Spano mob was nothing compared to Rocco's vast army and Bock knew that one word from Rocco could end the shakedown.

But the Spanos were mad-dog killers. Rumor had it a few years ago they had shot-gunned an elderly grocery storeowner and his wife for missing a ten dollar payment. Chucky and Chris Spano weren't in it for the money—they were in it for the excuse to kill somebody.

And Michael Bock had worked too hard for too long to get bumped off over a handful of change.

Chucky Spano was tall, slim and effeminate. But anyone who was believed to have whispered anything about his sexual preferences was likely to be gunned down by his brother Christopher. Chucky had gone in for the collegiate mode of dress; he preferred sweaters to suit coats and never wore a hat. Instead he kept his hair swept straight back and plastered down. The effect made him look even more like a weasel.

Bock knew he was coming even before he stepped into the office. Bock thought he could smell Spano's flowery perfume a block away. Chucky Spano entered the office without knocking and sat on the corner of the man's desk. "Mikey, how's business?"

"Fine," Bock said without emotion and pushed an envelope towards Spano.

Spano's lips peeled back from sharp teeth in a deranged grin as he thumbed through the envelope's contents. "You know, you're pretty well off. You got a few stores do a lot a business... I think you should give us another hundred."

Bock closed his eyes and bit his tongue. After a long pause, he said, "What do you think Rocco Petrelli would say if he knew you were trying to muscle me?"

Spano grinned again, and before Bock knew what happened, Spano had slugged him over the head with a small blackjack. Bock's vision was filled with purple circles as he lie holding on to the spinning floor, watching drops of blood from his own skull drip to the floor. He could hear Spano's high-pitched giggling. "That's what he'd say, sweetie."

Spano kicked Bock in the ribs, and then opened his suit coat. Taking his time while patting Bock down, he found the man's wallet and extracted the contents. He threw the empty wallet near Bock's head and hissed, "A hundred extra ev'ry month."

Spano delivered a final kick before letting himself out.

It was nearly a week later that Michael Bock found himself waiting outside of a phone booth on the city's west side. He glanced at his watch just as the phone rang. "Hello?"

"Mr. Bock, how can I help you?"

"You know," he wiggled a finger between his collar and his adam's apple. "Those Spanos."

"Yeah, I know. They're getting too big for their britches. That's why I want you to help me teach them a lesson."

"Me?" Bock had the insane vision of being forced to carry a machinegun or toss a firebomb. "What do you want me to do? I can't do anything."

"Don't be so modest, Mr. Bock. You're an artist with a pair of scissors, a needle and some cloth."

* * *

Christopher Spano, the older of the two brothers, had always tried to look out for Chucky. The Spanos had had a solid arrangement about their turf with the Amberg and Petrelli mobs for years now, and though Spano had to pay them for permission to operate and to keep adequate supplies of liquor, things had been very smooth. But Chris could see Chucky was getting hungry for more. He had always been a copious consumer. Chris turned a blind eye to many of Chucky's activities. Though he often saw Chucky escorting young men to and from his bedroom, it never registered in Chris' mind. When Chucky beat someone to death or shot them, it was as though Chris hadn't noticed, even if he was right there at his side. He even failed to notice when Chucky put his hand too far into the till.

He was seated in the upstairs office of the warehouse when all hell broke loose downstairs. A huge truck with a plow on its front end had barreled through the front door and a swarm of men in police uniforms poured forth.

For a brief instant, Tommy Trent was sure that they were going to obey his orders of "Hands up! This is a raid! Nobody move!" He motioned to the uniformed men behind him to move forward.

One of his men started towards the ladder where at least two men had escaped to the roof as the raiders burst in side, but Tommy motioned for them to let them be. If one of the Spanos escaped, Tommy would deal with them later.

Two men had apparently been in the act of trying to beat a gurgling still into submission when they put their hands up.

A short man in a cap was in the back of a truck bathing a barrel with block of ice. His eyes narrowed as they surveyed the crowd of coppers pouring in. The ice dropped from his hands, shattering at his feet as he reached for a revolver on his hip.

"Shit," Tommy Trent muttered and raised his machinegun. He let loose a short sweep left to right and could count the four bullets that hit the short man's wide chest, knocking him backwards off the truck.

The other workers began scrambling for the pistols and shotguns that lay waiting on the corner tables and soon a blazing battle was underway. But there wasn't much chance. Chris Spano watched from the office upstairs as the policemen with their heavy shotguns and Thompson machineguns began diving for cover and returning fire. Chris swore and pulled an ancient revolver out of the desk drawer and headed for rear office door. He could hear policemen coming in the back entrance of the warehouse downstairs, so he waited until they moved passed before venturing out of the stairway.

The smell of malt and fermenting mash hung on the air, but was quickly overpowered by the stench of gunpowder. Tommy judged there were about a dozen men all tolled, running in and out of pathways between crates of bottles and stacks of barrels. Most had pistols but there were a few who popped up from behind the crates with shotguns like bizarre jacks-in-the-box.

Streams of booze flowed from bullet holes in the barrels and onto the floor, making slippery spots where several men skidded as they ran for cover. It was apparent that Spano's men didn't have much idea of what to do in a shoot-out. Several men were too slow ducking back behind their cover to reload and Trent and his men would pop up and mow them down. Others were too slow to reload once they found cover and would be gunned down while still fumbling with their cartridges.

As the second group of men swept in the back way, Trent and his group began methodically searching each of the aisles between crates and barrels, taking turns in covering each other. It looked like some kind of well rehearsed military maneuver.

Chris Spano finally decided to chance making his way down the rest of the stairs and run for the back exit. As he turned into a dim corridor on the first floor, he tripped over something. He went sprawling, smashing his chin into the concrete floor. He turned to see what he had fallen over. It was Chucky.

Blood was gurgling from between Chucky's lips and his chest was heaving fitfully. "Chucky!" He crawled over to his brother and lifted him by the shoulders. "Oh, Chucky," he whimpered. Chucky tried to say something, but his brother shushed him. "Don't talk, Chucky. I'll get you outta here." He began the difficult task of dragging his brother to safety while still holding onto his pistol. As he pulled Chucky along he left behind a large smear of blood.

Tommy Trent stepped around the corner before they had moved twelve feet. Chris's eyes nearly popped out of his head as he raised his pistol and squeezed the trigger. The bullet bounced off of Tommy's vest. Tommy let loose with a long burst from his machinegun, spraying the brothers liberally with .45 caliber bullets.

By the time Gaetano Amato joined him, the smoke had cleared and Tommy was admiring his handiwork. "Get me that jar of glue."

20

Detective Sergeant Robert Alsop was a large man. His barrel chest always seemed to be straining the buttons of his overcoat; even more so when he was agitated. His thick bushy mustache, which in the grand old days gone by had been kept in the popular handlebar style, was now laced with gray. He had the bad habit of chewing at it with his lower teeth when he grew impatient, as he was now while waiting in the park.

The sun was just beginning to peer above the horizon and the Spano brothers hadn't been dead for more than six hours. He paced back and forth, his hands clasped behind his back, until Patsy Guarino finally appeared. Alsop remained pacing until he was close enough to strangle. Then the large man stopped. There would be none of the usual familiarities at this meeting. "What the hell are you doing to me, man?" The Sergeant's booming voice echoed through the park, scattering a handful of doves.

Guarino shook his head and shrugged. "I don't know what you're talking about."

"Ah, bullshit! I've got a dozen bodies on my hands in a warehouse in the Washington neighborhood and no time for fuckin' games!"

"Bob, I don't know what you're talking about."

"Alright, you wanna play your little games, play your fuckin' games. But tell Rocco this: He's finished. He's through."

"What?"

"Rocco might have wiped out some enemies tonight, but he's hung himself in the end. Jaysus, man, what were you thinking? Don't you know what happens when twelve bodies turn up in a warehouse full of booze? It attracts Federal men like shit attracts flies! He's just brought in an army of Prohibition Agents, the D.O.I and the whole goddam Treasury Department!" He took a step back and looked at Guarino as if he had something catching. He shook his head and said in a low voice, "The mayor and the governor can't help now. Rocco's through."

* * *

Fran Barrey smiled when Tommy stepped into Le Paris. She hitched her gown above her ankles and kicked her feet up on piano bench. "Hi, Tommy," she said with the cigarette holder clenched in her teeth. "Maxie had to run somewhere."

Tommy grabbed one of the chairs and placed it near Fran and sat on it backwards, his arms folded on the chair back. Fran handed him a thick envelope which he put in his pocket without looking at it. "Which is just as well. There's something I wanted to talk with you about, Tommy."

"What can I do for Frenchie?"

Her dark eyes glowed impishly. She grinned. "You know you shouldn't throw me a line like that." She removed her feet from the piano bench and crossed the empty club to fetch them each a drink. "Bourbon and ice, right?"

"Sure, kid."

She stood over him for a long moment before handing him the glass. "Thanks."

"You are welcome, Tommy dear." She sat on the piano bench and leaned towards him, the low cut gown catching his eye. She placed a hand on the smooth silky skin between her collar bones. "That silly little girl was in here again the other night."

"Who?"

"That little chick you brought in." She paused for a moment to think. "Sarah."

"No kiddin'?" Tommy chuckled, but there was a hint of melancholy behind it. "Looks like I've become a bad influence."

She reached out a hand to Tommy's knee. "You're not giving her the business, are you Tommy?"

"Naw. She's just Fat Eddie's daughter. A nice kid is all." He stopped, his drink halfway to his lips, "Now, don't look so skeptical, Frenchie."

Fran sighed and sat back with a satisfied smile. "Well, watch her, Tommy. She's… hungry for you."

Tommy gave a wicked half grin and spoke into his glass, "Now cut it out. You know I'm the shy bashful type. You'll make me blush."

She laughed and took a sip of her drink before placing it on the floor by the bench. She leaned back against the piano, folded her hands on her laps and studied Tommy.

After a long moment, Fran sat forward suddenly and placed a hand gently on the side of his face and kissed him. She pulled away with a smile. "A guy who plays the sap for a dame may be a little cute, Tommy, but he always ends up the loser. You know that neither Dottie or I would ever make a sap out of you." She gave him another quick peck on the lips again. "So just make sure that if you ever slip it to anyone other than Dottie… make sure it's me." She patted the side of his face. "Okay?"

Tommy stood up and laughed, "Ah, you dames." He shook his head and handed her the empty glass. "So you think I'm a sap?"

"No, Tommy! You're just… too sweet for your own good. But, this girl… she's got it bad for you…No matter what you've explained to her… She's got bad intentions. It would be for the best, Tommy."

Tommy nodded and then let out a long sigh. "I know you're right, Frenchie. I've been trying to get her together someone legit." Tommy chuckled, "Three years ago Fat Eddie'd rather have been dead than see his daughter with one of the guys, but now he thinks it's the greatest thing in the world." He laughed, "He thinks Sarah and I are romantically involved…"

"Maybe she wants him to think that…" When she saw Tommy wasn't going to answer, she stepped close to him. "Well, Tommy," she said draping her arms around his neck, "my handsome little lady-killer, if anything bad happens, I promise not to say 'I told you so.'"

* * *

Tommy Trent was showing Patsy Guarino and Fat Eddie around a new brewery Tommy had set up in the neighborhood. It would never be nearly as large an operation as the commercial breweries Rocco had purchased while Congress was debating the eighteenth amendment, but it would serve his purpose well. Tommy was interested in quality and not quantity for this brewery. They were high on the catwalk above the workers below who were busily filling barrels. "This is the real stuff. Good stuff, too."

"I'm glad to hear that. There's too much of that near-beer floating around." Eddie said. Near beer was made legally in the long-standing commercial breweries by running the brew over hot coils, which would burn off the alcohol content. It was customary for speakeasies to mix in wood alcohol after the delivery or place cakes of yeast in the barrels and allow them to ferment. This second process resulted in an interesting concoction often referred to as green beer.

"Uh-huh. I bought some of the components from Hymie Amberg, some from Marco, the Careli mob... They had some extra stuff in their breweries they didn't need."

Eddie chuckled, "How did you get that tight fisted old Jew to part with anything?"

Tommy shrugged. "He's a reasonable man. Talk to him reasonably, he's willing to come to an accommodation."

"I like this," Patsy said. "Where's this stuff going?"

"Most will stay in the neighborhood. Dottie's and I'm sending some over to Ruby's. They're killing those kids with all that junk."

Fat Eddie laughed, "What? You some kind a humanitarian now?"

"No, but nothing attracts Prohibition Agents faster than high school kids getting themselves killed."

"You're sending some to that place you're running with Hymie's nephew, ain't you?" Patsy asked.

"Yeah. I have a part interest, so..."

"And you have an agreement with Sal Careli." Patsy said.

Tommy didn't answer for a minute. Patsy was a well informed man. "Yeah. Part payment for some of the equipment."

Patsy nodded and counted the 3,500 gallon vats. There were only ten of them. Guarino pointed a finger at them. "I think I can get you some more. You don't want to spread this too thin."

"Hey, T?" A man on the brewery floor called up to him. "T? Could you come down a moment?"

"Sure." He turned to Patsy and Eddie. "You'll excuse me for a minute."

"Sure kid." They watched him head down the iron steps to the first floor. "That kid's a born diplomat," Eddie chuckled. "Nobody could ever get anything outta that old Jew." Patsy nodded. "Look, tell Tommy it looks great and he has my approval. I gotta run."

"Alright, Eddie." He shook his head as he watched the fat man waddle down the stairs. He leaned over on the railing and watched the men at work. "Huh," he murmured softly and rolled his eyes. "*Your* approval. I'm sure he'll be thrilled."

This was a nice operation. It looked as though Tommy had employed a good number of men and had brought back prosperity to the old neighborhood. The kid had done more good for the neighborhood in such a short time than Eddie had done in all the years since he took over. He met Tommy halfway down the iron staircase. "Hey, kid. Let's go see the Jew."

Hyman Amberg now owned the ghetto in the Jewish neighborhood that he had struggled so hard to escape from decades before. He owned the entire neighborhood and fair sized pieces of the adjoining territories.

He now sat in the back yard of his mansion with his two guests. An attractive young woman brought them a tray of drinks from the house. "Thanks, June, doll," Hymie said. "Put the tray on the table." The tall girl did as told, turned and winked a green eye at Tommy. When she had left, Hyman turned to his guests, handing them a drink apiece. "What can I do for you gentlemen?"

Patsy nodded for Tommy to go ahead. "We want your help to build a strong peace. A lasting peace. Between all the groups."

"Me and Rocco, we've never had any disputes."

"Yeah, I know. But this chaos that's everywhere—the Careli mob, Doyle, Rosen-DeMeo, they're all trying to battle their way to the top. If any one of them can consolidate the others, they're gonna come after us." Patsy said.

Amberg sighed, "Of course they are. These kids today, no one's content. There's so much out there and they think they can have it all."

Patsy nodded. "Now, we all know there's not enough room for *four* large factions. They'll come after you first. But if we start getting heavy with them like we did the Spanos, Conway will panic and start mobilizing his troops against us."

Tommy leaned closer in his chair, "There's no reason that we can't all devote our energies towards making each other rich instead of rubbing each other out, fighting for a bigger piece of the pie."

Hymie smiled. "True. I never understood all the violence myself. Blood is a big expense. The Spano hit—it was well done, mind you, but it brought too much heat on everyone. Now Rocco's got the treasury department searching his pockets."

"See, the problem is this:" Tommy said, "Too many people see America as a bunch of neighborhoods thrown together, side by side. But that's not it at all. It's one big country and it's ours for the taking if we all work together."

Hyman sat forward in his chair, trying to suppress a grin. "When my nephew introduced us, Tommy, he never told me you were so wise for one so young."

Tommy shrugged, "It's just common sense."

Amberg smiled. "What can I do for my friends?"

Patsy Guarino sat up, "Rocco's setting a meeting for all the gangs. He wants everyone to attend. If you support us in this thing, no one will straggle behind. And we'll help you with your policy racket in darkie town."

"Peace? Prosperity? Riches?" Hyman raised his glass in a toast. "What do we have to lose?"

21

The Williamson Hall was well known for its opulence. It was no coincidence it was within shouting distance of the mayoral mansion, his honor's country club, golf course and the racetrack. It was within these walls that some of the country's most powerful politicians celebrated New Years Eve and where their daughters' wedding receptions were held.

Now it was to be the site of a historic conference.

The long table in the dining room was covered with the finest lace from France, the china gold rimmed and a magnum of champagne stood within easy reach of every chair.

A second chair sat behind and to the right of each one of the settings. These chairs were for the guests Rocco had encouraged the attendees to bring along. They would be right-hand men, consiglieres and lawyers. Few would be bodyguards, although all had sworn not to bring weapons on the premises. Though oaths could not always be trusted, Rocco would not subject his guests to the indignity of being patted down and searched.

He knew there would be no bloodshed on this night.

The guests arrived in long black cars with purring motors. Rocco had picked Georgiana, the prettiest of all his prostitutes, to check their coats and hats before ushering them into the grand dinning room.

There the men mingled and drank the finest imported champagnes and liquors. They were encouraged to help themselves to a cigar from one of Rocco's personal humidors.

It looked like a meeting of the world's most successful businessmen.

But of course that's what they were.

And Rocco was sure that they all realized this. Prohibition had given a new and greater birth to the greatest of all industries: corruption.

Fat Eddie felt uncomfortable in his evening wear, but he'd be the first to admit that it was only when he was so attired that he truly looked presentable. He didn't notice his collar was tighter than it had been last year. Something else made him uncomfortable.

It was the ease with which Tommy Trent and Pasty Guarino were getting along. Eddie had brought Tommy along to take the second chair behind his place at the table. A part of him was pleased to see his protégé getting along so well with the mob's second-in-command, but the rest of him had had a hard time swallowing the envy.

Eddie was listening to Marco Messinio telling a long story that he supposed was intended to have a funny pay off, but his eyes kept returning to Patsy and Tommy across the room. Patsy looked like a demonic undertaker who smilingly helped all his customers into his mortuary prematurely. Tommy was even more suave and debonair than ever. When they had arrived, Eddie heard Georgiana the hat-check girl, whose personal preferences leaned more towards women, whisper crudely that she'd like Tommy to try to cure her of it.

"This was a smart call across the board," Patsy said in a low voice into his glass of champagne. He and Trent were surreptitiously surveying the crowd. "Just by showing up each one of these mugs is acknowledging Rocco as boss of the entire city." They watched as Hyman Amberg and his nephew entered. Amberg spotted them immediately and made a polite bow of his head in their direction. Guarino and Trent returned the gesture.

Guarino's eyebrow arched upwards as Sean Conway and his right hand man Pat Michelson stepped into the room. "Everybody showed."

"Of course they showed up," Tommy said. "Anyone who doesn't will be branded as an outsider and the instigator of any future problems."

Patsy Guarino looked at the young man in sincere admiration. "You sure you weren't a boss in a previous life?"

Tommy laughed. "Besides, Conway's convinced we're conspiring with the Jews to get rid of him."

Guarino chuckled. "Come, let us mingle."

As they moved through the room, Fat Eddie pulled Tommy aside. "Ain't this something?"

"Sure is."

"Everybody on earth is here. Come on, I'll introduce you to Rocco." He led Tommy to the north end of the room where Rocco was just delivering the punch line to one of his patented jokes. When the men's laughter died down, Eddie stepped forward into the circle pulling Tommy along behind. "Rocco. Rocco—"

Fat Eddie was never a student of people's eyes or the stories they could tell, but Tommy Trent was. He saw for a brief instant that there was no recognition in Rocco's eyes. This little fat man meant nothing to him.

"Eddie," Rocco said and pumped the man's hand up and down three times. "How you doin'?"

"Fine Rocco, Fine. Have you met Tommy Trent?"

Rocco paused ever so slightly, "Er—no, we never met. Hey, kid. How's it going?" This handshake was more enthusiastic and included a clapped hand on Trent's shoulder.

"Ain't he a good looking kid?" Fat Eddie said and slapped a hand on Tommy's other shoulder. "It's no wonder my daughter wants to marry him. All the dames is crazy about this kid. Even Georgiana propositioned him."

Rocco could barely contain his laughter. "Really?" He looked Trent over. "Huh... Ol' Georgi usually don't swing that way unless she's getting paid to." He was still trying not to laugh as he pushed Fat Eddie to the side and put an arm around Tommy's shoulder. He said in a soft chuckling voice, "If you can get Georgi to lose her taste for *la fica*...more power to you." He slapped a hand on Trent's chest and nodded towards the crowd. "So what do you think?"

"I'm impressed. This is a swell place and a good turn out."

"Well kid, it was yourself that got the ball rolling."

"Ah, I din't do nothing. Just idle chit chat with some kids I used to know. A couple of the Irish kids and Jewish kids and me used to get into scraps over who could sell papers on what corner. That kind of thing."

Rocco smiled as though he had similar memories. "Yeah, but they told other guys in their crews: 'Those guys in Rocco's mob ain't so bad after all. They got some good ideas if the bosses would just listen.' And word got around."

"Ah, come on, Mr. Petrelli. I didn't do anything. You said yourself a long time ago that butcherin' each other don't make sense."

Rocco was still grinning. Fat Eddie was beaming as the big boss thanked his protégé. In fact, Eddie felt he was going to burst with pride until Rocco clapped a hand on the young man's shoulder again and said, "Look, kid. I told you a hundred times. Call me Rocco."

When the grandfather clock chimed eight the men began moving to their seats at the table. Rocco would sit at the head of the table. Next to him would sit Patsy Guarino. Tommy was starting to sit down behind Fat Eddie as Patsy moved towards his seat. Patsy Guarino grabbed Tommy's arm. "C'mere." He led Tommy to the chair behind his and motioned for him to sit.

Fat Eddie watched in dismay and horror as his chosen second was shanghaied by Rocco's second in command. He looked down the Petrelli mob side of the table. He was now the only one without a second seated behind him. He was embarrassed; he felt like he stuck out like a sore thumb. It would take much longer before the other implications would sink in.

"Gentlemen," Rocco said, surveying the faces around the table. "I want to thank you all for being here on this historic evening." He motioned with the glass of champagne in his hand, "I'd like to thank Senator Whitehead for letting us meet here in his broom closet." The men all laughed. "You all know me, and I know all you, but for the sake of those who might not know each other, perhaps we should introduce ourselves…"

The meeting, which was little more than a lengthy speech by Rocco, lasted twenty minutes but would have far reaching consequences in the underworld. It was agreed that there would be no more unnecessary bloodshed. Nobody wanted another Spano massacre on their hands. Territorial concessions were made by the three big outfits: Petrelli, Conway, and Amberg with the understanding that they would be entitled to an extra cut of the profits from these territories. A few blocks of his turf was small price for Rocco to pay to have all of the rival gangs implicitly name him the overlord of the entire city. Rules were laid down. If there was a beef, the head of another gang would act as an intermediary. There was enough business out there for them all to share. They could share liquor resources, politicians, and their intelligence to battle the common enemy they all had: the law.

All of the gangs were represented by their highest leaders. The predominately Irish gangs of Sean Conway and Jimmy Doyle, Hyman Amberg and Nate Cohen who ran the 'Jewish mobs,' Sal Careli who ran the far south suburbs, and Henry Rosen and Mike DeMeo whose combine bordered the Conway territory to north. If any of them had a problem with any of the other gangs, they were to come to Rocco with their grievances before deciding to shoot it out. The gang leaders would all be responsible for disciplining anyone in their outfits who broke the rules. Otherwise all the other gangs would pool their resources to end the dispute before it disrupted business and "brought the heat down."

For dinner they all dined on dishes prepared by the greatest chefs in the city and it wasn't until midnight when the party had finally ended.

* * *

"Oh, hell. What a laugh that was!" Sean Conway laughed as he poured a drink for himself and Pat Michelson. "I have to hand it to him, though. That dago has a lot a balls. They think we we're not wise to them. They think we don't know they're in cahoots with the Jews. They buy up all the big breweries and the biggest politicians and they come to us and say: 'Sure, we'll share them all with you. For a price.'"

"Oh, yeah. Sure'n that's real white of them."

"Then he and that Jew tell us we have to give that greaseball Careli more room. What are we gonna do with these bums, huh? What are we gonna do?"

* * *

They were still wearing their evening attire when they stepped through the doors of Dottie's speakeasy. Rocco seemed to fill the doorway with his exuberance. Patsy was on his left, Tommy on his right. "All right, you mugs!" Rocco called in a triumphant voice. "Drink up because tonight everything's on Rocco!" A few of the customers turned and cheered and raised their glasses in salute. He led the men through the crowd to a large table, shaking hands with the customers he passed. A few women batted their eyelashes at his plump cherubic face. Rocco loved the celebrity.

The mob's entire hierarchy was present at the round table. To Rocco's right Patsy sat down, followed by Marco Messinio, Art Gagliano, Joey Bones, Felipe Migliore, and Raymond DeLaurentis. Tommy Trent sat at Rocco's left hand. Fat Eddie squeezed himself in somewhere in the middle.

As Dottie approached the table, Rocco snatched a chair from an adjacent table and placed it between himself and Tommy. "Dottie, c'mere. Siddown." She obeyed and put a hand on Tommy's knee and squeezed. Rocco smiled at them while pulling a thick roll of cash from his pocket. He thumbed off one thousand dollars and tossed it on the table. "Here y'are, Dottie. I'm buying for everybody in the place for the rest of the night."

"Why, Rocco. That's—" She shook her head in disbelief as she shoved the bills down the bodice of her dress.

"We're celebrating, tonight, kid."

"Oh?" She and Tommy were surreptitiously holding hands beneath the table.

"Yeah," Tommy said. "Tonight the whole county elected Rocco president."

Rocco laughed and nodded. "I like that, kid. That's a swell way of putting it."

The dancers were halfway through their final performance of the evening. Rocco craned his neck to survey the entire speak. He nodded with approval. He took Dottie's free hand and squeezed it. "I remember when this was your father's saloon. He'd be proud, Dottie."

Dottie blushed and swallowed the queasy feeling that accompanied Rocco's touch. "Thank you."

"You and Tommy make a nice looking couple. Don't you agree?" Everyone at the table nodded. Everyone but Fat Eddie, who merely sneered. Rocco fought the urge to laugh and changed the subject.

For a half hour he told the jokes he was so good at telling. Rocco had an enormous talent for captivating an audience and he used it as freely with his friends and fellow mobsters as he did with members of the press. When Rocco Petrelli was in a good mood, everyone was in a good mood. Everyone seemed to be having a good time except Fat Eddie. "Eddie, what's wrong?" Dottie asked. "You're not usually so nice and quiet."

"Fuck you," he muttered. Tommy and Patsy were the only ones who heard it.

"What?" Tommy flinched as though he was going to get up, but as fast as lightening Patsy Guarino put a hand on Tommy's shoulder to keep him still.

"I said sometimes you feel more like listening than talkin'."

Everyone's attention was drawn away as Rocco reached out a hand to grab a passing customer. "Alice, hi!"

Alice Byrd stopped and put a hand to her chest. "Oh! Hi, Rocco! I didn't see you," she said and then, for no good reason, threw in a giggle.

"How's your father doing?"

"Oh, much better. Thank you for the flowers and the fruit basket you sent him."

"Sure. He got the brandy too, didn't he?"

"Yeah. He said it was what made him better."

Rocco laughed. "Well, I'm glad. Your father's a good man, Alice."

"Thanks."

"Say, why don't you bring your boyfriend over and join us?" He pointed across the room to Frankie Sirico who was seated with his back to Rocco's table.

"Oh," Alice giggled then blushed, "He's shy."

"Shy, huh?" Rocco said. The young man looked more the anti-social type than the shy kind. "Well, tell your father I said hello and I'm glad he's doing better, huh?"

"Sure, Rocco," the girl giggled and waved her fingers as she continued on her way to the bar.

Rocco was grinning when he turned back to face the table. "That's one of the dippiest dames you'll ever meet. But she's a good kid." He motioned to Frankie's table again, "She's got herself a man, huh?"

Dottie nodded. "Oh, yeah. She's nuts about him."

"My, my," Rocco chuckled, "Little Alice finally discovered boys, huh?"

Seven young girls draped in furs, beads and pearls stepped into the speak. They made no motion to move father than the entryway. Instead they preened their furs and one lifted her skirt just high enough to adjust the rolled-down top of her stockings. Rocco grinned. "Hey guys, your broads are here. Go take your pick."

Tommy Trent grinned at Rocco, "You didn't invite Georgiana did you?"

Rocco laughed. "Don't worry kid. I didn't say a word. You're in the clear."

"Georgiana the Lesbian?" Dottie asked in an astonished tone.

"Yeah," Rocco said. "She got a load of your friend there all dolled up and decided she wants him to show her the errors of her ways."

They all laughed. Dottie pinched Tommy's thigh. "If he couldn't set her straight, no one could."

"All right, you mugs, clear outta here."

At Rocco's command, Messinio, Gagliano, Migliore, Bones and DeLaurentis excused themselves and met the girls at the door. They studied the girls for a moment and each put an arm around their selections and left. "Anyone else?" Rocco said nodding to the remaining two girls. When Tommy, Eddie and Patsy shook their heads, Rocco jerked a thumb towards the door. The girls nodded, pouted and left. Rocco sat back and belched quietly. He turned to Patsy, "I think I'm gonna go see my girl."

"Sure."

"That's alright with you two?" he asked Dottie and Tommy.

"Go on, Rocco. Have a good night."

"You too." He stopped as he passed Tommy Trent and tapped him on the shoulder. "I'll see you around, Tommy."

"Sure thing."

Fat Eddie stood up abruptly. "I'm gonna take off too."

"Good-night," they said together.

When Eddie had gone, Patsy Guarino, Tommy and Dottie were the last ones at the table. A well-endowed girl began clearing away the empty glasses. "Julia?" Tommy said and the girl looked up. "Has Tano been in tonight?"

She shook her head. "Not yet, anyway."

Dottie sighed, "I oughta go charm some of the other customers. I'll be back in a few, doll. Don't go away."

Patsy Guarino moved to the chair next to Trent and leaned close to him. "That crack Rocco made about you and Dottie looking good together—that really burned Eddie up didn't it?"

Tommy nodded sadly. "He thinks I should marry his daughter."

"How do you feel about it?"

"I think he oughta mind his own business."

"Tommy, I'm gonna say this just once then I won't nag you anymore. Dames are dangerous. Don't let them too close, Tommy. It's not a good idea for a guy in this racket to get too involved with dames. You can take them to dinner, take 'em dancing, fuck 'em, whatever. Just don't let them into your heart. A man who cares too much for a dame has a weakness and it affects his judgment." He finished his drink. "There. I'm done preachin' now."

Tommy didn't say anything. He was thinking about Fran Barrey's very similar thoughts.

Julia returned to the table and interrupted them. "Refills, guys?"

"Sure. Set 'em up," Guarino said sliding his glass towards her.

"Julia, have the new costumes come in?"

"No, not yet."

"Well, remember to take yours to the tailor's shop as soon as they come in so Dottie doesn't get on your case."

"Oh," the girl smiled and blushed. "Okay."

"Even though it'll break Tano's heart."

The girl laughed and took their empty glasses. Tommy leaned over and explained to Patsy, "She's so... *built* she keeps popping out of the costumes."

"I see," Patsy said with a crooked grin.

When she returned with the refills, she was still blushing. As she walked away Patsy shook his head in disbelief. "How do you do it?"

"Do what?"

"Every dame you lay eyes on wants to bed you. How do you do it?"

Trent shrugged. "It's that wood alcohol garbage they serve in the other joints. It makes them nuts."

Patsy laughed and sipped his drink. "This stuff don't come cheap."

"Yeah. I put most of my money in here, but Dottie's is worth it."

Patsy knew he meant Dottie the woman and not Dottie the speakeasy. He foresaw a lot of troubles ahead, but that wasn't unusual when there were dames in the mix.

"Fat Eddie's daughter don't drink that junk does she?"

"No. She never had anything other than wine until I took her out."

"You know, Fat Eddie's… delusional. He doesn't understand."

"Understand what?"

"Big Joe, Rocco's uncle who used to run things in the old days… Fat Eddie's father was Big Joe's cousin. That's the only reason they gave Eddie this neighborhood when Sally Nose died. And now, times what they are, and considering all that's going on…" He exhaled through his nose and addressed his glass, "there's too much to lose by keeping him at the helm, and too much to gain by putting someone else with a brain in." He lit one of Rocco's cigars and continued. "I know Eddie. By tomorrow he will have forgotten that crack about you and Dottie, he'll have forgotten she even exists. And he'll go on with these fantasies that someday you're going to marry his daughter and that he'll continue being the boss of the neighborhood." He looked Tommy straight in the eye. "You understand what I'm saying?"

"Yeah."

"Now, Marco's now the consigliere. Ray's been bumped up and given the old Spano turf. So who's left?"

Tommy Trent didn't answer for a long moment. He lit a cigarette and sighed.

"You're already doing the job…"

Tommy took a sip of his drink and put the glass on the table slowly. After a moment he said, "I'd like Eddie to go on thinking he's the boss."

"But why? Is this because the daughter? Do you love her?"

"Nah. It's not that… Give Eddie a demotion and he'll start making a beef. I don't want to end up having to whack the guy."

"Because of the daughter?"

"Yeah, I guess… I don't want to make her an orphan."

"Well, it won't be hard to let Eddie think he's runnin' things." Patsy laughed at an inner joke. "Can I break something to you, Tommy?"

"What's that?"

"Well, you're sittin' there lookin' like you just took on a massive responsibility…" He chuckled again, "You've already been running the neighborhood for a while now. Longer than you think. You didn't take over *anything*. It was given to you. And that doesn't come from me. That comes straight from Rocco. Even Mo knew that any orders that came from Eddie had to be cleared by you first. And I think that deep down, past those layers of fat in his head, Eddie knows it too. That's why he never made a beef when you took this joint over. Because he's afraid to be told what's what."

22

Le Paris closed around five or six in the morning, depending on the crowd. Max Aaronson usually cut out early and Dave Gold had taken the night off. But Jimmy Revel and the guys in his band had been kind enough to stay behind and help Fran and a few of the waitresses put all the chairs up on the tables so the two young Negro boys could sweep the floor.

The fresh cold air cut through the ghosts of cigarettes and heavy perfume as Tommy Trent opened the front door. He was a silhouette against the gray light of dawn which was breaking behind him. He stepped inside the club and closed the door. "Hiya, Frenchie."

He was still in his tux, but the tie hung loosely around his neck. It looked as if he had had a long but happy night. "Tommy?" Fran said. "What on earth are you doing, staggering in here at this time of the morning?"

"Can I talk to you Frenchie? Alone?" He nodded to the orchestra boys, "No offense, fellas." All speakeasy musicians developed a remarkable talent for seeing nothing and hearing nothing in the speaks. There would even be tales about jazz-age musicians who continued playing their hot jazz while a shoot-out was underway twelve feet from them.

"Sure, Tommy." She took him by the hand and led him to her office that accessible through a hidden wooden panel door behind the bar. Tommy noted another one of her nude postcards was framed on the wall. In any other woman, that desire to see herself might have seemed overly narcissistic, but like many things, it was different with Fran Barrey. She sat back on top of her desk. "What's the matter, Tommy?"

"Nothing. I was just on my way home and I thought I should stop in and see you." He took an envelope out of his pocket and tossed it on her desk. A few fifty dollar bills poked out of the open end. "And to give you this."

"What's this? A bonus?"

"No, ma'am. Not exactly…" He looked at the floor and scratched his chin with a thumbnail. "This is between you and me. Okay? Dottie is the only other person I've told this."

She grabbed his hand and pulled him closer so she could run her fingers over his five o'clock shadow. She pressed his hand against her heart. "On my honor, Tommy, I won't say a word to anyone."

"Fat Eddie's been retired."

"It's official now?"

He nodded.

She leapt off the desk and threw her arms around him. "Good for you, Tommy. I knew no one could keep you down." She stepped back, her hands on his elbows. "How did Fat Eddie take the news?"

"He doesn't know yet. I don't intend on telling him, if you get my drift."

"I see…" she said, but didn't. "But what if he starts thinking you should see his daughter and tries to make a beef? Thinking he's still running things?"

Tommy thought for a long moment. "I dunno. I guess he'll have to learn the hard way."

The smile slowly left Fran's face. She sat back on the corner of the desk. "You don't think he'll cause any trouble when he does figure it out, do you?"

"With any luck, he won't figure it out. But even if he does, I think he'll behave because he wants me to marry his daughter."

"Oh, Tommy," she proceeded to call him something in that French sounded highly erotic. She took his hands, kissed them and laughed. "I don't know of anyone around who'd like to cross you. You're a tough guy, Tommy. But not when it comes to the fair sex." She leaned back and narrowed her eyes. They seemed to twinkle. "You know what you're problem is? You're too nice. That's what it is. You are the world's biggest sweetheart trapped in one of the most corrupt and violent cities in the world."

"Is that how you see me?"

She nodded thoughtfully. "You're a throw-back, doll. I once knew this ancient Sicilian man. Very dark, very dangerous. If a man so much as looked at him cross-eyed, he's slit his throat. But any dame with big eyes and a sad story..." she pantomimed slitting her wrists, "and he'd bleed for them." She now was leaning back on the desk, propped up on one elbow, her free hand still holding his. "That's you, Tommy. That's you to a T."

"I'll have to mull that over for a while before I know whether or not I like it."

"It's not a question of whether you like it or not, Tommy. We are what we are." She shrugged it off. It was too early in the morning to get much more philosophical. "Is there anything else I could... *do* for you?" She hitched her skirt up to her mid-shins and waggled her eyebrows with a devious smile.

"No, no, angel," he grinned. "I've been up a million years and need to hit the hay. There's a lot to think about..." He leaned forward and kissed her on the forehead. "Goodnight, Frenchie."

"Goodnight, doll." She stared at the door for a long while after he closed it behind him. She let out a heavy sigh and smiled.

* * *

Tommy and Dottie were sitting side-by-side on one of the tables addressing the girls when Fat Eddie came in. Eddie was in an ebullient mood this afternoon. After he had left the speak the night before he had paid a visit to Mandy. She usually helped him clear his head and get rid of all the annoying questions nibbling away at the back of his brain. He clapped his hands together loudly, "Hey, girls," he called out, grinning. "How would you like to make some money with Uncle Eddie? Photographs?"

A mute chorus line of furrowed brows greeted him. "Come on, what d'ya say? There could be a lotta money in it."

The girls were all silent, gaping at him with expressions of deep disgust. Finally Julia Pennington stepped forward. "Eddie?"

"Yeah?" he said eagerly, unconsciously rubbing his hands together.

"If we told you where to stick your camera, wouldja take a picture of it so we could all laugh at you?"

The girls all broke up. Marie Evani laughed so hard she nearly fell over.

Eddie sneered and stepped forward with a raised hand, but an iron grip clasped his wrist. "Uh-uh, Eddie. Don't go crossing any lines, now." Tommy said. "These are my girls and anyone bothers them answers to me. Get it?"

There was a slight pause as Eddie scanned Tommy's face to see how serious he was. He was dead serious. "Sorry, Tommy," he said softly. He turned again and wagged a finger at Julie, "But that one with the big tits and the big mouth oughta watch it or else someone who don't respect Tommy'll knock her head off."

Eddie turned and stormed out of the speakeasy. "So much for his plans of moving into the pornography racket," Tommy muttered.

Tommy motioned to the girls. "Okay, girls, huddle up here." They all closed in a tight circle with their arms around each other. Julia's hand rested on Tommy's backside. Dottie wordlessly approached the group and gently moved Julia's hand to the middle of his back before returning to what she was doing.

"You gotta ignore Fatty. All that fat is pushing his brain out his ear." The girls giggled. "Now, if anyone ever bothers any one of you girls, let me know. And I promise you, they'll *never* do it again."

Dottie, who was now watching the scene from behind the bar, thought the girls were all going to swoon at his feet. She could only shake her head and smile. "That's my Tommy."

It had been six months since the newspapers dubbed it the Spano Massacre and the publicity was finally beginning to die down although the mystery would still remain. The shooters would never be identified.

The press never seemed to notice Tommy Trent or that his crew had gained a great deal of respect in the Petrelli mob. Even Fat Eddie DiStella, who felt like the last man on earth to find out anything, saw there were big changes coming for the gang. Rocco was planning a whole restructuring of the entire outfit—indeed, the entire Rocco empire.

It was time that Fat Eddie move up. He was sure of it. All of the other captains had a bigger piece of the action. Why not Eddie? Especially since he had Tommy to take care of the little piddly shit. For decades Eddie had been as loyal and faithful as he could be. He was the man who had taken a bullet for Sally Nose when the coppers got the drop on them during the so-called Election Riots. He was the man who had brought Tommy into the outfit. Therefore he was responsible for all the improvements in the neighborhood, responsible for getting rid of those no good Spanos. ... Indirectly.

But in any event, Eddie felt deserving of something more, a bigger piece of the pie. He suspected Tommy was holding out on him—the money he was giving Eddie wasn't much more than before he brought Tommy in and he knew for a fact that the neighborhood was now rolling in dough. It was flowing like water all around Tommy and Eddie was entitled to the lion's share. But he was willing to over look it. All good things to those who wait. Things were changing and he was sure when he got bumped up the money Tommy was holding out would look like peanuts. And, a part of him wanted his daughter to marry him and if Eddie started making a beef about the cash flow, he could kiss that good-bye.

If Tommy would marry Sarah, he knew she would be taken care of for the rest of her life and it wouldn't hurt Eddie to have someone as capable as Tommy for a son-in-law.

Tommy Trent was moving up in the world too, financially at least. He and some of his friends had moved into a nice little apartment complex at the edge of the old neighborhood, and though it would never rival the grand Carlisle Hotel for extravagance, it made Fat Eddie's nice little home above his furniture store look like a broom closet.

He would start pushing Tommy towards marrying Sarah. He had already been suggesting at every opportunity that Tommy take her to dinner, or take her shopping under the guise of running errands for him. There had once been a time when the thought of his daughter marrying anyone from the neighborhood would have given him heart failure, but Tommy was something different. Fat Eddie knew that he would never have a crack at the top spot, but having a son-in-law who, thirty years down the line, may very well run the entire city, would assure Fat Eddie a pleasant retirement.

But on the other hand, what would Fat Eddie do without her? For the last twenty years, his world had revolved around Sarah. She had always been first and foremost—before his business and even before his health. Sarah was the apple of his eye, the only person on earth to whom he could bitch about Guarino or Petrelli.

She was his all and she was counting the days until Tommy Trent asked her to marry him.

But there was one thing Fat Eddie needed to know before he could feel secure in such a union. He was sure that Tommy Trent had genuine feelings for Sarah, but he also knew that the seductive Dottie Deuce was madly in love with him.

He decided to call in Jimmy Brisone for a private chat.

Fat Eddie would be damned before he would let his one and only daughter marry a philanderer, future big-shot or not.

Gaetano Amato rolled over onto his back and rested against the headboard. He balanced an ashtray on his chest and lit a cigarette before taking up his glass of bourbon. Connie Banks smiled at him and snatched the cigarette from between his lips. "Excuse me," Tano said, "I thought that was my cigarette."

"Half of what's mine is yours and half of what's yours is mine." Connie Banks had raven black hair that just reached her bare shoulders. Her eyes were dark and had a violet cast to them and they regarded Tano now with genuine love shining in them. Tano had always been a ladies man; it was only natural considering his Mediterranean good-looks, his velvet voice, his cavalier manners and his sharp wit. But if there was anyone on earth who might tame his womanizing and get him to settle down, Connie believed she was the one.

"Not till we're married, kiddo," he said lighting a cigarette for himself.

The telephone rang and Connie answered it and said, "Yeah, he's here." She passed it to Tano. "It's T."

"Hello?"

"Tano, Dottie's at Maxim's Department Store. She's got some mug tailing her and she sounds a little frightened. You're closer than I am. Can you get over there right away and check it out?"

"Sure, Pally. She in some kind of trouble?"

"I dunno. She said she'll be by the jewelry department."

"Okay, Pally," he said and handed the phone back to Connie. "Come on, we gotta go."

"Where to?"

"We gotta meet Dottie at the department store."

* * *

It was the following night when Connie Banks stepped into the narrow dressing room. "Alright, girls! Get decent. A man's comin' through!"

She waited a moment and then led Tano through the room full of dancers, all of whom tried to say "Hi, there" and "Well, hello" a little more seductively than the last.

Tano laughed and clapped his hands together. "My, oh my! *Che petti! Mmm-mmmm!* We got us a smorgasbord here!"

Connie stopped walking and slapped at him playfully. "Okay, kids. You know the policy Dottie has regarding Tommy? Well, the same goes with Tano here."

Several dejected "Oh"s echoed through the room.

Tano leaned over Connie's shoulder, "What arrangement does the Deuce had about T?"

Connie smiled devilishly, "If any of the girls touch him, they not only loose their jobs, but they get their hands cut off too."

"Oh, hell, honey," Tano groaned. "You just spoiled me a ton of fun."

"Go on, ya' big lug. They're in there."

Tano was still smiling when he opened the door she had pointed to. He immediately averted his eyes to the ceiling, "Can I come in?"

"Sure," Tommy said.

Dottie Deuce and Tommy Trent sat on either side of a small table, drinking. Tano let himself into the small storage room, his smile broadening. "I wasn't sure if you kids were having a petting party."

"Tano!" Dottie called out as if he were a long lost brother she hadn't seen in an age. A lock of hair fell into her eyes as she put her fingers to her lips to stifle a hiccup. "Oh, hell, honey baby," she said to Tommy as she put her glass down, "I oughtta slow down."

"Hey," Tano said with a good-natured smile. "You're drinkin' like I'm supposed to." In all the years he had known Dottie Deuce, Tano had never even heard of her getting tipply. Tommy Trent, on the other hand, could drink anyone under the table and not show any effect.

"We're almost done," Dottie said. Tommy had a sheaf of papers balanced on his knee and he was marking items off as Dottie rummaged through a box. Dottie smiled as she caught Tano's eyes and she put a hand to the top of her dress as she leaned over. "And four makes twelve, Tommy."

Tommy marked off the final item on the list with a nod. He tossed the papers to the side and poured a drink for Tano. "So, what news?" Trent said sliding the whiskey towards him.

"Apparently Fat Eddie put Brisone up to following Dottie around."

Tommy nodded. He had already guessed that. "What for?"

"I can answer that, honey bunch," Dottie took a deep breath and then spoke slowly with great effort. "Fat Eddie's daughter is in love with you. … He thinks you're going t'marry her."

Tommy frowned and drummed his fingers on the arm of the chair. "I figured as much… The dumb sonuvabitch…" He turned to Tano, "So, what, is he gonna start trouble over this? Make a beef because I'm not in love with his daughter?"

Tano shrugged. "Who knows? I mean, we've all known that Eddie's a few bricks shy of a load."

"Yeah, but we can't whack the guy. I mean, he's got old ties to Rocco, even if he is a bumbling idiot. And Sarah's a good kid, I don't want to make her an orphan over this."

Dottie smiled lovingly at Tommy. "Ah, Tommy. You've always been an old softie. And I love you for it."

"Ah, hell… He actually thinks I had that kind of intention with his daughter?"

"Wishful thinking," Tano said. "He's gotta be starting to wise up to the fact he don't run things around here. And, if I may say so, boss, there's no telling what kind of thoughts the girl put in his head."

Tommy looked at his empty glass and then to the empty bottle. "I'm gonna get another drink. You want one, doll?"

"No, no," Dottie said. "You two go on ahead. I'm tired. I haven't had too much to drink," she protested, "It's just I had it too fast." She leaned over on the davenport, reminding Tano of a ship sinking. "I'm just going to lie down if you two boys'll excuse me."

The two men stood and started towards the door. As Tano flicked off the light, Tommy stopped. He took off his coat and placed it around Dottie like a blanket. He leaned forward and kissed her on the forehead. "Sleep tight, kid."

The dressing room was now empty as they crossed through it. The girls were all on the stage for the midnight floorshow. Tommy stopped halfway through the room and lit a cigarette. He sighed "What am I gonna do with this fat fuck?"

Tano shrugged and they moved a few more paces until Tano stopped him. He nodded his head towards the storage room. "You know, boss, that woman really loves you."

Tommy sighed. "Yeah, I know." He stuffed his hands into his pocket. "And I didn't have to save her life to make her feel that way."

Tano grinned, "See what kinda trouble you can get into just by trying to be a dame's friend?"

Laughing, Tommy slapped him on the shoulder. "C'mon. Let's go have a drink."

23

NEW AND INNOVATIVE WAYS TO GAIN AN EDGE over the competition or to steal money were generally regarded with admiration by fellow gangs until one crossed the invisible boundary into "too much" of an edge.

Tommy Trent had always understood that entertainment was one of the most important things a gangster needed to keep the customers spending money in their nightclubs. Sure, scantily clad women showing scandalous amounts of flesh was fine; but a fellow could find that in any nightclub or higher-end speak.

What was needed was a hot band and dynamite entertainers to add variety. Muscling entertainers wasn't Tommy's style; entertainers were usually honest joes trying to make a buck the best way they could. Besides, they could hardly be expected to give their best performance while wondering about the finality of the final curtain.

And paying top notch performers could lead to considerable

expenses.

But creating his own talent agency and allying himself with others and muscling agents who wouldn't play ball was right up Tommy's alley. It appealed to his 'inner gangster' and his organizational knack.

The United Theatrical and Musical Agency was born as an indirect result of hiring Jimmy Revel's orchestra as Fran's house band. The UTMA dealt in favors with other agencies that were kindly disposed towards it. Those who were not, usually found themselves lending acts to the UTMA minus the usual ten percent—the talent got paid their usual fee and the agent got to keep his limbs intact.

* * *

"This kid," Sean Conway fumed, shaking his fist at nothing in particular. Pat Michelson sat back patiently and lit a cigarette. He was getting used to this. "This kid, this goddam kid!" Conway shrieked.

"What's he done now?"

"You know what I just found out? My fuckin' bandleader just signed with the UTMA. That slimy little bastard!" As he grew more agitated, Conway's hair became more and more disheveled. He slammed the palms of both hands on the top of his desk. "I want that bastard dead. Make that first on your list, Pat."

"You want me to kill yer own bandleader?"

Sean Conway leaned across the desk, "I want that sonuvabitch and his goddam trumpet at the bottom of the harbor!"

Pat did not point out that this would be bad for business and decided instead to simply nod.

Pushing the hair back from his brow with one hand, Conway poured himself a drink with the other. He sat behind it and studied it for a moment before taking it in hand. "I can't get a good band for the club anymore," he groaned. "All the bands are signing up with this new agency—and who's the main backer? That fucking Trent kid. And he's got an in with some big shot guinea at the Conroy label to sweeten the deal. So who's getting all the good bands and all the good acts?" Conway stood up again and enumerated on his fingertips, "Dottie's, that French whore's place and that shithole The Jew runs. They get the pick of the litter! Why? Because this little prick has his fingers in all of 'em! And we get stuck wit' nothin'!"

He sat down again and sighed. "I mean, what's next? This asshole going to unionize the goddam cocktail waitresses too?"

Pat Michelson studied the end of his cigarette before answering. He shrugged, "The kid's just got good business sense, that's all."

"Well, that's just it," Conway sat forward in his chair and wagged his finger emphatically. "It's all in the name of Rocco Fuckin' Petrelli. We can't touch him without starting a war. A war we can't afford and that none of the other gangs will sit still for."

"So make him an offer."

"Wha?"

"The kid's in it for the money, Sean. Just like any other business man. He's not Rocco's favorite nephew, doing it out of love for the fat piece of shite. Make the kid a reasonable offer." He put the cigarette back in his mouth. "Or at least put out some feelers."

24

This had suddenly become a dangerous situation. Fat Eddie clenched his fists in rage as he stood over Jimmy Brisone's hospital bed. The kid was in a coma and Eddie doubted whether he would ever come out of it.

But how much did Tommy know?

It had been the natural thing for a concerned father to do. His daughter loved Tommy and Eddie wanted them to get married. But he wanted to be sure Tommy wasn't going to be seeing Dottie Deuce on the side. Eddie scolded himself for not hiring a private detective in the first place. He should have learned by now that Jimmy Brisone was too stupid to do anything right.

There was a chance, of course, that someone else had put Jimmy in his hospital bed for something entirely different. Jimmy Brisone was a punk kid who was always getting himself into trouble. That was why he was still hanging around Ruby's and Fats' poolroom while the kids Tommy ran around with had graduated to bigger things.

"If you squealed," Eddie muttered at the unconscious man's bed, "I'll make sure you never come out of that coma."

What a terrible thought. If Tommy suspected that Fat Eddie was going to be a meddlesome father-in-law, he might drop Sarah like a hot potato. And she was crazy about him. Her heart would be broken into a million pieces and Fat Eddie's easy retirement would be lost.

Eddie's face contorted into a snarl as he thought of his daughter weeping. His fat hands reached out and pulled the pillow from beneath Jimmy Brisone's head. Fat Eddie pressed it over Brisone's face and hissed, "Worthless bum." Fat Eddie's face turned red and the chords in his neck stood out from the layers of fat as he strained, smothering Brisone with all his strength.

* * *

It was after hours and Tommy, Gaetano and Dottie sat at a table in Dottie's watching the girls running through their new routines with the orchestra. Variety was a key factor when a club wanted customers to come back again and again, and Bob Harris' Orchestra and the girls always seemed to be learning the latest numbers. In the fad-mad Twenties, there was always something new.

Each time Connie Banks completed one of the pirouettes with the other girls, she'd stick her tongue out at Tano, making him grin. He always loved a little mischief. "There's something about a chorus line of pretty broads dancin' and singin' in unison in them little costumes gets me right here…" Tano paused for a moment before slapping a hand to his chest.

The girls completed the number and the three at the table applauded. "Ah, eat your heart out, Ziegfeld!" Tommy stood up and walked into the center of the chorus line, putting his arms around the shoulders of Connie and the girl next to her. "That was great kids." He looked over to Dottie and Tano, "We're gonna have to start screening customers. No Broadway talent scouts. We don't want them stealing our show."

The girls all giggled at the compliment. Dottie joined them and began adjusting one of the girl's costumes. "Julie, honey," she said fighting with the girl's bodice, "If you can't keep yourself in this outfit, we'll have to have it fixed again. This ain't no burlesque show."

"I'm sorry, Dottie. I know. It's just—"

Tano interrupted, "Hey, don't worry Julie. There ain't nothing wrong from where I'm sittin'!"

The girls laughed at his roguishness.

Tony Palermi appeared at Tommy Trent's side. "Fat Eddie's here."

"Oh, yeah?" He slapped Connie and the adjacent girl on the backside. "Alright, kids. That's enough for tonight. Go get yer beauty sleep." He turned to the boys in the orchestra. "That was swell, boys. You guys are soundin' better and better every night. Go getchersevles another drink on the house before you go." As the girls disappeared into the dressing room and the musicians crowded the bar, Tommy told Palermi, "Okay. Bring him in."

Fat Eddie held his hat in his hands when he approached Tommy's table. "Hey, Eddie. Sorry I missed you the other night."

Fat Eddie's eyes were tired. "I wanted to talk with you, Tommy."

"Sure. Sit down."

Fat Eddie pulled out a chair and cast a suspicious glance over his shoulder to Dottie. She was standing behind the bar filling glasses for the orchestra boys. Tano had joined them and was telling the piano player one of the latest jokes.

Fat Eddie leaned forward and spoke in a harsh whisper. "Are you fucking me, Tommy?"

"What?"

"Have you fucked me? Are you fucking me as we speak?"

"Wait a minute, wait a minute," he patted Eddie's shoulder and poured him a drink. "Slow down and tell me it from the beginning."

"You took this place from me. It made me some good money. But I let it slip by because you saved my daughter's life. I just looked at it as repayment. But—" He felt Dottie watching them from across the room. She was too far away to hear, but he could feel her eyes on him. He turned and glared at her before turning back to Trent. He threw his finger over his shoulder towards Dottie. "Are you fucking her? If you're two timing my daughter—"

"Is *that* what this is about?" Tommy laughed and leaned closer to him, "I would never do anything to hurt your daughter, Eddie. We're just friends."

Eddie blinked his eyes rapidly. He was stunned. "What do you mean, just friends?"

"Exactly that. I've never propositioned your daughter or made any inappropriate moves. "

"But she loves you, Tommy." Fat Eddie's jowls flapped for a moment but no more sound came.

"Tsk," Tommy said rolling his eyes with a smile. "We're just friends," he repeated.

Eddie found his voice again, "She wants to *marry* you, Tommy."

"Come on. No she doesn't. She thinks she does, but it's nothing. I explained to her on day one that I had someone else. Sarah and I are just friends. And this place—just business. You put me in charge of security for the booze in the neighborhood. *You* did that, Eddie. I never asked for it, I never *seized* the position. You selected me to manage the flow of booze. Now, Dottie's been loyal to this neighborhood her whole life. I just felt that charging her four hundred percent on the booze was like taking money from our own pockets. She's like one of the gang. And now look at the place. It's the biggest thing in the city. We've made a lot of very good contacts just by opening this place up to the wide world."

"Yeah. Good contacts," DiStella sneered. "You having dinner with Rocco Petrelli? You step over me and start dining with the top dog? You're fucking me, Tommy. You're treating me like nothing over here. I brought you in. If it wasn't for me, you'd still be busting your knuckles on two-bit thieves."

"Don't you think I'm grateful? Huh?" Tommy asked softly.

"Then why are you pushing me out?"

"What are you talking about?"

"Two days ago I had an appointment with Patsy. So I went up town and I was told he wasn't around. He was having meeting. With *you*."

Trent shrugged. "We had a couple of drinks. It was nothing."

Fat Eddie stood up and tossed a dollar on the table for his drink. "I just wanted you to know that I'm not as stupid as everybody thinks, Tommy. This is killing me. My daughter thinks the sun rises and sets around you, and in the meantime you're helping them put me out to pasture and you're treating her like she ain't even there. You're breaking my heart, Tommy."

25

Gaetano Amato and Frankie Sirico flanked Tommy as they entered the restaurant on the north side. Both wore their guns under their coats, but Tommy knew there would be no need of them. With a quick glance he studied Sean Conway's bodyguards and hoped they also knew there would be no need for gunplay.

Sean Conway put on his best business man's smile and stood from his booth. "Tommy! Nice of you to come." They shook hands, "Come, sit down."

Tommy removed his hat and placed it on the table. Frankie and Tano, their coats unbuttoned, took the nearest table. "What can I do for you, Mr. Conway?"

Conway motioned to one of his bodyguards who quickly grabbed the coffee pot. As he refilled Conway's cup, Conway offered, "Coffee?"

"No, thank you."

Sean Conway took his time putting the sugar and cream into his coffee and stirring it. When he finally rested the spoon on the saucer, he raised the cup to his lips. "I have an offer to make you, Tommy." He took a sip and put the cup down. "No one can help but notice how many improvements have graced Fat Eddie's neighborhood since you joined him. The truce you initiated… the way Dottie's is stealing all my best costumers…" Conway shrugged, "I'd like you to come work for me." Tommy didn't answer. "I realize that you have a personal attachment to Eddie's neighborhood. You grew up there.

"You and me, Tommy, we're a lot alike. We both come from nothing and made our own way in the world. It's just that I'd like to see you succeed." He paused for a moment and tried to read Tommy's face. It betrayed no thoughts or emotion. "Fat Eddie is a well meaning fellow, but let's be honest, Tommy. You're running things over there now, aren't you? But Eddie gets all the credit."

Still no reaction. "I'd like you come over with us, Tommy. I'll beat any offer Eddie can make for you and your men. After all, it's 1926 now and things aren't going to stay the same forever. Every day the Carelli mob and the others are getting bigger, wanting a bigger piece of the pie… Sooner or later there's gonna be trouble and I would like to have a capable young man like yourself at my side when the shit flies."

"With all due respect, Mr. Conway, I think you may have heard some exaggerated stories."

Conway laughed. "Yeah. I read all about the Spano hit. Good work, kid. And the UTMA… genius. Tommy, anybody'd be happy to have a guy like you on their side."

Tommy lit a cigarette and said nothing. Conway laughed. "What? You think I got the district attorney hiding in the booth behind us, with a stenographer waiting for you to confess? Everyone knows you were the one who buried the fuckin' Spanos and good riddance…" He waited. Tommy smoked in silence. "All right, you don't have to admit it, Tommy. You don't have to accept my offer right away. Do me the favor of *thinking* about my offer. You know you won't rise any farther in Rocco's mob with Eddie in your way."

Tommy picked his hat up. "It's been nice to meet you, Mr. Conway."

"Same here, Tommy. Same here."

Frankie and Tano fell in behind Tommy as he left the restaurant. It wasn't until they had started the car and pulled away from the curb that Tano spoke. "So what's it all mean, chief?"

Tommy shrugged. "It means Conway's getting antsy and he's expecting war any time now. And it means that I'm first on his hit list."

* * *

"I took the kid in. I gave him his start," Fat Eddie whined softly. "You know? I saw he had potential so I gave him some things to do to help out my crew. I know you and Rocco really like the kid. I thought that would mean something to me and the rest of my crew." Fat Eddie beat his breast, "My crew! Now I'm not free to do anything in my neighborhood without his approval? This punk kid? Even Mo, my right hand, goes sneakin' behind my back to check my orders with Tommy."

Patsy Guarino sat in his large office chair, his chin in his hand with the index finger massaging the side of his long nose. His dark eyes seemed to be piercing Fat Eddie as he listened patiently. Guarino knew it was only a matter of time before he started getting complaints.

"I look like a fuckin' nobody in my own neighborhood. I'm this kid's stooge. But what am I gonna do? My daughter loves him. I love him too. In some ways he's like my own blood, but this has got to stop. His head is so swelled he's neglecting my daughter who is dying of a broken heart before my very eyes."

"Eddie, my friend, what do you want me to do?"

"I want you to get him to lay off. I want you to help me regain control." Guarino regarded him blankly. Fat Eddie waited for what felt like a very long time for an answer. None came.

Fear flashed through Eddie's eyes. The take-over hadn't been Tommy's idea after all. "I always did a good job, didn't I? Didn't I? And you're gonna let this kid who's still fuckin' wet behind the ears take over my neighborhood? I was buying and selling cops when this kid was in the cradle!" As Eddie scooted forward in his chair with each sentence. Patsy wondered if he'd fall off the chair or, considering the deepening red hue of his face, if Eddie'd have a stroke first. "You know the people in the neighborhood pay him for protection? They don't fuckin' pay me no more. They pay *him*. Everybody pays him. I don't see a fraction of the money. You know that?"

Guarino's patience was beginning to wear thin. "You think I don't know what's going on, Eddie? Do you think I'm blind? Why do you come here and tell me things I already know?"

"Then you approve?"

"Be patient, Eddie."

"How can I be patient when this kid is making a fool of me? When he makes a fool of my daughter? What are the people in the neighborhood going to think when a long time friend of yours is pushed out by some upstart? It's *my* neighborhood."

It happened so fast, Eddie didn't see Guarino clear the desk. He had Fat Eddie by the collar and was lifting him off of his feet, slamming his back into the wall. A picture on the other side fell from its hook and crashed to the floor in the next room. Guarino was very tall; his dark sunken eyes and his bony frame gave him the appearance of Death walking. "Listen you fat fuck! That neighborhood and whole goddam city is mine and Rocco's, see? Don't ever forget that. You come in here and question me?" He shook the fat man violently and hissed, "*Figlio di troia!* Who do you think you are? You come in here whining like some old woman and think its going to get you respect?"

He let go of Eddie with a powerful push towards the doorway. Eddie stumbled to the floor. "You want the honest truth? Tommy was trying to spare your self-respect. You're out, Eddie. You've *been* out. Finished, see? Get that through your head. Over. So just keep your trap shut, and go along for the ride." Guarino straightened his tie. "Now get the fuck out of here and quit your bitching."

26

Fat Eddie was starting to feel better now as he lie on the bed in the Golden Swan. He had had too much to drink after his meeting with Guarino and it was all nibbling away at the corner of his mind. He couldn't see it, but something ominous was just outside his field of vision.

He lie on his back, with his fingers intertwined beneath his head, staring up at the tulip shaped glass covers over the four dim light bulbs overhead. In the far corner of the ceiling a small spider swung lazily in a draft as he spun himself a web. Fat Eddie sneered at it and closed his eyes. He supposed he had figured it out long ago, but it didn't make it hurt any less. He thought they called it denial. Years of dedication and loyalty. For nothing. He was out. Finished. *Finito.* If Sarah didn't marry Tommy...

—'Just friends'? What was that about? Sarah loved Tommy and Eddie thought—

Mandy sighed at his cold silence, stood up from the bed and began dressing. She was tall and slim with long black hair. She hadn't changed much over the years. She was still beautiful. She turned to him, "You want me to go, Eddie?"

"Yeah," he grunted.

Mandy began pulling on her stockings. It was unlike Eddie to be so distant and inhospitable. She was used to other men taking out their daily frustrations on her, but this was a first for Eddie. "What's the matter, Eddie?" Again his only response was a grunt. "You wanna talk about it?"

"No."

Her black curls bobbed as she nodded her head, admitting defeat. "Well, could— could I have my money, Eddie?"

"No."

The girl looked crushed. "What?" They had known each other for years and this was the first night Eddie had treated her so miserably. She had always thought that he was a little in love with her because he had once told her that she was the only woman with whom he had cheated on his wife.

"*No,*" he repeated. "I'm the boss of this neighborhood. The boss don't pay." He put a cigar between his lips and lit it. "Besides, you were lousy."

"Eddie, do you know we only get twenty cents out of every dollar?"

"Go cry me a river."

"But Eddie—"

"I said no! I'm the chief around here and I don't have to pay. Even if I did, I wouldn't because you were lousy!"

Tears welled up in Mandy's eyes. "Why are you being so mean? Are you mad at me for something? You never complained before."

"No. Tonight you were lousy. Maybe you're gettin' too used."

"Well, fuck you!" she cried. "You think I get anything out of that tiny little thing of yours?"

Eddie snapped. He hadn't moved so quickly in years as he launched himself off the bed. He punched her, throwing all his weight into it. Her head snapped around and she staggered into the wall and fell. When her hand came away from her mouth, it was covered in blood. She put her fingers to her lips again and this time as she pulled them away, one of her front teeth came with it. "Why, Eddie?" She began sobbing.

Her crying seemed to enrage Eddie more. He grabbed her by the throat and hair and dragged her back to the bed where he straddled her and pounded her face repeatedly with his right fist. The transformation her face underwent was remarkable. She had been an attractive woman a moment ago, but with each punch her face changed. Her jaw was hanging crookedly, several teeth on the pillow next to her. Her left eye was already starting to swell shut, a thin trickle of blood oozed from the corner of her eye. Her nose was now so flattened and bloodied it was hard to distinguish from the rest of her features.

Finally Eddie wrapped his fat hands around her throat and squeezed.

* * *

It was three o'clock in the morning and Tommy and Dottie had fallen asleep in her parlor upstairs. A good number of their evenings ended this way. They had been sitting on the davenport listening to phonograph records one minute and in dreamland the next.

The telephone awoke them.

Tommy answered, still half asleep, thinking he was home. "Hello?"

"T-tommy?"

"Eddie?" Tommy blinked several times and looked around the room. "How'd you get this number?"

"I had Mo track down your friend Tano. I'm in trouble, Tommy."

"How bad?"

"Bad."

"What happened..." By this time he was fully awake and aware that Dottie was leaning close to him wearing an expression of deep concern. "Oh, Jesus, Eddie, you didn't... Where?" He sighed. "Sit tight. Don't go anywhere."

He placed the receiver back on the cradle and ran a hand through his hair. "What is it?" Dottie asked.

Tommy stood up and reached for his coat. He shrugged, "It all comes with moving with Rocco and Patsy, I guess." She followed him to the door. He turned and gave her a quick kiss on the forehead. "I'll be by tomorrow night. Get some sleep, doll."

* * *

Fat Eddie was still naked, holding his head in his hands and sitting on the edge of the bed next to the dead woman. The smell of bodily fluids and excrement nearly knocked Trent off his feet as he stepped into the room. "Oh, Jesus, Eddie," he sighed. Eddie hadn't simply killed her. He had ripped Mandy apart with his bare hands.

"I don't know what happened," Eddie explained weakly.

"What the fuck did you do?"

Eddie suddenly thought about Tommy's affinity for women and how he always seemed to have a soft spot for them. Maybe calling him for help wasn't the brightest move, but there was no one else on earth Eddie thought he could turn to. "I just… snapped." His eyes were wet. Tommy sneered at the blood on his hands and chest. He seemed to be splattered from head to toe with it. "I was drunk… we got into an argument and I just snapped."

Tommy had rounded to the other side of the bed. He inclined his head and leaned over for a closer look. The corpse was almost unrecognizable. "Was that Mandy?"

"Yeah," Eddie said, his voice cracking. "She was a good woman. I've known her for *years*. I— I don't know what came over me…" Tommy was now standing in front of him. His eyes were very dark. For a moment Eddie thought he might shoot him. "You won't tell anyone, will you? You can fix it, right? You—you won't tell Sarah?"

Tommy didn't answer for a long time. He stared down at Eddie with thorough contempt and disgust. He was breathing though his flared nostrils and his right hand kept opening and closing at his side. Finally he spoke, "Listen to me, you fat pile shit. You know what would have happened if you'd done this in The Victoria? Rocco'd be pulling your guts out right at this very moment. Personally."

"I know. I know." He couldn't look at Tommy anymore.

"Maybe Sarah *should* know what kind of monster her father is."

"No, Tommy, no. Anything but that. She loves me." He began rocking back and forth, his arms wrapped around his barrel chest. Tears coursed down his face and between his chins. "She loves me…"

Tommy was silent for another long moment, but Eddie was too afraid to look at him. "You know, you should thank your daughter. Because if it wasn't for her, I'd break your fucking neck for you right now."

"Don't, Tommy. Don't kill me." Eddie knew that in the pause that followed, Tommy Trent, the kid he had taken in and given his start, the kid who had saved his daughter's life, was seriously considering murdering him.

"Alright. Get your shit. Get dressed. Get the fuck out of here. I'll tell the broad that runs the place it was a big-shot politician that did it. That'll keep everybody's trap shut."

"Thank you, Tommy," Eddie said gathering his clothing.

Tommy grabbed him by the throat as he passed by. There was certain death in his eyes. "If I ever see you near one of these places again, you won't make it to the front door."

27

Fat Eddie hadn't been able to look Sarah in the eye since the night at the Golden Swan. He was starting to realize what was happening: The world was coming down around him.

Not only had Tommy Trent passed him up, but the entire outfit had soured on him. His only income during the last week and a half had come from two pieces of furniture his daughter had sold in the shop downstairs and a handful of watches, lighters and jewels he had fenced for the kids in the pool room.

Fat Eddie had been put out of action.

Tommy hadn't been by at all to give Eddie a cut of any of the rackets he was now running in the neighborhood. There was no reason to carry on the charade. Eddie was a has-been and everybody knew it.

And poor Sarah. The poor kid. Not only was her father unable to hide his melancholy—which alone was enough to worry and upset her, but she had no idea why Tommy wasn't coming over every other day anymore. She had no idea he was avoiding her father. She had no idea that her father had beaten a woman to death with his bare hands for no reason.

—Poor Mandy—

"Ah!" Eddie bellowed, pushing away a stack of invoices he was working on. "She was just a whore!"

But now she was a dead whore. A whore who over the years had given Eddie an education about English literature because she loved Lord Byron and Percy Shelley and would recite their poetry at the drop of a hat. She was just a four-dollar whore who for years made Eddie laugh and feel young again. She was just a whore who dreamed of one day living in a small house by the Pacific Ocean with a piano in the parlor....

But now she was just a dead whore.

Her death ended Eddie's career. Even he could see that. There would be no come-back for Fat Eddie DiStella. If he made a beef about anything, all Tommy would have to do would be whisper "Mandy."

There was but one remaining hope.

If Sarah's dream of marrying Tommy came true, there would be a chance Tommy would throw his father-in-law a bone; some small racket he could keep his hand in.

There was still that chance.

Wasn't there?

Deep within him, he knew the answer.

The only reason he was still alive was because Tommy had cared for his daughter and didn't want to make her an orphan. And Eddie had probably sealed that love's doom.

Why would Tommy want to come within a hundred yards of a man he had looked upon with such unabiding disgust? And what hope could Eddie have that his daughter would steal Tommy's heart from Dottie Deuce if he never came around?

"That fucking beer-soaked whore," he muttered to the empty room.

"Poppa?" Sarah called, stepping inside the front door. "I've got your medicine."

Eddie moved slowly and met her in the parlor. "Sarah... I need to talk to you." He took her hands and guided her to the sofa. They sat down and he kept her hands in his. "Tommy told me that you and him are just friends…" He waited for a moment, hoping she would break down and cry and deny it, admitting that they were lovers. But she simply nodded slowly. Eddie was bewildered. "But you love him?"

"Poppa, I don't want to talk about it. It's over."

Eddie's eyes were panic-stricken. "No. Sarah, you've got to tell me. I *need* to know."

Sarah was now bewildered. She hadn't expected her father to be so curious about her personal affairs. He never had been in the past. But maybe, like most things, when Tommy was involved things were suddenly completely different. "Yes. I love him. But he's had someone else. He told me all about it. I told him I wanted to at least be friends… So I could be near him… I thought I could steal him away. And now, he doesn't even return my phone calls…" She looked away, "I guess I deserve it."

"Come on," Eddie chuckled encouragingly, "What could any broad he might find have that could compare with you?"

She shrugged. "I don't know. Whatever it was, I never found it."

Eddie's mind raced. He sighed and squeezed her hands. He tried to sound reassuring. "Well, don't give up hope just yet. There maybe more to Tommy's not coming around than you think. See… Tommy's mad at me… "

"Why? What did you do?"

"It was just… a misunderstanding. Business. It'll blow over in time."

"But what would your business have to do with me?" Her eyes were edged with tears.

"Nothing. That's what I want you to understand. If he doesn't come over it's because of me. Not you."

"But he doesn't even call anymore. And I deserve it." A tear rolled down one of her soft rosy cheeks. "I've been a terrible person, Poppa. Now he doesn't even want to be friends."

"C'mon, don't cry." He brushed her hair from her shoulder and tried to smile. "I'm sorry Sarah. You try callin' him?"

"I tried," she sniffled. "He doesn't answer."

"Oh," he said quietly, "I'm sorry, Sarah." He pulled her close and hugged her to him, patting her head with his hand. The same hand he had used to beat the life from Mandy. He stopped patting her head. "But don't give up hope yet, Sarah. You're a beautiful girl. Maybe Tommy'll come around…I love you, Sarah."

"I know, Poppa." Her voice was muffled. "I love you too."

Eddie sighed and squeezed her tighter. "You are all I have to live for."

* * *

Giovanni DeStefano was one of the countless men with criminal records who had fled Mussolini's purges in Sicily. The first time Tommy met him someone made the mistake of mentioning the name Benito Mussolini. DeStefano spat on Dottie's clean floor and launched himself into a long tirade in Sicilian, vehemently cursing Mussolini and Mussolini's mother. He concluded with a solemn vow: "One day I piss ona their grave!"

The forty-some year-old DeStefano was now Patsy Guarino's chauffeur and bodyguard. With his thick accent and broken English he now addressed Joey Russo, "Mr. Guarino. To see Tommy. Please. Important."

Russo nodded and motioned to the human telegram. (Joey was surprised he didn't end each fragmentary sentence with the word 'Stop'.) He crossed through the crowded nightclub to Dottie's office. He heard the sounds of a heavy petting session going on behind the doors. He swallowed hard and tapped lightly on the door.

"Yeah?…" Russo thought he could hear panting. "What is it?"

"Mr. Trent? G is outside in his car. His driver says it's important."

"Yeah. Gimme a minute."

Russo retired to his post at the front door and made an effort to speak clearly and distinctly to DeStefano. "Mr. Trent will be with you presently."

DeStefano knitted his eyebrows, translated the message and nodded slowly. He returned to the car waiting outside.

Joey grew nervous as he waited for Tommy to get his pants back on and join Mr. Guarino in his car. This was the part of the job Joey didn't care for. He always held a deep suspicion that he would be held accountable if Tommy did not appear quickly enough to suit Mr. Guarino.

He breathed a sigh of relief when Tommy finally appeared. "Sorry, Tommy, I—" He stopped himself, wishing he hadn't said anything to indicate he heard anything unusual coming from inside the office. "It's okay, Joey," Tommy said and marched past him.

Tommy hid the fact he felt a little uncomfortable as he climbed into the back seat of the car to sit with Patsy Guarino. Guarino patted the driver on the shoulder, "Okay, Johnny. Drive around a bit."

"What can I do for you, Mr. Guarino?" Tommy asked.

"When were you going to tell me what happened at The Golden Swan?" Tommy nodded his head almost imperceptibly. He should have known. "And don't give me any shit about not wanting to make his daughter an orphan, Tommy. Those kinds of decisions are not yours to make. That's why there's a boss."

Tommy took his time answering. "Eddie got passed over and he took it out on that girl. Until then I had been thinking about giving him something to do, but… I was waiting to see how he was going to act after he calmed down. Got his head clear."

Patsy Guarino was only in his mid thirties, but he had taken a paternal shine to Tommy. "Do me a favor, Tommy," he said, "next time something like this happens, don't play games. Don't fuck around." Guarino paused and seemed to collect himself. "I ain't pissed at you, Tommy. Just worried. Sometimes…"

"What?"

Patsy Guarino shook his head. "Skip it. Okay, listen: Rocco's at his mansion down in Florida. Fishing. Next weekend Ray, Art, Bones and Marco are heading down there. I want you to go too. Go learn how to fish. Get yerself some sun. Have a bit of fun… And give Rocco the straight dope about this, huh? Nobody's buying that thing of blamin' it on a politician, Tommy. Give it to him straight and leave the decisions to the boss, huh?"

"Sure."

"You're a good kid, Tommy. But there's one thing you have to remember and keep with you always: This thing of ours—business before anything. Remember that, Tommy and you'll be okay."

28

It felt good to be behind the bar. It felt natural. For nearly a decade and a half she had been there every night and she enjoyed it. But there was an added enjoyment with Prohibition. The colorful characters she met seemed even more colorful. Even the old timers. She was serving up drinks and talking with some of the regulars she had known since before the Amendment. "How about a song, Dottie?"

Dottie blushed, "Nah. Not tonight. Besides, it's only a few minutes till the floorshow starts."

"Is that French friend of yours going to sing tonight?"

"Tomorrow night."

"That's right." Earl Moreni had been a regular since he returned from the Spanish-American War and had known Dottie since she was an infant. He had watched her blossom into the glamorous young woman who now stood behind the bar, chatting knowledgably with ease about any topic the customers chose.

Earl turned to the man on the stool next to him, "You know that Dottie here's a pioneer?" He nodded his head in answer to the man's expression. "She was the first doll in the neighborhood to run her own business all alone."

"Is that so? The independent type, huh?"

"Yeah," Dottie said, "but don't get me wrong. I wasn't one of those gals beating the drum for the right to vote or forming temperance leagues." She smiled and her eyes twinkled, "Of course, if I had known how much fun Prohibition was going to be, I would have!"

The men and women crowded around the bar laughed. Earl looked around him wonderingly. All the men loved Dottie and all the women seemed to really admire her. She was everybody's pal.

"Dottie, can I ask you a question?"

"Sure, Earl. What is it?"

"How come you haven't married yet? You're what? Twenty…"

Dottie cut him off with a smile, "I'm getting older, let's say. Think I'm getting to be an old maid Earl?"

"No!" Moreni laughed. "It's just you're a… well, if I wasn't old enough to be your father, I'd be on you doorstep every night."

Dottie smiled and pointed to the landing over head that led to her living quarters. "But Earl, you *have* been at my doorstep every night."

Moreni's eyes brightened. "Well, I'll be!" He laughed. "I guess I have!" He laughed more and slapped a hand on the bar, "I hope my wife don't find out!"

"You never know, Earl," Dottie said stuffing a towel into a glass to dry it. "I may surprise you all yet and get married some day."

"Dottie?" Tommy had appeared in the crowd and was now coming around the bar.

"There he is now," Dottie smiled and winked.

Earl nodded his approval. If it had been any other gangster, he might have tried to warn her against it. But they had known each other forever and if they wanted to get married, it was their business. She knew that young gangster better than anybody and if Dottie loved him, there had to be something more than just gangster to him.

Tommy stood behind Dottie and rested his hands on her hips. "Just in time for the floor show," she said.

"How's business tonight?"

That was something of a silly question. Business was booming. The club attracted a high-profile clientele that her father's old saloon could never dreamed of drawing, and Dottie's charm and personality had kept all the old timers coming in as well. "We'll need more rye by Friday."

"Consider it done," Tommy said. He leaned over her shoulder. "Can I talk to you upstairs?"

"Sure." She turned to Angelo Zonis, the barman. "If you get bogged down, just call one of the girls."

"Sure, Miss Dottie."

Dottie led Tommy up the stairs to her what had been her family's living quarters. Tommy put his hat on the hook by the door and sat on the sofa. "Drink, Tommy?"

"No. I've had enough for tonight."

Dottie pulled a chair across the floor and sat close to him, "What's up, doll?"

"Do you trust Connie?"

That was a shocking question. "Of course! Why, she's like a sister, you know that."

Tommy nodded, "Would you trust her and Tano to look after the speak for the weekend?"

"I guess so..."

"Good. I've gotta go down to Florida on business. Sorta a business-vacation. Rocco's got a cottage down there and some of the boys are going down to see it." He leaned forward and grabbed Dottie's hand. "It won't be all business, though and I'll have a lot of free time. I thought maybe we could hit the beach together... I'll be bored out of my mind without you."

Dottie smiled and felt herself turning red. The thought of not being in the saloon for the first time in so long... and yet a little vacation with Tommy...

It didn't take much consideration.

"Sure, Tommy. I'd love to."

Tommy grinned. He hadn't thought prying her away from the speakeasy would be so easy. "Great. Only…" he leaned closer, "Don't tell anyone where we're going, okay?"

"Oh. Is it that secretive?"

"It's not exactly a secret, but I don't want it broadcast either."

* * *

They sat close together on a mound of white sand beneath the beach umbrella watching their men stroll along the water's edge discussing business. While Tommy had been visiting Rocco's mansion in the morning, Dottie had been shopping for a bathing suit and heard a familiar voice cursing in French. Dottie followed the voice to find Fran Barrey standing in an aisle with a bathing suit draped over one arm, rummaging through her hand bag.

"Frenchie?"

Fran looked up and smiled. "Dottie! What are you doing here?"

"I'm with Tommy."

"Oh. So he convinced you to come along?" She dropped her voice to a low conspiratorial mutter, "I don't think that anyone but Tommy is supposed to know we're here." She put a finger across her lips and winked before resuming her search of the handbag.

"What's wrong?"

Fran sighed with frustration, "I must have left my money at the hotel."

"Well, I've got enough to cover for you. If you'll help me pick out a bathing suit." And so Fran had helped Dottie choose a bathing suit, which, as Dottie had discovered, clung immodestly to her chest when wet.

She was now seated on the beach towel with her knees pulled up to her chest to keep the young men from gawking at the way the material seemed to sculpt itself around her nipples. Fran sat in a similar posture, hugging her knees to her. "I envy you," she said. She extended a finger in the direction of Tommy and Max. "I've told you before that you're a lucky woman."

Dottie smiled at the compliment. "Tommy says that you and I are the only people on earth he can't hide anything from. He says we must be mind readers. He can put on a poker face for anyone else. But not us."

"When did you meet him?"

Dottie forgot herself and stretched her legs out and leaned back. "Nineteen… eleven. Yes. Tommy was about seven or so." Fran indicated that she wanted to hear more of the story by inclining her head. "My mother and father and I were walking to church. We saw these boys about my age kicking around a scrawny little pile of rags and bones. Ah, but he was a fighter. Even then." Dottie smiled at the memory. "He was tough and wouldn't give in. They were after a nickel he had.

"My father chased away the bullies and picked this kid up off the pavement. He asked him his name and where he lived. But Tommy didn't say anything. He just turned and ran away. But before he turned, he looked at me. He had the most remarkable dark blue eyes… They were the eyes of a boy who knew the world wasn't going to keep him down forever."

Dottie looked down at the sand and picked up a handful. She toyed with it absently, letting it trickle between her fingers. She said sadly, "Of course, there wasn't any place for him to go but up…" After a long pause she continued, "A few days later I started seeing him across the street from my father's saloon. For the first week or two, I thought he was a mute because he never said anything. He'd just stand there until he knew one of us had spotted him. Then he'd run away.

"Mamma said, 'Oh, he's like a scared lost kitten afraid to come in out of the cold!'" Dottie smiled, "But I saw it differently. Tommy didn't want to be taken in by anyone. He…"

She interrupted herself, "Then he started walking me to school. And we've been friends ever since."

A tall sandy-haired man with spidery pale legs took his time walking past the girls. Fran smiled sweetly and said something in French. The man smiled and nodded as though he had been complimented.

After he was out of hearing range, Dottie asked, "What did you say to him?"

Fran grinned devilishly, "I told him that his mother commits obscenities with dogs." The girls laughed and lit cigarettes.

"I know nothing of mob politics," Fran said with a sigh of smoke. "I believe the less I know, the better. But I can't help but wonder why Max has been so secretive about our coming down here. His uncle doesn't even know. He said something about Rocco wasn't even supposed to know Max is here."

Dottie had tried to stop listening after the first sentence. Although she believed Tommy to be the most capable man around, she could not keep from worrying about him; especially as they grew closer and closer and Tommy got bigger and bigger.

"I don't trust Max's uncle," Fran added.

Dottie changed subjects, "Tommy told me you set him straight about Sarah."

Fran shrugged. "I only reminded him of what he knew already."

"It's a shame. She's an alright kid. She could have fit in with the crowd at the speak. She got along swell with the other girls."

"I believe she's a good actress with bad intentions." Fran smiled and put a hand on Dottie's arm. "Now, I lust after your Tommy, but I am decent enough to admit it. And I would never have him betray you." She turned away and looked out over the ocean. "I once loved a man who betrayed me. I could never make another human feel the way that made me feel. I just couldn't do that to anyone."

"Well, I never worried about that. Sure, in days gone by Tommy ran around with his share of girls—just like I was entitled to see whoever I wanted. But I knew in the end, when our age difference didn't seem so great, when things fell into place, I think we both knew we'd end up together."

"How lucky you are," Fran observed. "You and Tommy are quite extraordinary. It's a privilege to know such people, let alone call them my dearest friends." Her thoughts seemed to trail off as she watched two seagulls wheeling lazily through the bright sky above the ocean.

"I am very lucky, too," Fran said. "In Europe, I never had friends like you or Tommy. Only... *acquaintances.* When I achieved some measure of fame, I met all kinds of people: actors, painters, dignitaries... I ran around with the crème of society. And one day I realized that they were all so arrogant, full of themselves... it took a simple American doughboy to steal me away from it all.

"I loved him very much. I treasure the memory of those six months we had together." She thought of her murdered husband lying in a pool of blood in a darkened alley. She shook the vision away, smiled and looked at Dottie, "Do you know I haven't been with anyone since he was murdered?"

"What about Max?"

Fran smiled wistfully, "Max loves me but knows we will never be more than companions… It's funny isn't it?"

"What?"

"Go to any of the guys in any of the gangs and mention 'the French whore' and they'll say 'Oh, yes. That dame who runs Le Paris and is fucking Max.'" Dottie started to deny the existence of such scandalous rumors, but Fran cut her off. "No, no. It's okay. They call me a whore because in Paris I took off my clothes before a camera for all the world to see." She frowned thoughtfully, "I'm not ashamed of that—in fact, I am proud, as I believe the models of the great painters were proud. …I know it sounds terribly arrogant and conceited but it is, in a way, reassuring to know that my beauty will remain on film long after it fades in life… Does that sound too terribly egotistical?"

"No," Dottie said softly.

Fran hugged her knees closer to her and sighed. "They think of me as a whore even though I haven't slept with anyone since my husband was murdered and there were only three lovers before him… They think of me as the *French* whore, even though I'm half English." She shrugged and smiled again, "What does it matter? As long as my friends, like you and Tommy know the truth?"

Dottie Deuce said nothing and hugged her knees to her chest again. She had never thought of the fun loving Fran Barrey as a tragic figure until now. For a brief instant, she had seen Fran as an old woman who had already lost the love of her life and was merely waiting for death to claim her. Dottie looked along the beach to see Max and Tommy strolling back to them. She made a vow to treasure every moment she had with Tommy Trent.

"It's just Americans don't understand your photographs," Dottie said, but she knew it sounded like a weak excuse.

Fran laughed. "Your Tommy and I had a very similar discussion! I told him that this country was too puritanical to produce a great artist." She added quickly, "But don't get me wrong. I believe that the cinema will be America's great contribution to the world of art."

"Moving pictures?" Dottie asked incredulously.

Fran nodded firmly. "And now they've thought of adding sound." They fell silent as they watched the men in the distance. They had stopped walking and were facing each other. Tommy was speaking animatedly and finally Max nodded his head, which seemed to end the discussion. As they continued walking towards Fran and Dottie again, Fran sighed. "Do you know why he has done all of this?"

"Hmmm?"

"Why Tommy has worked his way up. Made something of himself."

Because he's Sicilian and Sicilians never forget and they never forgive, Dottie thought. She decided to let Fran give her the answer. "It was all for you, doll. He had to make something of himself before he would give himself to you."

Dottie smiled at the sand. "I am lucky. I guess I've always known that…"

As the men approached they could hear Max saying, "What about Meyer and Cuba?"

"I think it's a goldmine," Tommy said. "More power to them."

"Hi, guys!" Dottie cried cheerfully.

Max dropped to his knees by the picnic basket. "Anyone else hungry?"

"Sure."

Tommy sat next to Dottie and brushed a bit of sand from her knee. "Gotta cigarette, doll?"

"Sure." She handed him a cigarette and a lighter. He lit the cigarette and then took her hand. Dottie thought of her friend, the French widow and squeezed his hand tightly. *Treasure every moment, Dottie,* she told herself.

* * *

Rocco Petrelli called it his tug-boat, but the Isabella was one of the most luxurious yachts to ever set sail from Florida. Dottie was the only girl from home on board tonight. Art Gagliano, Joey Bones, Marco Messinio and Raymond DeLaurentis had all picked up local girls for the party. Rocco had several for himself and some for his guests who were local big-wigs. Dottie was introduced to them by first name only, and if Dottie knew gangsters—which she did—they weren't their right names either.

These were Rocco's new business partners. American Gangland was beginning to unite. She guessed these men would be involved in running sugar and rum between Cuba and the United States and laundering money. There was also a great deal of talk about gambling going on as well.

The only guest she was introduced to formally was a small Spaniard in a military uniform. Dottie wondered how he could stand up with all the medals hanging from his chest. His Latin name sounded so exotic to her that she wouldn't be able to remember it a half hour later. He was supposed to be a high ranking official of the new regime in Cuba. When Tommy introduced him, the small Spaniard smiled, took her hand, bent low and placed his lips above her knuckles. "In all my days I have never seen such a beautiful senorita." His thin mustache, which appeared to be penciled on, rose at the ends when he grinned. It gave her the willies. He turned to Tommy, "You are a lucky man, Signor Tommy."

It was eerie too, to see Tommy laughing and joking with Rocco Petrelli. Ten years ago she would never have believed it.

But the music, the food and the champagne were marvelous. Dottie and Tommy spent an hour dancing on the yacht's wide deck in the moonlight with the warm sea air enveloping them. It had been a long time since Dottie had had so much fun.

The party ended after midnight when the yacht returned to the dock. Dottie had never been on a boat before and had been afraid she would be sea sick, but now she seemed to be floating on the champagne bubbles and couldn't remember ever having a worry in the world.

Rocco stopped Tommy as they were heading towards their hired cars. "Tommy," he paused and slipped a cigar into Tommy's pocket. "You learn anything tonight?"

Tommy nodded. "Yeah, I think so."

"Good." he smiled and patted Tommy's chest. "Go ahead with yer plans—" Dottie did not catch the way Rocco's eyes flickered to her and then back again. "—then, regarding our friend... do what you gotta do. Okay?"

"Sure, Rocco."

"You two leaving tomorrow?" Tommy nodded. "I'll be back up in a few days. I'll see you then. Goodnight, Tommy. Dottie."

"Goodnight, Rocco," they echoed.

Tommy opened the car door for her and rounded to the other side to let himself in. As the car turned around and aimed itself towards the hotel, Tommy grabbed her by elbows and kissed her so passionately she was stunned. "I love you, Dottie." His eyes were sober, his face dead serious. "Always remember that."

29

JIMMIE'S RESTAURANT ON THE NORTH SIDE WAS A phantom. Of course those who were not in-the-know could get served something resembling a meal there but they were few and far between. Stepping in through the front door one first noticed the bright brassy lights and the old gay-nineties style bar that was nothing more than a show piece now. A handful of tables were squeezed in between the booths and from the front door one could see the window to the kitchen. A bored looking chef sat reading a dime novel just behind it. A waitress was seated in a booth to the left reading an issue of Photoplay and glancing at her watch at regular intervals. Behind the bar, where the cash register sat, was an ex-boxer Liam McKee. Liam McKee was known for more than his distinguished career in the ring. A war-hero and a known ace-triggerman, he was also rumored to be very good with a knife. He was reading the lines of the waitress's curves.

He ignored Fat Eddie as he came in. Eddie knew the drill. He walked straight through the curtains on the far side of dining room, drew them closed and knocked three times on the wall. A small slot in the wall opened and strains of jazz greeted Eddie. He noted immediately that the orchestra at Dottie's was better. A pair of eyes behind the slot narrowed. "What do you want?"

"I— I need to see the boss."

The man studied him for a long tense moment. "Hold on."

There were muffled voices above the crowd noises and the music. The telephone rang in the dining room behind him, but Eddie thought nothing of it. He was too busy moving from one foot to the other like a small boy who had to use the bathroom.

The curtains behind him opened with a startling metallic "whoosh!" Eddie spun around to find Liam McKee had him by the tie. "Don't hurt me!" Eddie babbled. The ex-fighter grinned.

"Shaddup an' get yer arms up."

Fat Eddie obeyed and closed his eyes. Instead of feeling a knife entering his ribs, or a bullet tearing through his skull, he only felt Liam's giant hands searching him for a weapon. He took Eddie's penknife. "I'll hold this till youse come through again." Liam tapped on the wall. "He's clean."

Liam stepped back and closed the curtains. The wall opened inward and there appeared the weasely looking man to whom the eyes had belonged. "Alright. Mr. Conway will see you."

* * *

Pat Michelson stepped into the office to find Sean Conway seated with his feet upon the desk. He also had one of the club's dancers there, lighting his cigarette for him. "Hello, Pat. Siddown." He pinched the girl's thigh lightly. "Okay, doll. Scram." He gave her bottom a pinch for good luck as she made her exit.

Conway poured a drink for himself and one for Michelson. "I had an interesting conversation today."

"Anyone I know?"

Conway pursed his lips and nodded. "Fat Eddie DiStella."

Michelson rolled his eyes. "More peace plans? He and the Jew want us to fork over more territory to Careli?"

"No, no. Quite the opposite, in fact. Remember I told you a couple of weeks ago a private dick I know was hired to get photographs of this Trent kid fucking Dottie Deuce?"

"Sure. He get any?"

"I dunno. But if Eddie suspects enough to hire a detective..." he shrugged. "Things could get ugly over there."

"What did the fat piece of shite have to say?"

"It looks like Rocco's restructuring his whole outfit. Seems they forced Fat Eddie into early retirement and he's not too pleased. He says Patsy is moving himself away from the muscle end of the outfit and it looks like this Trent kid is going to take over that end."

"Him?"

"Did you see the job that was done on the Spano brothers?"

"Of course." The newspapers had gone over the top with their coverage of the "Spano Massacre." They printed every detail they could find, including how a bottle of glue had been poured over the corpses' hands to show the Spanos had developed sticky fingers.

"It was this Trent kid who hit them."

Michelson's brow dropped incredulously. "No. That kid?" He gave a soft low whistle. "Imagine a wee little dago like that balling Dottie Deuce *and* wiping out the Spano mob." Michelson chuckled. "I'm beginning to have a little respect for this kid."

"Fat Eddie tells me we have a squealer in our midst."

"How so?"

"Our long term plans—the guns, cars and apartments... Trent knows about it all. Someone's kept him well informed. And I imagine he's been keeping Patsy and Rocco well informed too."

"Oh, hell... Did Fat Ass say anything else?"

"Other than he'd like Dottie Deuce to have an accident?... No." Sean Conway stood up and stretched. He finished his drink and placed the glass on the desk with a dramatic clank. "Of course, we had enough cause to make a beef over the whole Dorchester Gold thing." Dorchester Gold was an imported whiskey that Conway had been getting from Rocco for an exorbitant price. Finally Conway decided to move to a cheaper

Canadian whiskey from an outside source and pocket the difference. When the orders dropped off, Conway asked Rocco to put him back onto the Dorchester Gold, but Rocco had laughed contemptuously. "You're too late. Somebody picked up your share. It's all spoken for."

Conway sat on the corner of his desk and flipped open the lid of his humidor. After a moment's consideration, he selected a cigar, trimmed the end and lit it. "The question I'm going to put to you is this:" He jabbed the cigar in the direction of Michelson's chest. "Why is Rocco restructuring his organization?"

Michelson shrugged. "If they have any idea how many guns we've been building up..."

"Exactly, boy-o. I bet Rocco's been busy as well. It's going to be all out war. You know damned well this kid would never have hit the Spanos without Hymie's okay. Then Rocco and the Jew divvied up their territory. They're both getting greedy. Rocco wants this Trent kid to do to us what he did to the Spanos."

"So what do we do?"

"Hit them first. We hit the mattresses tonight."

30

It was unusual for Dottie to get out of bed so early. She felt as though she had just fallen asleep and it was morning already. The night before she had promised him that she would be up and waiting for him when he arrived.

She was just finishing her second cup of coffee when Tommy and Tano arrived. "Hi, Dottie. How are you this fine morning?"

Dottie harrumphed. "Can you boys tell me what I'm doing up at this ungodly hour?"

"Now, now," Tommy scolded. He held up her fur coat for her as she slipped into it. "Let's not be grumpy."

Tano stepped behind her. "Okay. I'm sorry, doll, but I have to blindfold you."

"Blindfold me? What are you guys—" Tommy gently held her arms at her side as Tano tied a strip of cloth across her eyes. "Tommy?"

"It's okay, doll. Trust me." He kissed her, picked her up and carried her outside to the car. "Get the door, Tano."

He leapt ahead of them and opened the rear door. Tommy deposited her gingerly on the backseat and went around to the other side and got in next to her. He held her hand as Tano started the car and drove away.

"What's going on, Tommy?"

"Shhh. You'll see."

The car hadn't traveled very far—at least Dottie didn't think it had, when it came to a stop. She could hear Tano and Tommy getting out and coming to her side of the car. The door opened and Tommy scooped her into his arms. He stood her up and put his left arm around her shoulders. "Ready?"

"Yeah. What's this—?"

Tommy pulled the blindfold away and Dottie found herself standing twenty yards in front of a large Victorian house. It was too small to call a mansion but it was an impressive looking structure. It stood on a hill which over looked a stretch of woodland in back. The sun was still rising over the hill. "Tommy, what did you guys bring me out here for?"

She spotted Connie Banks sitting on a porch swing.

Tommy gave her a squeeze. "It's our home, Dottie."

"What?" She closed her eyes and put her fingers to her forehead. She was much too tired for games. "Tommy, what are you talking about?"

"Shhh," Tommy said putting a finger to her lips. He motioned Connie to come over. When she joined the group, Tommy cleared his throat. "Quiet, now Dottie. I have a very important question to ask Tano."

Gaetano straightened his tie and corrected his posture. He cleared his throat. "Yes?"

"Will you be my best man at the wedding when Dottie and I get married next month?" As he spoke, the fingers of his left hand manipulated a diamond ring so it appeared to come out of Dottie's ear.

Dottie's mouth hung open for a moment, her eyes wide and moist. "Oh, Tommy," she said softly. Then she leapt into his arms and he hugged her and swung her around. "Oh, Tommy, God, I thought you'd never ask." She kissed him for a very long time.

"Don't you wanna look at the ring?" Tommy asked.

She kissed him again and smiled at the ring. "It's beautiful, Tommy." She slipped it on and kissed him again before turning to show the ring to Connie. Connie was dabbing at the corners of her eyes with a handkerchief.

* * *

Her father had been acting peculiar all day long. Eddie had never been very good at hiding when his jittery nerves were acting up. In the afternoon he had asked her to cancel any plans she might have had. "I want you to stay home tonight." There was something in the tone of his voice that discouraged any argument. It was unlike her father to be so serious. So dead serious.

And so she had spent the afternoon in the furniture shop listening to phonographs and playing solitaire. After what felt like the hundredth game, Sarah groaned and set the cards aside. This was ridiculous. She was a grown woman—she had every right to go out if she wanted to, didn't she?

Then she remembered the dead look in her father's eyes.

He had always succeeded in sheltering her from his gangster world and surely this was more of the same. But the way his "I want you to stay home tonight" had sounded so final...

Eddie was in trouble. That had to be it. A chill ran up Sarah's spine. Tommy had taken over the neighborhood, hadn't he? Poppa had been passed up—

She suddenly wished she could see Tommy.

Sarah rose from the chair behind the counter and placed the "closed" sign in the window. She paused and watched a few people going in and out of the sandwich shop across the street. It was getting on towards evening; the sun would be setting before long.

Upstairs she followed the sound of her father's voice. He was on the telephone. As she drew closer to his office, Eddie's tone sounded more and more hysterical. "No, I'm not trying anything funny... How do I know? He's always at the speak... You got a post at the French whore's?... Well, be patient. They'll show up. And fer crying out loud, don't fuck up. This is my ass on the line."

Suddenly Sarah DiStella knew.

* * *

The three words the man on the telephone spoke made Micah Collin's blood run cold. He hadn't felt such panic since the day he thought Conway's boys found out he had sold out Felim Strong's crew and warehouse to Tommy Trent.

Three words.

"Hit the mattresses."

The phone went dead. He slammed down the receiver and shakily lit a cigarette. The peace had been too good to last, he supposed, and wondered who had fired the first shot. In any event, upon receiving that signal, he had thirty minutes to make his way to a small apartment across town where he would hole up and run operations with a handful of other men for the duration. He looked at the clock and decided he would have just enough time.

He tore through his bedroom closet, moving everything out of his way so he could reach the far corner. Tucked under a piece of wood molding he kept a piece of paper. He retrieved it and rushed for the telephone. There was no one at the first number he tried. He swore and tried the second.

* * *

Vic Nash was just passing the small office in Dottie's when he heard the telephone ringing. He had a box full of new sparkling headbands for the girls he was taking to the dressing room and he debated ignoring the telephone. Frowning, he stepped into the office and set the box down. "Hello?"

"Is Tommy Trent there?"

The slight hint of Irish brogue on the other end of the line made Vic suspicious. "No."

He started to hang up but heard the man's desperate question. "Is Dottie there? Or any of his gang?"

"No."

"This is important. You need to find them. *Now.*"

"Hey, fuck you. Why don't you go back to your little green isle and quit bustin' my balls?"

"Dammit, man! Sean Conway's given the orders to hit the mattresses! We're at war!"

31

ANGELO'S WAS ONE OF THE BEST FAMILY RUN restaurants in the city. On weekends it was usually hard to get a table without a long wait. Except, of course, for Rocco Petrelli, Patsy Guarino or one of Rocco's captains like Tommaso Trentino. Tables and maître d's would appear like magic for one of Rocco's gang.

And it had been so tonight—Tommy and his guests were escorted to a table with great pomp and circumstance past ordinary citizens, politicians and policemen who waited in line with their husbands, wives and mistresses, all with impatient and envious frowns distorting their faces.

The gangsters had taken over.

The table was set up at the front of the restaurant, near the band, who began playing all of Dottie's favorite romantic tunes. A lavish floral arrangement and bucket of champagne were placed in the center of the table as they were seated.

Dottie Deuce's head and heart were still whirling. She had known for so long that Tommy would someday ask her to marry him, that she had taken it for granted; it had slipped past the realm of hope and waiting and lie dormant in the cradle of her heart for so long that a part of her had nearly forgotten that someday it would really happen. That someday she would be Mrs. Tommy Trent.

It had been one of the best dinners Dottie Deuce could remember and now she was walking hand-in-hand with Tommy back to the speak. It was a chilly evening, March had not wrestled the cold sting away from winter, but Dottie was too preoccupied to notice. The six of them, Tommy and Dottie, Tano and Connie and Tony Palermi and his girl Marie Evani had such a great evening and Dottie was on top of the world. Nothing could go wrong now.

"Tommy! Tommy!" the voice called. They all turned to see Sarah DiStella running down the street after them, waving her hand. Her other hand was clutching her fur coat closed as her steps took on a staggery fashion. Tommy wondered if she hadn't run all the way from home. When she caught up with them, Tommy had to catch her by the shoulders to keep her momentum from knocking them over. "Tommy, I need to talk to you."

"Sarah—what's the matter? "

The girl panted to catch her breath. "Tommy, it's Poppa."

"He in trouble?"

She shook her head and swallowed hard. "Oh, Tommy, I don't know." Her eyes, wide with fear and moist with tears, scanned the faces around them. "I think he's trying to set you up, Tommy. If anything happened to you, I'd die—"

A car whirled around the corner with screeching tires. Two men were standing on the running board on the left side of the car. One held a shotgun, the other a machinegun over the car's roof. Two more men were leaning out of the passenger side windows with pistols.

The glass storefront behind them exploded inward. The noise from the guns was terrific, sending people scattering for shelter all along the block. Drawing their guns was only their second instinct. Their first was the safety of the girls. The three men on the sidewalk grabbed them and fell on top of them.

Tommy knew he was hit before his knees touched the pavement. He could feel Sarah's tear-soaked cheek against his face. His other arm was wrapped around Dottie who said "Ow" quite calmly as though she pricked her finger while sewing instead of landing hard on her tailbone.

The gunshots were too numerous and too close together to count. But the car hadn't slowed down much as it passed by. When they heard the car whirl around the next corner, turning off the block, Tommy began to sit up to look around.

Marie Evani was lying beneath Tony Palermi, her face covered in a mask of blood. Her eyes were wide and startled but did not react as blood flowed into them. Palermi lie on top of her, blood splattered all over his face and more fountaining from his mouth and throat. His legs were convulsing and he was shitting himself. He had taken the brunt of the tommygun's burst. A bullet had gone through his neck and into Marie's forehead. He died as Tommy laid eyes on him.

Tano rolled over, holding his arm and cringing. Connie seemed unhurt and was trying to examine his arm. Dottie was sitting up now and rubbing her backside while shaking shards of glass from her hair. As Tommy lifted himself up to his knees, Dottie's eyes grew wild. "Oh, Jesus, Tommy!"

He looked down to his side. The coat and shirt were shredded and blood flowed freely down his hip and over his thigh. His side was on fire. Sarah was lying on her back, tears still in her eyes and her mouth half open. She blinked her eyes twice and looked to Tommy. "Oh, God," he said and lifted her shoulders into his lap. Her dress was purple but a large area under her left breast was growing black. She reached a hand up and gently caressed his face.

"Tommy?" Sarah DiStella said and died.

32

Patsy Guarino proved he was still physically fit as he took the four flights of stairs at the Carlisle Hotel two steps at a time. He kept up the swift pace until he reached the door of Rocco Petrelli's penthouse suite. "Okay, boys," he said to the two guards outside Rocco's door. "You better call for reinforcement."

The guards took the news as unemotionally as they took everything else. They wordlessly unlocked the door and let Guarino into Rocco's suite. He looked around the lavish room. "Rocco? Rocco!"

Petrelli emerged from the bedroom, closing the door behind him quickly to keep Guarino from seeing inside. Guarino already knew who he had with him. "Conway's boys hit Trent's crew fifteen minutes ago."

"He hurt?"

"He's getting patched up. Half his crew is there on guard duty."

"How bad is it?"

"One of Tommy's boys, named Palermi's dead. Tano, T's right hand caught one in the arm. There are two dead girls. Rocco… one of them was Fat Eddie's daughter."

Rocco Petrelli gnawed on the end of his cigar for a moment, contemplating. "Oh, hell. Fat boy's not gonna like that. Who was the other one?"

"A dancer at Dottie's place."

"I suppose Conway thinks we're not wise. Suppose he thinks we've been sitting around for the last six months picking our noses. Yeah. He wants to play rough, does he? Well," Rocco chuckled, "If that's how he wants it, that's how he gets it, see?"

* * *

Dottie Deuce was seated next to his bed in his apartment, holding his hand as the doctor used long tweezers to remove buck-shot from his side. A nurse was following behind putting a tiny stitch wherever needed, wishing that the lighting was better. Tommy's lips pressed together in a thin white line of anger and pain.

Dottie squeezed his hand. "It's not your fault, Tommy. Bad things like this just happen." She blinked back a few tears. "I…"

Tommy shook his head and tried to say something, but the words didn't come. His eyes softened as he pulled his hand free and touched Dottie's face. "I love you, doll. I hope you know that."

She smiled. "I suspected as much."

"I've been in love with you since I was twelve years old. No…. Since the moment I saw you." He winced. "Hey, careful Doc. I think you just tweezed my spleen."

The doctor grinned. "You're a lucky guy, Tommy. Another foot closer and you wouldn't be here." He dropped another piece of buckshot into the porcelain bowl and set the tweezers aside. "I think that's it. We can take some pictures tomorrow to be sure."

"Thanks, Doc." Tommy took a roll of bills from his trouser pocket and peeled off two hundred dollars. He placed the bills in the doctor's hands.

The doctor smiled and nodded his thanks. He stepped aside to let the nurse put a large bandage over the Tommy's left side. While waiting for her to finish, he looked into the bowl and let out a low whistle. "If these were gold, you'd be rich."

Tommy thanked the doctor and the nurse again as they left the room and added: "I'll remember to make sure they use golden bullets next time they come gunnin' for me."

As the door shut, Tommy sat up in the bed. "Gimme my clothes, doll."

"You don't think you're going anywhere, do you?"

"Come on, sweetheart. I'm a sitting duck here. Let's go home."

She helped him dress without saying anything further. He still hadn't moved all of his belongings to the new house and he was fighting with a case in the closet. His left side hampered his mobility. Dottie stepped forward and helped him pull a large heavy case out of the closet. He set it on the bed and opened it up to reveal an unassembled tommygun. He assembled it with lightening speed and clicked the drum magazine into place. He studied it for a moment and removed the stock. From a tall wardrobe he selected a long overcoat and Dottie helped him into it. The right pocket was cut through on the inside, allowing him to conceal the machinegun beneath the coat while keeping his finger on the trigger. Dottie picked up the case to bring along without being asked to, and it made Tommy Trent smile. He turned for the door.

It wasn't until he had his hand on the doorknob that she spoke. "Tommy, I'm afraid."

He turned to her. "What? Dottie Deuce afraid? The Deuce is a legendary dame!" he grinned. He brushed aside the hair from her shoulder and gently caressed the back of her neck. "She's never been afraid in her life!"

She took his hand. "I am now. Besides, I'm not Dottie Deuce for much longer, remember?" She raised her hand to show him the ring. "I'm Dottie Trentino."

"You got that right, doll." He said and kissed her. "But you're still the toughest, smartest most beautiful dame in the whole city. Always remember sweetheart: If you have no fear, your enemies will."

33

Fat Eddie still seemed to be in a trance when the police dropped him off at home. He had said nothing that made any sense since Detective Alsop had opened the cold metal drawer in the morgue. And there lie Eddie's daughter, his baby girl, her eyes closed, her skin ghostly pale and her brow furrowed as if asking "Why, Poppa? Why?" His only daughter had walked into a trap Eddie had had a hand in laying.

He stood in the doorway of Sarah's bedroom for a long time, staring into the darkness, knowing the room would now remain empty forever. Sarah had been the kind of girl who lit up an entire room just by coming in, and when she left the absence of her light made everything seem all the more dark.

And tonight the world had lost a great deal of light forever.

He walked like a very old man as he tore himself away from her room and went to his office. He sat at his desk and found a pen and a piece of paper. He wrote absently, like some kind of automated machine. His mind, heart and soul were elsewhere.

With the same slow mechanical movements he went to the bathroom, undressed and tried to look into his eyes in the mirror. Nothing there remained. Only a brief fleeting image of himself in formal wear, tossing rice at his beautiful daughter as she scurried down the church steps with her handsome husband on a hot bright day in June that was never to be.

He turned on the faucets to draw a nice hot bath. The sound of the rushing water seemed to roar and wail in the still night. The pipes beneath the floor rattled angrily. He tested the water's temperature and nodded slowly that it was satisfactory. He turned the handles off.

Before he climbed in, he went to the medicine chest and removed his straight-razor. The handle was long, smooth and black. The long blade gleamed as though it were polished silver.

Eddie DiStella made sure the blade was sharp.

* * *

"Here ya' go, doll," Dottie said placing a drink in Tommy's hand. He was reclining on the davenport in their new home.

"This is a helluva way to spend our first evening in our house, hon."

She shushed him and patted the top of his head as she walked away. The entire place had come furnished with furniture Tommy had picked for her. It proved how well he knew her because there wasn't a thing in the house that she wouldn't have picked herself. She was back at the drinks cupboard pouring one for herself and looking at her reflection in the mirror. On the mantelpiece behind her was the solid gold apple Tommy had given to her. Apples, she thought. Always apples. She would treasure it forever.

"I should move someplace where there's a telephone."

Crossing the room, she sat next to him on the edge of the davenport and put a hand on his chest. "Tommy, you're safe here. They'll be looking for you at your place and my place."

"I know. I know."

There was a period of silence that seemed to last for minutes. She sighed. "Tommy, if this had happened yesterday, I wouldn't ask. But I'm going to be your wife now and—"

"I know. You're entitled to know what happened. Fat Eddie flipped, doll. He's the one who set me up to get killed."

"But why would Eddie do a thing like that?"

"He didn't have the balls to do it himself."

"But it doesn't make sense, Tommy."

"Rocco passed him over and put me in charge. And he figured out I never wanted to marry Sarah. And without that he hadn't any hope of staying in the rackets."

"Jesus…. Eddie," she bowed her head and shook it.

He took Dottie's hand and squeezed it. "Hey, babe. Don't be blue, huh? Eddie wasn't the comical fat buffoon everyone thought he was, doll. He had a lot of nastiness deep inside. Believe me. He wanted me out of the way so he could reclaim control. He just picked a time when Conway was itching for an excuse to hit the mattresses."

"I wonder where he is now."

"Unless my guess is very, very wrong, he's already dead."

When the knock came at the door, Dottie went to answer it. "What is it?" she called through the shut door.

He could hear Tano's voice, "Frankie's here."

"Tommy, Frankie's here," Dottie repeated.

"Show him in."

Frankie Sirico's eyes were blazing as he entered the room. He marched quickly to the davenport and dropped to his knees. His lips were pressed together in a tight white line of anger. "Tell me who did it, T."

"Frankie—"

"I swore an oath to you and Tano. Say the word T, and I'll make the scumbags suffer."

"I will Frankie. But not right now. It's what they're expecting. They're waiting for another Spano raid. But I'm gonna make them wait."

* * *

Fran Barrey spent most of the late evening on the telephone trying to find some trace of Tommy or Dottie. Word of the shooting had reached the west side speakeasy a little more than an hour after it took place. Shootings were not that uncommon. The smaller gangs had been fighting among themselves since Prohibition began. So she paid little attention to the gossip until she heard a man mention Tommy's neighborhood. "Hey, mister. What did you say?"

The man turned in his chair and Fran recognized him as a local policeman. "Well, it's just a rumor. If there's any truth to it, though, there could be the biggest mob war in history."

"What? Where?"

"You know that club on the east side? Dottie's?"

Fran nodded.

"Down the street from there. Some boys shot up a bunch of Rocco Petrelli's men. One or two guys got it and some of their girlfriends got killed in the crossfire. The whole block is cordoned off."

"Oh, Jesus," she whispered softly. The glasses she had been carrying slipped from her hands and shattered at her feet. Tommy was going to take Dottie to dinner at Angelo's just down the street from the speak before they came to Le Paris to celebrate. She had to grab the back of the man's chair to steady herself against the rising tide of panic.

After a moment, she whirled around and trotted to the front door. "Cockeye, I need your car."

Without hesitation, he produced the keys from his pocket. "Sure, Miss Barrey. What's the matter?"

She snatched the keys from him and was halfway through the door. "If Max comes in, tell him there's trouble on the east side."

"Hey, your coat!" he called after her, but she waved him off impatiently.

The policeman had been right about one thing. The entire block north of Dottie's was still closed off. Fran had to make a quick detour to reach the club. As she stepped inside, the suppressed atmosphere hit her like a physical blow. Bob Harris and his band were playing, but only half heartedly. There seemed to be none of the usual light hearted festive exuberance. It felt more like a funeral parlor than a nightclub.

She grabbed the door man, Joey Russo by the arm. "Joey, what's going on?"

"Oh. Hi, Miss Barrey." Joey frowned and examined his shoes. "I dunno. Nobody's saying nothing… I don't think they want the shooters to know if they hit or missed just yet."

"Nobody's said anything?"

Russo shook his head sadly.

"Who was shot at?"

"Miss Barrey—"

She shook Joey's arm. "Who, dammit!"

Russo frowned and again bowed his head to address his shoes. "Tommy... Dottie... Tano... Marie... Tony... and Connie. They was comin' back from dinner."

"And nobody knows if they're alive?"

He shook his head again without looking up.

"Oh, God," she groaned. Her heart wanted to give one last thunderous beat and stop. "This can't be happening. You know of anybody in city hall who might be able to tell me? Any of Tommy's friends?"

Russo shrugged helplessly. "I don't know Tommy's connections, Miss Barrey. If they don't want the shooters to know..." He shrugged again. "All we can do is wait."

Fran drove around the neighborhood feeling like she was caught in a bad dream, trying to think things through. Nobody would try hitting one of Rocco Petrelli's captains without the backing of one of the other big gangs. That meant Conway or Max's uncle. There was no one else big enough.

She shook her head to get rid of the thoughts. She didn't know enough about mob politics to start making guesses. All she knew was that someone had shot at her two best friends and no one seemed to know if they were dead or alive.

She returned to Le Paris and locked herself in her office and began making phone calls. It seemed no one knew anything more than poor Joey Russo.

Fran had put a sizable dent in a bottle of imported Irish whiskey and had smoked half a package of cigarettes when her private telephone rang. Only a handful of people had that number.

"Hello?"

"Miss Barrey?" the voice was vaguely familiar.

"Yes. Who is this?"

"This is Frankie."

It took a second for a connection to be made through the whiskey. "Tommy's Frankie?"

"Yes, ma'am. Now, what I have to tell you is for your ears and your ears only. You understand that?"

"Yes."

"T and The Deuce are okay. They're some place safe, but there's no phone there. T sent me to call you up because he knew you'd be worried."

"Oh, thank God," Fran breathed a huge sigh of relief. The weight of the world had been lifted from her shoulders. For a brief instant, she felt faint. "Is there anything I can do, Frankie?"

"Just don't say nothing to no one. Not to Max or Rocco—not even to your mother… And if you could keep your ears open for the latest gossip. Can you do that?"

"Sure. Sure thing, Frankie."

"Okay. One of them will probably be in touch tomorrow. Goodnight, Miss Barrcy."

"Goodnight, Frankie. Thank you," she said, but the line was already dead. She supposed that Frankie had a lot of things to do. Fran sat back and stared at the bottle of whiskey. "And you had the nerve to scold Tommy for caring about someone too much?"

* * *

They slept very little that night. Tano, in spite of his wound, Joe Mitchner, Marty Rossini and Frankie Sirico worked in shifts keeping guard outside the house. Connie Banks slept in the guest room. It was about three in the morning when Tommy got tired of tossing and turning, thinking everything through. He slipped out of the bed carefully so as to not wake Dottie, grabbed a robe and went downstairs. Yeah, it was a helluva way to spend the first night in their new home together.

He opened the front door and stepped out on to the porch. "Tano, Frankie. C'mere." He led them inside and motioned to them to make themselves comfortable. "How's the arm, Tano?"

"Eh. It'll make it a little harder to fight all the women off, but," he sighed bravely, "I shall have to endure."

Tommy smiled and clapped a hand on Tano's good shoulder. "Thanks. I needed a chuckle. You sure you're up to prowlin' around all night?"

Tano spotted a bulge in the pocket of Trent's robe. From the size and shape he could tell it was a small hammerless automatic pistol. "Yeah. I'm fine."

"I'm sorry about the girl, T," Frankie said.

"I'm sorry for all of them. But hell, she was barely twenty."

"Come on, pally," Tano said. "You can't see everything that's coming."

"I know," Tommy said. "And that's exactly how people wind up dead in this business."

"What can we do for you, T?"

Tommy lit a cigarette and drew them together in a conspiratorial huddle. "They're gonna try to nab Dottie."

"How do you know?" Frankie asked.

"If they want me, that's what they'll do. To draw me out in the open. God only knows what Eddie told them. And you know Dottie. She won't be able to keep herself away from the speak forever. Now, you two are the only men on the face of the earth I can trust with this. This woman is going to be my wife. The mother of my children. Keep her safe."

"I'll give my life, T."

"They won't get within a block of her," Tano pledged.

"I know." He sighed and sat back. His side was throbbing again. "The breaks are with us, guys. They botched the hit so now they have to worry about us *and* the other crews. And Hymie's not going to lie down and ignore this either. Conway thinks he will, but he won't. He doesn't know Hymie. I do. This war is going to disrupt *everybody's* business and Hymie won't sit still for it."

"How bad's it gonna be, T?"

"This is going to be the biggest thing to ever hit the city. Probably any city. It's gonna be bloody and nasty, but it's gonna be over quick."

34

Do you think this place is safe?   On the second floor, just outside the entrance to Dottie's old living quarters above the speakeasy there was a landing with a high railing. Tommy had stationed two soldiers there wearing long coats to hide their weapons. He had called Joey Russo in early and he was seated near the front door with a machinegun within easy reach. He also knew that Frankie and Tano were packing at least two pistols apiece and Connie was carrying a third for Tano in her purse.

"It'll be safe for now as long as you can keep the high-profile customers coming in. Nobody'd bomb the place if they thought it was full of politicians and coppers." He reached a hand out to touch the side of her face.

"Hi," a voice said sleepily. They all turned to see Julia Pennington approaching the table. She was rubbing her blurry eyes and her hair was a mess. It looked as though she had slept in her clothes.

"Julie? What are you doing here?"

She sat with them and stifled a yawn, "When I couldn't get a hold of you or Connie last night, I was worried. So I slept in the dressing room in case you came home."

"Oh," Dottie said and hugged her. "Everything's okay, kid."

"I know. It's just—" she trailed off again and rubbed her eye some more. "Poor Marie. And someone came in last night and said that Fat Eddie was a rat and he had killed himself."

"What?" Tommy had figured Conway or Patsy would have gotten to him first.

Julia nodded sleepily. "They said he cut his wrists. And with all the talk of shootings and bombings, I was worried. You guys okay?"

She looked around the table at Dottie, Tano and Connie, each one of them nodding in turn. She put a hand on Tommy's leg. "How bad you hurt?"

"Just a scratch, Jules," he said and gave her hand a squeeze. "Don't worry about it."

"T?" Frankie called from across the speak. "Telephone." When Tommy was close enough, Frankie put a hand over the mouth piece and whispered, "Tony's sister."

"Oh, shit," Tommy muttered. He sighed, braced himself and took the receiver. Florence Palermi was weeping on the other end.

"You bastard," she said.

"Now, Flo—"

"You bastard," the girl repeated. "You killed my brother. It's your fault. You killed my brother and my friend Sarah."

"I didn't. I—"

"I hope you rot in hell." The voice said and the line went dead. Tommy put the receiver back on the cradle and frowned at it for a long time.

He pulled Frankie close and spoke softly, "Look, make sure her family's taken care of, okay? And make sure the funeral arrangements are all settled."

"Sure thing, T."

"Who was it?" Dottie asked.

"Just one of my fan club," he murmured. He returned to the table and put a hand on Dottie's shoulder. "I've gotta run. I think everybody should clear out of here until closer to opening time, okay?"

"I can make breakfast for everybody," Julia offered.

"I can't stay. I've got things to take care of. Thanks anyway."

"Aw, Tommy," Dottie teased, "She's always wanted to make breakfast for you."

Tommy grinned and put a hand on each of Dottie's shoulders. "I'm sure she has." He gave her a kiss. "I'll be back in a little while, okay? Don't worry about me."

Dottie winked. "I'll try not too."

"That's my girl."

* * *

It was an hour later when Tommy used the employee's entrance of the Carlisle Hotel to slip into the building and up four flights of the back staircase. When the body guards let him into Rocco Petrelli's suite, he found the other caporegimes gathered in a circle with Rocco, Patsy and Marco Messinio.

"Hey, there's the kid!" Rocco grinned and stood up to greet him. "Boy, those lousy bastards gave us a start, Tommy. But we'll show them what's for, won't we?"

Tommy nodded and joined the circle. "So what's the latest?"

"It's been quiet in my neighborhood," Art Gagliano said.

Felipe Migliore reached for a cigar. "I had a truck hijacked last night. They shot the driver like a dog." He shook his head sadly, "Had a wife and three kids."

"Tsk," Joey Bones said, shaking his head. "Animals. Other than that and them bums firebombing Fat's and Ruby's, it looks like they weren't too well organized."

"Jesus Christ," Art said. "The place is full of kids. Why didn't they just go blow up the college, fer chrissakes."

"Well," Bones said, "The place was closed at the time, thank God. I don't think these guys have their shit together."

"Well, let's not start underestimating Conway," Patsy cautioned. "He's shrewd. He's not dumb. He won't underestimate us and we shouldn't do the same. He's already hiring cops from the 10th precinct as his bodyguards."

"He's sure that you want me to send him to see the Spano brothers," Tommy said. "He's had that idea all along. He's got soldiers scattered in little apartments all over the area. My guy on the inside could only give me three of the addresses."

"Boy," Rocco said, "This guy you got sure gives good information."

Tommy shrugged. "We grew up together."

"I don't mean anything by it, Tommy," Marco Messinio said putting up a cautionary hand, "but why was the hit so amateurish?"

"I think they planned to hit me at Dottie's, but when they found out I wasn't around, they went looking for me. They only have one real pro but everybody over there is afraid of him. Even Conway's afraid of him."

"Oh, yeah," Patsy said. "That punchy."

"That's him. His name is Liam McKee. Ex-prizefighter, ex-army war hero. They lost count of how many men he killed during the war. When he came home, he worked as a freelance hitman until Conway saved his brother's life. He's been sworn to him ever since."

Rocco plucked the cigar from his mouth, "This guy's some kind of screwball, huh?"

"A fanatic. Too many rounds in the ring and too much blood on his hands. He's not running on all cylinders. His outfit was trapped in this forest by the Kaiser's men. They were outnumbered three to one, but McKee somehow got them out."

Rocco chuckled, "What, you read this guy's biography?"

Tommy shrugged again. "Just a little research. I remember there was an article about him in the sports pages when he came home from the war, before he started hiring himself out as a killer. And compared to this guy, *everyone* looks like an amateur."

Patsy leaned forward to take the floor. "Conway's been making overtures to the other mobs. He's been trying to convince them that they'd be better off under his patronage than they are with us or The Jew. He knows he doesn't have much of a chance without their help. He's gonna lose money on this war too and he's out numbered. If he can win all of Hymie's gangs over to his side, Hymie won't have the muscle left to step in. Whether or not any of the other gangs go along with him, he's gonna send McKee to hit Rocco. I'd bet you whatever you want. He thinks if he can show his muscle and disrupt the power structure, he can at least

221

win the peace."

Tommy nodded. "Sure. He wants to hit Rocco, but he knows that won't be easy. He's got his finger on me because he thinks the Spano hit shows I'm the family muscle. He'd love to hit Rocco and take me along the way. This guy doesn't really want peace, but it's the least he will settle for. He'll rebuild his arms and start it again because he's convinced we're gonna rub him out and take over his territory."

"You know what?" Rocco said, taking the cigar from his mouth. "The cocksucker's right now."

* * *

Sean Conway had made his wartime headquarters in the warehouse on 132nd and Lincoln Avenues, in the heart of his territory. He could not have found a better strategical place to run his war. A short drive from his home, the warehouse was within two blocks of the 10th precinct police house and his best nightclub. The windows of the first floor had all been painted black from the inside to prevent the stray prohibition agent from looking in. The windows on the second floor, from his office and from the catwalk above the warehouse floor, gave a sweeping view of the neighborhood. With his armed look-outs parading along the catwalk, it would have been impossible for anyone—prohibition agents or otherwise—to stage a raid without being spotted. Two ladders provided escape routes in the event a raiding party was spotted. The first was in the warehouse proper, the second in Conway's office, both leading to the roof. From there a crude drawbridge could be lowered to the roof of the textile factory across the alley. Once the men were across, the drawbridge could be disengaged and pulled over to prevent anyone following. By the time a raiding party was inside Conway's warehouse, all his men would be safely inside the neighboring building.

Charles Coneer, the 10th precinct police captain had been elected by his fellow officers and the ward aldermen to voice their concerns to Conway. For years they had been dreading a clash between any of the three big mobs and now it was up to Sean Conway to convince Coneer to convince the others to remain patient.

"But what the hell were you thinking?"

"That I can win," Conway was seated behind the desk in his shirtsleeves, his coat hanging lazily over the back of his chair. He had his feet upon the desk and the chair rested on its hind legs, appearing cool and confident.

"Everyone's tired of these greedy bastards like Rocco and that Jew-fuck."

The police captain seemed less secure as he paced in front of Conway's desk. "You realize this puts every lawman in the state in a bad spot regardless of whose side he's on?"

Conway placed his chair on all four legs and rested his elbows on the desk blotter. "I understand that, Charlie. But everyone knew that Rocco had something big up his sleeve. He's been planning on a takeover for a long time. It was a matter of kill or be killed. Believe me."

"Look, Sean," Coneer sat in the chair on the opposite side of the desk and calmed down. "You know we're all grateful to you for keeping the dagos from setting up their whorehouses here. And we'll always be grateful for that. But we're powerless to help you now and as long as this war lasts. Nobody will be tipping you—or anyone else, for that matter—about raids."

"Because they're going to wait to see who comes out on top?"

"Ah, hell man. It's never occurred to you that there are some who are loyal to you because you *pay* them, and not because of the things you've done for the district? There's a lot of men who are more loyal to a handful of cash than they are to any man. And they're all going to mind their own business until this thing is over. Then they'll be loyal to whoever is left standing."

"Okay," Sean said and sat back in his chair. He formed a pyramid with his fingers and thumbs and placed the point to his lips. "Spread the word through your precinct: A hundred dollar bonus for any tips that come in time for us to take precautions."

"That will cost you a fortune!"

"No it won't. In four weeks, Rocco and all his captains or chiefs or capos or whatever he calls them, will all be dead and buried."

* * *

Joey Russo considered himself now to be Guard of Dottie's Club and he took the job was seriously as any of the King of England's Royal Palace Guards might. He insisted on being present when anyone was in the building, even after hours and in the hectic days and weeks following the outbreak of war, this meant many trips to the club. Fran Barrey noticed how tired the poor man looked, and she smiled sweetly as she entered the club. She patted Joey's face. "You poor thing. You look all-in. Why don't you ask Dottie if you can move in here?"

Russo shrugged, "I'd rather not be stuck inside when Conway decides to burn it down. But I want to make sure that I'm around in case anyone starts any trouble while Ms. Dottie or Tommy are around."

Fran smiled. "You're a good man, Joe."

"Thank you, Miss Barrey." He stepped aside to let her through, "You're expected."

Gaetano Amato was seated at the piano lazily plucking a melancholy tune. Fran leaned against the wall, folded her arms and listened for a while. He was good. "Where did you learn to play like that?"

Tano didn't miss a beat, "The first broad I ever took to bed was a piano teacher."

Fran chuckled. "Fine. Don't tell me."

"—*My* piano teacher," Tano said with a grin. Fran laughed and Tano sounded indignant: "Well, hell, it was better than paying *money* for them lessons!"

She laughed again and put a hand on his shoulder. "Where's Dottie?"

"Upstairs. Connie's helping her pack her things. You want I should call for them?"

"No. Go on playing. I'll go up."

Tano paused and nodded towards the large heavy book she carried under her arm. "What have you got there?"

"Naked pictures of myself," she grinned.

Tano's eyes grew wide and he reached out to snatch the book, but Fran moved it away with a laugh. "No, no."

"Ah, phooey," Tano grunted and resumed playing.

She was still smiling as she moved to the stairs. Frankie Sirico was sitting on top of the bar with a rifle across his lap and a newspaper in his hands. "Hi, Frankie."

"Hi, mademoiselle. What's the good word?"

"Booze. What else?"

She knocked gently on the door of Dottie's living quarters and stepped in when she heard the voice say "Come in."

She let herself in and followed the noises until she found Connie

Banks loading a pile a clothing into a box while Dottie was sorting through framed photographs in the bedroom. "Frenchie!" Dottie exclaimed. "Come to help?"

"Sure. What can I do?"

Dottie looked around her and sighed so that it blew a curl of hair out of her eyes. "I don't know. This is… strange. I've lived here all my life." She threw her hands up with a smile, "I'm not sure where to begin."

Fran stepped forward, placed the book on the bed and took the stack of frames from Dottie. "Here. Now go get me a box and all your towels."

"Towels?"

"Yes. You use them to protect the frames when you put them in a box. That way you're packing two things at once. See?"

"Oh. Makes sense to me." She nodded to the oversized book Fran had placed on the bed. "What have you got there?"

Fran smiled, "In Florida, I told you I would show you my scrapbook."

"Oh!" Dottie and Connie both dropped what they were doing and sat close together on the edge of the bed with the scrapbook balanced on their knees.

"Here," Fran said, leaning over and opening the scrapbook for them. She selected a page with two of her nude postcards on it. "What do you see?"

A great deal of thought had gone into the poses on the postcards. Dottie remembered hearing someone speak of balance, symmetry and other similar things when talking about paintings and she could see it applied to the postcards. In the picture Fran sat in a regal high-back chair, holding a large bouquet of roses to her bare chest.

"It's beautiful…" Connie said, but she sounded unsure of herself.

"Thank you. My American friends have vindicated me," Fran Barrey was smiling triumphantly. "Do you understand? When a woman sees a *dirty* picture of another woman, she sees obscenity. But when she looks upon a work of art, she sees beauty."

The girls nodded. They flipped the scrapbook to the beginning and found a whole series of magazine advertisements featuring photos and drawings of Fran Barrey. Connie stopped when she came to an ad with Fran sitting at a desk writing a letter. Though she couldn't read the French, it was apparent it was an ad for a pen. In the photo, Fran looked all of sixteen years old.

"How old were you?"

Fran leaned over, "Oh, yes! That was one of my first appearances in a national magazine. I was so proud. I was thirteen." They perused through the scrapbook and found that the first third was filled with similar advertisements. The last section of the scrapbook was devoted to newspaper and magazine articles about Fran's career as a singer. The smallest section was the section of nudes in the middle. She had kept only her favorites. Connie was surprised by how tasteful they were. From the way people talked about Fran Barrey, she would have thought the pictures would have been pornographic in the most vulgar terms.

"How do you become a model... like that?" Connie said and felt herself flush.

"I was thirteen years old, trying to break into show business as a singer and I answered an advertisement for models. And, as you can see, I spent a good three years singing in small clubs and modeling for magazine and newspaper advertisements: coffee, stockings, hats, wine, cheese... I think I appeared in an ad for almost everything. After three years or so, I was posing for an illustration—it must have been for coffee or tea, because I remember holding the cup—when one of the ad men came in to show me a letter.

"It was addressed to the ad company from Jean A. Mondell, one of the most famous of photographers. He was known the world-over for his landscapes as well as his work with nudes. In the letter he pleaded with them for an introduction to the young woman who had been appearing in so many of their ads.

"So, I arranged to meet with him and he took me to dinner. He was a very charming man and explained to me the nude as an art form. I was flattered, but I didn't believe it was the right thing for me until he took me to his studio, showed me some of his work and let me watch as he worked with another model.

"After a short while, I was convinced. We worked together for nearly a year until our personal relationship got in the way. We broke it off professionally and personally. But by then I was famous enough to pick and choose any modeling job I wanted and I was singing in the brightest clubs in Paris. My face and my breasts were seen the world-over because of Jean's work and I was determined that my voice would be just as famous."

She smiled wistfully and shrugged. "But it was not to be."

"But you have a great voice," Dottie said.

Connie stopped turning the pages of the scrapbook, "Why don't you have Tommy and Bob Harris set you up with that label he records for?"

Fran shrugged shyly. "He asked me to sing on one of his records, but… I can croon old love ballads to a room full of people, but the thought of a microphone in a recording studio frightens me to death." She smiled, "It's silly, I know… I'm sorry. I'm keeping you from packing." She hopped off the bed and reached her hands out. "Get me some boxes!"

The girls were strangely silent as they sorted through a lifetime of Dottie's belongings. A photograph fell from between the pages of a book and Dottie knelt to pick it up. "My God," she whispered with a smile. It seemed as though the picture was ancient but it couldn't have been more than ten or twelve years old. The photograph was of a teenage Dottie and an eleven year-old Tommy Trent, standing outside of what was then her father's saloon. In the photo Dottie looked as though she was laughing and Tommy was grinning like a cat who had just swiped a bowl of cream. Through the window behind them she could see her ailing father shaking his head.

Fran and Connie leaned over her shoulder and smiled at the photograph. "You two looked good together even then," Connie observed.

"I remember that day very clearly," Dottie said softly and then shook her head at the ridiculous urge to cry. "You know he's taking care of all the funerals? Even Eddie's?"

* * *

The small apartment was in the heart of an overcrowded mixed neighborhood near Tommy Trent's base of operations. It resembled a tenement flophouse more than an apartment dwelling and likewise, the inside of the apartment looked more like an armory than anything else. The three rooms were crowded enough for the four men who would live there for the duration, without the masses of ammunition, bomb making equipment, the rifles, machineguns and pistols.

An ashtray on the small coffee table was overflowing and spilled onto a neatly typed piece of paper that had been delivered by "special courier" during the night. It was a detailed list of addresses. Fat Eddie's poolroom and the Ruby speakeasy had checks by them. Fat Eddie's furniture store and home had been marked out as no longer being necessary. The other addresses included the new brewery Tommy had shown Fat Eddie and Patsy Guarino, the apartment complex where Gaetano Amato lived and where, until the war started, Tommy had lived. Both were unmarked. It continued to list other speakeasies around the neighborhood including Dottie's, with a note 'Hit after hours.'

It was a detailed list that could keep the four men busy for months.

Angelo Corocco snorted after reading through it and slipped it into his pocket. "These boys think highly of themselves," he said. "Philsy will be interested in seeing this." He turned to the three other men. "Alright, pack up the gats and then make yerself comfortable. We'll give these mugs a homecomin' like no other."

35

A WRITER FOR THE HERALD EXAMINER LOST HIS job when he submitted the following editorial for publication:

> "For as long as anyone cares to remember, the mayor has repeatedly stated that there is no corruption at city hall and that the war against bootleggers is being won. One can only wonder where his honor is getting his information.
>
> Has he forgotten that he himself attended "Big Joe" LaCava's funeral, along with a host of other city, county and state officials? Did he not notice the grand reception given for Sean Conway, the second biggest bootleg kingpin in the city—a party given by his many close political allies? Nobody has noticed either, I assume, that

since the Amendment was ratified, there have been more than three hundred gangland murders in the city and only ten arrests and one conviction.

The crime commission estimates some twenty thousand speakeasies are operating throughout the county, and less than a hundred have been closed down by Prohibition agents.

A year and a half ago, when the gangland skirmishes exploded into a night of total war resulting in the Spano Massacre in the Washington neighborhood, every lawman and politician in the country vowed to bring such things to an end. Eighteen months later nothing has come of the much fanfared investigations.

And now a new rash of gangland violence is plaguing the city and this time it is total all-out war between the bootleggers. Gangs of armed men patrol the streets looking for each other to murder, oft times asking policemen on the beat if they've seen their intended victims. The random shootings, shoot-outs and bombings have become anything but random. A collegiate football star, a big swarthy tough-looking fellow, stated that he was too afraid to go out in public dressed in the new hat and graycoat he received for Christmas, lest he be mistakenly shot down by one of the marauding patrols of gunmen.

It is a sad commentary when a traveler heading into town asked for directions and was told: "When you smell gunpowder, you're there."

Our fair city, always known as being a rough and tumble town, has sunk to new lows, becoming an embarrassment to the entire country. Where else in the country, indeed in all the world, is such lawlessness aided so egregiously by those sworn to uphold the law?

It seems that since the local and federal law enforcement agencies are powerless or unwilling to stop the insanity, only an act of Congress can save our beloved city from permanent scandal. The Eighteenth Amendment and the Volstead Act must be repealed immediately."

It was no coincidence that the police department had put extra officers on the beat around the Carlisle Hotel. They were joined by roving pairs of Rocco's soldiers dressed in police uniforms who seemed to circle the block endlessly.

On the fourth floor, in Rocco's suite of rooms the hierarchy of his gang had begun holding regular meetings to coordinate their campaigns. Joey Bones had successfully sprung a trap for some of Conway's stick-up men. Conway's men had stolen two truckloads of beer from one of Bone's warehouses, only to have the police hijack them a mile further down the road. The shipment was back safe and sound in the warehouse.

Felipe Migliore handed Tommy a list of addresses. "Some of my boys raided two of the apartments your contact mentioned. They nailed all eight guys. And they found this."

Tommy read through the list and nodded slowly. "Thanks."

* * *

Frankie Sirico's telephone began ringing. "Get off me," he panted and tried to reach the phone. He was too far away. "Get off me," he said again. He wriggled his shoulders closer and tried again, but his fingers fell a few inches short. He repeated himself a third time and grabbed her firmly by the hips and lifted her to the side before depositing her on the edge of the bed.

As he spoke into the telephone, Alice Byrd stood up and slipped into her silk knickers. She turned, planted a fist on each hip and stuck her little pink tongue out at him. When he threw his shirt at her, she giggled.

When he hung up the phone, he frowned at Alice. "You dumb broad. Dintchew hear the telephone?" She gave a non-committal shrug. "Don't you realize with all the shit's that's going on, I'm on call twenty-four hours a day? It coulda been important!"

She was now watching out the window with her arms folded, coming as close to sulking as Alice Byrd ever came. Frankie frowned and slipped his arms around her waist. "Come away from that window. You want the whole world to see your tits?"

It seemed as though Alice wasn't quite bright enough to think of that. But—even though Frankie would never admit it—he loved her anyway.

She turned around and placed her forehead against Frankie's. "Frankie,

I have something important to ask you."

"Yeah? What's that?"

"Daddy's having a big party for his friends. There's gonna be all kinds of people my age there with their dates… I want you to come with me."

Frankie tried not to laugh. "Don't you think I'd be conspicuous?"

"What do you mean?"

"All those kids of your father's friends'll be bringing lawyers and coppers and politicians as their dates."

"Yes?"

"I think I'd stick out like a sore thumb."

"But Frankie—"

"Come on," Frankie said, but he was genuinely touched. It was something he was unaccustomed to. "I don't think your old man'd approve. I mean, his political opponents would have a field day if his daughter showed up at a swanky party with a guy who just did five years in the can."

Alice pouted. "But it won't be any fun without you."

Frankie kissed her and said, "Well, we'll see." He patted her bottom. "Now go t'bed. I gotta go out."

She crawled back into bed and watched him get dressed. As he pulled on his coat she said, "Can I come?"

"Nah. I gotta go whack someone."

"Oh," She said. After a pause, she smiled and waved, saying cheerily, "Have fun!"

Frankie stopped halfway through the door and smiled wonderingly at her while shaking his head. He was still smiling when he got into his car, checked his shotgun and drove away.

* * *

Flynn deftly picked the lock and pushed the door open just enough for Morse to slip inside. Flynn followed and carefully closed the door behind them, his hand on the handle to keep the bolt from making a racket. The two men stood there in the complete silence, listening.

They were moments away from striking a major blow for Sean Conway.

They stood like statues for a few minutes on either side of the door before nodding to each other that their eyes had adjusted to the low light level. They could now distinguish between furniture and walls.

Silently they stepped out of their shoes and made their way down the hall. The bedroom was on the left and Flynn could just make out the bottom of Tommy Trent's foot without stepping into the room. He smiled at Morse and crept in.

The important thing was silence. They were sure that Trent slept with a pistol under his pillow and another on the bedside stand. Morse could just see the shape of a Colt automatic by the lamp.

They lifted their tommyguns and opened fire. "Take that ya' bastard!" Flynn cried above the roaring machine guns.

After fifteen seconds, they stopped squeezing the triggers. The room was filled with smoke and feathers drifted through the air like falling snow. Though both men were smiling triumphantly, there was something wrong.

Morse stepped forward to rip the blanket away from Tommy Trent, but the store mannequin in the bed was so light weight that it moved with the blanket and crashed to the floor. "Oh, shit."

The two men looked across the room, expecting someone to burst out of the closet with guns blazing. "C'mon," Morse said. "Let's get outta here!"

They left their shoes behind as they ran into the hallway and made for the stairs. Flynn made a complete revolution to see if anyone was following, but he did it too soon to see Frankie Sirico step out of an apartment behind them and let loose with two quick shotgun blasts.

Both men flew forward, Flynn careening off the wall and landing on his back. Morse was reaching feebly for his machine gun. Flynn looked down the hallway to see Frankie walking towards them with a grin as though he were an old friend who hadn't seen them in a long time. His hands were opening a long bladed knife. It gleamed wickedly.

Flynn could not feel his legs and they would not move to propel him towards the gun that had flown from his hands. Morse was lying face down, still scratching at the floor, trying to reach his gun. "No, ya' don't," Frankie muttered and lifted Morse's head up by the hair. One sweep of his arm lay Morse's throat open from ear to ear. Flynn never realized that a human body could contain so much blood.

"Don't worry," Frankie grinned. "It don't hurt." He nudged Morse's corpse with his foot and asked it, "Does it?" He shrugged, smiled and turned back to Flynn, "See? He says it don't hurt."

The last thing Flynn saw before he closed his eyes forever was the silver flash of the blade as Frankie placed it under his chin.

* * *

"Mr. Petrelli! Mr. Petrelli!" The members of the press began clamoring as Rocco and his entourage appeared on top of the first landing above the wide spacious lobby of the Carlisle Hotel. They were all trying to talk over one another, but the questions were nearly all the same.

Rocco smiled patiently and motioned politely for them to calm down. "Mr. Petrelli, what can you tell us about the newest rash of gang violence plaguing the city?"

"What do I know about gang violence?" Rocco smiled. "I'm in the import business. It's just a bunch of maniacs out there."

Another reporter chimed in, "What do you think of the grand jury investigation regarding the charges of income tax evasion?"

"It's a lot of hooey, boys. They can rig statistics to prove anything and that's what they're trying to do. And they had to bring in a load of boys from Washington to do it… Why, they could probably come up with figures to prove that Shipwreck Kelly was a better fighter than John L. Sullivan."

The men all laughed. A photographer stepped forward, motioning cautiously with his bulky camera. "Sure," Rocco said. "Get me from this side, though. This is my best side." Several photographs were snapped of the dapper man in his pearl-gray hat and long coat. He managed to look like a big friendly lug.

One of the braver reporters among them stepped forward, "What do you think of the accusations that you arranged the Spano Massacre? Is this new wave of violence related?"

"Ah, that's bunk, too. I'm just a business man is all."

Another voice spoke, "Why do you think the Treasury Department is after you?"

"I dunno. If you boys could find out, I'd be appreciative." Rocco grinned, "A thousand bucks and a big box of cigars for the first one of you to get the dirt on them."

The reporters laughed. A small man forced his way to the front of the crowd. "Is it because of your charm and good looks?"

"Could be. Could be they want to seize my yacht and go fishing." They all laughed again. Rocco and his entourage began moving as one. "But, sorry, boys. I have an appointment with the dentist."

The voices began crowding each other again as the reporters tried to get one last comment. "Ah, my public," Rocco sighed while grinning at one of his bodyguards. "They can't get enough of me."

* * *

Pat Michelson was startled by the party being held in Conway's office. As he stepped in, a champagne cork whizzed past his right ear. "What goes on?"

Conway was grinning with a cigar clamped between his teeth. He had a crowd of men around him, all in high spirits. "We hit Art Gagliano this morning." He poured out the champagne and raised his glass. "One down, five to go!"

"Cheers!" the men cried in unison.

Conway tugged at one of his sleeve garters and laughed. "A couple of the boys stumbled onto him coming out of one of his bookie joints. Never knew what hit him!"

"Well, I hate to bring bad news," Michelson said, "We missed Trent again."

"Eh. T'hell with them. After ole' Artie gettin' hit, they'll soon be on the run when they find out I just made a deal with Careli."

"You did?"

"Mm-hmm. He's jumping ship. Just Rocco and the old Jew don't know it yet. And with him comes a third of the territory that used to belong to the Spanos. All Hymie has left is Doyle's gang and his own handful of men. And it gets better..." He handed a glass of champagne to Michelson. "You know that French whore Hymie's nephew's so hot for?" Michelson nodded vaguely. Conway grinned, "Rumor has it she's doing Trent behind Maxie's back. He might set this Trent kid up for us. And with Maxie on board, before you know it, all of The Jew's political friends will be our friends." He pointed to Michelson's champagne glass. Michelson regarded it without enthusiasm. Conway chuckled again. "You know, you spend so much time brooding, I bet there's a Scotsman in your woodpile." He nudged the bottom of Michelson's glass. "Here. It's a good day, Pat. Drink up."

"I don't think we should let up on them."

"Oh, hell no." Conway emptied his glass and sat on the corner of his desk. The glass clanked against his desk top as he set it down and jabbed a finger at Michelson. "Don't get me wrong, Pat. I'm not getting soft. I still intend to start hammering away at every money making operation Rocco has. The more we can strangle his cash-flow, the more pressure he'll have."

"I think we should call for Liam." He noticed Conway winced when he mentioned the name. "We're on the verge of taking the upper hand, we oughtta really start putting it to them."

"Where's Liam now?"

"He's still babysitting that speak for you."

Conway considered it for a long moment. "Let him be for now."

* * *

As they charged into Jimmie's restaurant, George Hoffman only caught a glimpse of Liam McKee as he ducked behind the old antique bar. As the others surged forward with their axes swinging, he motioned to the tired chef behind the kitchen window. "Get him." The stubble-cheeked chef raised his eyebrows in surprised and the cigarette drooped from his lips. Hoffman pointed to the bored looking waitress, "Her too."

A police officer grabbed her by the elbow. "Getcher paws off me," she sneered. "I'm goin', I'm goin'." The officer led her outside to the waiting wagon.

The "secret" door to the speakeasy gave way with only three forceful blows from the axes. The other agents and officers surged in, identifying themselves loudly over the rising panic inside.

Hoffman went to the antique bar. "All right, you—" but there was no one there. He stared at the floor, puzzled. He never saw Liam McKee materialize seemingly out of nowhere behind him with a pistol in each hand. McKee needed only one shot, which he placed squarely in the back of Hoffman's head. The agent's body pitched forward like someone in a Mack Sennett comedy having a rug yanked out from under him.

McKee whirled around and into the street. The policeman who was putting the girl into the back of the wagon never got his hand to his belt.

He fell dead with two holes in his chest. His partner returned fire but was shot down before he got the third round off. McKee scooped the waitress under one massive arm and placed her gently on the ground before pushing her towards the anonymity of the gathering crowd across the street.

He whirled around again and walked over the hood of a touring car without apparently exerting himself. From the other side of the car he exchanged fire with the agents inside the restaurant.

He took four steps backwards into the street. A truck roared past and Liam McKee was gone.

Sean Conway's bulldog was on the loose.

36

She was known as Carol Sage and she had known Rocco Petrelli since the days when he worked in The Victoria, the most luxurious and exclusive bordellos of them all.

Now she was madam of the old Victorian building which had been servicing only the richest and most influential men for more than three decades. It was a grand life for her now, since she had surpassed the age where she'd be expected to service anyone other than the oldest and dearest of friends. She simply took care of the girls and made sure the guests helped themselves to the buckets of French champagne and caviar that stood prominently on the banquet table in the grand lounge where the customers could mingle with the girls before making their selections and retiring to the girls room.

Someday she would retire altogether and find a house by the ocean with a long stretch of white beach as its backyard where she would live out the rest of her days. She had already chosen Georgiana to take her place when she retired. Though Georgiana preferred women, she was an expert at fulfilling the needs, wishes and desires of the powerful men who came to The Victoria for escape.

Georgiana saw, just as Carol did, that the stocky man with white hair in the expensive graycoat who had just entered the Victoria was more of a traditionalist. There would be no need for exotic costumes or role playing with this one.

They watched as the newcomer handed his wallet to the bouncer, who examined some of the contents and handed it back. The bouncer politely smiled and led him towards Carol. "Ma'am?" the bouncer said politely.

"Yes, Louis?"

"This is Judge Clarence Carter."

"How do you do?" She extended her hand to the bespectacled man and he took it, bent low and placed a kiss on it.

"I have heard good things about you, ma'am, from Senator Whitehead."

"Really? How delightful! May I introduce Georgiana?"

The man repeated the polite gestures with Georgiana.

"Shall I issue him a card, ma'am?" Louis asked. No one could partake of the pleasures within The Victoria without a membership card.

"Of course!" Carol smiled. "Any friend of the Senator's is a *dear* friend of mine."

They had not noticed the other man who entered until he was a few steps away. He seemed like a giant compared to the stocky judge. His eyes were very dark and his nose was crooked, remnants of being broken many times. He had a cauliflower ear.

When he was behind the judge and the bouncer, the judge removed a revolver from his coat and shot the bouncer twice in the chest before stepping out of the way. A woman who had been escorting a customer up the stairs to the private rooms above screamed. Carol and Georgiana were held fixed with terror.

The large man produced a shotgun from beneath his long coat and calmly leveled it at Georgiana. He shot her in the face from about twelve inches away. Georgiana's beautiful face disintegrated and Carol was vaguely aware of one of Georgiana's teeth bouncing off her cheek.

Without moving his feet, the large man swiveled and shot Carol in the face. She fell backwards over the divan and was still.

He looked around the lobby as his accomplice went to the front door to keep watch. Through the large curtained doorway was the lounge. The customers had started scrambling in every direction the moment the shooting started. They thought it was a police raid.

The lounge was empty when the large man entered. He went into the ladies' powder room where he found Senator Whitehead hiding with a young prostitute in one of the immaculate stalls. The large man smiled at the Senator, grabbed him by the throat and tossed him across the room. He cocked the shotgun once more and dragged the girl out by the hair. He threw her to the floor and put a foot on her stomach. Her eyes were wide with terror as he forced the shotgun barrel between her breasts. "No," she pleaded trying to cringe away from the cold gun barrel against her flesh.

He smiled and moved the shotgun away. For a brief instant the prostitute thought she had been given a reprieve. She tried to clutch her robe shut but the gunman kept his foot on her stomach, a slight deranged smile as his gaze moved from her naked chest to her face and back again. With a surprisingly sudden movement, he swung the gun down again, placed it against her lips and squeezed the trigger. The Senator screamed like a woman as the blood splattered him. "Don't kill me! Don't kill me!"

The large man smiled, tipped his hat politely and left the room. As he passed through the lounge again he overturned the banquet tables, showering the floor with wine, caviar and countless gourmet dishes. As an afterthought, he tore an expensive looking oil painting from the wall and tossed it onto the pool of champagne and caviar.

He turned the corner and stood at the bottom of the lavish staircase. A woman was crouching on the middle landing. She too wore nothing but stockings, garters and a robe. The gunman reloaded, and took aim. The woman stood up, prepared to run, but before she could turn, the shotgun blast caught her in the belly and forced her backwards against the wall. She whimpered and was still.

As he started up the stairs, the man watching the door whistled loudly. "Liam!"

Liam frowned, and came back down the stairs. The police sirens were growing louder. He had been hoping to have enough time to tour the rooms upstairs, but he knew The Victoria had an alarm wired directly to the police station. "Oh, well," Liam sighed. "There's always another day."

* * *

The two bodyguards burst into the suite with their guns drawn when they heard the loud noises.

Rocco stood in the center of the room glowering at them, absently rubbing the hand he had just put through a wall. "What do you want? Scram!" The bodyguards said nothing and returned to their posts.

"I'm sorry, Rocco," Patsy said as sincerely as he could manage.

"Why it's not fair. Carol? Georgiana? Both of them?" Patsy nodded again as Rocco set himself into a chair. His rage had now dissolved into disbelief. "Why, it's not cricket! It's— That yellow rat bastard! That's not— No, it's—" His mouth worked silently for a moment as he searched for the words.

It was the first time Patsy could recall seeing Rocco speechless.

"That's playing dirty," Rocco finally managed. "They wanna play dirty? We'll play dirty. Patsy, I want this bum's head on a silver platter."

* * *

There was probably only one truck like it in the entire world. Rocco had designed it himself just for amusement only weeks after the amendment became law. It looked like any other canvas covered lorry but it was much more. The cab was protected by a windshield of inch-thick bulletproof glass. The canvas cover over the back was lined with pockets that held ceramic plates like a bulletproof vest. Behind this was a thin layer of metal as an added precaution. There were thin slits in the canvas and the metal—two on each side—to accommodate machineguns.

Rocco was one of the few people who knew of the truck's existence and he now gave it to Tommy Trent to use to guard a $200,000 shipment of Canadian whiskey that had come in by railcar. There would be little chance of Conway's men raiding the rail yard to steal the shipment; there would be too many police officers overseeing the unloading. But to pass up the opportunity of stealing $200,000 worth of Rocco's incoming whiskey would be an admission of defeat. Conway had purposefully targeted The Victoria because he knew it would shake Rocco up personally. That had taken the war from the business level to the personal level, a new and more dangerous plane. Two hundred thousand dollars worth of booze wasn't going to break Rocco financially, but it would make him feel insecure. "Rocco's getting nervous," Conway grinned, "Let's see how this makes him feel."

He assigned Peter Calan to select as many men as he needed to plan and execute the hijacking. Calan assumed there would be a lead car filled with gunmen to protect the caravan. Given the value of the shipment, he wouldn't be surprised if Rocco assigned Tommy Trent's crew to guard it. The lead car would probably keep a constant distance in front of the trucks, perhaps no more than thirty yards ahead, which would make the timing and placement for the hijacking critical.

Calan scouted the most direct routes between the rail yards and Rocco's nearest warehouses. To take the caravan on a route longer than absolutely necessary would be asking for trouble. He selected a perfect place only a half mile from the rail yards where a long straightaway turned sharply on a blind curve. On the left side of the road was a four foot ditch and on the right side a dense row of trees. His men on either side of the road would be able to fire freely at the trucks in the center without having to worry about friendly cross fire.

Timing would now be the important factor. He would have a car waiting to speed into the roadway and separate the lead car from the truck as the lead car disappeared around the blind curve. On the other side of the curve Calan set up two machineguns to take care of the lead car when it turned back to come to the caravan's aid.

With the lead car and its gunmen thus disposed, the other men, some in the ditch, some among the trees could open fire on the truck cabs without having to worry. During peace time when hijacking a truck from a rival gang, the drivers were usually given a chance to surrender, but this was all out war. His men would just move down the line of trucks shooting. Of course, if any of the drivers escaped, he wouldn't waste time hunting them down—not with the rail yards and the police a half mile away. The important thing was getting the shipment away safely.

He decided a second car would be necessary to block the road behind them, so none of the trucks would be able to back out of the line of fire. He had all the angles covered and Calan himself would drive the first car that would separate the lead car from the caravan of trucks.

When the caravan's lead car came into view on the long straightaway Calan started his car's motor. He could count three trucks behind the oncoming car growing larger and larger as the seconds ticked away. The lead car was coming up quickly on his right side now. He put the car in gear and began counting.

Three, two, one...

The car lurched into the roadway, narrowly missing the back of the caravan's lead car. The squealing of the truck's brakes filled the air. Calan could hear the lead car that had disappeared around the blind curve speeding up, away into the distance. "Must have seen the trap," he muttered, reaching for his shotgun.

Six men on either side of the first truck began firing. It took Calan a moment to realize that the bullets were bouncing off the first truck's cab. The noise was deafening, but then another louder sound joined them. Calan had seen just enough service in The Great War to recognize the sounds of heavy machinegun fire.

His men who had surrounded the truck were dropping like flies. Tongues of flame were spitting out of the sides of the first lorry. Calan was dumbfounded. It was so simple, it was unimaginable.

The two men who had been manning the trap for the lead car around the blind curve were now running towards Calan, on his left. Their eyes grew wide when they saw heavy machinegun fire pouring into the night from the sides of the truck.

A handful of Rocco's men emerged from the back of the truck and a brief second later there was more small arms fire in the distance. They had neutralized the car blocking the escape route in the distance.

Calan slipped out of the side of the car and used it for cover as he placed the shot gun over the hood and began firing. His two remaining men joined them. The heavy machineguns could only reach them if the truck maneuvered itself sideways on the road and they had Rocco's men pinned down.

Then the truck started moving towards Calan, gaining frightening speed. He could see the crazed look on the truck driver's face as he peered from behind his bulletproof enclosure. Calan didn't clear the road in time and as the truck hit the front end of the car, the back end whirled around and sent Calan flying through the air. He thought it was as though the hammer of Thor had swung down from the heavens and smashed into the middle of his back. He could hear one of his men screaming in pain. He could feel the earth rumbling as the trucks moved passed him on the road. The battle seemed as though it lasted hours, but it was all finished in less than two minutes.

37

SEAN CONWAY'S THREE STORY MANSION UNDERSTANDABLY RESEMBLED A fortress. Guards armed with rifles paced along the stone wall that ran the perimeter of the property. A car was parked sideways blocking the entrance to the drive. Two guards with machineguns stood on either side. Forty yards further along the drive, two more men watched the front entrance.

Hyman Amberg was unused to the indignity of being frisked, but he understood completely. The night that shots were fired at Tommy Trent, all the old allegiances and alliances were wiped away. He was frisked at the driveway entry; they would not allow his car on to the property, and frisked again on the front steps of the house. Yet another guard opened the door for him and led him inside the mansion. He marveled for a moment that he had not seen Liam McKee's face among the army of guards, and wondered if the stories about McKee making even Conway

244

nervous were true.

The guard led him down a long hallway and into a large library. Sean Conway stood from his leather chair behind the desk and motioned Amberg forward. "Hyman, come in."

Hyman seated himself in the leather chair across from Conway. He noted the guard stayed about ten feet behind him. A leather bound edition of The Dubliners sat opened on Conway's desk. He had noticed how Conway had been bent low over the book when he entered the room, as though he was having trouble seeing the words or understanding them. Amberg guessed the latter. "What can I do for you, Mr. Amberg?"

"Aren't you even going to offer me a drink first?"

Conway considered it for a moment and sniggered softly while nodding. "Sure." He crossed the room to the small bar and retrieved a tiny glass. "But if this is just some offer for making a peace, you'll excuse me if I'm not receptive." He filled the glass and stood by Amberg's chair. "Try this liqueur. Fresh off the boat from Belfast. The best in the world."

He returned to his seat behind the desk and folded his hands by the book. He watched as Amberg sipped the thick amber liquid and nodded his approval. "What can I do for you, Mr. Amberg?"

"The question is, what can I do for you, Mr. Conway?" Conway's brow furrowed. Amberg offered an explanation: "You remember a while ago… that bit of trouble I ran into?"

Conway nodded, remembering the newspaper photograph of Amberg's car sticking out of the side of a police station after two gunmen had tried to kill him. "Sure, I remember. The Spanos tried to have you clipped."

"Yes," Amberg smiled wistfully, as if he had enjoyed it. "But it wasn't Chris Spano. It was Rocco Petrelli who tried to have me killed."

* * *

Giuseppe Osso, aka Joey Bones thought back to the night Rocco had held a meeting for his gang at Welman Hotel, when he introduced Joey as the newest member of the Petrelli mob. It had been the right move. The other gang leaders, Careli, Cohen, Doyle and the Rosen-DeMeo faction would be left behind in the dust when the war was over. By joining Rocco Petrelli's mob and becoming his fifth captain, Bones had guaranteed himself a piece of the Conway territory.

Of the remaining small mobs, Careli was likely to fare the best. Bones knew that Hyman Amberg had convinced him to make Sean Conway think he'd play ball and join the war against Petrelli. Then Careli could do his bit to shake things up from inside Conway's ranks. For this, when the war was won, Careli might get an extra taste of the Conway turf. But the other mobs would just dry up and blow away.

But not Joey Bones. He'd still be around, operating the second largest crew in Rocco's army, which was just as good as being a small boss if not better.

The war was a tough one. Sean Conway had started playing dirty when he hit The Victoria. The place hadn't had a customer since the shootings.

If they wanted to play dirty, they'd play dirty. Joey Bones was on his way to meet with George Peterson, an explosives expert under Hyman Amberg's wing. They were going to turn 132nd Avenue into a pile of rubble.

Keaton's was just like any other bar in the city. The bootlegger's political influence had been so great from the very beginning that the number of blind-pig speakeasies hidden in the backs of ice cream parlors was only a fraction of the numbers in other cities. Ninety percent of the speakeasies were run in the open, just like pre-prohibition taverns.

Joey Bones was a short wide man and his shoulders seemed to span the doorway as he stepped into Keaton's. The place was dim, but it was before operating hours. He could just make out George Peterson sitting at the bar toying with some dynamite. "Hey, Joey!" Peterson grinned. "Come on in!"

Bones hung his coat up and joined Peterson at the bar. "Whatcha got there?"

"This?" Peterson held up the ingenious little device. "See, ya' put this on the underside of a truck, near the gas tank. Break the seal here and you've got ten minutes to get out of the neighborhood. Then the truck—and everything else in the garage—goes up like the fourth of July."

Bones nodded his approval. "Where and when?"

"Conway's got a garage on south Lincoln. He keeps about a half dozen lorries there. Lightly guarded early in the morning. We'll be able to slip this in with no problem."

Bones chuckled, "I'd like to see where he thinks he could get replacements for those trucks."

His chuckling was stopped abruptly. A thick wire had cinched around his throat and he felt himself—all two hundred forty five pounds—being lifted off the bar stool. His eyes wheeled back enough to just make out Liam McKee's face smiling down from behind him.

It didn't make sense! He was here under Hyman Amberg's protection. What was Conway's bulldog doing here?

Bones put his hands to his throat to try to loosen the garrote. There was no use. Liam McKee was too strong. His feet began kicking wildly, knocking over a bottle of juniper-juice gin and thumping into the suitcase of dynamite.

"Aw, shit!" Peterson wailed. "He's pissing all over!"

Bones' face was turning from red to purple as he managed to wriggle a revolver from his shoulder holster. Peterson leapt across the bar and grabbed the gun. A shot went wild and shattered a mirror behind the bar. Bones was thrashing wildly now, foam dripping from the corners of his mouth and snot bubbling from his wide nostrils.

Peterson's face was ashen, his eyes frightened. He got the gun away from Bones and panicked. He pressed the gun against Bones' side and squeezed the trigger three times screaming "Die! Die!"

Bones stopped struggling, but Liam did not release his grip from the ends of the garrote. Peterson dropped the gun and collapsed onto a bar stool, running his fingers through his hair. He hadn't expected dying to be so nasty.

It seemed like an eternity before Liam McKee loosened the garrote and let Bones slump to the floor. He was grinning at Peterson's sickened face. "You screamed like a girl," McKee giggled.

"Yeah, yeah," Peterson sighed. "Look, you get rid of him. Make sure he's never found. If Rocco finds out where he was when he disappeared, it's all over for Hymie." He stood up and pointed to the floor. He said weakly, "I'll start cleaning up."

38

Jack Billister owned the office building across the street from Dottie's speakeasy. It was a nice neighborhood now and it was becoming a nicer place to own real estate. After years of renting to small businesses that had trouble making the rent payments on time, he now had a reliable paying tenant renting the first floor of the office, a young lawyer who was on the rise in the city's political front.

The woman who visited Billister was tall and attractive, dressed in furs and pearls. She was, as the neighborhood youths might have said, a high-class dame. She introduced herself as a Mrs. Donald Frompton, the wife of a dentist who was looking to move his practice to the neighborhood. She seemed pleased when he told her the upstairs office was vacant and would make an ideal place for a dentist office. Billister showed her around the empty office with its wide front window, which could bear the dentist's name in letters large enough to be seen halfway across the block. The office was filled with her heavenly perfume. This dentist must be rich.

His suspicions were confirmed when she paid out four months rent in advance in cash. "It will take at least that long to move all the equipment over," she explained. "And we'll have to repaint first. Brighten up the place a bit."

"Of course, Mrs. Frompton," Billister smiled, taking the money from her quickly before she could change her mind. "If there is anything I could do for you, please let me know." He pressed a business card into her gloved hand.

The woman's green eyes appraised him hungrily. "I am sure that if there is anything you could *do* for me or my husband, we will let you know."

Billister had read a great deal into that statement and had waited eagerly for further development. But that had been four weeks ago. He checked with the receptionist in the lawyer's office down stairs, but she said she had seen no sign of either of the Fromptons. In fact, the only people she saw were two men in painter's overalls who had appeared four weeks ago. The funny thing was, she never heard any noise coming from the office upstairs. "If they're remodeling," she said, "They're doing it very quietly." She fell silent for a moment. "And one of those two guys... He's the size of a house and looks like he's had his nose broken a dozen times. I've only seen him once or twice, but... that guy gives me the creeps."

* * *

Since the war began, it had become a familiar thing to see the street outside of Dottie's lined with gunmen and police officers at closing time. If The Victoria, with it's powerful and influential patrons wasn't safe, Dottie's wasn't safe either. Frankie Sirico, Tano, Connie and Dottie were always the last to leave. They were all living in the new house Tommy had bought for Dottie. It was an arrangement that would last as long as the war.

Or until Liam McKee killed Tommy Trent.

The ranks were thinning. Art Gagliano had been killed early in the war, purely a target of opportunity. But the disappearance of Joey Bones hinted at a capable executioner and a carefully executed plan.

The remaining targets were Tommy, Marco Messinio, Felipe Migliore, Ray DeLaurentis, Patsy Guarino and Rocco himself. Although Conway's gang didn't have a military style chain of command, he understood it well. He had successfully removed two names on the list, hindered Rocco's business and made some of his political allies nervous with the raid on the Victoria.

Though greatly outnumbered, Sean Conway seemed frighteningly close to winning the war. All he needed was to hit one or two more caporegimes, sending Rocco's chain of command, and therefore his army into chaos and close up the places like Dottie's to send all the wet politicians and policemen to Conway's safer speakeasies.

Liam McKee sat in the darkness of the upstairs office across the street from Dottie's watching them leave. It was clear that they were expecting something and they obviously felt secure enough with their police protection that Joe Russo, the bouncer, was covering them from the doorway with a Thompson machinegun. Tano and Frankie were leading the girls to the car by the curb, looking each way for signs of trouble. They were an alert group. Dottie was wearing a tight gold lamé gown and a fur coat. McKee focused the field glasses on the great Dottie Deuce and smiled while thinking of the things he would do to her.

39

Jimmy Revel and the Reveleers were hot tonight. **Every night** Fran thought they were getting just a little bit better—an outstanding accomplishment considering how good they had been when she and Max hired them.

In fact, as she thought about it, Le Paris was hot tonight. They had already reached their goal of having the night club be second only to Dottie Deuce's. Even Rocco Petrelli had paid more than one visit to Le Paris and had promised to come back again. From where she stood by the bar, she could count three politicians and a couple of high ranking police officials. It wasn't a bad crowd: rich, energetic and thirsty. Fran grabbed Max Aaronson's elbow as he passed her. She pulled him close and whispered, "Who's that big guy at table twenty three?"

Max followed her gaze. "That's Liam McKee. Sean Conway's bulldog. He's got a contract on Rocco and Tommy."

"Oh?" An eyebrow arched high on her forehead. "Well, introduce me, won't you?"

Max studied her for a moment but her eyes betrayed no secrets. It was an art she had learned while modeling. "Okay." He led her to the table, paused and cleared his throat before speaking. "Liam, this is Fran. She runs the place with me."

"How do?" Liam McKee was a man of as few words as possible.

"Fine, fine. Uh, have one of the girls bring us some drinks, will you Max?"

"Sure."

Fran pulled a chair close to McKee and sat down. "When I saw you from across the room, I thought you were somebody else. A bullfighter I met in Paris."

"You French?"

"Yes."

McKee nodded that his suspicion had been correct. The girl with the light French accent *was* French. He thought for a long moment. The only girl he had ever truly loved was a peasant girl he had met in France during the war. She had the same sort of youthful face, but without the dark enchanting eyes. He breathed deeply through his nose. The French perfume reminded him of something.

"Yes," she repeated. "I came to America right after the war. Did you fight?"

McKee nodded.

When she realized he was not going to say anything, Fran gave her best throaty laugh, "You are remarkably like that bullfighter I mentioned. He didn't talk much either, but..." She placed her left hand high on his thigh and cooed something in French.

McKee studied her face, the dark eyes, the wide mouth with its full lips... It had been a long time since he had met a woman who wasn't frightened away by him. This one, in spite of the youthful face and its diametric mixture of innocence and mischief, knew exactly what she wanted. Her hand slid up to his groin. "He was remarkable," she translated. It had been a long time since McKee hadn't had to pay for sex or force it.

It took every ounce of her strength and self-control to not flinch away when he put his large sweaty hand on her leg. He swallowed hard and his cheeks twitched upwards into a smile. Fran smiled back and leaned close. "Are you busy later this morning?"

McKee shook his head.

"Well, my house is right behind the club here… Why don't you stop in for a few later on, huh?"

McKee hesitated until she squeezed lightly with her left hand. "Okay."

* * *

Fran Barrey's heart was lodged in her throat when the knock came at the door. She finished her drink with a vicious thrust of her head and then smoothed down the thin silk robe she wore. Liam McKee seemed to fill the entire doorway when she opened the door. "I was beginning to think you had changed your mind. Come in."

McKee examined the room as he stepped inside. It was apparent that this was no peasant. Fran Barrey had done well for herself in America. His eyes stopped on the portrait of her that hung over the fireplace. It was done by one of the most famous painters in Europe.

Fran closed the door behind him and motioned for him to go further into the room. McKee pointed a finger at the ceiling. "Don't go nowheres." He turned, thrust his hand under his coat and began touring the house.

When he returned to the parlor, he found Barrey with a cigarette holder in one hand and her other on her hip. She smiled. "The trusting sort, hmm?"

McKee shook his head and rushed to her, sweeping her into his arms and pressing his lips on hers. She kissed him back and then pulled away with a coy smile. She poked him in the ribs with her fingertips. "Do you always wear a bullet proof vest when you make love to a woman?"

He shook off his coat and let it fall to the floor. Then he removed the shoulder holster and placed it on the divan. Next the bullet proof vest came off. "That's better," she said returning to his arms. She nibbled at his neck and unbuttoned his shirt. As she tugged it out, a small revolver fell from the small of his back. He grinned, blushed and leaned over to pick it up.

When he looked up again, Fran was standing in the kitchen doorway, wiggling a finger for him to come closer. He pulled his undershirt off and tossed it to the floor and began walking towards her slowly.

Fran Barrey opened her robe to show she was bare beneath and let it fall at her feet. McKee was frozen in his place. His eyes had to go over her again and again as though her beauty was too much to drink in all at once. He had never seen such beauty; indeed no such beauty seemed possible. She took his breath away.

She backed up a few more steps and he tried to lick his lips but his mouth and throat were bone dry. Fran's eyes twinkled, and as though she had thrown the switch on some giant electromagnet, Liam McKee found himself drawn to her. He was unaware of his feet moving. He stood before her, her perfume gently caressing him, enveloping him in a milieu of fantasy. His eyes swept her again and again. He reached a massive hand out to touch her breast and found his hand hesitated, sure that the mirage would vanish if he touched it. She stepped into him to prove she was very real and very warm. Liam kissed her and his other hand found the small of her back and moved down. His hands had never touched such soft, smooth skin and he had to will them not to tremble. She unbuckled his belt and pulled it away.

Then she stepped away from him and he found himself still partially paralyzed by her beauty. Liam could feel his pulse beating in his ears. She moved behind him and nibbled his shoulder blade as her hand undid his trousers and slipped inside. "Like a bull," she cooed and then shoved a butcher knife into his back between the ribs.

For a moment he made no movement as she stepped away, her heart pounding so loud she thought even he could hear it. The black handle of the knife met the flesh of his massive back, and yet he hadn't fallen. She reached a hand forward, knowing she'd have to grab the knife and put it someplace else, but her feet dared not carry her any closer.

A scream of rage filled the house. Liam McKee grabbed the large dining table and without seeming to strain, he flipped it so it sailed across the room and splintered against the wall. The unintelligible bellow echoed through the house. It was not a cry of physical pain. It was a cry of anguish. He had been cheated. He had been lied to. He had seen the most beautiful of all creatures and had believed she wanted to give him that beauty. She had cast a spell over him with her beauty and for those brief moments he had been happy; he had wanted her to be his all. But she had lied.

Finally he moved. His hands whipped this way and that, trying to reach the knife blade in his back. He gave up the attempt quickly with a vicious snarl.

He turned stiff-legged to face her. His eyes were the devil's. His hands at his sides were massive claws ready to squeeze the life from her. He approached, slowly, menacingly, hate and rage and shame burning in him.

Fran Barrey had never been so frightened in all her life. She had tried to save Tommy Trent's life and she screwed up. And now she was going to die.

She whirled around, tripped over a coffee table and went sprawling. She felt rug burned from her nose to her knees, but that would be the least of her pain. Liam McKee would have his way with her while tearing her limb from limb. The devil in his eyes would be unleashed and he would make Jack The Ripper look like an amateur.

Scrambling on her hands and knees now, she could feel the floor shake with each of his stiff legged steps. He was closing in on her. The front door was too far away. Her eyes focused on the revolver on the divan. Her fingers had just closed around the handle when he grabbed her by the foot. She felt like a rag doll in his hands. He dragged her backwards and flipped her over onto her back with one hand. She raised the gun and pointed it at his belly. She squeezed the trigger and whimpered at the explosion and at the way he seemed not to notice the small neat hole that appeared on the left side of his chest.

He took three more lumbering steps, dropped to his knees before her and forced his way between her legs. His hands found their way to her neck. Tears of rage and shame dripped from his eyes and onto her breasts. Fran Barrey saw her life flash before her eyes, ending with the surrealistic vision of her head coming away from her body. She closed her eyes and fired again.

* * *

Sean Conway gave little thought to the sound of the car roaring around corner from 132nd Avenue onto Lincoln and speeding away into the night. Cars overflowing with drunken youngsters were commonly seen careening from one speakeasy to the next. He was waiting for the telephone to ring, occasionally exchanging anxious glances with Pat Michelson. For weeks now Liam McKee and William Powers had been casing Dottie's speakeasy from the office across the street. The two had arranged the most feasible plan they could manage. In the early afternoons Dottie usually arrived at the speakeasy escorted by only two men. McKee and Powers were to grab her this afternoon and burn the speakeasy to the ground.

With Dottie Deuce in their hands Conway could bargain with Tommy. It was no secret that Tommy was a soft touch when it came to dames. Especially his beloved Deuce. At best Conway could get Tommy to set Rocco up in exchange for the woman he loved. At worst, he could lure Tommy into the open and kill him. Then he'd let Liam do as he pleased with the "beloved Deuce." Conway chuckled at the thought that leaving The Deuce's mangled and defiled naked corpse on the charred remains of her front door step would do wonders for the morale in Tommy's neighborhood.

One of the guards from downstairs appeared at the door. "Mr. Conway?" His eyes were wide and his face pale. "You should come see this."

"What?"

The man's lips moved silently. He wiped a bead of sweat from his forehead and left. Conway and Michelson looked at each other questioningly. As they passed through the outer office, he motioned to Charles Coneer. "Come on, Charlie. Something's up." Coneer put down the magazine he had been lazily perusing and unbuttoned his holster.

Conway and Michelson let Coneer take the lead as they followed him down the stairs, through the warehouse and into the street. As they passed, a few of the men in the warehouse shrugged that they didn't know what was going on. Outside, one of the other guards was hunched over, hanging onto the brick wall, vomiting. The first guard pointed to something lying on the curb.

They stepped forward for a closer look. Conway's face went pale and his jaw dropped. His knees became watery.

"Oh, Jaysus," Michelson muttered, staring down at the body.

They had taken a sharp knife and laid Liam McKee's belly open from ribcage down to his belly button before tossing him out of the speeding car. His intestines left a grizzly trail into the street. McKee seemed to be staring up at them in surprise.

The most frightening thing of all, though, was they had somehow made Liam McKee cry before killing him.

Charles Coneer put a hand to his forehead and turned away. Conway could not take his eyes off the dead man. It didn't seem possible that anything could kill Liam McKee.

It was Michelson who broke the eerie silence. "I think I'm going to catch the first boat home and rejoin the revolution. It's safer there."

* * *

He held her close until she stopped crying. She had handled herself surprisingly well after she came to and crawled out from under Liam McKee's body. She couldn't remember emptying the gun. She only remembered firing three times, but there were four holes in the man's side and another in the wall.

After she had crawled out from under him, it took her a full three minutes to drag herself to the divan. There was no telling how long she sat there, holding her throat which was slicked with blood, waiting for the pain and numbness to leave her legs. The giant's three hundred pound frame had apparently pinched a nerve somewhere when he finally died and collapsed on her.

Then she forced herself to walk on needles and pins to the telephone where she called Tommy. Speaking took a great deal of effort and even then it came out as a raspy whisper. She had no idea why she chose to call him instead of Max, but her mind kept repeating Tommy's name as she lifted the receiver.

While waiting for Tommy to drive across town, she went to the bathroom, spat some blood and washed the dead man's blood off of her. Then she returned to the parlor, picked up her silk robe and slipped into it. Then she sat on the divan near the dead man's body and waited.

She had even kept calm as Tommy and his friend Gaetano carried the corpse from the house. When Tommy returned, he put an arm around her and led her to the bedroom and sat with her until the doctor arrived.

Tommy had waited outside in the hallway while his doctor friend examined her and then held a brief conference with him in the hallway. Tommy came back into the room and sat beside her. He put an arm around her shoulder and held her while she broke down and cried.

The tears were subsiding now and she sniffled into a handkerchief. "Better?" Tommy asked.

She nodded and then chuckled, though it hurt her throat. "Yeah. I don't think I'll ever want another adventure as long as I live."

Tommy smiled back at her and gave her a squeeze, kissing her forehead. It made her feel better. She thought it was no wonder that she loved him so. "Dr. Talbert says you'll be okay. He's gonna come by first thing in the morning and put a brace on your neck to cover the bruises and protect your throat. I want you stay home and outta sight until he gets here, okay?"

Fran Barrey nodded. "Do you think we should call Max?"

"No," Tommy said, shaking his head. "I don't think Max really ever needs to know about this."

The dark eyes lit up. "Really?"

"Sure. Guys like Liam have a habit of disappearing. It can be our little secret."

She sighed and put her head on his shoulder. "Thanks, Tommy."

Then he left her there to fall asleep which she did with surprising ease. When she awoke, Tommy and Tano were gone. Apart from a tiny bullet hole in the parlor wall and the fact that the dining room table was gone, there was nothing to show there had even been a struggle.

It was almost as though Liam McKee had never been there.

* * *

It was ten o'clock in the morning when William Powers arrived at Conway's office on 132nd. It looked as though Sean Conway and Pat Michelson hadn't slept in days. Powers didn't seem to be doing much better himself. He had been pacing the rented office across the street from Dottie's for hours, waiting for that creepy bastard to return. He resented the fact that McKee came and went as he pleased, running other errands for Sean Conway, while Powers had been stuck watching the comings and goings around the busy nightclub. But no one was brave enough to complain about McKee—especially not William Powers.

"Come in, Bill." Conway poured a cup of coffee for him and sat back in his chair. "Do you know where Liam is?"

"No," Powers said. "I thought we were gonna grab the girl today. He didn't say where he was going when he left last night. I assumed he was going to get laid and that he'da been back hours ago."

Conway believed him. "Okay, Bill. We're postponing plans for a while. I want you to go take a break. I know you been stuck up in that office for weeks. Pick a new partner and go back there in two days and just watch, okay?"

"Sure. What about Liam?"

"Don't worry about him. Just go home and get some rest."

"Okay, Mr. Conway," Powers grinned. Not having to work with Liam anymore was the best news he had had in a long time.

When Powers had left the office, Conway turned to Michelson. "He doesn't know anything. They nabbed Liam wherever he wandered off to last night. Probably one of Rocco's whorehouses…"

"So what do we do?"

Conway shrugged. "We can nab The Deuce if we need to later…"

"Hyman might be able to set Rocco up for us. I don't think Rocco's wise to him yet."

"I don't trust the old Jew. He's a rat bastard. I'd rather talk to Maxie. See if he is willing to help us get to Trent and Rocco."

"Does he even know Rocco?"

"Rocco's gone to Le Paris a few times." Conway stretched and yawned. "But anyway, I wanna see what Maxie's got up his sleeve. If he's that steamed up over the French tart…"

Michelson raised his eyebrows and motioned for Conway to go on with what he was thinking. "I've been shopping around for some torpedoes from outta town. Italians. So they'll think Rocco's behind it… I wanna size Maxie up before they hit his uncle."

* * *

William Powers was tied to a chair in the next room in the old abandoned building. He had proven to be a softie. Tommy was putting his coat back on as he addressed Tano and Joey Mitchner. "Give this guy a while, Joe. He'll come too and then slip out the window. I want you to keep an eye on him."

"Think he was telling the truth?" Tano asked.

"I think so. There's something in the way he described that dentist's wife. Something rings a bell. I'm gonna go check up on it." He turned back to Joe, "Meanwhile, keep tabs on what this joker does next. Where he goes, who he sees. Give Tano a ring-a-ding-ding to keep him updated, while I go see what's what."

"And then?" Tano asked.

"Well, it's like this… If I find what I think I'm going to find… We'll have Frankie take care of this mug. If not, we pull him back in for another little chat."

Again Tano could see the wheels spinning in Tommy's head. He raised an eyebrow and gave Tommy a stern expression.

Tommy grinned, "Well, if I am right…. I just figured out what happened to Joey Bones."

* * *

"Frankie?" Alice Byrd's child-like voice flowed over his shoulder. They were dancing to a slow number recently recorded by Bob Harris and His Orchestra. She was dancing on the tip of her toes to rest her head against his shoulder.

"What is it?"

"Daddy's running for the House of Representatives. Will you vote for him?"

Frankie leaned back to look at her and smiled. "Twenty times. A hundred times!"

Alice giggled and put her head back on his shoulder. After another long pause she said again, "Frankie?"

"Mm-hmmm."

"When are we gonna be married? Like Tommy and Dottie?"

"What are you talking about?"

"Well… you bought me this beautiful ring."

"I didn't buy it, you dippy dame," Frankie grinned. "I *stole* it."

"Stole, bought," Alice shrugged. "I think we should be married. Make an honest woman out of me."

Frankie laughed. "That's all your old man needs for his campaign. Vote for Byrd and his gangster son-in-law."

"Senator Whitehead's son-in-law is facing a murder trial."

"Yeah, but listen, Brainy: The Senator's daughter married that bum after the old man was elected. Besides, he ain't in the rackets. He's just a scumbag."

"Oh." There was another long pause while Alice Byrd tried to digest the information. "Then can we get married after Daddy wins?"

Frankie sighed and sounded exasperated. "Sure. If you're gonna keep needling me about it." But the way he squeezed her betrayed his gruff response. He was very happy.

The telephone rang. "Oh, phooey!" Alice exclaimed and stamped a foot. "Why's that gotta ring every time we're alone?"

"Watch your language," Frankie said, pointing a warning finger at her as he crossed the room. "Besides, if we're gonna get married, you gotta get used to it." He lifted the receiver and listened. He hung up without speaking.

Alice's eyes were directed towards the floor. "You gotta go bump somebody else off?" Frankie took her in his arms and gave her a squeeze. He didn't answer. "Well, do it quick, Frankie. I was gonna make you a special dinner tonight."

"All right. Then you and me's going to Dottie's to celebrate our engagement," he smiled.

Alice brightened, "Oh, Frankie!"

"Pending your father's election, sweet-cheeks."

* * *

Liam McKee hadn't been dead twelve hours when William Powers decided to disappear. He now supposed that he was the luckiest man alive, even though he knew he was hunted. He was one of the few people to ever survive being taken for a ride.

But then again, they hadn't really seemed too intent on sending him to join McKee after he had talked. In fact, he had slipped out of a window in the old abandoned building so easily, it was as though they had let him. Perhaps they had let him live until they could verify the information about the apartment across the street from Dottie's nightclub.

But nonetheless, if they ran across him again, he knew he would be a dead man.

At first he told himself he was being paranoid, but now he was sure someone was keeping tabs on him. They knew he was broke and too afraid to come out of hiding long enough to make many traveling arrangements.

Maybe they were going to nab him again.

After having been tortured once, he wasn't going to stick around any

261

longer to give anyone another crack at him. Powers sang like a canary about the dentist's office across the street from the speakeasy, about the long creepy hours with Liam McKee who would sit with an erection while spying on his intended victims.

Now it was time for Powers to get the hell out of the city anyway he could.

If Sean Conway wanted to kidnap Dottie Deuce, he'd have to do it himself.

Powers limped into the telephone booth, closed the door and deposited the coin in the slot. "C'mon, c'mon," he muttered, waiting for the operator to connect him.

A shadow fell across the booth. He turned in time to see Frankie Sirico with his hat pulled low over his eyes. Powers shrieked and threw his hands up in self-defense as the bullets crashed through the door. He was dead by the time his body slumped to the ground.

If Sean Conway wanted to nab Dottie Deuce, he'd have to do it himself.

40

Nate Cohen laughed when they called him a mob boss. "I'm a glorified saloon-keeper!" he'd say. He certainly didn't look the part of a gangster. He was short and chubby—a jolly cherry-cheeked fellow who might have been mistaken for a thirty year-old beardless Santa Claus. He never wore the stereotypical sharp suits or the snap-brim hats that were so fashionable among gangsters. Indeed, if he wore anything on his head, it was likely to be a yarmulke.

He ran a very nice little family style Yiddish restaurant and spent much of his time waiting tables there.

But looks could be deceiving. Nate Cohen was every bit as powerful as Sal Careli or Jimmy Doyle and was capable of being just as ruthless. And though he made a small fortune controlling the bootlegging and gambling operations over the southwest corner of the city and the southwest suburbs, they were only sidelines to him. The restaurant, which had been founded by his late father was his number one operation.

While the Rosen-DeMeo mob relentlessly stirred up trouble between the forever-warring Doyle and Careli gangs, Nate Cohen lived quietly and as peaceably as possible.

Apart from favors for his political allies and occasionally having to have someone taken for a one-way ride, Nate Cohen's neighborhood was last among headline grabbers.

Which was why, after the Conway-Petrelli war began and the short-lived agreements made at the Williamson hall were wiped away, Cohen's turf was the only neutral zone in the city.

He opened his restaurant three hours early and had his chef come in just long enough to prepare lunch for Sean Conway, his police captain bodyguard Charles Coneer and Max Aaronson. The three sat around a circular table with a red and white checked table cloth. Conway and Aaronson did all the talking; Coneer was simply there so that his presence would assure Conway's safety. A policeman being killed in the line of duty in a gun battle with mobsters was one thing, but to assassinate a police captain would send the city into a furor and every political backer would run for cover. Without their support, the gangs would be unable to operate.

So Charles Coneer simply ate quietly, not paying much attention to the conversation. His .38 was tucked securely under his coat on the one-in-a-million chance someone might try to get past him and hit Conway.

But it would never come to that. Sean Conway was secure in his new ally. "Well, I'll be honest, Maxie. There's been rumors for a while. Even your uncle's mentioned something about it."

Max Aaronson lowered his fork slowly. "You mean even he knew?"

Conway held up a hand defensively. "Just a rumor. It's no secret that this kid can't keep it in his pants."

"Yeah," Max said, taking a sip of wine. "That's Tommy."

"But," Conway said cheerfully, "guys who can't keep it in their pants are easy to get to. That's how they got Liam."

"Oh?"

"Sure! The dumb sonuvabitch decided he wanted to get laid so he went to one of Rocco's whorehouses. And of course, after what happened with The Victoria, Rocco had all his places under surveillance. They spotted him and got lucky. They got the drop on him. Otherwise, Liam would've been untouchable. He was too much of a pro to get caught any other way except with his pants around his ankles."

"You ever find out who the shooter was?"

"Nah. This Tommy kid never mentioned it to you?"

Aaronson shook his head sadly. "No. He doesn't talk much about anything anymore. Which is another reason I can't trust him."

Conway's face loosened into a frown. "You don't think he might suspect you guys had something to do with Joey Bones disappearing, do you?"

Aaronson could only shrug. "I dunno... I dunno... For my uncle's sake, I hope not. I guess Tommy might have started clamming up when he and Fran started fooling around."

"And you know they're messing around for sure?"

Aaronson gave a crazy laugh. "I found out the hard way. I decided to stop by Le Paris early one day with some flowers for Fran. The place is empty so I check the office. And there they are, both naked as newborns, him on the desk, and her kneeling on the floor sucking him off."

"Jaysus," Conway sighed. "I'm sorry."

"Ah," Aaronson shrugged again. "I still love her. But she's gotta understand that this ain't Paris where everybody fucks everybody's uncle and gets away with it. So she's gonna have to learn the hard way."

Conway raised his eyebrows and waited for a further explanation. Aaronson smiled and drained the last of the wine from the bottle into their glasses. He picked up his glass and studied it before taking a long slow sip. Finally he said, "I'm gonna give her Tommy Trent's penis in a little black velvet box."

Conway smiled. The smile broadened into a hearty belly laugh. "I think—I think that'll get the point across!" He laughed again and finished his glass of wine. "You Jews. I had you all wrong all along," he chuckled.

Aaronson smirked and shook his head. "I gotta be honest with you, Sean. My Uncle and I are more than happy to help you bury Rocco and his boys. But for different reasons." He leaned forward and said softly, "I love Fran. Everyone knows it. And I'd do anything to keep her. But my uncle...."

Conway raised an eyebrow again.

"My Uncle and Rocco.... They've always respected each other. But they've never *trusted* each other."

"In this day and age," Conway observed, "a wise policy."

Aaronson nodded gravely in agreement. Then he leaned forward eagerly. "So when can we do this?"

"Hmm?"

"When can we take care of this? Now they know I know, they're not so discreet anymore. When he's not giving it to Dottie Deuce, he's giving it to my Fran and I want to stop him 'fore he knocks her up."

Conway spoke slowly, thoughtfully. "Well... we were gonna nab The Deuce and use her to get Tommy to set Rocco up for us... But if you can get us close to Rocco... I know he comes to your club sometimes..." He shrugged, "Then name the time and place and my boys'll be more than happy to castrate this kid for you."

Aaronson sat back in his chair and scratched his chin. "Let me think... There's gotta be a way to get Rocco for you..."

Charles Coneer, who they had nearly forgotten was there, cleared his throat and pushed his chair back. "I gotta take a leak." He started from the table, stopped and returned. He placed a small automatic pistol by Conway's plate. "I'll be back in a minute."

Conway pointed to the wine bottle. "That empty?"

"Yeah."

"It's pretty good. Nate! Hey, Nate!" Conway groaned, "Where'd the fuck he go?"

"I'll get another bottle. Don't worry."

Max Aaronson had no sooner left the room than the front door burst open. Three men stepped inside. "Holy shit," Conway whispered as he recognized Tommy Trent. "Charlie! Charlie!" he called. He grabbed the automatic and aimed it squarely at Trent's chest. He squeezed the trigger and the gun clicked impotently. It wasn't loaded.

"Hi, Sean," Tommy smiled sweetly. "This is for Sarah and Marie."

Conway leapt to his feet, knocking the chair backwards, his hand reaching for the gun in his waistband. The three men opened fire with their pistols, sending Conway into a jerky dance. The last shot hit him between the collar bones, knocking him backwards over the upturned chair. A pink mist hovered over him before settling to the floor. "Mama?" he whispered quietly. Frankie Sirico grinned and stood over him. He fired

266

once more, hitting Conway between the eyes.

"And that's that." He turned to Gaetano Amato. "I'll go find a mop and a bucket."

Tano nodded. "I'll get the body bags."

Tommy shrugged. "I guess I'll clear the table. The staff will be here in an hour."

41

Hyman Amberg wasn't easily surprised, but he hadn't expected his bodyguard Hank to come in and announce the arrival of Pat Michelson. "What does he want?"

Hank shrugged. "Dunno."

"He clean?"

"Yeah, I searched him."

"Okay, send him in."

Pat Michelson stepped in and took off his hat. "Hello, Mr. Amberg."

Amberg motioned for him to sit down. "What can I do for you?"

Michelson pulled a blood-stained pocket watch from an inside pocket and placed it on the desk. "Sean is dead." He put his hands in his pockets and studied Conway's watch for a long time. "They sent me that to let me know. I'm next." He sat down in the leather chair across from Amberg and toyed absently with his hat. "I want you to know he hired three torpedoes from outta town to clip you. I don't know who they are, but he hired Italians so your nephew'd blame Rocco."

"And why are you telling me this?"

"Because I'm taking over all of Conway's operations. And I want this war to stop now."

"Well," Amberg sighed. "That's easier said than done. Your departed boss made this war personal with that business at the Victoria. I don't know if Rocco will listen to reason."

Michelson leaned forward and jabbed his hat towards Amberg. "But it's gonna become more personal if we don't stop it now. Your nephew's ordered a hit on Tommy Trent. If he gets nailed, Rocco will come after *you*... There won't be anything or anybody left to save if we don't make the peace *now*."

Amberg narrowed his eyes. "All because of a bit of French pussy?"

Michelson had been gravely serious and calm. But that eloquent summation made him laugh. "Yeah. That's about it."

"You sure?"

"Positive. He's been negotiating with Sean about it for a while now. We were gonna hit Trent for him and he was going to let us hit Rocco in his club... Then Sean was going to have those torpedoes knock you and your nephew off and declare himself emperor."

Amberg's brow shaded his eyes. "I'm sorry, Pat. I find that hard to believe. Max loves Le Paris and would never allow a hit on Rocco to take place there. They'd close it up forever."

"He was willing to give up the club to keep the broad."

Hyman Amberg leaned forward and flipped open his humidor. He motioned for Michelson to take a cigar, but he declined with a polite gesture. Amberg extracted a cigar and closed the lid. He took his time trimming the end and lighting it, turning it back and forth over his lighter's flame until the tip glowed evenly. When satisfied, he removed it from his mouth and licked his lips. "Maybe if I had this French broad picked up for prostitution. She could have an accident. That'd take care of the situation."

Michelson had to think about it for a long time. It was so simple it hadn't occurred to him. If two guys were dumb enough to start a war over something so trivial… Remove the bone of contention, remove the disagreement and bad blood.

Amberg went on, "I gotta copper over here I'm not happy with. Maybe he could stand trial for getting carried away during the interrogation and strangling this whore." He shrugged, "It'd take care of two thorns in my side. This cowboy copper and Max and Tommy could make their peace."

"Yeah… Yeah, it could work."

"Now, straightening things out between your boys and Rocco… That's a different story. You killed two of his captains… His underboss is a Sicilian and you know how they are. Blood for blood and all that old world shit."

Pat Michelson's eyes went cold. "And who helped set up Joey Bones for us?"

Hyman Amberg stood up from his chair and paced three steps before sitting on the edge of his desk. He poured himself a drink. "Max is to never know anything about that," he said with great finality.

After a long moment, Michelson shifted and his seat and went on, "Well, I got word out to cancel the contract Sean had on you. I've offered double for you alive than what he offered for you dead. We can hope they get word in time."

Amberg motioned with his cigar, "Start having the coppers in your district pick up every out of towner. I'll get in touch with Rocco and have him do the same. That might take care of that."

"Sure. Just tell Rocco that a new administration is running the north side now. I'm cleaning house starting today… Then we can see about that French broad."

* * *

He was never expecting this to be like the Irish Republican Brotherhood. There was no unifying cause like a free Ireland here. It was all bluff and blunder and money. Every man for himself.

But he had never expected it to be so dangerous.

A bloody pocket watch was all the remained of Sean Conway. It was the same handsome watch awarded to Conway by a county clerk during a political banquet in Sean Conway's honor. Pat Michelson had decided he would carry it always as a reminder.

He was sitting in his car across the street from the Conway wartime headquarters, disappointed by the number of men going inside. He turned to George Reagan who sat beside him, "Not as many as I thought."

Regan shrugged. "Since word of Conway getting bumped off hit, a lot of people have been disappearing from their posts. Micah Collins... Jake..."

"As far as I'm concerned, the war with Rocco will be buried with Sean. I asked the Jew to negotiate a deal." Pat Michelson sighed. He seemed to have aged a decade since Liam McKee turned up dead. "We need to reorganize and regroup. We gotta sort out the bloody traitors."

"And not everybody's going to agree that you're the rightful heir to the North Side," Reagan offered, saying what Michelson hadn't wanted to. Pat Michelson now understood why the Italians ran their mobs with a military style chain-of-command.

"Yer right. We gotta be ready for them too. But I know most of Sean's political allies. I'll sway them over. And if we make a peace with Rocco and get him and The Jew to support us, the police will follow along."

"And then? When everything gets back to normal?"

Michelson smiled. "Then we pay a visit to Rocco for old Sean."

An explosion rocked the night air, shaking Michelson's car. Shattered glass, flaming pieces of wood and a few bricks rained down around the car. A brick smashed through the windscreen and cracked Reagan's elbow. Men scrambled out of the warehouse on 132nd and Lincoln. One of them seemed to be on fire from head to toe, screaming for Jesus to help him. "Holy shit," Michelson whispered in an awed tone.

A car whirled around the corner and a machinegunner began spraying the men fleeing the burning building. Michelson and Reagan ducked inside the car.

When the car was gone, Michelson sat up cautiously. A few cans of wood alcohol inside the warehouse exploded, making him wince. He turned to Reagan. "You alright?"

"Yeah," Reagan hissed, "It's not broken."

Michelson turned his attention back to the burning warehouse. Now the ranks of men loyal to the old regime were even thinner. "Rocco?" he asked.

Reagan was still holding his elbow and making faces. "Either that or the civil war has come to the North Side."

Micah Collins had tried to defect twice before, but now he was dead serious. "Tommy, I told ya it's all gone to hell since Conway got bumped off."

"They don't respect Michelson?"

"Naw! They aren't acknowledging his claim. Everybody was afraid of Conway and his bulldog—that, that punchy fuck. But they're both gone and it's like the entire North Side is up for grabs. I knew a lot of those guys that got themselves blown up in that warehouse." He sat up straight and squared his shoulders. "Tommy, we've known each other for a lotta years. I wanna jump ship. Me and some of the boys wanna work for you. And this time I mean it."

Tommy nodded and pretended to consider it for a moment. "Sure. Let me talk to Patsy."

Collin's relief exploded in a grin. "Thanks, Tommy." Collins shrank back in his chair and lit a cigarette with great effort. "You know, even when we was kids I knew you'd be big someday. Lookitcha now. Runnin' your own piece of turf, marrying a fantastic woman like Dottie Deuce..." Micah raised his glass, "You're a credit to guys like us everywhere." He took a drink and then smiled again. "You know, I thought I was done for. *Twice.* When I helped you clean out Felim's warehouse to force that truce..."

"Yeah," Tommy smiled wistfully. "Seems like a long time ago."

"And then after we hit the mattresses, I thought they suspected something when my little group couldn't accomplish any of its tasks."

"Micah, me ole' friend," Tommy said, scooting forward in his chair. "I will tell you something between you and me. There are things in the works now that'll solve a lot of problems. And believe me, all the things you've done for me will be repaid well."

42

Max Aaronson had known this was coming for a while now, but knowing didn't make it any easier. They sat in the office at Dottie's, comparing notes over a few glasses of whiskey. "You know what has to be done, Max."

"I know, Tom. How he boxed himself in like this," Max sighed and shook his head, "I'll never know."

Tommy shrugged. "The old fox out-foxed himself. He should have listened to you more." Tommy sat forward in his chair and jabbed the air at Max with his cigarette, "And I don't want to blame yourself for not getting him to open his foolish old eyes. Your uncle was a true businessman, but he was too hardheaded and too smart for his own good."

Max Aaronson shook his head sadly. "My uncle's been a fool," he said. "He never believed in me and he underestimated you, Tommy. So he picked the wrong side."

Max looked into the glass of amber fluid for a long time. Finally he said, "I know he's a crazy rat bastard, and I know he almost got us all killed…. But he's still my Uncle. Can I talk to him one last time, Tommy?"

Tommy stood up and circled behind Max's chair. He patted his shoulder, "Sure thing, Maxie. Sure thing."

Ever since Max Aaronson's mother had died some twenty years before, his Uncle Hyman had been his mentor and guiding force. Hyman was harsh but loving, tender but cruel. In the early days when Amberg was still on the rise, Max could always count on him. But as he grew older and Amberg became more influential and rich, he was there for Max less and less. Max Aaronson had always believed it was his way of teaching Max some independence and self-reliance. Still, even though Max was now a grown man, he felt a certain trepidation when he needed to enter his Uncle's study during the afternoon.

But this was not the time for childhood fears. It was the time, as his Uncle had taught him so very well, when a man had to act like a man.

"Uncle Hyman…. You've put me in a bad spot." He sat down on the edge of his uncle's desk. "I have to ask you to retire early."

"What are you talking about?" Hyman Amberg stuck an index finger in the book he was reading to mark his spot. He had always detested being disturbed in the afternoon, especially by his nephew's nonsense. "After the repeal," he said impatiently. "Then you can have the unions and the gambling. When I move down to Florida." He resumed his reading, as though Max had gone.

"See, this is how it is, Uncle Hymie: You're gonna retire early, or not at all. You out-foxed yourself and now you're in deep trouble and don't even know it."

"What are you playing at, Max?"

Max Aaronson sighed heavily, wondering if his Uncle was just pretending to be ignorant.

His uncle had always used his finger as a bookmark when Max interrupted him with his trifles. It was an impatient, disdainful gesture. Not for the first time, Max had the urge to slam the book on that finger to break it. "You screwed up big time playing both ends, courting the fucking Micks. Me? I went along with Tommy Trent. You think they don't know you set up Joey Bones for Conway?"

"Max, I don't know what you're talking about."

"You know who set Sean Conway up to get hit? Me. I did. Me and that copper bodyguard of his. We made up that story about bad blood over Fran to lure Conway out. We got him confident, we got him unsuspecting and we let Tommy walk in and blow him away."

Amberg's face was pale. "You dumb—"

"I ain't through yet… And meantime, you're yanking Patsy Guarino's chain about helping them out. Then you tell Sean Conway it was Rocco who tried to have you clipped, and not the Spano brothers, which we both know is bullshit. You just wanted to gain Sean's confidence. But that's what gave him the idea of bringing in some outside dagos to kill you. Then you turn around and set up Joey Bones and Tommy Trent."

"I never did anything to Tommy." The old man was sweating now.

"See, that's where you made your fatal mistake, Uncle Hymie." Max smiled. His uncle looked frightened, his book was forgotten. "See, a little birdie told Tommy that Bill Powers was Liam McKee's partner. So Tommy had a little chat with him. Then Tommy tracked down the broad who rented the office across from Dottie's speakeasy. That Mrs. Frompton."

"No."

Max nodded. "Uh-huh. That little hooker friend of yours. The one who served drinks to Tommy Trent and Patsy Guarino on the day they invited you to Rocco's big meeting." Max was still smiling as he wagged a finger at his uncle. "That was pretty stupid of you, unc. Must be getting slow in your old age."

He gave the old man a moment to speak, but he said nothing. Max went on, "And when Tommy made that connection, your whole game fell into place. Sure, you threw a little help Rocco's way now and then, but you were cahoots with the fucking Micks all along. You were hoping that Conway'd drive Rocco's gang into the ground so it'd be just you and him and the whole city. But you fuckholes double-crossed each other one too many times. And now, Conway's dead, Rocco's more powerful than ever, my friend Tommy's his star captain, and you're pissing your pants.

"Looks like I'm on the winning team, unc."

"That broad," Amberg stuttered, "That office—that wasn't my girl!"

"Don't give me that. See, my friend Tommy has a way with women. He never forgets an ass when he sees one. And this dame was all too happy to sing for him."

"Max, you don't understand! Me and Rocco are—"

Aaronson interrupted him again. "Let's forget that old guinea goombah. This is about me, you, Tommy and a couple of dead Irishmen." Aaronson let out a long sigh. "You should have listened to me a little more, unc. You should have trusted and valued my counsel. I'd've never let you get in this jam! But when you let me open up Le Paris without ever complaining, and when you quit using me as your go-between for city hall… I knew you had given up on ever retiring. You thought you saw a way you could get the competition to wipe each other out, leaving you to reap all the rewards.

"Now, *that* you'd never be willing to hand over to me. The whole city in your hands? You'd never let that go. So you forgot about the agreement that you were gonna retire when the repeal came and leave me nothing but a couple of bookie joints and the nightclub.

"Greed's a terrible thing, Uncle. It destroyed Conway, and it's done the same to you. I thought you knew better."

"What are you going to do?" Amberg asked softly.

"Maybe those wandering torpedoes will find you. I doubt Michelson looked for them too hard. Maybe Rocco'll send someone around with warm regards." Aaronson shrugged. "Maybe he'll let you live. But if he did that and thought you were still running the west side, what would keep him from suspecting that you wouldn't convince the Irishmen to take another crack at him?

"Now, if I put you on a train with a few trunks full of money, Conway's hired guns might miss you, but Rocco won't. If you disappear, I'll have to tell Rocco where to find you when he comes to shake it out of me. Otherwise, he'd never be able to trust me and he'd have Tommy send me to join Conway and the Spano brothers. So finally…" Aaronson sighed. "I find myself in a position where I have to kill my mother's brother, or set him up, which is just as bad."

Amberg thought his nephew's eyes had grown moist, but the young man's jaw was firmly set. "I don't like it, Uncle Hymie. But you backed me into this corner. You're the one who put me in this position."

Hyman Amberg crawled out of his chair, and for the first time in his life, onto his knees. "Please, Maxie." He clasped his hands together and began weeping. "Please, Max. You can't do this…"

He grabbed the old man gently just above the elbows and raised him to his feet. "That's why you have to leave today. I've got a ticket for you on the train to Florida this afternoon. I've got some phony papers—they're not the best, but they should work. Maybe in a couple of weeks I can arrange for you to go to Cuba and you can retire there or see if you can't get into one of them gambling joints.

"But this is the important thing you have to remember. For both of our sakes: When you get on that train, as far as the world is concerned, Hyman Amberg is dead. I've got a hell of an acting job to do tonight to convince Tommy that your body guard and I disposed of you quietly and discretely. Rocco's got a lot of friends everywhere, Unc. If anyone figures out who you are, we are *both* dead men and everything we have worked for will have been for nothing."

He put a hand on his uncle's shoulder and gently shook it. *"Nothing,* you understand?" The old man's eyes were moist. Somehow Max knew he was thinking about how he rose from the poverty of the Jewish ghetto to build an empire and a comfortable life for his sister.

As if the old man knew Max was trailing his train of thought, "Your mother was a good woman, Max." The old man put a hand on the back of Max's neck. "And you're a good boy. You're a lot like her."

The two embraced. A lump appeared in Max's throat. "I love you, unc."

"I love you, *boytshikl, leeb plimenik.*"

Max smiled. He hadn't heard anyone speak Yiddish since his mother had died. "Go on. You've got an hour to get ready."

They had a tearful farewell in the driveway after Max helped Amberg load the suitcase in the back of a stolen car. Max instructed Hank, Amberg's bodyguard to take the back roads and to make sure Hyman kept his coat collar up and his hat turned down low.

It was a gray, dreary day as the car took Hyman Amberg from his mansion one last time. His mind rolled over the years and over recent events. Perhaps he had grown too greedy. In the slums of the Jewish ghetto, he had simply dreamed of being rich enough to take care of his family. But his mother and father had passed away at young ages, leaving only his sister to look after.

He had done well. Though his sister, a widower, had died at the age of thirty, she had spent the last ten years of her life comfortably. And when she succumbed to the raging fever that racked her body, she knew her son

Max would never be in want for anything.

"Mr. Amberg?" The bodyguard said. "Mr. Amberg?"

Hyman looked up to Hank, trying to pull his mind back from the memories. The car had stopped. They were miles from anywhere.

Hank frowned and shook his head sadly. "Tommy says he's sorry it has to end this way. He always respected you. *Gezegenung,*" Hank said and shot Hyman Amberg six times.

43

It was one of the grandest parties gangland **America had ever seen.**
It was a combination wedding reception/victory celebration held in the
elaborate Williamson Hall which Rocco Petrelli had commandeered for
the occasion. He had never had one of his captains get married while "in
office" and felt, owing to the couple's popularity and the way Tommy had
proved himself during the course of the war, that it was only proper that
Rocco organize things.

Dottie Deuce almost laughed when she heard the news. "To think
Rocco Petrelli is throwing a wedding reception for you. Oh, Tommy…"
she said sadly, putting her forehead against his. "I don't know what to
think."

More than three hundred people attended the wedding and the
reception: Max Aaronson, the new boss of the west side, as well as
representatives from every other mob except the civil-war strafed north

side rubbed elbows with police captains, aldermen, Senators, the assistant DA, and a host of other politicians. It was virtually impossible for Rocco Petrelli not to dominate a party he attended, but he made a gallant effort at deflecting the attention onto Dottie and Tommy and their friends.

Her old acquaintances among Paris's social elite would have been stunned and scoffed to see the way Fran Barrey had teared up during the wedding. The woman they had known, the most famous in the nightlife of all France would never allowed herself to make such an emotional spectacle of herself.

But that Fran Barrey had been left behind long ago. She had found her calling. She was not a glamorous model or a famous singer: she was a saloon keeper, just like Dottie. And Fran Barrey would have it no other way.

Connie Banks had been unable to keep the waterworks from flowing during the wedding either. This union had been more than a decade in the making and Connie thought she had never seen anything so beautiful as the ceremony.

Mountains of caviar and rivers of champagne were consumed during the course of the evening as Bob Harris and His Orchestra serenaded the guests. The chorus girls from Dottie's thrilled at the change of pace: instead of being the ones slinging drinks, they were being served by other gorgeous dames. Tommy had purchased suits for the five neighborhood boys he had dubbed the Jackrabbits and gave them a hundred dollars a piece to check coats and hats and guide the guests along the banquet tables that overflowed with food. The boy swelled with pride that Tommy had thought enough of them to include them in the celebration.

Gaetano Amato, Tommy's best man, in spite of his image as a wine, women and song rogue, made an eloquent speech and then Rocco stood to make a speech of his own. To have Rocco dedicating a toast on the day of their wedding made Dottie feel a little ill.

By the end of the evening, every important politician in the state knew Tommy Trent. Some had heard the name, and most knew little about him before the reception other than he was the only one of Rocco's captains who was not yet thirty years-old. Ronald Byrd, Alice's father, who was running for the House of Representatives, danced with Dottie Deuce and pretended not to notice his beautiful, if somewhat backwards daughter dancing with Frankie Sirico. "Frankie's a good guy, Mr. Byrd," Dottie said softly. "He loves your daughter even if he tries not to show it in public. They want to be married."

The old politician frowned and thought for a long moment. "If Rocco and your husband can help me with the election, Alice can marry whomever she chooses. As long as it is done quietly and is kept quiet."

Dottie smiled and hugged him. "That's great. You're an old doll!"

The stoic politician felt himself flush when Dottie put her arms around him. He cleared his throat and muttered a hasty excuse and made a quick retreat to the rear of the hall.

Few had ever seen Patsy Guarino in such a celebratory mood. He beamed as though he were Tommy's father as he introduced Kenneth Fraley. "Tommy, I'd like you to meet Commissioner Fraley. Commissioner, this is Tommy Trent."

"How do, young man? Thanks for inviting me. It's a grand party."

"Sure, Commissioner."

The police commissioner turned and kissed Dottie's hand. "And a lovely bride. I've visited your club a few times, Mrs. Trent. I always thought you were a radiant beauty." Dottie smiled at the compliment. She had been doing a great deal of that this evening and her cheeks were starting to hurt. Fraley turned back to Tommy and clapped a hand on his arm. "You're a lucky fella, Tommy."

"I know it," Tommy grinned.

Jeremey Fosch, the lieutenant governor was the next to introduce himself and extend his congratulations and those of the governor. "Any friend of Rocco's," Fosch grinned, waving his glass of champagne.

The party lasted for hours and was continued when Tommy and Dottie took their intimate friends back to the speakeasy. For the first time since before January 17, 1920 Dottie's speakeasy was closed to the public. Bob Harris and his band joined the group. "Put down yer instruments," Tommy demanded with a smile. "You're not here to work. You're here to enjoy yourselves!"

The musicians proceeded to consume copious amounts of booze and danced with the chorus girls to phonograph records played on the old Victrola in the corner.

Gaetano Amato and Connie Banks, arm-in-arm approached the newlyweds wearing similarly sheepish expressions. "Hey, guys," Tano began and then licked his lips nervously. "We've got a... Well, I mean.... We want to know—"

Connie laughed and said it for him, "We want you guys to stand up at our wedding."

"You've decided to get hitched?" Tommy asked. When the couple nodded, he and Dottie gave them each a hug. Tommy chucked Connie playfully under the chin. "So you've finally decided you've got this guy tame enough to marry, huh?"

Tano stood behind Connie and slipped his arms around her waist. "Well," he explained, "we figure if we want our bambinos to play with your bambinos, they should be about the same age. So that means we've got to throw caution to the wind and get it over with."

Connie mocked offense. "Oh! 'Get it over with!' How romantic!"

Tano laughed and kissed her ear. "Alright, you old ball and chain. Sounds like you need a few more drinks."

"After that crack, you better get me something!"

Fran Barrey pulled the newlyweds aside to speak privately, "Not to be a wet blanket, but Prohibition won't last forever... I'll have a lot of time on my hands..." She smiled, "So if you two ever decide you want a half-French, half-English nanny for your children, lemme know, huh?"

Tommy laughed and put an arm around her, "No, no. If you think Le Paris is just a thing for the Prohibition age, Frenchie, you're wrong. After the repeal, we're gonna turn it into a world-class French restaurant."

Fran chuckled, thinking at first that Tommy was joking. But when she saw he was serious, her eyes lit up and her jaw dropped. "You don't mean it."

"The hell I don't!" Tommy said and Dottie laughed.

Fran felt like weeping again. She threw an arm around her American friends and squeezed them tightly. When she pulled away, she grinned devilishly, "But... I guess this means I will have to learn how to cook!"

Tommy and Dottie made their exit around two in the morning, inviting the others to stay in the speak and continue the party until they all passed out. Some would do just that.

Dottie turned as she opened the speakeasy door and looked back at her crowd of friends. She hugged Tommy. "On top of the world, doll?"

He smiled. "On top of the world, Baby."

44

THE POLICE COMMISSIONER WAS SITTING IN THE LOBBY of the LaCava-Petrelli Imports building toying anxiously with his hat. The governor had thought it would have been in bad taste to have the lieutenant governor bring it up at the wedding reception, and so now, three weeks later it was up to the commissioner. The chaos on the north side had reached an unacceptable level.

Kenneth Fraley assumed it was just another hood who stepped out of Guarino's office until he looked up. "Tommy!" He got to his feet and shook Tommy Trent's hand. "Back from your honeymoon?"

"Yes, commissioner."

"Have a good time?"

Tommy's grin was answer enough. "Yes. It was wonderful."

"Swell, swell."

"How long you been sittin' out here?"

"Not long," the commissioner lied. "Not long."

"I'm sorry. You should have come in. Go on, Mr. Guarino's expecting you."

Fraley shook Tommy's hand again before stepping into Guarino's office.

As Commissioner Fraley seated himself in front of Guarino's desk, he took one of the cigars he was offered. "I'm sorry Rocco couldn't be here this morning," Patsy said. "But he's meeting with his lawyers about this indictment."

Fraley nodded sadly. "You know we did all we could."

"I know that. Rocco knows that too."

"We couldn't get the stool pigeon. We tried, but," Fraley shrugged helplessly.

Patsy nodded. "But I didn't think you came here to talk about Rocco's legal troubles."

"No. No, I didn't." Fraley scooted forward to the edge of the chair. "The Mayor understands that the trouble with Conway wasn't Rocco's fault. But the press made a helluva time for His Honor and for me."

"I understand. I apologize. You should know we'd never intentionally do anything to jeopardize your position or the Mayor's."

"Yes, yes. I know. But all hell's going on on the north side. We've counted at least five groups who have sprung up to challenge Pat's control of the old Conway territory. It's a civil war up there. Everybody's killing everybody up there and the press is killing the Mayor."

"What can we do for His Honor?"

"Stop the war. The Mayor and I will back you in any decision you make as long as you can bring some sanity back to the north side. We don't care what you have to do to restore peace and order, but it has to be done soon. Before the election."

Patsy pretended to mull it over. He and Max Aaronson had simply been waiting for a green-light. This was it. "I'll see what I can do. Give us… a month."

"Ah, that's grand!" the commissioner beamed and thrust a large hand over the desk.

Guarino took it and smiled. "Is there anything else we can do for you or His Honor?"

The two men were still shaking hands and smiling as they walked to the door of the office. "Well, now... the campaign fund is a might low..."

"Sure," Patsy grinned. "I'll talk to my treasurer. We've already got things in the works."

The Commissioner grinned a final time before he closed the door behind him. "Bless you, lad. And tell Rocco we're still trying everything we can for him. The city wouldn't be the same without Rocco!"

* * *

Patsy Guarino was pondering the words Rocco had spoken so long ago at the Williamson hall. "The old days are gone and with them, the old ways." He understood what Rocco had been getting at, but it was all wrong.

The fundamentals never change.

The village where Patsy Guarino grew up had been controlled by Don Croxifficio Diligatio, a man of ageless character and infinite resources. Diligatio had lived and died by the credo that family comes first.

If anything, the world was going back to the old ways. Ten, twenty years from now when Prohibition and the Petrelli-Conway war were nothing more than stories repeated over glasses of beer in saloons, it would be only the oldest of traditions that remained.

The Sicilian way, born of centuries of invasions and oppression, where anyone who was not blood was an outsider not to be trusted, where the only law that mattered was the ancient Sicilian code.

But Rocco Petrelli was a Neapolitan, not a Sicilian. He was not bound to the old world by centuries of his family's bloodshed. He was not born with the innate cynicism or the ability to view the whole objectively.

But Tommy Trent was. Though his blue eyes told tales of a northerner in his bloodline, Tommy Trent was Sicilian through and through. Patsy Guarino had seen that all along, but it was something Tommy was just beginning to understand.

Spring was now leaning towards summer. It seemed that earth was warming itself to the new period of peace. Pat Michelson had fled the country and the north side had been tamed by Max Aaronson and Patsy Guarino's mobs. It had been a long time since the world seemed so peaceful.

Patsy Guarino and Tommy sat in lawn chairs sipping anisette and watching the girls.

"This is a magical time we're living in, Tommy. But it's not gonna last forever." Patsy could feel the younger man's eyes on him, waiting for him to continue. "With this prohibition thing, everybody wants to help. Everybody wants a piece of the action. But mark my words," he jabbed two thick fingers in Tommy's direction, "when the repeal comes, ninety percent of the coppers and politicians who are our friends now will become our enemies. We'll be back to not being able to trust anyone or anything again."

"So we should enjoy it while it lasts, huh?"

Patsy smiled and raised his glass. "Damn straight." He took a sip and then sighed. "But it's a good thing we've got the unions and the gambling. We'll be okay."

"What about the drugs?"

Patsy frowned. "Narcotics… There's a lot of money there. But a lot of danger, too. Now, booze is nothing. Everybody drinks. Mothers, teachers, priests… Public opinion is generally on our side… But with narcotics…" he shook his head sadly, "Nobody but the addicts and the most greedy will support it… When they decide to repeal prohibition—and they will, eventually—I will miss it very, very much."

"Me too."

There followed a long pause during which the two men gave thanks to live in such interesting times and to think of how they would mourn its passing. Gone would be the speakeasies, the juniper juice gin and the green beer, the flamboyant politicians rubbing elbows in public with known killers, the hot jazz bands and the scantily clad flappers kicking up their heels. Gone would be the little thrill people got from sipping a little illicit whiskey. Americans would have to move on to new avenues to fulfill their need for mischief.

"It's only a matter of time before they lock Rocco away now." Patsy sighed and took a sip of anisette. "And I don't mean years. Soon. That bookkeeper they got their hands on is singing like a canary."

"Can we get to him?"

"It'd be too late anyway. The damage is already done." He grabbed Tommy's arm and leaned closer. He whispered in a conspiratorial tone, "I told Rocco a million times: 'Keep your name outta the papers.' And he goes around posin' for photographs like he's Theda Bara."

He sat back and watched Dottie and Connie Banks playing badminton as Fran Barrey looked on, laughing. It was a picturesque scene: The three beautiful dolls dressed in outfits that would have gotten them locked up ten years ago, playing badminton in the middle of the huge manicured lawn, a stretch of woodland in the distance behind them. The sunlight was shining in the girls' hair and above all a few wisps of clouds strolled lazily across the blue sky. In more than one way, Patsy envied Tommy Trent.

"Well, things'll cool down when you're bumped up."

Patsy snorted, "You think I want the fuckin' job? Sure, it'll be low-key for a while until they realize they may have put Rocco away, but his empire's still there." Patsy disparaged the thought. "Then the heat and the press will come back, looking for the celebrity gangster's heir."

Tommy shrugged. "I could be your front man."

Patsy laughed. "Yeah. About like you were Eddie's errand boy."

"Just a suggestion."

"No, no. It's just the way things are now, I guess. Everybody wants their gangster to be a guy like Rocco."

"A forty-some year-old guy who likes to sleep with thirteen year old girls?" Tommy said.

Patsy's reaction was a mixture of shock and anger. That was something that no one was supposed to know about. "A guy I know…" Tommy explained, "When Rocco was starting his way up, white slavery and all that… he turned this guy's aunt. She was barely thirteen."

The explanation was satisfactory. Patsy nodded. "That's one of the sides the American public has never seen." He lit a cigar and admitted morosely, "Yeah, he's gotta little girl locked away in secret like she was in the Tower of London."

They fell silent for a long moment. Patsy seemed to be asking himself how he could have gotten in with such a man. He had always done a remarkable job of hiding the contempt he held for his boss, but he couldn't help but wonder just how much of it Tommy could see.

He heard Fran Barrey cursing in French in the distance. She and

Connie had traded places and now Connie was the one watching and laughing. Patsy Guarino smiled to himself.

An inch of gray ash stretched from the tip of his cigar when he next spoke. "The worst thing is, these feds, these Treasury Department Mama's Boys, will be strutting around like a peacock that's got it's first hard-on."

Arrogance was something Patsy only tolerated from Rocco Petrelli and even then it was only grudgingly.

"Their heads will get so big," Tommy agreed, "they'll think they can take on anyone."

Patsy nodded slowly. He tapped the cigar and the inch of gray ash tumbled to the ground where it was held suspended by the blades of grass. "It'd be a shame to see that happen."

45

Rocco Peirelli was feeling particularly good when he woke up. He felt refreshed and revitalized. He rolled over on to his side and slid a hand under the silk blanket to pinch Hannah's bottom. "Hey," he said softly. The thirteen year old slapped absently at his hand without opening her eyes. She grumbled something unintelligible. Rocco reached a hand around her and lightly pinched her nipple. "Hey, you want breakfast?"

For a moment the girl did not answer. Then she rolled onto her back, one hand rubbing the sleep from her eyes. "Okay." When she sat up she made no effort to keep the silk sheet covering her. She regarded Rocco and the suspicious lump in the blanket with equal aplomb. "I have time to wash up?"

"Sure," he said and sat up. He leaned against the headboard with an arm around the girl. "How they treatin' you over there?" Hanna lived in a private suite in The Victoria, but she was not available to the public. Only a handful of men other than Rocco even knew of her existence.

The girl sighed and shrugged. "Okay, I guess, but…"

"But what, sweetie?"

"All the other girls act like I must be too good for them," she said looking down at her belly button. "I don't have any friends, Rocco." She fought the urge to sniffle and lost.

"Hey, come on. Don't be blue, angel." He lifted her face to his. "Come on, you wouldn't want to know those other broads anyway. Come on, smile."

"I'd like to have a friend."

"Listen," he pushed a lock of hair from her forehead and put his hand on her shoulder. "When you got Rocco Petrelli, you don't *need* nobody else. Come on. Give me a smile."

The girl forced herself to smile. Hannah had become a very good actress. "Okay."

"Okay? Good. Now go wash up."

"Okay, Rocco."

They both got out of the bed and as Hannah passed him, he gave her a playful smack on the behind. He picked up his pajama bottoms and thought better of it. "Hey, Hannah?" he called, sitting down on the foot of the bed.

"Yes, Rocco?"

"Leave the door open. I wanna watch."

Rocco was pulling on his robe as he stepped out of the bedroom. "Gloria?" he called and waited the usual five seconds it took his maid to reply. He repeated himself. There was no answer.

Hannah was still in the bath and he wanted to have breakfast brought up to them by room service. He cursed under his breath and crossed the suite to Gloria's quarters. He threw open the door and said, "Gloria!" in a sharp commanding tone to an empty room.

"Where the hell is she?" He glanced around for a note but decided he didn't feel like looking any further.

He marched to the entrance of the suite and threw the double doors open. "Hey, you mugs, where's that—"

The bodyguards were gone. His eyebrows drooped as he tried to puzzle it out. The man down the hall wasn't at his post either.

"Hi, Rocco."

Rocco whirled around to find two men standing in his parlor. His eyes narrowed as he tried to make the connections. "Tommy?" His eyes dropped to the guns the men were carrying. "What is this? What are you birds playing at?" he demanded. He looked at the second man. "Who are you?"

"My name is Frankie."

"So? What kind of game is this?"

"We've got a couple stories we'd like you to hear," Tommy said conversationally.

"Stories? What do you mugs think you're doing here?"

Frankie nodded for Tommy to go first. "Once upon a time there was a guy named Big Joe LaCava," Tommy began.

"Say, what is this?"

Tommy continued as though he hadn't noticed the interruption. "His nephew was a guy named Rocco. Rocco did a lot of things for Big Joe. He got the people in the neighborhood to fall in line and pay their respects to Big Joe. One of the things Rocco did that convinced them was he torched an apartment building. The landlords all started paying up immediately after that and everyone else fell in line…"

There was a darkness, an emptiness, a hell that Dante could not have dreamed of in Tommy Trent's eyes. "….My mother and father died in that fire."

The look of horror on Rocco's face was slow to dawn, but it was genuine. "No, Tommy. No. I'd never— Why, I—"

"I grew up in a shit-hole orphanage with two kids to a bed, half of them dying of disease."

"Tommy, I don't know what to— Why, I— Now, Tommy ya' gotta understand— Why, I'd never—"

Frankie took a half step forward and began his story. "This also happened a long time ago, but I'm sure you don't remember it."

"Boys, please. Listen—"

"—There was a girl named Angelina Sirico. She was thirteen years old when you kidnapped her and forced her into a life of prostitution. They found her four years later and she's been in an insane asylum ever since. This is for my Aunt Angie." He stepped forward and fired his pistol into Rocco's groin.

The great Rocco Petrelli, The Babe Ruth of Crime, let out a squawk like a bird being hit by a truck and crashed to his knees. His hands groped frantically between his legs. Blood poured from between his fingers, down his thighs and onto the blood red carpet. His mouth was working soundlessly as he watched the spectacle.

"Sorry, Rocco," Tommy Trentino said, "but this'll be your last fuckin' headline." He stepped forward, raising his gun. He hissed in Sicilian, "This is for my mother and father," and the two men emptied their revolvers into Rocco Petrelli.

As the smoke cleared, Rocco was still on his knees, swaying in a heady circle. His eyes were aimed upwards as if imploring the same heavenly body who had blessed him with prohibition to now come down and save him. His jaw was still moving but no sound came forth. He gave one final sway and toppled over onto his back with a thud that was nearly as loud as the gunfire. His legs worked twice as though he were riding a bicycle, then stopped.

Tommy Trent calmly put two cartridges into the gun's cylinder and then walked around the corpse. He leaned over, holding the gun to Rocco's head and fired twice.

There would be no doubt. Rocco Petrelli would never hustle another dame or set another fire.

* * *

There would be no lavish send off for Rocco Petrelli. When his uncle Big Joe LaCava died, nearly half of the politicians and police chiefs in the state attended. His pallbearers had included a senator. His coffin was buried under a $30,000 mountain of flowers.

But not so for Rocco Petrelli.

In the three hours following the death of the king of gangsters, the outcry was terrific. The press scrambled to release special editions dedicated to the murder and memory of Rocco Petrelli. All across the nation there seemed to be an outcry for vengeance and justice. An eccentric Texan, who had no ties to the world of crime, offered $5,000 reward for the capture or killing of Rocco's murderers.

The nation seemed to be in mourning as if the president had been assassinated.

But four hours after the shooting, the headlines were stolen away by "Girl H."

The police, during their second press conference on what would be the biggest day of the decade for the newsmen, discussed the murder scene in greater detail and revealed that a thirteen year-old prostitute had been discovered cowering in Rocco's bathtub. Identified only as "Girl H" to the public, it was revealed that she had been Rocco's lover for more than a year and she had first met him at Christmas at one of the annual holiday dinners Rocco gave for the homeless— the dinners that had helped make him a national hero, the bad boy America loved to love.

Girl H had been a homeless twelve year old orphan when Rocco spotted her at the dinner. He immediately whisked her away to a secret hideaway and she had little human contact during the next sixteen months apart from those who brought her her food and those who escorted her to and from Rocco's hotel.

The national uproar over Rocco's death dwindled to a sickened disillusioned silence. The police stated that the girl had not seen the killers—she had spent the night with Rocco and was bathing when the gunfire started.

The police declined to give many details about the girl, like the fact she had contracted syphilis from Rocco nor did they answer the questions like: How often during the sixteen months had Rocco called for her services and what did those services include? The answer to the latter question was "Whatever Rocco wanted."

The District Attorney spearheaded an investigation into the Carlisle Hotel. "How is it possible," he asked, "that for sixteen months a young girl, the victim of the most horrid kidnapping, forced into a life of prostitution, could be brought to the hotel repeatedly with no one noticing?"

The scandal ended the Carlisle Hotel's life of opulence. It folded during the course of the investigation and one of the managers was jailed after admitting he knew about Girl H. His defense had been that he feared for his life, but the prosecution proved he lived a life style far more extravagant than could be explained by his tax returns.

The morale of the Treasury Department had been dealt a vicious blow. A special team of Treasury Department Agents along with agents of the Prohibition Bureau had worked long and hard and had been on the verge of toppling the gangster of all gangsters, only to have it all snatched away from them in the eleventh hour, most likely by Rocco's very own men.

Through all the scandals and uproar, the investigation into the murder itself was virtually forgotten and fell by the wayside. It remains an "unsolved case."

Three weeks after the murder, a happy ending was given to the newspapers: A relative of Girl H had been discovered in St. Louis (though it was actually Dallas, Texas). At the time the story was given to the press, the girl was on a train to go live with an aunt and try to put back the pieces and try to live the life of a normal thirteen year-old girl.

46

THE SPRING THE FOLLOWING YEAR WAS EVEN COLDER than the one before. It had been two years to the day now that the Petrelli-Conway war began. In so many ways it seemed like it had been a lifetime ago. Dottie Deuce was wrapped in a fur coat as she sat in the back of the long black car parked inside Mount Carmel Cemetery.

She watched as the love of her life strolled through the maze of gravestones, which peered bleakly from under a blanket of snow. The sky was gray and the clouds seemed to hang so low over the cemetery that she thought she could step out of the car and reach up to touch the sky's underbelly.

Tommy stood still in the distance, his shoulders hunched against the cold. He was so still he might have been another headstone.

Dottie ran a hand over her rounded stomach. She could feel a tiny foot kick against the palm of her hand. "Shh…" she whispered. "Daddy'll be back in a minute."

Fran Barrey was seated on her right side. She smiled and put a hand on Dottie's shoulder. Dottie managed a wan grin in return. "It's been a two years now," she said softly.

She turned her eyes back to the gray world outside. "He still blames himself," she said and watched the figure in the distance. Tommy Trent knelt and placed a red rose on the grave of Sarah DiStella.

NICK DEFFENBAUGH IS A FREELANCE WRITER FROM NORTHWEST Indiana. He is a student of early 20th Century American history and culture.

Printed in the United States
151104LV00002B/25/P